A DUET OF SWORD AND SONG

LISA CASSIDY

National Library of Australia Cataloguing-in-Publication Entry

Creator: Lisa Cassidy

Publisher: Tate House

ISBN: 9780648539285

Cover design: Jessica Bell

Map design: Oscar Paludi

Music and lyrics: Peny Bohan

This one is for the real Sari, Cynia, and Leviana.

Just as amazing in reality as in this series.

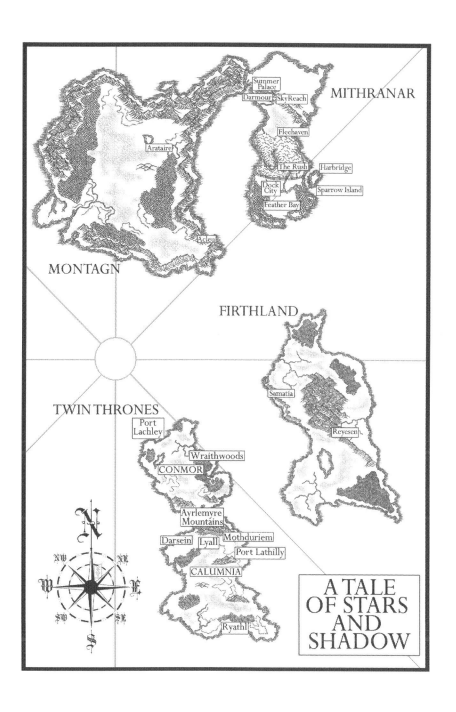

MITHRANAR

Summer
Palace
Darmour SkyReach

Flechaven

Arataire

The Rush   Harbridge

Dock
City   Sparrow Island

Feather Bay

Acleu

MONTAGN

FIRTHLAND

Samatia

TWIN THRONES

Port
Lachley

Reyesen

Wraithwoods

CONMOR

Ayrlemyre
Mountains

Darsein Lyall Mothduriem

Port Lathilly

CALUMNIA

Ryathl

A TALE
OF STARS
AND
SHADOW

CHAPTER 1

a chair scraped across the floor, its legs cutting through the narrow slices of sunlight that shone through the gaps in the wooden planks nailed to the window. Cuinn tracked the movement with a distant stare.

He'd drifted awake a few moments earlier and decided that the light meant it was day... but which day? How long since... His thoughts trailed off, growing muddled in a tangle of memory: blood and fighting and his brother's triumphant face.

A soft yowl came from the foot of the bed, making Cuinn aware of the weight pressing against his legs. Jasper. He blinked again as the chair stopped by his bed and someone sat on it, their form cutting off most of the light from the window. "It's me, Prince Cuinn. Jystar."

The healer's dark-skinned face moved into his line of vision. Cuinn licked his dry lips, then decided he'd try and sit up. Maybe that would restore some clarity to his groggy mind. Stabbing pain between his shoulders and down his back stopped him before he'd moved more than an inch.

He gave a grunt of pain, tried to turn his head to see what the cause of it was, then froze at the realisation he couldn't see his wings.

His heart seemed to stop in his chest.

"I'm sorry, Prince Cuinn. I couldn't save them." Jystar spoke again, soft but firm, leaving no room for Cuinn to hope that he might mean something else. "You're okay, but I've kept you unconscious to help the healing. You're going to feel out of it for a while. You lost a lot of blood."

Cuinn's eyes closed and he pressed his face into the pillow, not wanting to betray the horror and nausea rising through him. He tried to suck in a breath, fists clenching, nails digging into his palms. "Talyn?" he managed to ask. If she were here, it would be okay. He could get through anything if she was here with him.

A hesitation, then, "We don't know. She and Zamaril are still missing."

The words hit him like a physical blow. He buried his face deeper in the pillow, pain and grief and horror roping through him in unrelenting waves. The weight on his feet shifted and moved up the bed, steering clear of his back. A damp nose nudged his cheek, then the weight settled at his left side.

"We're in a safe house in the Poor Quarter." Jystar kept talking, but seemed to give up after a few moments when Cuinn gave no appearance of hearing him.

The door opened and brisk footsteps crossed to the chair. Saniya's voice sounded. "Is he awake?"

"He is." Jystar sighed, sounding tired, worn. "I told him about his wings. He asked about the Ciantar. Have your people found any sign of her yet?"

"Nothing so far." A hesitation. "Not even a single sign of what happened."

Jystar said nothing. Cuinn tried to breathe through the pain.

A brief silence, then, "The last group left on the dawn tide. Far as I could tell they made it out safely. You can't linger here much longer. The patrols are increasing—they're moving into the deepest parts of the Poor Quarter now."

"He's in no condition to travel, even if we could be sure he was going somewhere safe." Worry filled Jystar's voice, weighing unbearably against Cuinn's song magic and making it impossible to escape the miasma of despair filling every inch of him.

Saniya's voice sharpened. "You're going to compromise me and my people if you stay here much longer."

"We're appreciative of your help, but—"

"I don't care if you're appreciative. There was a debt owed. I paid it, but my patience is running thin and you're risking exposing all of us." Another pause. "Let me know when he's more alert. I want to talk to him."

The door opened. Closed. Its sharp click jolted Cuinn out of the daze of emotion and pain he'd sunk into.

"Your Highness?" Jystar asked. "I'm going to work on your back, all right?"

"Wolves?" he managed.

"Vengeance has been moving them out in small groups, helping them get north to Darmour." Jystar swallowed. "I hope they reached it safely. You and I are all that's left now. Saniya made the talons leave, insisted it was easier to keep you hidden here without a pack of Wolves surrounding you at all times." A light touch on his back made him wince as pain rippled down his spine. "I'll make it as painless as possible, Your Highness."

It didn't matter. Nothing Jystar did could hurt worse than what he was already feeling. His wings were gone. Talyn was lost. His throne was lost. Wolves had died. The rest had fled to uncertain safety. Silent tears streaked his cheeks.

How did he come back from that?

CHAPTER 2

*S*omeone was trying to talk to her. Badgering her thoughts, drumming at her mind, pushing hard, but there was a block. An empty gap the voice couldn't penetrate. And in that gap was fear. Terror. Something stalking her in complete darkness.

The woman's eyes flew open with a strangled cry.

Her heart thundered in her chest, and it took several moments before she calmed enough to become aware of the sweat slicking her skin and the weakness trembling through her muscles. The terror of the dream lingered, clinging to her like cobwebs. She shifted, forcing herself to widen her awareness in an attempt to banish the nightmare.

The effort required for that was almost impossible to summon. It shouldn't be. Terror uncurled again, threatening to overwhelm her, but she forced it down. Seeking distraction, her gaze landed on the only source of light nearby, a small fire flickering in the middle of a dirt floor. A woman hunched over it, stirring something in a pot, staring at the smoke rising from the flames as if it held the answers to everything.

She blinked. This woman was familiar. The answer came grudgingly, drawn from the depths of her blurry memories. Kaeri. The woman had shared the name during one of her previous lucid moments, though she couldn't remember which one, nor how many there'd been. They all blurred into one feverish dream.

She tried to speak, to get Kaeri's attention, but a faint rasping sound was all she could manage.

Kaeri heard it, though. She swung around, green eyes taking her in with a single assessing glance. "Another nightmare?"

She swallowed and nodded. The feelings roused by the dream still filled her so thoroughly that it was hard to summon the coherence for speech. If only she could *remember*. Remember what terrors stalked her dreams. And why.

"Did it help you remember who you are? What happened to you?" Kaeri asked.

"No." Her voice was hoarse, barely audible.

Kaeri's mouth thinned. "Then the dreams are doing you no good at all. You need rest if you're ever going to recover."

The words were brisk, well meant, but the woman had caught Kaeri looking at her when Kaeri didn't realise she was awake. Kaeri didn't think she *was* going to recover. Too tired to keep fighting to stay alert, she allowed her eyes to slide closed, wondering if she was going to die.

As muddled and weak as she was, she understood that she was hurt. Badly. The unceasing, throbbing pain in her back and side told her that. And she wasn't healing. Kaeri had said something about infection last time she was awake, and the fevers and weakness certainly bore that out.

Dimly, through a restless doze, she heard the other women who lived in the shared hut return. Voices sounded as they greeted Kaeri, asking after her as they always did, but silence soon returned. The women rarely stayed awake long, usually going straight to their narrow pallets to sleep. Only Kaeri ever spoke to her. She hadn't yet been able to summon the clarity of thought to do more than wonder why that was. Or where the women came from... what they did in daylight hours.

She didn't even know *where* she was. She was sure she'd asked the question before. Sure Kaeri had answered. But that memory was lost in the fever.

Time passed—it could have been seconds or hours—then Kaeri shook her gently and forced her to drink water from a wooden cup. Hot tea, slightly bitter, touched her tongue.

"Where am I?" She managed to force the words out. Her back felt like it was on fire, but the pain was both immediate and distant, shrouded in a haze of fever and grogginess.

"A labour camp." Kaeri's tone indicated she'd answered this more than once.

"Where?" Her eyes slid shut and she fought against the unconsciousness tugging insistently at her mind. Summoning every bit of will she had, she forced her eyes back open.

"Montagn." Kaeri sat by her pallet, cross legged. Her fair skin was marred with soot, lank brown hair tied roughly at her neck. There was no softness, no give, in her eyes or voice. "I'm doing the best I can to treat you, but we don't get proper healing supplies. Your wounds are infected and your body has no strength to fight it because you're not eating or getting restful sleep. I'm barely getting enough water into you to keep you alive."

"You're saying I'm going to die?"

Kaeri nodded slightly. "It's likely. I'm sorry."

Did that upset her? She wasn't sure. It should, but death would be an escape from the unending pain and illness. "It's... all right."

Again she had that sensation, like a voice was battering at her mind, trying to get through. But before she could grasp it, it was gone, faded away into nothingness. The gap loomed large, threatening to swallow her whole.

"I'll do the best I can for you." Kaeri moved away and the woman forced herself to summon enough energy to speak again.

"Kaeri?"

Kaeri heard the faint whisper and turned. "Yes?"

"Thank... thank you."

Kaeri made a dismissive gesture and turned away, filling a cup with water from their shared jug and bringing it over. "Thank me by drinking this."

The woman tried to drink. Tried even harder to remember.

But she couldn't do either.

CHAPTER 3

*H*e'd been hurt worse than this before, after the avalanche Vengeance had used to ambush him. He'd attacked that recovery with every ounce of determination he'd possessed, working relentlessly with Tiercelin's help until he was well again. Strong again. He hadn't even *thought* about giving up.

This time… Jystar did everything he could. The wounds on his back closed over. There was no infection or fever. Within days Cuinn could sit and stand and walk without much pain. But he didn't have the determination he'd had before.

He tried to find it. He *wanted* to find it. But every time he stood up and almost fell over without the weight of his wings balancing him, every time he woke from a restless sleep to remember Talyn was missing and Halun had died, remembered his brother had betrayed him and taken away his one chance to make things better for his country, his people—the weight of those realisations crashed down over him with a force he couldn't shoulder. And they buried him.

Jasper refused to leave the room, stuck as close to him as he could, but his tawncat couldn't make a dent in Cuinn's despair. Even good news from Andres—amongst the first group of Wolves to reach Darmour—failed to restore his will.

"They got to Darmour safely and Andres managed to contact Windsong at the Summer Palace." Jystar's hands trembled as he read the note to Cuinn, his relief so strong it soothed the edge of Cuinn's pain for a few moments. "He was apparently waiting for us and had prepared a place to hide. Andres is in Darmour, shepherding each group of escaping Wolves to Windsong's hideout."

"Where?" Cuinn asked.

"Andres wouldn't say in the note in case it was intercepted. But he says it's secure, and isolated. He says Windsong might have saved us all." Jystar sounded close to tears.

Part of Cuinn sagged with relief to hear that. To know what was left of Talyn's Wolves were safe. He trusted Windsong as he trusted Talyn and her talons and he knew the man would look after them when Cuinn couldn't.

That knowledge had a weight of its own, though, tainting his relief. They couldn't hide forever. They'd be waiting for Cuinn to do something. Fix this somehow. Find a way forward.

But he didn't even know where to begin. Not without Talyn, his general, who could turn any loss into a victory. Not when he had lost his wings and therefore any chance of the winged folk accepting him as king.

He had no hope left to offer them.

THE OPENING DOOR broke him from the constant cycle of hopeless thoughts. It was Saniya, and she clutched a piece of torn parchment in her hand. She tucked it into a pocket before dropping into the chair by his bed. Her expression was masked, and the sapphire eyes that marked her as a member of one of Mithranar's most powerful families were duller than Talyn's luminous Dumnorix eyes. Still, a glance from Saniya could immediately hold anyone's attention, and it compelled Cuinn's now.

"I think we can help each other, princeling."

"How's that?" His voice was flat, lifeless.

She gave him an impatient look. "You're really giving up? After years of beating your head against the wall as the Shadowhawk, *now* is when you decide to quit?"

"No." The word escaped him before he even thought about it, the response instinctive and raw. He swallowed. "I just don't... I don't know what to do next."

"I do. Get out of the city before they catch you and kill you. Jystar is babying you. You're strong enough to leave."

He nodded, accepting the truth of that.

"And like I said, we can help each other." She eyed him, reluctance for what she was about to say written all over her face. Cuinn could feel it with his magic, too. "You have a network here and in Darmour. So do I."

"We destroyed your network."

Saniya's face tightened. "We've still got contacts, infrastructure and knowledge. And you didn't kill all my people—it's why I asked for the truce, to save what we had left. Slaves from Montagn who just wanted a better life, mostly. Your Ciantar granted me that. Which is why I'm here now. I propose an alliance."

He shifted, tried to force himself to pay better attention. "An alliance to do what?"

"To merge what's left of our people, knowledge and infrastructure. Then start stealing and moving supplies again. Your people in the north are going to need them."

He huffed a bitter laugh. "You want to use my network to rebuild your own."

"Exactly. And then I want to use our combined resources to go back to doing what we always did together, Shadowhawk." Her eyes gleamed, her anticipation almost palpable.

He shook his head. "I'm not going back to being the Shadowhawk. It didn't solve anything then, and it won't now."

She smiled without warmth, sitting back in her chair. "I figured you'd be looking to take the crown from your brother. So here's my proposal. Our merged network undercuts Azrilan when and where we can to help the humans here, plus we provide supplies and infor-mation to your hidden army."

He opened his mouth. To tell her there was no point, that there was no chance he could take the throne back, that even *thinking* there was a chance was foolish in the extreme. But that same instinct that had denied he'd given up earlier flared inside him again. So instead he asked, "Who would run this merged network?"

"We'll have co-leads," she said promptly. Clearly she'd put a lot of thought into this. Talyn's cousin indeed. "Myself and one of your people. No decisions will be made without both leaders' agreement." She sat forward. "But this would be a logistical alliance only. We work together to irritate a common enemy. I'm not here to fight for you and I still have no desire to see winged folk on the Mithranan throne."

"I'll think about it." It didn't pay with someone as canny as Saniya to agree to anything too quickly. Weeks ago they'd been at war. She'd wanted his death. "Now tell me what you really came in here to say." He'd sensed it nagging at her the whole conversation.

She tugged the parchment out of her pocket, passed it to him. "These were placed on all the city noticeboards this morning. Your mother died a few days ago. Azrilan is king of Mithranar."

He stared, unseeing, at the words on the parchment.

His mother was dead. He was too hollow to even know how he felt about that.

"The coronation will be tomorrow night." The chair scraped as Saniya stood and headed for the door. "You should be gone by then."

He crumpled the note and let it drop from his hands. Saniya was right. If he wasn't going to give up—even though he truly saw no way out of this—then he had to leave, go north to Darmour and re-join his Wolves. That was the first step.

But there was something he needed to do first.

CHAPTER 4

*T*he shadows lengthened as dusk turned the day into night. Music drifted in the stillness, a hint of melody, not enough to overpower the hum of conversation or the occasional burst of laughter.

Azrilan Acondor-Manunin stood in the centre of the open air platform, the focus of attention, those attending the reception in his honour circling him like he held a gravitational pull.

Already ahara of Montagn, Azrilan was now king of Mithranar.

He looked the part—handsome, debonair, his dark hair cut neatly, charcoal wings glimmering in the lamplight. He held himself straighter than he ever had before, sloughing off all of the languidness, the deference he'd once pretended.

There was no more powerful man in the world now. Not with the Dumnorix king dead and the new warlord of Firthland presumably still stabilising his rule after launching a coup against his uncle.

Tarcos. Cuinn's lip curled, but he pushed away thoughts of that man before they could take hold and threaten to destroy his focus.

A glass of wine hung loosely from Azrilan's fingers, almost forgotten as he smiled and chatted with Irial Swiftwing and Jenseno Blacksoar—the eldest sons of Kingcouncil lords once Cuinn's friends but now clearly in Azrilan's favour. The entire court was present for the celebration of the crowning of a king, some hovering in the humid air while others gathered in groups on the platform.

Falcons were there too. More than had ever been present at an official reception before. Cuinn couldn't do more than glance at the winged folk in the sky before he had to look away, despair roping through him. He'd never identified himself via his wings, had often been frustrated that they set him apart from the humans in Mithranar in a way they shouldn't. But losing the ability to fly... it ate at him. He couldn't stop it even though he told himself he should let it go. That there were far more important things to despair about.

But the thought of never feeling the air in his face, through his feathers, of looking down on the world from above... it was devastating.

He swallowed, tried to force those thoughts away and concentrate. He stood well hidden by a pillar on the eastern side of the platform, the shadows wrapped around him so tightly he was invisible as long as he didn't move. His back ached, his legs trembled—he'd been there too long already.

But he stayed.

He'd needed to do this. To see Azrilan and the Mithranan court one last time before he fled Dock City.

Another burst of laughter erupted nearby. Annae Ravensweep was chuckling with her father-in-law and Lord Jurian Stormflight. Charl Nightdrift was with the group too, but his face was stony, shoulders hunched slightly. Tirin Goldfeather lingered on the edges of the platform, clearly uncomfortable.

Cuinn noted those things.

He also noted the lack of Firthlander Bearmen amongst the Falcon guards.

Saniya's people had reported that Tarcos had taken his warriors with him when he'd departed a week earlier, leaving behind only his naval ships blockading Feather Bay. Azrilan had also been confident enough not to bring any Montagni soldiers with him to Mithranar apart from a small Berserker honour guard. They weren't here tonight

—no doubt a result of Azrilan's understanding they would make his winged court uneasy. After all, as fearsome as they were, they were human. Azrilan was no fool.

Bitterness curled in Cuinn, edged with the familiar despairing hopelessness he did his best to push away. The shadows around him flickered, his hold loosening, and he swore inwardly. His energy was draining—he needed to focus better.

His gaze fell on Azrilan again. There was no trace of sadness in his face, of grief at their mother's loss. There was only triumph and satisfaction, both clear in his expression and stance but also broadcasting for any song mage to read. He wasn't even trying to hide the glee he felt in his victory.

For the first time since waking in the safehouse, Cuinn felt something other than pain or despair or hopelessness. He felt anger. It flared in his chest, burning through the other emotions. He grabbed onto it, welcoming it, feeding it. Allowing it to bring back a spark of life to his heart.

He *hated* what Azrilan had done. Hated his brother in a way he'd never hated Mithanis.

Before he'd even realised what he was doing, Cuinn began moving, shrouding himself in just enough shadow to keep his features and form largely hidden from anyone glancing his way. The servant's uniform he wore and his lack of wings did the rest.

After all, humans were beneath most winged folk's notice.

By the time he'd moved closer to where Azrilan stood, he was sweating through his clothes. But he barely noticed. His entire attention focused on his target, the source of the fury winding through him.

The prince of games.

The brother who'd always had a word of affection for Cuinn when Mithanis never had and his mother rarely did. Who'd winked at Cuinn every time Mithanis was furious at him or lost his temper. Who'd made him feel sometimes like he was on Cuinn's side when nobody else was.

A brother who'd been pretending and lying for years. Manipulating him. A man who'd killed Halun and ripped out his wings. Who'd torn Talyn from his life.

Cuinn's mouth curled. He forgot his aching back and his weariness, sinking fully into his building fury and using it to gather his magic. He sent out a tendril of emotion towards his brother, just a little push of anger, enough to make the winged king start suddenly and look around. Eventually Azrilan's dark eyes fell on the shadowy area where Cuinn stood.

For a heartbeat, he dropped the shadows, letting Azrilan see him standing there, using glamour to make himself look healthy, strong.

And he smiled. Let Azrilan feel the rage winding through him.

Then he lifted his hand in a mocking wave.

And mouthed, *"I'm coming for you."*

They were silly words. Hopeless. An empty threat. But despite all of that, Cuinn wanted to make them come true. He wanted it with every fibre of his being. Wanted it more than he'd ever wanted anything in his life before.

And in that moment, standing there staring at Azrilan, he found that determination he thought he'd lost. The same determination that had sent him out on the streets of Dock City night after night, year after year, to keep trying. This would be no different.

He would do everything he could to *take* what Azrilan had stolen away from him.

He would bring Azrilan down. Or he would die trying. There was no middle ground anymore.

Before the prince of games could twitch, take a step, begin yelling for the Falcons, Cuinn drew the shadows around him completely and turned, striding away, hidden in darkness.

Shouts erupted on the platform behind him. The hum of wings beating furiously sounded as Falcons lifted off or moved in his direction. The music was drowned out completely for a moment.

But Cuinn moved through the darkness, avoiding the pools of light from lit lanterns and torches, stilling every time a Falcon passed above, trusting his shadow ability to hide him. In this slow, cautious way he eventually made it down to the lowest sections of the citadel, below where the Wolves' barracks had been.

The anger faded the further he got, stripping him of its strength and leaving only heartsick weariness in its place. Once he was certain that he'd evaded any pursuit, he stopped in a dark corner, pressed his palms against warm marble, and began to cry.

When Saniya had passed him the announcement about his mother's death, he'd brushed off the news, unable to properly feel it amidst everything else. But seeing her court tonight. Everyone drinking wine and talking. *Her* court. Without her there. Knowing she'd never be amongst them again.

His mother hadn't been loyal to him. Hadn't protected him from his brothers. Had actively made life for humans in Mithranar worse. But he'd loved her anyway, and she had loved him, at least a little. The tears streamed down his face and he swallowed back the sobs, not wanting to make a sound.

Here, alone and protected by the shadows, he allowed himself to grieve. Not just for her. For his wings. For Talyn and Zamaril and Halun. The other Wolves that had died.

Once the tears had run dry, he used the hem of his tunic to scrub his face clean and then a hint of glamour to remove any trace he'd been crying. Then he shifted away from the wall and moved for the rendezvous point. He was limping by then, the pain in his back a constant throbbing, his energy almost completely deserting him.

Saniya and Jystar waited for him in a dark walkway, both looking incredibly disapproving. Jasper broke from the shadows to pad over and bump his head against Cuinn's leg.

"You didn't let any of them see you?" Saniya asked sharply.

"Azrilan did."

Jystar paled visibly, while Saniya's expression tightened. Cuinn almost staggered with the force of the fear that leapt off them. "What is it?"

"My people have been moving about discreetly, looking for traces of Talyn. One of them found a message in the old spot we used to communicate with Navis."

Cuinn frowned. "Navis? What—"

Saniya moved closer, voice filled with a low fury that he sensed wasn't directed at him. "Navis and Savin are one and the same man."

As Cuinn stared at her, uncomprehending, Saniya dug into her pocket, yanked out a dirty, torn page and passed it to him. "This is the message we found."

BROTHER DEAREST,

YOU DO HAVE FRIENDS IN LOW PLACES, DON'T YOU? I ASSUME THOSE FRIENDS WILL GET THIS MESSAGE TO YOU—MY FRIEND USED THIS SPOT TO COMMUNICATE WITH THEM. SHADOWS ARE THE MOST USEFUL OF CREATURES, AREN'T THEY? BUT YOU WOULD KNOW THAT, WOULDN'T YOU, CUINN?

Cuinn glanced up at Saniya. "A Shadow..."

"Gaping fools, the lot of us, missing that." Saniya hissed. "Try re-arranging the flea-shitting letters of his name."

Savin. Navis. Cold fingers of horror trailed down Cuinn's spine. Had Navis been a plant from the beginning, guiding him along the path Azrilan wanted him to follow? He must have been. Pushing down the horror of that, he returned to the note.

ENOUGH WITH THE NICETIES. MITHANIS IS DEALT WITH, AND YOU'RE THE ONLY THREAT REMAINING TO ME. TARCOS LEFT ME A USEFUL LITTLE GROUP OF SPIES AND KILLERS; "HOUNDS," HE CALLED THEM. HE SAID THEY WOULD HUNT AND KILL ANYTHING I ASK THEM TO.

THEY'RE COMING FOR YOU. UNLESS YOU COME TO ME FIRST. I DON'T WANT YOU DEAD, BUT I CAN'T AFFORD FOR YOU TO BE OUTSIDE OF MY CONTROL EITHER. YOUR CHOICE, BROTHER DEAREST. TURN YOURSELF IN OR FIND A KNIFE AT YOUR THROAT ONE NIGHT VERY SOON.

AZ

"Cuinn, you need to go now. Tonight." Saniya snatched the note from his hands. "They could already be on your tail, especially now you basically just paraded yourself in front of him."

"She's right." Jystar glanced around as he spoke, as if expecting assassins to jump out at them any moment. "The Ciantar taught us about Shadows and Armun. It's not a matter of *if* they find you, but *when*."

"All right." He held up a hand, trying to stop them from talking so he could have a moment to think. They were right. He couldn't face down Shadows on his own, especially without the Wolves around him. He had to go... but wherever he went they would follow.

Which meant if he went north to Darmour, he'd only be placing the Wolves in danger, not to mention revealing their hideout to any Shadow tracking him there. But turning himself in to Azrilan wasn't an option, because after what he'd just done, Cuinn felt a glimmer of hope amidst the ache in his chest, enough to keep him on his feet despite his exhaustion and pain.

Azrilan had been scared at the sight of Cuinn.

Absolutely terrified.

And he hadn't been able to hide it.

He looked up, nodded at Saniya and Jystar. "We go tonight."

Saniya's shoulders relaxed. "We'll separate here just in case, and instead of going back to the safehouse, we meet at the docks. Cuinn—the alley where you used to leave messages for me?"

"Agreed. Jystar, you take Jasper and I'll meet you both there."

"I think you should have protection," Jystar protested. "I'll come with you—"

"A winged man, a human and a tawncat together will be far too visible. I am the Shadowhawk. If I can't move through these streets safely, then nobody can," he said firmly. "As a winged man, you can talk your way out of trouble better if you're alone. Jasper knows how to disappear if needed."

"He's right," Saniya said crisply. "Go, both of you."

Cuinn didn't look back.

As HE WALKED, he focused his glamour, ensuring his face showed the bland human features of the Shadowhawk. It was easier now, not having to hide his wings. Pain stabbed at him—reminders that they were lost to him were constant and unrelenting. As was the surge of devastating loss he couldn't control.

He tried to stop himself from glancing over his shoulder, tried to ignore the prickle down the back of his neck at the thought of Shadows or Armun following him through the streets. Talyn had told him all about Firthland's spy and assassin force. Cuinn had no chance if Azrilan's hounds caught up to him. Fear lurked in the pit of his belly.

There were fewer people on the streets than he was accustomed to, and more Falcons patrolling the skies above—Azrilan clearly didn't trust the City Patrol. Fear and unease hung heavy on the air, enough of Dock City's citizens feeling it that it had become a palpable presence to a song mage as powerful as Cuinn. He didn't try and shield himself from it, instead letting himself soak in it.

He wanted to remember. To use it as fuel.

As he walked, he looked for her, even though he told himself it was pointless. She'd come down to the city with Zamaril right before the attack and nobody had seen either of them since.

Aching loss ripped through him, like it had every second moment since he'd woken in the safehouse. She was gone and he didn't know where or how.

It hurt too much to think about, so he pushed thoughts of her away, to deal with when he was stronger, when he could think of some way of trying to find her or... he swallowed and re-focused on his immediate surroundings.

One by one he left messages in all the usual places for his contacts in each Quarter. Navis had never known his other drop locations, but even so, he approached each cautiously, wrapped deep in shadow. At each one, he left a note to wait for further word, that he would have news for them soon. He warned them to stay hidden and quiet until then.

His footsteps eventually came to a halt at the end of a quiet street looking out over the sprawling, tangled series of jetties making up the docks. Although his gaze ran over the ships and smaller fishing vessels, his thoughts were distant.

He didn't want to leave. Had to constantly fight the feeling that he was abandoning his home and his people by running away. But there was no other choice. He couldn't do anything while hiding out in the

Poor Quarter. Especially if Shadows were after him; they could be on his tail already. A shudder went through him at the thought.

The determination he'd found earlier roused in his chest, battling with the fear and sense of hopelessness. He didn't know how he would defeat Azrilan. He knew he couldn't do it as he was now. Not on the run, afraid for his life, with no army, no resources, no...

A thought occurred to him as he stood there, staring towards the south. Over miles of ocean. A crazy, wild thought.

Unbidden, a smile tugged at his mouth. Talyn's plans were often crazy and wild.

A possible next step revealed itself. One Azrilan would never expect... wouldn't *know* enough to expect.

After all, he had no idea that the Acondors weren't Cuinn's only family.

SANIYA AND JYSTAR waited for him at the meeting spot, deep in a narrow alley between two popular sailors' inns. Jasper was with them, only his green eyes visible in the shadows.

"Saniya, I'm taking you up on your offer." He forced briskness to his voice despite his own doubts telling him he was crazy for doing this. Allying himself with people who had murdered innocents and tried to kill him was far from the easiest thing he'd done, and after everything, he wasn't sure he could trust Vengeance. Yet his network and Vengeance had both successfully undermined the Acondors for years, and Cuinn was willing to do whatever it took to take down Azrilan. "With one extra condition."

Her gaze narrowed. "Which is what, exactly?"

"You use our combined resources to find Talyn and Zamaril. Or at least learn what happened to them."

"Agreed." There was no hesitation in Saniya's response.

He tugged a creased piece of parchment from his pocket and gave it to Jystar. "Talon Tye will be the co-lead of our allied network. Jystar, you'll take those orders to Andres and the Wolves—the note includes a list of all the codes and locations for communicating with my network in each Quarter. You tell the Wolves to stay safe and grow strong. Windsong is in charge until I return."

"Until you return." Jystar looked blank. "What are you talking about?"

He turned his gaze to Saniya. "I'm not going to Darmour with Jystar. I'm going south instead. Can you get me there?"

"Not directly, not with the blockade," she said. "But I can get you across the channel to Acleu. From there you'll be able to get on a merchant ship heading south."

"Prince Cuinn, I—"

Cuinn lay a hand on Jystar's shoulder, cutting him off. "Your orders are to get yourself safely north. Tell the Wolves I'm well and that I will return. In the meantime, they're to train hard and grow strong." He looked at Saniya again. "Recruit where you can."

She hesitated. "I proposed an alliance to rebuild our networks for mutual benefit. I'm not fighting for you or risking my people's lives any more than necessary."

"I'm not asking you to fight for me, but you said you were willing to help support my army. I want your help recruiting. Will you agree to those terms?" Cuinn offered his hand.

"Yes." Saniya shook it, her grip sure and confident. He felt only determination and sincerity from her, but used more of his magic to probe deeper, make sure there was nothing under the surface. When he did, he found only regret, bitterness, and a hint of relief?

Saniya glanced away. "Give us a moment, Jystar."

Looking significantly unhappy, the healer moved out of hearing distance. Saniya seemed suddenly… uneasy. Cuinn's magic told him she was wrestling with something. He waited her out.

She took a breath, met his gaze. "My second's name is Leon. I trust him implicitly. I'll have him contact Andres as soon as he gets Jystar's message and returns to Dock City—they can coordinate the merge of our groups together."

Cuinn frowned. Saniya was a known quantity, Talyn's cousin. He knew nothing of this Leon. "That wasn't what you proposed. Where will you be?"

A thick silence fell before Saniya answered. "Talyn let me live. She let me go free, and she did it because she knew it was what her father would have wanted." She scowled. "And I know that my father would want me to find Trystaan's daughter. Leon and Andres will be busy rebuilding our resources and undercutting Azrilan—they won't have the time or opportunity to properly search. So I'm going to."

Cuinn swallowed, one hand reaching out to brace himself against the alley wall as the strength threatened to leave his legs. There was nobody better to look for Talyn. The weight lifting from his shoulders made him momentarily dizzy. "Thank you."

Her voice turned brisk again. She was clearly made uncomfortable by the gratitude in his tone. "Wait here. I'll get Jystar on his boat and then send someone to collect you once I've organised another trip across the channel." She hesitated. "Good luck wherever you're going."

And then she turned and strode away, stopping at the edge of the alley to wait for Jystar to make his farewells.

"Mithranar will be mine," Cuinn spoke fiercely as Jystar re-joined him. "Azrilan will not win. He will die, along with Tarcos Hadvezer. Tell them that, Jystar."

Jystar stilled, then bowed, one hand over his heart. "Your Highness."

"Tell Windsong I will always be grateful for what he's done. Tell the Wolves I'll be back." He reached to grip the healer's shoulder. "And tell them Talyn will be back too."

Jystar's breath hissed. "Your Highness, I don't think—"

"She's not dead." He lifted a hand. "I know it's foolish to stand here and say that to you knowing what we know. But she's not dead. She's out there somewhere, and I know that wherever she is, she'll be fighting to come back to you and the Wolves. And you need to tell them to be ready for when she does."

Something like hope flashed over Jystar's face then, and his shoulders straightened. "I'll make sure they get the message, Your Highness."

. . .

ONCE JYSTAR WAS GONE with Saniya, Cuinn hunkered down, humming a small note. Jasper instantly looked at him, green eyes locked on Cuinn's.

Cuinn reached out to press his hand against the tawncat's soft black fur. Jasper let out a purr. "When Vengeance kidnapped me and hid me away in those tunnels, you knew I was in trouble, and you found me. Because we're family." He stared into the cat's fixed gaze. "Now I need you to find Talyn for me, because I can't. Help Saniya. Bring Talyn home."

Jasper turned his head, pressed it into Cuinn's palm, then bumped his nose against Cuinn's shoulder.

Cuinn lifted himself gingerly to his feet.

Jasper gave him one final look and he was gone.

Cuinn found himself alone, with his thoughts and memories. Again the realisations crashed through him: his wings gone, Talyn missing, Halun dead.

His grief seemed endless sometimes, like it was going to drown him in its agony. But whereas in those first few days after the attack it had taken him down and held him there, now each time, breath by breath, he fought his way back to the surface.

Talyn had felt this pain after Sari's death. He'd sensed it in her. Felt how she'd fought so hard to manage it. Watched her win that battle over and over again. He could do that too. He would keep doing it. And each time he did, some of the pain turned to scar tissue, to a hardness inside him that had never been there before. But he welcomed that too, because he was going to need that hardness in the days and months ahead.

Cuinn walked forward to the end of the alley, eyes fixed on the docks and the harbour beyond it. He stared to the south.

The time of the Shadowhawk was gone.

Now he needed to be more.

CHAPTER 5

*E*ven when she was conscious, it was like being trapped in a feverish, restless nightmare from which there was no escape.

If Kaeri had held any hope whatsoever, it seemed to fade as her condition grew considerably worse. She drifted endlessly from fever dream to fever dream. And still that... something... trying to batter through her dreams, to reach her somehow. Failing every time.

She'd come awake screaming, stay conscious long enough to take a few sips of water and swallow some soup, before her strength would give out again and she'd sink back into the nightmares.

Days passed, one bleeding into another, until she had no idea of time anymore. Just endless illness. Some core part of her knew she was getting worse. But she didn't know what to do about it.

And then came a different dream. First it was only flashes, a glimpse of green grass and the brightest blue sky she'd ever seen. She scrambled after those images, tried to hold onto them, to escape the nightmares.

Was this dying? She thought maybe it was.

In the snatches she could grab, a man's voice spoke, indistinct at first, but becoming clearer the harder she tried to reach that place with the blue sky.

Her body grew sicker, weaker. And the glimpses grew more frequent, stayed a little longer. Eventually, she didn't have to scramble for them anymore. Wherever that place was, she began to sink towards it.

Then a man's face flashed before her, older, beautiful, tanned skin with sapphire eyes. She knew that face—but couldn't find the memory associated with it. And then another man appeared with him, this one familiar too, with dark skin and hazel eyes. She tried harder to reach him, reach *them*, and in her struggles the pain flared white-hot, breaking through the fog of fever. She screamed, writhing, but kept trying, kept fighting.

They helped her. With indistinct voices the two men encouraged her over and over. Once she swore the man with the sapphire eyes had taken hold of her arm—with rough, calloused palms like those of a farmer—and helped her when she needed just a little bit extra to fight.

They stayed with her, never leaving, as the pain worsened and the fever grew hotter, burning through her, taking what was left of her life.

And then, suddenly, she was *in* that place. The grass under her feet. Blue sky above. All of it with a dreamlike quality, as if it might vanish at any second.

"Talyn?"

A man stood before her. He had magnificent wings that gleamed the same blue as his eyes and wore a familiar smile on his face.

"Da?" The word came out without thinking.

At his nod, his smile—the soft one he'd always reserved for her alone—the knowledge of who she was came crashing down around her, followed by a rush of memory that had her swaying on her feet. Not all of it was there, not why she was here or how she'd gotten so hurt. Those memories remained locked away and she didn't go chasing them.

"I…" Tears filled her eyes. "Am I dead?"

"Very close to it, I'm afraid." He stepped forward. "Which is why we're talking right now. Talyn, you've got a fight on your hands, but I'm here to help."

She swallowed, for a moment struck by the sheer wonder of seeing her father standing in front of her. She opened her mouth, tried to figure out what to say, and simply said, "I miss you. I miss you so much, Da."

"I miss you too, my girl." He drew her into a fierce hug. He wasn't quite solid under her hands, but she hugged him back anyway. Her da was here. It was overwhelming and wonderful and heartbreaking all at once and for a long moment, she buried her head in his chest and closed her eyes, allowing him to rock her gently back and forth.

"Where are we?" She pulled away reluctantly.

"An in-between place that only the most experienced of winged folk healers know about," Trystaan said. "You're here because you're close to death, Talyn. But being here means I can reach you, which is a good thing."

"It's better than good." Tears welled in her eyes. "You're helping me," she said in wonder.

She could feel it, distantly, a little bit of strength returning, some of the fever easing.

"Tiercelin told me how—I have secondary healing magic. He wanted to come too, but it's not... it wasn't possible for all of us."

All of us?

"Tiercelin..." She bit her lip as more tears welled. She missed him too, so much. "What do I do?" she asked helplessly.

"My magic is helping your body to beat the infection," he said soberly. "But I can't heal your wounds, do you understand? Tiercelin thinks the blow to your head is the source of your memory loss, but he says it probably won't last. You'll have to be strong. You have a difficult road ahead."

She managed a smile. "I've done difficult before."

"You have." He framed her cheek with his hand. "Be the Ciantar I could never be, Talyn."

"I love you." She swallowed back more tears. "Please don't go."

26

"It's time, Talyn. And I love you," he whispered. "Always."

She searched for all the words she needed to say, found some of them. "Say hello to Tiercelin for me. Tell him I love him and miss him. Tell him we all do."

"He loves you too." He pressed a gentle kiss to her forehead.

He was gone before she was ready, fading from view until she stood alone under the blue sky.

The fields and the sky faded too, and with it Talyn's awareness. For a long time there was pain and restless nightmares and a horrible weakness. Dimly, she sensed her body fighting, doing its best to rally now the infection was gone.

But she was so, so tired. There was nothing left to fight with.

When she opened her eyes and found herself in the field again, she blinked in confusion. But before she could follow that thought, wonder why she was back, her gaze was caught by movement in her peripheral vision.

She turned to see a tall warrior striding over the grass, Callanan cloak hanging from her shoulders, her face stretched in a laughing smile. The bright light of reckless confidence lit up her hazel eyes, and her hands glimmered with her silver Callanan magic like they always had when she was excited.

"Sari," Talyn breathed.

Then she ran.

"Oh Tal, it's good to see you." Sari threw her arms around Talyn as they collided.

She couldn't breathe. Couldn't think. Couldn't do anything but stand there and hold onto her partner as fiercely as she knew how, fiercely enough to stop her ever being pulled away again. Each day since Sari's death she'd hoped for this, wanting her back with every breath she took, every single moment, every time she opened her eyes in the morning. Now it was here she couldn't even comprehend the complete and utter relief and joy of it.

"You going to say something?" Sari chuckled.

Talyn shook her head, forced herself to swallow around the lump in her throat and loosen her grip enough to stand back. "You... you have no idea," she whispered.

The laughter faded from Sari's face. "I can imagine. If you had died and I had lived..."

"I didn't want to live. I didn't know how."

Another smile spread across her partner's face. "But you've learned how. You've been amazing."

Talyn's eyes flooded with tears. "I didn't want to. I still don't want to. You have no idea how much I miss you, how hard it was to lose you. I want it all back, Sari."

"I'm so sorry," Sari said softly.

"I didn't even get to say goodbye." The pain of that surged, broke through her, had her biting her lip hard. "Not even a moment to tell you what you meant to me, to thank you for always having my back, no matter what."

"I didn't need you to tell me, Talyn. Just like you don't need me to tell you. We just knew," Sari said simply.

Talyn nodded acknowledgement of that. "And you didn't leave me completely."

"I had no idea Callanan magic worked like that." Sari's laugh pealed out. "Doesn't it get annoying, having me in your head all the time?"

"No." Talyn huffed a laugh. "No. It's the most wonderful thing that ever happened to me."

"I don't know. I think I'd want to kick you out regularly if you were in my head."

Talyn grinned. "No you wouldn't."

"Yes I would."

Her smile faded. "I don't suppose there's any way you can come back with me?"

"I *am* with you, Tal," Sari whispered. "Always."

She nodded. Tried to accept it.

"And I'm here now for a reason." Sari took hold of her hands. "You have to fight harder. For me, please?"

"I am fighting." Talyn frowned, confused.

"I need you to do more," Sari said. "Your body has lost too much blood and it's failing, even with the fever gone."

"I'm trying to—"

"I know you miss me, and your dad and Tiercelin. I know part of you probably wants to stay here." Sadness filled Sari's face. "*I* would, if I were in your shoes. But you can't. You have to fight with everything you have, no doubts, no hesitation. I know you don't remember everything yet, but there's someone waiting back there for you, Tal, someone you love just as much as me or your da. Trust me like you always have. You have to go."

Talyn swallowed, opened her mouth to deny Sari's words, before she realised she couldn't. Part of her *did* want this. To be back with Sari properly. With her father and the Wolves she'd lost. To not have to hurt anymore.

"It feels like losing you again," she admitted, mortified as her eyes flooded with tears. "But I know I can't stay. I know, I just…"

Sari's voice firmed, and she took Talyn's hands. "You need to hold on, fight back to awareness so you can drink and eat, help your body heal. Let me in. Let me help you. I'm your partner. Always and forever."

Sari's grip on her hands tightened and she felt their Callanan partnership bond strengthen, expand. With it came a rush of dizzying strength. "I'll fight."

"Good. As hard as you can, Tal."

"With everything I have," Talyn promised.

She wanted to say more, to tell Sari how big Tarquin had gotten, how Leviana and Cynia still missed her every day too, but before she could even open her mouth, their combined Callanan power surged and she was wrenched away in flash of silver and sapphire light.

The field was gone.

The darkness faded.

And she fought. With everything she had, she fought to return to life.

. . .

TALYN BLINKED AWAKE. It was dark, and she hurt all over. Sweat dried on her skin from the fever that had been burning her up but was now broken.

Her back arched at the intensity of the pain no longer hidden by delirium, her hands digging into the cool dirt floor as agony flooded through her head like stitches being torn out of a wound.

The pain dug deeper into her bones, bringing everything into sharp awareness. More memories came flooding back.

She remembered pitch darkness. Being underground. Savin's dying body sprawled on the dirt as too-strong arms dragged her away. She'd been dizzy, in pain, blood flowing freely from the stab wound in her right side.

Bearmen.

Why were Bearmen helping Savin? He'd ambushed them... Zamaril! Where was Zamaril?

The man holding her had asked a question. Another one replied. His words were mostly indistinct but she made out the words 'warlord' and 'orders'.

She was dying. She and Zamaril had walked straight into Savin's trap and now she was dying.

Talyn drowned in her memories, and the more she remembered, the more she came back to herself. Slowly the pain began to abate and as it did, a sweet rush flooded her body.

Her magic.

This power, she remembered this. Her winged folk blood.

Winged folk.

She was Ciantar. She was Dumnorix. She was Callanan and Aimsir.

Callanan. She was Callanan. Her Callanan partner...

"*SARI!*" she screamed, didn't know if it was audible or not, didn't care. She just needed...

"*I'm here.*" Her partner collided with her, wrapping Talyn with her magic, the two of them slamming back together. "*You did it!*"

"*That was you, all this time nagging in the back of my head.*" She was almost delirious with relief. Her partner was still there. She hadn't gone.

"*I was shouting, screaming, but you couldn't hear me. You couldn't hear me.*" Sari's voice sobbed with relief and sadness.

"*I can hear you now. What happened to me?*"

"*You were hit on the head and lost your memories.*" Sari held on tight. "*Let's bring them back.*"

Images flashed through Talyn's mind then, so fast she could barely recognise them, but each one bought back everything she'd forgotten.

The citadel in Mithranar, glittering in its splendour on a sunny afternoon.

The grey and white of the Wolves' uniforms as they drilled in the barracks.

Zamaril's mocking tone.

Theac and his scowl.

The light in Corrin's green eyes when he played the flute.

The sober look Andres would get on his face when he was thinking deeply about something.

Halun's way of talking without using any words.

A winged prince. Golden and silver and full of magic. His voice, his song, his *everything*. The unexpected joy of loving him.

Her heart stopped. Cuinn. Where was he?

"You're awake?" Kaeri's face appeared in her field of vision as the woman leaned over her, astonishment in her face and voice. "Can you hear me?"

Talyn blinked. "I hear you," she said, the words rasping.

"Drink this, now!"

The command in Kaeri's voice had Talyn shifting her mouth towards the cup of water before she knew what she was doing. Pain stabbed through her again, but she ignored it, sipping the water. Sari said she needed to drink to heal. She'd promised.

"All of it," Kaeri insisted when she began slumping back to the pallet. "Drink."

Somehow she forced herself to drink all the water. The last of it trickled down her chin as her strength gave out and her head sank back to the ground.

"*Sari?*"

"*I'm here. You're back. We're back.*"

Talyn swallowed, her consciousness already slipping away again, this time from exhaustion. "*I am Talyn Ciantar.*"

And then she slept.

CHAPTER 6

*N*ext time Talyn woke she lay still, marvelling. There had been no nightmare. She'd come awake from real sleep.

But pain quickly followed on the heels of lucidity. Her body ached all over, with several sharp lines of burning pain down her back and one hot ball of agony on her lower right side, under her ribs. The pain there was so strong a sharp gasp of breath escaped her, unbidden.

The next thing she became aware of was a rhythmic tapping on the roof. A slight turn of her head and she was looking out at a curtain of falling rain through the arched opening that served as a doorway. The light of the day was fading, but she could still make out the muddy ground beyond the door, spotted with deep puddles. It must have been raining a while.

She blinked. That had been a clear thought.

Immediately she reached for her memories. The green field was still there. Sari and her father… before that… a dark tunnel. Savin, triumph twisting his face. She'd killed him, remembered clearly the sensation of his warm blood soaking her hands.

She'd been stabbed. She'd lost sight of Zamaril. And after that… the first thing she remembered was this hut.

A cold slide of dread in her chest followed. Cuinn. Her Wolves.

What had happened? If they'd ambushed her and Zamaril... surely that meant they were going after Cuinn too. But who? Had she hallucinated the Bearmen?

She needed to find Cuinn and her Wolves. Get to wherever they were. But she had no idea how much time had passed, or where she was. Heart racing, she was quickly spiralling into a breathless panic when there was movement at the doorway and Kaeri entered the hut, rain soaking her shoulders and hair.

The instinct to lunge upwards, to demand answers to her questions, was close to overwhelming.

"Calm, Talyn. Learn your situation first," Sari counselled urgently. *"Wherever you are, it looks like you're a prisoner, but those holding you might not know who you are, and if so, you're probably safer that way."*

Kaeri came over and crouched beside the pallet. And Talyn, her memories restored, recognised her instantly.

Kaeri Venador.

Paler, gaunt, definitely less polished than the last time Talyn had seen her. But it was Ahara Venador's daughter nonetheless.

Shock and confusion jolted through her, dislodging some of the panic still swirling in her gut. What was the favourite child of the Montagni ahara doing in this hut, dirty and careworn, tending to Talyn's wounds? She opened her mouth to ask the question, but shut it just as abruptly. Sari was right... best to understand what was going on before revealing anything.

She tried to draw on her self-control, as she always had before, to manage her fear and pain and panic. It was harder than it had ever been. Her desperate desire to know what had happened to Cuinn, to her Wolves, was so strong it came perilously close to overpowering common sense.

"Talyn, I'm here." Sari wrapped her in reassurance. *"You could put Cuinn in more danger if you talk about him. Just be patient."*

"Something wrong?" Kaeri asked, presumably seeing the surprise that had flashed over Talyn's face and then the subsequent battle with her emotions.

"Your name... Kaeri?" she managed. Her throat was so parched it hurt to talk.

Kaeri's eyes widened in surprise. "You remember me telling you that?"

"Not dead... yet."

"No." Disbelief edged Kaeri's blunt voice. "Your fever broke two days ago. You've been sleeping normally ever since. I don't understand how, but I think you've turned a corner. It should have been impossible."

"What... happened?"

"Have some water before you keep talking." Kaeri placed a wooden mug at Talyn's mouth and she shifted her head to drink. The liquid was cold and clear, but the movement caused agony to rip down her spine and right side.

She gasped, choking on the water.

"Keep as still as you can. Your wounds haven't closed over properly. Hopefully you'll heal faster now the infection has cleared."

Talyn summoned all her strength. "Tell me... my injuries?"

Kaeri coaxed her to take another sip, then set the cup down. "You must have fought hard when you arrived here because the guards beat you, then whipped you into submission. The whipping tore several layers of skin from your back. The injuries you already had—the worst of which was a stab wound just under your right ribs—were infected when you got here. By some stroke of luck the strike missed your kidney or you would have died weeks ago."

Even so, that was bad. Very bad. "Anything... else?"

"You've got a nasty cut on your forehead—it was swollen and bruised. I think that's why you can't remember anything."

Talyn closed her eyes as a wave of weakness washed over her.

"Drink more," Kaeri urged.

Talyn did as she was bidden; the cool water soothed her throat, helped her marshal her thoughts. She needed to know where they were. "Did you say... labour camp?"

"That's right." Kaeri hesitated. "We're in a labour camp for slaves."

Slaves. It was only then that Talyn registered the swirling blue tattoo on Kaeri's left cheek. Her chest tightened. If Kaeri was a slave then so was Talyn. She didn't even know where to start with processing that, so for now she pushed the knowledge away. "How long?"

"You've been here just over two weeks. Do you remember anything?"

So long... so much could have happened. Fear for Cuinn, for her Wolves, swept through her so profoundly she could do nothing but lie there for a long moment and ride it out. Once again she had to fight down the desire to ask Kaeri about them. Not now, not when she was so weary and sick she could barely think straight.

"I remember a little bit. Not much," she whispered, eventually.

"Good." Kaeri touched her head softly. "Sleep now. Your body needs the rest. We can talk next time you wake."

Another wave of weariness washed over her and despite her fear and pain, Talyn sank into a deep sleep.

IT WAS ALMOST another full day before Talyn woke again. Kaeri was hovering over the fire, the two other women from their hut settling on their pallets on the other side of the open space. Both had fair skin and brown hair, but the tattoo mark on their cheeks wasn't as fresh and bright as the one Kaeri wore. Neither spoke to Talyn, though they glanced her way frequently when they didn't think she was looking. She wondered what it was about her that unsettled them so much.

"How are you feeling?" Kaeri asked, noticing she'd woken.

Talyn frowned. "In pain. Tired. Thirsty." *Terrified.*

"Thirsty is good." Kaeri carried over a cup of water. "Drink all of this and then you have to eat something."

Her stomach turned at the very thought of food, but Talyn dutifully sipped at the water until it was all gone. Kaeri then helped her to a half-sitting position, pain tearing through her with every movement. Once she was up, Kaeri presented her with a small bowl of rice. "Eat."

It was dark out, and the other two women were already asleep.

Talyn scooped up a spoon of rice, forced half of it into her mouth, and chewed slowly. Her stomach roiled. Her back throbbed.

"You don't seem to sleep much," Talyn noted, focusing on the small fire where Kaeri was boiling water for tea. Maybe the distraction of conversation would help her get the food down before she vomited it all back up. Not to mention help her learn more about her situation.

"I don't sleep well."

"How did you know how to help me?" It was hard to imagine the favoured child of the ahara learning healing skills.

"The favoured child of the ahara has somehow become a slave, and her healing skills are what's confusing you?" Sari asked.

"Leave me alone, I'm recovering from a head wound."

"Excuses, excuses." Sari sniffed.

Talyn smiled inwardly, taking strength from her partner's presence.

"I learned the basics of healing from some of my father's soldiers."

Talyn thought on that a moment, decided to try and probe further to see whether Kaeri would reveal who she was. "Your father is a Montagni lord?"

"Of sorts." Kaeri flashed a bitter smile. Then she sighed and reached for the bubbling kettle. Her hands busied themselves adding herbs into two cups and then pouring the liquid over them. The sharp scent of the tea filled the room—something sweet edged with a sourer smell.

"Montagni woman aren't allowed to fight, are they? Like in Mithranar?"

"You remember that?"

"I do," she hedged. "It was just there, in my mind, the knowledge."

Kaeri brought the tea over, flashing an approving glance at the empty rice bowl. "You're mostly right. Slave women are expected to fight if necessary, but female citizens do not. It's not considered proper. I trained with my father's soldiers when he wasn't paying attention."

Talyn shifted, wincing. Her stomach had not enjoyed the food, but the tea and conversation were helping keep it down. "If you're the daughter of a lord, then what are you doing here?"

"The answer to that is the reason I don't sleep anymore." Her tone was curt, dismissive, clearly flagging that she didn't want to talk about it any further. But underlying the words was a pain Talyn recognised all too well. She nodded and sipped at her tea.

"And you don't know who I am? The guards didn't tell you?" Talyn tried to probe further.

"They dragged you in here, dumped you on the ground, then barked at me to look after you," Kaeri said in disgust. "There was no polite exchange of names."

"I remember some flashes from my nightmares, like the citadel in Mithranar," she said carefully.

Interest flashed over Kaeri's face. "You're Mithranan?"

"Maybe." Talyn shrugged, pretending casualness she didn't feel. "Did something happen there that might have led to me ending up a slave in Montagn?"

Kaeri's face closed over. "A lot has happened in Montagn recently that will no doubt effect Mithranar. But I was dumped in here not long before you. I have no idea what's happened in the outside world since."

Rising, Kaeri crossed back to the fire, her rigid bearing indicating she had no desire to discuss the subject any further. Talyn tried to swallow down her disappointment.

"*What do you think?*" she asked Sari.

"*Honestly? I think she might be an ally. But best to hold counsel for a little longer.*"

"Tomorrow you should start moving about," Kaeri said, voice lighter. "If you're not on your feet soon, the guards here will force you up. Right now you're a burden, and they don't tolerate slaves being burdens for very long."

The words hung in the air. Talyn carefully put her cup down. Time to address that development head on. "So I'm really a slave?"

Kaeri grimaced. "I guess the pain from your back is masking the one from the healing tattoo they put on your left cheek. Yes, you're a slave."

Talyn instinctively lifted a hand to check, wincing as the movement caused agony to flare in her right side.

She was a slave.

"Oh, Talyn."

Her thoughts went straight to Halun. She wondered if the big man was okay, where he was at this moment. Wished he was there with her. His silent presence had always been a comfort.

Did it matter that she was a slave? She wasn't sure… suspected that the panic and fear she was barely holding at bay regarding Cuinn and her Wolves dwarfed any negative emotion she might have over learning she was a slave.

From the simmering fire in Kaeri's eyes, Talyn had a feeling the ahara's daughter wasn't coping with the idea well. Weariness stole over her, and she stifled a yawn, wanting to try and find out more before she slept again. "What sort of work do slaves do here?" she asked.

"We make weapons," Kaeri said grimly. "Everything you could think of. Swords, axes, arrows, bows, knives, daggers."

"Oh." Something about Kaeri's words stirred something in Talyn, but the thought was too distant and she couldn't quite manage to pin it down. Kaeri said something more, but Talyn didn't hear as exhaustion claimed her and she slid back down onto her stomach, eyes closing before her head hit the surface.

Even so, worry followed her into restful sleep. Cuinn. Where was he?

CHAPTER 7

*C*uinn didn't sleep much on the journey south, unable to bear being alone with his thoughts in the dark quiet of his bunk. To keep himself busy he worked at simple tasks to help the crew. While he coiled rope or helped in the galley, he tried to keep his thinking productive, focused on the present and the future instead of dwelling on what had happened. Often he failed. There was too much pain inside him to win that battle regularly.

It still took his breath away—not only learning the truth of who his brother was, but knowing that he'd missed it for so long. Cuinn Acondor, the most powerful song mage of his generation, nicknamed the prince of song for his power, and he'd completely missed Azrilan using that same magic on all of them to hide his ambition, his planning.

And Talyn had missed it too. Missed Tarcos Hadvezer trying to use her as a strategic piece to take the Twin Thrones from the Dumnorix. Missed him teaming up with Azrilan and throwing her life away when she chose to marry Cuinn instead of him.

He loved her more than life itself. The thought that she was out there, possibly hurt, in trouble, and he couldn't help... and more than that, he just missed her. Missed her smile, her laugh, the way her sharp sapphire gaze softened whenever they were together.

He pushed the despair away with little success.

Tarcos had made clear his intentions to invade the Twin Thrones and take them for his own. And it had been equally clear that Azrilan was willing to help him in that endeavour if necessary.

But Azrilan couldn't help Tarcos immediately. Cuinn understood enough about Montagni politics to know it was going to take time for Azrilan—especially as a winged man—to establish his rule over all the powerful Houses. And even when he did, it would take some convincing to send them to war on Tarcos's behalf.

Cuinn had a little time to figure out a plan, a way forward. He needed allies, and the Dumnorix were powerful. *If* they'd managed to rally themselves after Aethain's death. *If* Tarcos hadn't already invaded and taken their kingdom out from under them.

His chest tightened with doubt and anxiety at the thought of what he was trying to do. It was a constant nagging shadow in the back of his mind. He felt weak and vulnerable without his wings. Unable to confidently pick the right path forward without Talyn. Unable to focus through the grief and fear weighing him down.

He couldn't hide in the shadows as a criminal anymore. That mask was gone. Now he was just a winged man without wings. A prince without a throne. And the closer he came to his destination, the more it felt like he'd made a terrible mistake.

What could he offer the Dumnorix?

He forced himself to take a deep, shuddering breath, reaching for the spark of determination that had brought him this far. It was faint, but he held onto it with everything he had. It didn't stop the doubt curdling his belly, but it gave him enough to keep moving forward despite that doubt.

One step at a time.

He'd just gotten himself under control when shouts came from high in the rigging—Port Lachley harbour had come into sight. Cuinn dropped the rope he'd been coiling without thinking, going to the railing to stare at the approaching landmass.

The Twin Thrones.

The last time he'd made this approach, it had been with Talyn and a ship full of Wolves, seeking sanctuary after Mithanis had attacked them. Or had it been Azrilan?

All that time it must have been Azrilan whispering in Mithanis' ear, urging him on, sowing the seeds of conflict, setting Cuinn and Mithanis up for inevitable confrontation. And whichever brother defeated the other, well, that was one less powerful brother for Azrilan to deal with.

A prince of games indeed.

And now Cuinn was here, in Port Lachley. Where the family he hadn't realised existed lived, a family he barely knew. He had to hope Theac and Corrin had made it safely. If they had, then Talyn's family would also know that she was missing. They must be devastated. They probably blamed Cuinn, and so they should.

As the ship drew closer, what had on first appearances looked like a crowded approach to the port resolved to four Conmoran navy vessels patrolling the ocean around it. His breath caught in his chest and for a moment his pain was eclipsed by relief.

The Twin Thrones was on war footing.

Which meant Theac and Corrin had probably made it and warned them.

Abruptly turning away from the railing, he went down to the sleeping quarters of the ship. With quick movements he tugged off the clothes he'd been working in and changed.

It was still strange how easy it was to put on a shirt and jacket without the awkwardness of wings. Dressing himself took moments now, where before it had taken almost a quarter-turn depending on what he'd chosen to wear. He wondered whether he'd ever grow accustomed to the change. Whether it would ever start feeling like a good thing, rather than the tight ball of pain and vulnerability that lodged in his chest every time he thought about it.

Once dressed, he ran a hand over the growing stubble on his scalp —he'd shaved it before leaving Dock City to reduce the chances of being recognised—and straightened his jacket.

It wouldn't do to have the Kingshield refuse to allow him anywhere near the castle fortress because he looked more like a street ruffian than Prince Cuinn Acondor. Scrutinising himself, he added a touch of glamour to make the clothes seem a little finer, the cut a little better. Satisfied, he let go of the magic so as not to waste energy, then finished packing his bag.

Within a full-turn he was disembarking onto a narrow jetty amidst the handful of other passengers on the ship. Back on solid ground, he had to re-adjust to the feeling of being off balance as he walked without his wings to steady him. Tears flooded his eyes and he scrubbed roughly at them.

His gait mustn't look too strange though, because nobody glanced in his direction with anything but passing interest as he walked through the city. He marked the soldiers patrolling the streets in their midnight-blue Conmoran uniforms—they hadn't been there when he'd visited with Talyn—but kept his head down and stride long. They weren't bothering anyone, just keeping a watchful eye out.

It was a long walk from the harbour to the eastern city gates where the main road led out to the east of Conmor, splitting off not far beyond the city to wind its way up to the castle fortress perched on the eastern bluff of the harbour.

Plenty of traffic was heading to or from the castle so Cuinn didn't stand out as he joined them, though his legs soon burned from the steady incline of the winding road.

The main gates of the castle stood open and the large entry court-yard was even busier than the road, packed with people, horses and carts carrying supplies in and out of the castle or wealthier folk waiting to attend meetings with one or more of the lords in residence. The sharp crack of chisel on stone resounded through the morning air from a group of workers reinforcing a section of the outer wall.

The gates bristled with soldiers, though again, they weren't harassing anyone, just asking the occasional question or looking over some of the larger loads coming in on carts.

It struck him, for a moment, how different this was. The palace at the citadel wasn't open to its citizens like this place clearly was. The

Dumnorix fortress was formidable, and he'd seen how it could be locked down on the night Aethain had been murdered, but it was also clearly a place Conmoran citizens should feel welcome to enter. Even in a time of trouble.

Dismissing his idle thoughts, he cast his gaze around, searching the chaotic throng of people and animals, until he spotted six Kingshield guarding the entrance into the inner courtyard of the castle—an area decidedly not for the public.

His shoulders relaxed in relief. He hadn't been certain any of the Dumnorix would be in residence at Port Lachley. Talyn had left them two months earlier and they'd had no news of the family since. But the presence of Kingshield meant at least one of them was here.

On the heels of relief came nerves and apprehension.

As glad as he was to have found them, he was equally anxious about what came next. He wasn't at all certain that he could pull it off.

But that didn't mean he wasn't going to try.

Four sharp gazes landed on Cuinn, watching his approach to the inner gates, while the other two Kingshield continued scanning the courtyard. So well-trained, these men and women. They were the model off which Talyn had built his Wolves.

"Can we help you?" One of the guards stepped forward. She was slight, but the unusual grace in her movement indicated she'd been Callanan once. The *sabai* they all learned gave them a winged folk-like agility.

"Yes." Briefly he hesitated. He wasn't known to these guards and he no longer had wings to prove his identity. So instead he hoped Talyn's name would get him in. He hadn't failed to notice when he was here last that the other warriors in the castle idolised her. Not that *she'd* noticed. "I am a friend of Lady Talyn Dumnorix, and I was hoping you would convey a message to her family that I'd like to see them."

The guard stilled, and two of the other Kingshield stepped towards them at the sound of Talyn's name. Holding to their duty, the other three merely glanced in his direction before returning to watching the courtyard. "You have news of Lady Talyn?" the ex-Callanan asked.

"Is she coming back?" another added. A flash of his emotion

washed over Cuinn, a touch of recklessness with a hint of his bond with his horse—this one had been Aimsir.

"Wait!" the woman said sharply, before Cuinn could answer. "Are you with the two soldiers that came from Mithranar?"

"Yes. I am." His voice flooded with eagerness, relief. "They made it here?"

"They're staying as guests of the family." She hesitated, running her eyes over him. "I'm Kila."

"Cuinn Acondor." He offered his hand.

"You're the Mithranan prince?" The male Kingshield started in surprise and he and Kila shared a shocked glance. "The one Lady Talyn was to marry?"

"That's me." He swallowed the surge of pain, though he was sure it was obvious on his face. "Will you take me to see whoever of the family is in residence?"

"Right away." Kila waved for one of the other Kingshield to open the inner gates. "Come through. This is Felix."

The Aimsir nodded in a friendly fashion as he fell into step with Cuinn. Apparently he was now getting an escort. Talyn's name had worked the magic he'd hoped for.

"Is she okay? Lady Talyn? We haven't had any news of her since she left."

He should have prepared himself for this, but he hadn't. The pain curled, but he fought it down. He took a breath, shook his head. "I'm sorry, I don't know."

Kila and Felix shared another look but fell silent, asking him no more questions as they escorted him up another set of steps and into a cavernous entrance hall. They turned right off the hall and walked down a wide corridor decorated with rich tapestries.

Cuinn's stomach clenched, the anxiety he'd already been feeling surging through him in a wave. He didn't know these people, and being here without Talyn felt awkward, uncomfortable.

The Kingshield had no such hesitations. Felix spoke briefly with the two guards standing outside a set of closed doors on the left, then waved Cuinn over before pushing them open.

Felix winked at him. "Good luck in there. The Dumnorix are a fierce, intimidating lot, but they're good people."

Bolstered by the unexpected support of these two Kingshield he'd never met before, Cuinn walked into the great hall. The massive arched windows down the western side showed grey ocean and equally grey sky.

Both Alyna and Ariar were there, leaning over a table covered in rolled and unrolled parchment. Soar, the SkyRider Chieftain, sat frowning in a chair. An unfamiliar woman was there too, wearing the green Callanan cloak, her short stature eclipsed by the fierceness of her scowl. The First Blade?

They all turned at the sound of the opening doors and his boots rapping on the floor.

Alyna's hand went to her mouth at the sight of him, and her eyes widened with shock. Ariar paled, straightening up from the table and heading towards him in quick strides. "Cuinn!"

Ariar had dropped Cuinn's title unconsciously, a habit of all Dumnorix when speaking to family. A sharp look from Alyna indicated she'd picked up his mistake, but Cuinn pretended not to notice. Her next look was for the First Blade, who immediately turned and left the hall via a side exit, leaving only family behind.

"Do you have news on Talyn?" Alyna asked, violet gaze on Cuinn's face, pleading. Ariar paused halfway to him, hope lighting his blue eyes. Soar's hand curled on the arm of his chair.

"I'm sorry." Tears filled his eyes, his song magic flooding him with the family's grief and worry. It was overwhelming, and it took a moment before he could speak again. He fought hard to disassociate himself from their emotion, hold it at bay, but even so, he was sure he must look like a miserable fool rather than the strong prince he'd wanted to show them. "I don't."

Ariar swallowed, but resumed walking, stopping at Cuinn's side and lifting a hand to his shoulder. "You look awful. Come and sit down."

"I'm fine." Cuinn shook his head.

"We didn't know if you were even still alive." Soar rose to his feet.

"Your Wolves said you'd been badly hurt, that your wings..." Soar's voice trailed off and every single Dumnorix in the room flinched as they all realised that his wings were gone.

It was Alyna who spoke next, her eyes still unwaveringly on Cuinn. Grief drew deep lines on her face. "Is she dead?"

Cuinn met her gaze. "She lives, Alyna. I don't know how, or where she is, or even what happened to her. But she lives."

"How do you know?"

"I can't explain that to you." He filled his voice with the conviction he felt, used it to keep his fear at bay. "But I'm certain."

Ariar's hand returned to his shoulder, squeezing tightly before letting go. Soar leaned forward, eyes closing briefly. And Alyna let out a sob, sinking into a chair. She took a long, shuddering breath, then nodded. "Then we'll find her. No matter what."

"I don't want to give you false hope. Whatever happened... there's no trace. Not a single clue to follow," he said, then turned to Alyna, urgency thrumming through him. He had to make sure... "The King-shield told me Theac and Corrin made it here. They warned you about Tarcos?"

Ariar turned grim. "They did. Two days before a force of Montagni and Firthlander soldiers boiled out of the Ayrlemyre Mountains, trying to march north into Conmor. We're at war, Cuinn."

"Without their warning, we wouldn't have had forces ready. We may not have contained their first push," Soar said quietly.

"As it is, for now they remain contained in the mountains." Ariar's words were positive, but his voice was laced with bitterness. "It's Viscarin all over again."

Cuinn searched his memory. Viscarin, architect of the Firthlander invasion of Conmor and Calumnia generations earlier. The man Cuinn's ancestor Rianna had killed before giving the Twin Thrones to her younger brother Alendor, the ancestor of the people gathered in this room now.

"Has Aeris been found?" he asked quietly.

A moment's silence, then, "He remains missing," Soar said.

And presumed dead. Soar didn't have to say the words aloud.

Tarcos had sent a Shadow to kill the king of the Twin Thrones—he would not have left his heir alive.

"I'm sorry." Cuinn wrapped his words in magic, reassurance mixed with empathy and a touch of shared grief. "Have you chosen a regent?"

"We're ruling by committee." Ariar's eyes strayed to Alyna. "With war so suddenly upon us we figure that's best for now. At least until we know for certain about Aeris. And Talyn now too."

"And the lords?" he asked.

"The Conmoran Lords' Council is furious at the incursion into our territory and we fight daily to talk them down from their insistence on launching an all out invasion of Firthland and stretching our forces too thinly in the process. Fortunately, declaration of war remains in the remit of the Dumnorix," Alyna said. "The Calumnian lords are anxious, but they trust us. For now."

Alyna's glance in Cuinn's direction spoke volumes. They needed Talyn here. As much as she would deny it until her dying breath, Talyn had been born to lead. And her strategic mind would have been the asset they needed to win the war. They needed her as regent.

"Cuinn, we need to know what happened, what's going on," Alyna said sharply. "Your Wolves were only able to tell us pieces, enough to warn us, but that's all. We can't plan properly if we don't know the whole story."

"That's why I came." Cuinn took a steadying breath. "To help you in any way I can." And to ask for their help in return. But he couldn't ask that straight out. He'd have to approach it carefully. Try and win their trust first.

"Sit." Soar pointed to a chair. "Tell us."

"It will be best if I start from the beginning," he said, settling himself before he started talking.

When he got to telling them about that horrible night, he did his best to relate the events calmly, but mostly failed. In several places his voice broke and he had to stop, gather himself, before continuing on. "Mithranar is fully under Azrilan's control. Falcons loyal to me have either escaped Dock City or been killed. The harbour remains blockaded. Montagni merchant ships are still trading south to Firth-land and the Twin Thrones, but there's not much getting in and out of Dock City or Darmour. Plenty of smuggling traffic is sneaking across the channel in both directions, though, which is how I got out."

There was a long silence while each of them processed Cuinn's story. He was glad of the respite. His mouth was dry and cracked and his palms were slicked with sweat; saying all that out loud had left him feeling like he'd run up a mountain and back.

"You said..." Alyna visibly calmed herself. "You said there was no trace of what happened to Talyn, but you must have some idea."

It was in her cracking voice, in the flinch that rippled across both Soar and Ariar's faces. They thought Talyn was dead. To them there could be no other explanation. They knew as well as Cuinn did that Talyn wouldn't be missing if she were still alive. She would have found a way, she would have been there fighting with her Wolves, with Cuinn.

Because she was warrior born. And she loved them. For a moment he couldn't breathe. But Alyna's question still hung on the air. And he did have an answer—he'd had enough time to think about what had happened, to put all the pieces he'd missed together in his mind.

"My guess is that Savin led her and Zamaril into an ambush of some sort." Cuinn forced the words out. Forced away that memory of the two of them walking away from him, off to meet the Shadow, unknowing of everything that was coming. "They disappeared after going to meet him."

Ariar rubbed a hand over his face, looking weary and beaten. "That's the Shadow you said was posted to Mithranar on the Firth-lander warlord's orders?"

"That's what we thought," Cuinn said bitterly. "Instead he was clearly loyal to Tarcos, and there to help Azrilan."

"You're telling me you think a Shadow orchestrated Vengeance, half the Shadowhawk's activities, Mithanis learning of Talyn's parentage and almost getting her executed. All of it." Soar's expression was an odd mix of disbelieving and horrified.

Cuinn frowned at his words. Something about them created a half-formed thought, an *almost* idea. But he couldn't quite grab onto it.

Alyna frowned. "Vengeance was never working for Montagn?"

"They're not innocent in all this, but no, they were manipulated by Savin." Cuinn's mouth curled, bitterness leaking from his words. "Used as a tool by Azrilan to seed unrest. Their original purpose— trying to make life better for the humans—was twisted to meet those ends. Tarcos wants to throw off the yoke of the Twin Thrones and claim your kingdom for his own. Azrilan wanted Mithranar and Montagn. They figured out they could help each other do that."

Bitterness and anger flared in the room, and Cuinn used a touch of magic to dampen it. He understood it, but the emotions were still too raw in himself for him to be able to manage those flaring around him too. Instead he changed the subject to practicalities. "Tarcos is not Viscarin, starting a war alone," he said. "He has a powerful ally in my brother. Azrilan will bring Montagn into this war sooner rather than later."

"Are you sure?" Ariar asked.

Cuinn nodded. "He will need time to establish his leadership in Arataire but as soon as he's done that..."

A heavy silence settled over the room.

"When your Wolves told us about their alliance..." Alyna started, pausing before continuing. "I could scarcely believe it. I never saw this in Tarcos. He seemed a strong, capable young man. The perfect heir."

"None of us saw it," Cuinn said bitterly. "But he hated that the Firthlander warlord was under the thumb of a Dumnorix sovereign, and he fomented that discontent amongst the niever-flyers and Armun. His uncle thought they were deserting. They weren't—they were joining Tarcos's secret army."

"We know," Ariar said grimly. "The strange brigand movements into the foothills this past year? It was a distraction to keep our attention from the deeper mountains where Tarcos was ferrying in his traitor niever-flyers and Bearmen. Montagni too, we think, though only a token force."

Impotent frustration replaced the bitterness that had been hanging like a cloud over the room. The Dumnorix were berating themselves, furiously guilty they hadn't noticed what was going on under their noses. The emotion was strikingly familiar—identical to how Cuinn felt—and oddly it comforted him. Made him feel a touch less out of place amongst them.

"Forget what's happened," Cuinn said firmly, the same thing he'd told himself a hundred times. "You need to plan how to contain their invading force to the mountains once Azrilan starts sending Montagni troops in force. He's got a big navy, and he'll try to hit you in other places, probably your ports."

"And what about you?" Alyna asked carefully. "Why are you here, Prince Cuinn?"

"I'm going to take back my throne," he said quietly. "I'm no fool. I know I can't do it now, not weakened and without support. I know it will take time. But I am determined."

"You should start with getting a healer to look at you," Alyna said. "We'll summon your Wolves too. They'll want to see you."

He hesitated. Alyna's words and tone were a clear dismissal, but impatience rose in him, unexpectedly strong. The sooner he secured the Dumnorix's help, the sooner he could return home, start *doing* something to destroy his brother.

But sense intervened. If he asked them now, when they still barely knew him and he looked like a trembling, grieving wreck, there would be no help forthcoming. No, he needed to win them to his side with something substantial. So he nodded. "Thank you. I'd really like to see them too."

HE WAS SO CAUGHT up in his thoughts, tossing over Soar's words about Savin again and again to try and catch hold of the idea that had been sparked by them, that it took him a few moments to register the two familiar Callanan waiting for him outside. He stopped dead when he saw them, but had no idea what to say.

Their gaze took in his lack of wings, his no doubt ragged appearance, and the fact he was alone.

"She's not with you?" Leviana asked.

"No, I'm sorry. I…" He gritted his teeth at having to say the words aloud again. "We think she was lured to an ambush by a Shadow loyal to Tarcos, but after that… we just don't know." He cleared his throat. "It's good to see you both."

"And you, Prince Cuinn." Cynia tried for a smile, but didn't quite succeed. His words hit both Callanan like a blow. It weighed hard on his magic. His shoulders sagged.

After a moment, Leviana gave herself a little shake, as if trying to dispel her worry. "We're sorry too, for what happened in Mithranar."

Cuinn took a breath. "I need to go and see my Wolves. Will you walk with me?"

"We'd love to." Leviana fell into step with him, Cynia flanking his other side. "How long are you staying?"

"Hopefully not long," he said in a non-committal tone.

A shared glance full of something he couldn't read.

"And then what?" Cynia asked.

"I'm still thinking on that." It was as close as he was willing to get to an admission that he had no idea.

"What about getting Talyn back?" Leviana said sharply.

He sucked in a breath, stung. "If I had any idea where she was, there is *nothing* that could stop me from… but there are people looking for her. Good people who have the skills I don't. Wherever she is, I know she's fighting too," he added. "You know that. She'll find her way back."

Neither of them disputed his words. Cynia reached out to touch his shoulder briefly. He instantly felt better.

Soon after they came to a stop outside a non-descript door in a relatively busy hallway. He searched for a way to break the awkward silence that had fallen, and his mind once again went to Soar's words earlier. "Can I ask something?"

"Anything," Leviana said.

"The Armun and Shadows that were posted in Calumnia and Conmor when Tarcos invaded. What happened to them?"

"They were arrested and taken south to be held at Callanan Tower. Indefinitely." Cynia's voice was cold.

"Has anyone thought to ask them whether they support what Tarcos is doing? Surely you could use the services of a good spy or assassin right now."

"Armun and Shadows are trained in manipulation and lies. We couldn't be sure anything they were telling us was the truth." This from Leviana.

Cuinn mulled that over for a moment. The idea tickled at his mind again. Savin. What he'd done in Dock City. How he'd... Cuinn's eyes widened as he realised what his brain had been trying to tell him.

"What?" Leviana asked suspiciously.

He tried to tamp down the excitement that flared in him. It was crazy, crazier than deciding to leave Mithranar entirely and come to Port Lachley. He didn't care. "Is there an Armun you *do* trust? Someone you've worked with before, someone Talyn and Sari trusted too?"

Leviana and Cynia looked at each other. Turned back to Cuinn.

"Saundin." They spoke at the same time.

"Do you have a way of getting in contact with him, discreetly?"

Another shared glance. "It's possible."

Relief loosened some of the constant tightness he carried around his chest. Maybe he *could* find a way. One step at a time.

Until he could fix everything.

CHAPTER 8

Once Cynia and Leviana left him, Cuinn knocked on the door they'd led him to. He wasn't sure how to describe how he felt as he stood there and waited for one of his Wolves to answer. Whatever the tumult of emotion was, it left his heart thundering and sweat slicking his palms.

It felt like an age before the door swung open and Theac Parksin stood there.

The veteran warrior's grizzled face stilled in shock at the sight of Cuinn. He only had to take half a step forward and Cuinn moved to meet him, finding himself enveloped in the brawny man's fierce hug.

He'd lived his whole life without a father, but sometimes Cuinn thought having Theac at his side this past year more than made up for that.

Theac let him go too quickly, eyes widening in horror as he registered Cuinn's lack of wings. "The flea-bitten bastards, what did they do to you?"

"Jystar couldn't save my wings. But I'm okay, truly." Cuinn forced the words out. "You have no idea how good it is to see you. I couldn't be sure you'd made it here safely, and... your wife? Corrin and his sisters? Evani?"

"All safe here," Theac assured him, then seemed to realise they were still standing in the doorway. "Come in."

He followed Theac through to a small sitting area where a fire burned happily in the grate. Neither sat down. Cuinn wasn't sure what to say next, but Theac spoke before he needed to.

"I've wanted to go back, every minute of every day, since we got here," Theac said roughly. "But I didn't know what happened to you, and with the Ciantar gone too... I didn't even know where to start."

"Your priority was to keep your family safe and warn the Dumnorix. Those were your orders," Cuinn said, infusing his voice with magic to impress upon the man how sincere he was. "Theac, you did the right thing."

"I felt a traitor to you, lad."

"I would never consider you a traitor." Cuinn added more magic to his voice, calming the man's guilt. Theac visibly relaxed before him.

"You're okay?" Theac asked.

He wasn't asking about Cuinn's physical health, and they both knew it. Cuinn took a breath, met his gaze, and told the truth. "I'm so terrified for Talyn that I can't think straight sometimes, and I miss her like a constant, fierce ache, and I grieve terribly for those we lost. I'm not certain I *can* do what I need to do next. But I am going to try anyway. I'm going to fight. You have my word."

Theac took a steadying breath. "I'm glad to hear it, Your Highness."

"Tell me about your family, Corrin, they're well?"

"Corrin and Evani are out training with the Kingshield—they spend most of their days in the yards with them. And Errana is helping in the kitchens, she insisted on it as a way to repay your family's kindness in letting us stay here. Her girls are at lessons with the other children of court."

"Evani is training?" Cuinn finally sat in one of the chairs by the fire, hoping Theac would do the same.

"Halun's loss tore her up. After so long apart, for them to be reunited, and then..." Theac cleared his throat, eyes glistening. It took him a moment before he could go on, and Cuinn was glad, it gave him time to manage his own clawing grief. Theac sat eventually, hands clasped. "She wants to be a Wolf like him. And the training gives them both a purpose. Something to hold onto."

"You're worried about Corrin?" He sensed it in the man's voice.

"He trains obsessively." Theac scowled. "He has no other outlet for the rage and grief he feels."

"And you?" Cuinn asked quietly.

"I struggle too." Theac relaxed into his chair. "But Errana calms the worst of it, and the girls' smiles help me forget, even if just for a moment."

The door opened before Cuinn could say any more and Errana entered, carrying a steaming pot. Its delicious scent made Cuinn's stomach growl. Theac rose quickly to take it from her and carry it over to the family's dining table.

Errana looked as overcome as her husband had been to see Cuinn standing in her lounge. Their sheer joy at seeing him made Cuinn feel loved, and another piece of his strength returned, more pain turning to tough scar tissue.

Corrin's sisters arrived soon after, home for their lunch, and Errana fussed over Cuinn, placing a large bowl of stew, warm bread and a mug of cider in front of him. While he ate, she and Theac took turns telling him of what their lives had been like in Port Lachley.

Both girls were reluctant to leave to return to their afternoon lessons, but eventually Errana shooed them out, leaving Theac and Cuinn sitting alone.

"Tell me everything, laddie," Theac instructed.

He did, passing on everything that had happened since they'd parted on the streets of Dock City on that horrible night. Theac's habitual scowl didn't change much throughout the recounting, except to show a flash of surprise at how helpful Saniya had been.

Once Cuinn had finished, Theac scratched his beard and looked away. "No news on the Ciantar?"

Cuinn merely shook his head.

"What do you intend to do next?" Theac asked, voice gruffer than usual.

"I barely know where to start, but I'm here to ask the Dumnorix for help, if they'll give it. I have another idea too, but I need some time to mull it over more."

"And these hounds of Azrilan's, you think they'll track you here?"

"I have no doubt." Fear thrilled through Cuinn, and he was glad Theac had no song magic to pick it up. "It's just a matter of time. I can't stay too long."

"Understood." Theac grunted. "Nobody will touch you while you're with me, Your Highness."

Cuinn smiled for the first time since Talyn's disappearance. Theac's response, his tone and the words, were just so... Theac, that he couldn't help it.

Bootsteps sounded approaching the door, and Theac instinctively reached for his axe, but Cuinn stopped him. "It's Corrin."

"You can tell that?"

"His emotions are familiar to me." Cuinn paused. "He has an edge of heartbreak to his feelings, ever since..."

Theac nodded in understanding. Since Talyn and Zamaril had gone. Sharing a look with Theac, Errana left the room.

Moments later Corrin came through the front door. He halted halfway across the room, gaze taking in Cuinn sitting with Theac. "Your Highness." Undisguised relief and hope shone from the young man's green eyes. "You're alive."

Cuinn stood. "Yes, Corrin. And I'm gladder than I can say to see you standing in front of me."

"I..." Corrin's grief hit Cuinn like a hammer. "I thought... I thought everything was gone, that we'd lost everything."

"We've lost a lot," Cuinn said somberly. "But not everything." As he said the words, he realised how true they were. There were things left to fight for. And he would fight.

"The Ciantar?"

Cuinn forced himself not to wince as Corrin's hope and grief slammed into him again. It wasn't just Talyn that Corrin was so desperately worried about either. "I don't know. We haven't been able to learn anything about what happened to her or Zamaril. I'm sorry."

Corrin's shoulders sagged and the light went out of his eyes. The

Wolf's pain echoed Cuinn's own so much that for a moment he couldn't breathe. To try and quell the emotion he stepped away and returned to his seat. "To take back the throne, I'll need the Wolves. They're hiding in the north, under Windsong's command. I've given orders for them to stay hidden and recruit where they can."

"What about us?" Corrin asked. Already he was pulling himself back together, shoulders straightening, determination flashing on his face.

"Theac, I'd like you and Evani to stay with me for now." He needed the man more than he was willing to admit, and it would be foolish to send away all his Talyn-trained bodyguards, reluctant as he was to place them in any kind of danger. "Corrin, you'll leave now, this afternoon. Go down to the harbour and get on the next ship to Acleu." He paused. "You'll have to rely on Saniya's people to get you from Acleu to Darmour, but the Wolves need you with them."

Corrin's eyes glittered with relief and excitement and he bowed low. "I'll farewell Mam and leave now, Your Highness."

Cuinn reached out to grip his shoulder. "Thank you. Knowing you're there with them will ease my mind."

Corrin saluted. His eyes closed briefly, then he opened them, smiled and was gone.

THREE DAYS LATER, Cynia and Leviana visited, and the three of them took a walk along the battlements, braving the cold air to discreetly discuss a message for their Armun friend, Saundin.

"We don't know how long this will take to get to him," Cynia warned. "Especially now. It could be weeks. Months even."

He chafed at those words. It wasn't quick enough. Nothing felt quick enough. But there was no fast way to bring Azrilan down. He was in such a position of strength and power that only time and clever planning had a chance. He knew that. He just wished that the constant ball of anxiety that resided in his stomach would ease. "I appreciate you doing this, no matter how long it takes."

"Are you going to tell us why you want to talk to him?" Leviana's curiosity was bursting from her.

"No. Not until I speak to him and figure out if my idea is even viable."

"Are you just going to stay here in the meantime?" Cynia asked. "Wait for the Dumnorix to warm up enough to agree to ally with you? In all honesty, Prince Cuinn, without Talyn here, I think you've set yourself an impossible task."

He shrugged, trying not to let on that he didn't have a good answer to that. He'd come to win an alliance with the Dumnorix, but how long could he afford to linger before Azrilan's hounds found him? Cynia was right. From reading their emotions the other day, it was clear the Dumnorix family's minds were preoccupied by the war, worried about their ability to win it. There was no way they were going to be willing to tie their fortunes to him, not unless he gave them a reason to. "I have to try anyway."

Besides, even if he did leave, where would he go? Back to Darmour, and place his Wolves in danger while they were still recovering, trying to rebuild? Back to Dock City, where he risked exposing Saniya's new network?

He was a liability, and he *hated* that.

An ear-piercing scream sounded above, drawing all their attention to where a SkyRider rode the icy drafts high in the sky. The eagle drifted through cloudbanks, appearing for a few moments before disappearing again.

"I sometimes wonder if I should have chosen SkyRiding over the Callanan," Leviana mused. "Imagine soaring through the sky like that?"

Cuinn's heart clenched, and he looked away, fingers curling into fists at his sides.

Cynia snorted. "You? Living most of the year inside a rocky mountain in the middle of a freezing mountain range? Never."

"You make a fair point."

"I'm going to go before Theac starts to panic that I've been out of his sight for too long," he said abruptly. "Thanks for your help."

They let him go, their sympathy and concern following him all the way to the edge of his magical range. He tried to ignore it, to focus on figuring out his next steps instead.

How was he going to win the Dumnorix to him?

CHAPTER 9

*H*e blinked awake into darkness, a shudder rippling through his song magic.

For a moment he had no idea what had awoken him so suddenly. The room was quiet. Faint moonlight shone through the curtained window.

Slow to catch up, his sleepy thoughts didn't process what the faint blurring of the shadows by his bed meant until something heavy landed on his chest and he found himself staring up into a pair of eyes filled with cold resolve.

"THEAC!" he managed to bellow as he lurched upward, throwing out his song magic desperately. The wave of fear he flooded the assassin with was enough to give him the leverage he needed to throw off their weight, but it wasn't fast enough to completely avoid the glinting blade slicing towards his throat.

It cut into his left arm, a stabbing line of agony. Blood sprayed, and Cuinn grunted in pain as he moved for the edge of the bed. The knife slashed again, slicing along his side as he threw himself to the floor in a desperate attempt to get clear.

He hit the stone hard, legs half tangled in the blankets, at the same moment the door slammed open and light flooded the room. The

Shadow, about to lunge at Cuinn again, reacted with enviable speed, throwing the knife at Theac's throat instead.

A quick *sabai* move saved the Wolf, and the blade chipped into the stone wall before falling to the floor with a clatter. Theac was moving before it landed, axe swinging, trying to get in between the Shadow and Cuinn.

Cuinn scrambled back towards the window, knowing Theac needed room to fight and for Cuinn to keep himself clear so he wasn't a distraction. The Shadow hesitated for single heartbeat between the two targets, before making the same decision Talyn would have made —Cuinn was trapped against the wall with nowhere to go and Theac was the more dangerous adversary.

He went for Theac, two more knives flashing in his hands.

"You picked the wrong target to assassinate, you piece of fleashit." Theac's scowl was fiercer than Cuinn had ever seen it, his focus utterly locked in on his target, mouth curled in a silent snarl.

Cuinn's magic could sense his confidence, his skill, matched against the Shadow's darkness. He controlled his fear to prevent it leaking to Theac and distracting him. Instead, he wrapped the Shadow in it. He filled him with unease, lack of confidence, tugged at his focus.

Theac's first swing barely missed the Shadow, who sidestepped, recovered, but then faltered as Cuinn pounded him with more doubt and fear. He did it remorselessly, not allowing himself to think of the Shadow's inevitable death. He had to save himself and Theac.

Theac's next strike was too fast, sweeping in to take the man's head off in a single strike. Cuinn flinched as blood sprayed, then doubled over when the Shadow's death and fear slammed into him. He gasped in a breath.

"You all right?" Theac barked, gaze scanning the room, axe held ready.

"Fine," Cuinn forced out. After a few more moments of focus, he was able to sit up. It was then he became aware of the stinging pain in his arm and side. "He got a few cuts in, but nothing life threatening. I think."

"That a Shadow?"

"Yep."

Theac sheathed his axe and reached down to help him up. "Nasty piece of work. Let's get you to one of the Dumnorix and call the Kingshield."

"Not yet." Cuinn managed to straighten, get to his feet. The stinging in his arm was turning into fiery pain, and he gritted his teeth against it. "Can you go and find Levs and Cynia? I want to talk to them first."

A HALF-TURN LATER, the four of them sat in Theac's rooms, talking by the fire while Cynia briskly cleaned and bandaged Cuinn's wounds. He bore her ministrations as stoically as he could even though it hurt like crazy. Luckily neither was life threatening, though the gash on his arm was deep.

The two Callanan had informed the Kingshield commander in the castle and sent a message to the Dumnorix. A servant had arrived a quarter-turn earlier with a politely worded request to come and speak with the family immediately.

He'd promised to come soon, and then Evani had closed the door on the poor man.

"You can't stay in Port Lachley," Cynia said as she wrapped gauze around his stitched arm. "They found you remarkably quickly and it's pure luck they only sent one Shadow to test the waters. You'll have to leave, and fast, before they try again."

"That's not entirely true," Leviana disagreed. "Even a bunch of Shadow assassins won't get through a full Kingshield detail. Not after what happened to King Aethain. The Kingshield have trained for that happening again."

"I don't warrant a Kingshield detail," Cuinn said simply. "They're for Dumnorix only."

He could almost hear Talyn's voice in his head then, telling him to demand a detail, that he had as much right to one as her family did. But he couldn't. His identity was a secret—if he started walking around with a Kingshield detail, the secret risked getting exposed. Then he would lose any trust he was building with the Dumnorix.

Leviana waved a hand. "Don't play coy. Talyn told us your little secret. You ask for a guard, you'll get one."

Theac cleared his throat. "What are they talking about?"

"It doesn't matter," Cuinn said firmly. "Azrilan wants me dead. He *needs* me dead. His hounds will keep coming for me."

He couldn't stay. If nothing else, tonight had made something very clear. His people had no hope if he was killed; without Cuinn, who could successfully challenge Azrilan? His responsibility was to stay alive.

But to do that, he had to be stronger. Better equipped to defend himself. He had to somehow learn to fight despite his song magic. So that if another assassin came for him, he could survive without help. So that he could go home without putting them all in danger.

He thought back to his walk with the two Callanan earlier that day. What they'd discussed.

And he wondered if maybe there was a way he could both learn to defend himself and get out of Port Lachley to somewhere much more difficult for a Shadow or Armun to get to him.

A way to make the Dumnorix see him differently. A way to spend his time productively while he waited for Saundin.

He rose abruptly. "Let's go talk to the family."

DESPITE EXHAUSTION AND LINGERING SORENESS, not to mention he'd come inches from dying only a full-turn earlier, Cuinn felt buoyant, energised, as he walked through the halls. Talyn had always said that big problems just needed to be broken down into small steps.

He had some of those steps now, and the path ahead felt clearer. Confidence in his decision to come to Port Lachley rose, dispelling the doubt that had been weighing so heavily in his chest.

The Dumnorix were all on their feet, on edge, their unease hitting Cuinn like a wall as he approached them. The attack on Cuinn had been too much like the night when their king had been assassinated.

"There you are," Alyna snapped. "Where have you been?"

"Deciding what to do next with my advisors," he said simply.

Alyna's gaze flicked to the closed doors—Theac, Cynia and Leviana had stayed outside instead of coming in. As deeply as he trusted them, if Shadows were on his tail, then the fewer people who knew his plans, the safer he'd be.

"And?"

"Tarcos gave Azrilan a group of Armun and Shadows—Azrilan sent them after me, though I didn't realise they'd find me here so quickly," Cuinn said. "I can't stay here now. Not where I'm so visible."

"You have our protection here, Cuinn," Ariar said. "What happened tonight won't occur again. We've increased the Kingshield presence throughout the castle and—"

Cuinn raised a hand, stopping him. "I didn't come here to hide out in your castle forever. I have strong magic, but I need more than that if I want to take my throne back." His gaze settled on the Sky Chieftain. "I want to learn to fly again."

Soar's eyebrows shot upwards in surprise. "You want to train to be a SkyRider?"

"I do."

"Prince Cuinn, no," Alyna said firmly. "The mountains are the most dangerous place in the Twin Thrones right now. SkyRiders are flying and fighting every day."

"Mothduriem remains safe—it's too high for the nievers to fly. And these hounds of Azrilan's will find it difficult to get into the mountains without being noticed, no matter how good they are. Besides, if nobody but us knows where Cuinn has gone, they likely won't even learn where he is, at least for a while," Soar pointed out.

"He's a foreign prince," Alyna protested. "He can't be a SkyRider."

A tense silence fell. Cuinn debated whether to reveal that Talyn had told him the truth about his blood—he was increasingly confident this was the best way forward. Not only could he fly again, but he could learn to fight, and Soar was right about the hounds finding it hard to track him to Mothduriem. But rather than making them feel threatened by telling them he knew he was a Dumnorix and demanding it as his right, perhaps instead he could use a touch of song magic to convince them—

"Cuinn is one of us," Ariar spoke suddenly, determinedly. "It is his right. Callanan, SkyRider or Aimsir." He aimed a small smile at Cuinn. "You picked wrong, Cousin. I would have welcomed you into my Aimsir."

At the look on Ariar's face, warmth unfolded inside Cuinn like a comforting blanket on a cold winter's day. There was welcome in that look. Family. A smile curled at Cuinn's mouth. "You knew?"

Ariar shrugged. "I know Talyn. When she trusts, she doesn't hold back. I have no doubts she told you."

Cuinn bit his lip, throat closing over in an utterly embarrassing fashion.

"She would never have betrayed..." Alyna's words died as she saw the look on Cuinn's face, and horrified shock rippled over her expression.

"How long have you known?" Soar asked, grim and worried.

"A few months," he said, and left it at that. These people were his family, but he didn't know them, and they didn't trust him, especially with Talyn gone. He wouldn't make promises he couldn't keep.

"Nobody can know." Alyna was firm, uncompromising. "No matter what Talyn said to you, the consequences of this getting out—"

"I'm fully aware," Cuinn cut over her. "Nobody will hear it from me. I swear it."

"And we should trust you?" Soar's voice had a note of helplessness to it.

"I would never betray Talyn's confidence," he said quietly. "You can trust that."

Alyna was upset, but she didn't protest any further. Soar rubbed a hand over his face. "Ariar is correct. If you want to be a SkyRider, Cuinn, it is your right."

"Thank you," Cuinn said.

"We'll leave for Mothduriem at dawn," Soar said simply. "Just the two of us. That way we make sure nobody knows where we've gone."

"That's too dangerous—" Alyna began, but Soar cut her off.

"No assassin would ever think two Dumnorix would travel alone without any guards," he pointed out. "A single SkyRider departing the castle won't draw any undue attention."

"I agree that I need to go as soon as possible, but there's more for me to tell you. Things that might help you." Cuinn had filled them in on the most important details of what had happened over the past couple of days, but not everything. "If you don't mind skipping some sleep tonight, I'd like to do that before I leave."

Alyna eyed him for a long moment, then gave a short nod. "I'll send for the First Blade and First Shield, and ask the servants for some hot tea and food."

"I DIDN'T SEE any warships docked in Acleu when I left, but I wouldn't be surprised if Azrilan begins gathering a fleet sooner rather than later." Cuinn spoke to those gathered at the table. Candles flickered. Outside was the deep night of the pre-dawn hours. The scent of herbal tea and buttery cake filled his nose. He hadn't touched either.

"There's no chance your brother reneges on their deal now he's got everything he wants from Tarcos?" Alyna asked.

Cuinn thought back to that night. Tarcos and Azrilan standing together, the way they'd glanced at each other. There'd been trust there, his magic sensing an odd kind of kinship, maybe even something more. "I think Azrilan will honour their deal," he said.

"A Montagni war fleet will hit us everywhere they can," Ariar said. "But we have the advantage of our shallow coastline."

Cuinn threw him a questioning look. "They don't have to anchor at port, right, they can offload soldiers onto smaller boats offshore to ferry them in?"

"True, but they need to be able to anchor close enough to make ferrying soldiers in practical," Alyna said. "If you combine that with sections of the coastline that aren't too rugged for landing troops, it still limits the number of places they could attempt it."

"Where?" Cuinn asked.

Soar leaned forward and began pointing out places on the map.

"Port Lachley, Ryathl, Darsein, two uninhabited spots on the east and west coast of the Ayrlemyre range. Plus here near the Wraithwoods, and here, here and here." He stabbed at Port Lathilly last.

"Two of those spots are on Conmor's north coast." Cuinn frowned. Alyna was right—there were limited locations, but if Montagn hit them all at once... He wished Talyn were here, she'd be able to pick apart Azrilan's likely attack strategy in moments, but his brain didn't work like hers.

"Tarcos is already coming at us from the east, trying to push more and more troops into the mountains, so they in turn can put pressure on our lines trying to hold them there," Ariar said. "We'll be in trouble if Azrilan opens up another front to the north."

"Why is Tarcos pushing troops into rugged mountain territory instead of hitting Port Lathilly or other populated spots down the west coast?" Cuinn asked.

"He's been using the uninhabited mountain coastline to ferry warriors in under our noses for at least a year now, preparing," Ariar said. "That's given him an established beachhead to securely land ships and more troops. And it's not like we can just go in there and take them out. The Ayrlemyre region is so massive we could waste months just trying to find them in there."

"He's playing the long game," Soar added. "Rather than risking splitting his naval strength to hit well-defended ports along the east coast, he's funneling his forces through the mountains to try and break out into southern Conmor. He knows once that happens, we're in trouble. Bearmen and niever-flyers marching into the vulnerable farmland of southern Conmor? Let's just say it would be difficult to contain."

"As it stands, we're in a good position. Our SkyRiders, Aimsir and Callanan bolstering the regular army are effective enough to hold the Firthlanders penned in the mountains indefinitely," Alyna said briskly. "But that is why Montagn worries us so much."

"If Azrilan has smart commanders, they'll hit us in the north, wait till we divert troops from the mountains to defend, then send more ships south to hit the west coast and Ryathl. We're still several months from winter, so the western seas will be navigable," Soar said grimly. "Once that happens, it's over. We'll lose. We don't have the numbers to fight on that many fronts—not against the sheer numbers Montagn and Firthland combined can throw at us."

A heavy silence fell. It was clear they'd discussed this before—they'd simply been repeating it for Cuinn's benefit. He stared at the map, putting together what he'd seen in Acleu with trying to imagine how Talyn would attack the problem. Before he left the Dumnorix, he needed to make an impression on them. Something to build off when he returned.

An answer sprang out at him.

"You need to take out Azrilan's ships before they reach your coast." He looked up, energy coursing through him. "Destroy them with your SkyRiders. You can use flaming arrows spiked with izerdia, yes? The Montagni don't have niever-flyers, their ships will be vulnerable. And if Tarcos sends his niever-flyers to help them, then *his* ships coming from the east will be easier targets."

The Dumnorix glanced at each other. Cuinn's eagerness died—of course they'd already thought of this.

"Two problems with that." Soar sat forward. "First, my legions are finite. I need almost the entire force to hold the Firthlanders inside the mountains while also hitting his ships crossing the channel carrying more troops. I could only spare a legion or two for what you're suggesting. Second, the ocean between us and Montagn is massive… with only a handful of legions to spare, there's no way for us to cover the ground we'd need in order to spot them before they hit us."

Another thrill of excitement went through him. They *hadn't* thought of everything. The excitement died a little when he considered how Saniya would react to what he was about to suggest, but he shrugged it off. She had suggested an alliance, after all.

"I can help with that. So can your Callanan."

Several pairs of eyes snapped to him. His song magic picked up a flash of hope, quickly buried.

"How?" Alyna frowned.

"I have contacts in an… underground network in Dock City and Acleu. Smugglers and criminals by trade. They can send warning by bird when the Montagni warships leave port, how many there are, how they're armed, all that stuff—then you'll know when they're coming and can make some educated guesses to help narrow your search window for the SkyRiders."

"Where do my Callanan come into this?" The First Blade lifted an eyebrow.

"Deploy your warriors to Acleu. I've seen what Talyn can do, what she trained my Wolves to do. They can sabotage the ships before they leave port, kill their captains and officers, help my network find information on when the next assault force is leaving. Maybe even steal any izerdia they're carrying." Cuinn's eagerness was back. "They can reduce the threat before it even reaches you."

Alyna held his gaze, considering. "How would we get them into Acleu?"

"Merchant traffic is still operating between Port Lachley and Acleu, it's how I got here. Your Callanan can travel that way and take as many messenger birds as they can with them. It's not foolproof— you'll need to figure out how to replenish the birds or work out some other way to communicate discreetly, especially if trade shuts down when Montagn joins the war. But my people might be able to help with that too."

"What do you think?" Ariar looked at the First Blade.

"I think my warriors can do everything he's suggesting," Shia said evenly, her small frame vibrating with supressed excitement. "Send us in, Your Highness."

"If we know when the ships leave port and how many there are, we have a much greater chance of targeting a search to intercept them out at sea," Soar said slowly. "And if the force is already weakened by Callanan sabotage, then a single legion should be all that's needed to take them out."

"We can take the plan to the Lords' Council today," Ariar said.

Alyna rose. "We'll do it. Shia, have your warriors ready to leave as soon as possible."

"Thank you, Cuinn." Ariar nodded at him.

It was on the tip of his tongue to ask for an alliance in that moment—the assistance of his network in Acleu contingent on their agreement. But he held himself back. Even if they did agree now, he still couldn't remain in Port Lachley. No, he'd go to the SkyRiders, learn to be a warrior, and by the time he returned, Saniya's people and his would hopefully have provided substantial help. Then he'd have leverage to work with. "I just hope it helps."

As the meeting broke up, Cuinn crossed to the First Blade. "May I make a suggestion, First Blade?"

Faint irritation rippled across the woman's face. "Let me guess, you want me to send Warriors Seinn and Leed with the Callanan contingent I deploy to Acleu?"

He smiled faintly. "I do."

"It will be done."

"Cuinn?" Soar's voice called across the hall; the Sky Chieftain was lingering by the door. "Ready to go?"

Cuinn straightened. "I'm ready."

Time to go to Mothduriem. And learn to fly again.

CHAPTER 10

*T*alyn limped beside Kaeri, doing her best not to wince with every step and failing miserably. Even though the wounds on her back were finally closing over, forming tender, tight scar tissue, she couldn't raise her arms above her head without them pulling painfully, and even walking she constantly felt them tugging.

Kaeri had warned her not to overextend herself. "If the scars open up, there's a high chance of infection setting in again, and your body won't survive that."

A fortnight had passed.

Two weeks since Talyn had first woken free of fever and begun her recovery. Kaeri had forced her to her feet, moving slowly, within the limits of pain she could handle. After a while, boredom had become as much of a problem as the lingering weakness and pain. Once her mind had regained its lucidity, sitting or lying endlessly on her pallet with nothing to do for full-turn after full-turn each day while Kaeri and the other women were gone came close to driving her mad.

Sari had saved her. They'd talked, mostly about small things, good memories from their time in the Callanan, anything to stop Talyn worrying about what had happened to Cuinn, her family, the Wolves.

As the pain receded and her strength returned, the need to know what had happened grew stronger and stronger. As much as she tried, she was never able to banish the ball of worry and fear that constantly resided in the pit of her stomach.

She still hadn't told Kaeri who she was, but was confident now that the ahara's daughter hadn't recognised Talyn. Neither of the other two women sharing the hut had shown a shred of recognition around her either.

Someone had put her in this camp, though. The terrible but obvious conclusion was that Montagn had invaded Mithranar as the Callanan informant had warned them, and they'd taken out the threat Talyn had posed by sending Savin to ambush her.

Which meant Talyn had failed miserably at being Ciantar. At protecting her home.

Sari's hesitated. *"Even if you're right, that theory doesn't explain why they left you alive. Or how Kaeri ended up in here too."*

Talyn agreed—and that wasn't the only thing that was nagging at her. *"If it was Montagn that invaded, why were Bearmen there when Savin ambushed us?"*

"Are you sure that's what you saw? You'd been stabbed, and then you were in a fever a long time. You might not be remembering accurately."

"Maybe." She swallowed, then whispered her deepest fear. *"They might be dead."*

"Or they might not be. Have some faith in the warriors you trained, Tal. Have faith in Cuinn," Sari said briskly. *"You need to talk to Kaeri."*

"I do." But she had wanted to wait until she was out of the hut first, until she got a better idea of the camp, the guards. Of her situation. At least that's what she told herself. The truth was, part of her was too afraid to hear the answers Kaeri might have. She wasn't sure she was strong enough yet.

But now there were no further excuses to delay. Kaeri had returned to their hut the previous night to tell her that the guards insisted she begin working, delivering the news with her typical bluntness. "It's either that or they decide you're worthless and they kill you."

So Talyn had joined Kaeri and the other two women of their hut when they left not long after dawn. She followed as they formed a line that then joined other snaking lines of women moving along muddy paths leading through the collection of living huts towards another part of the camp.

Emerging from the dim confines of the hut into fresh air and open space gave Talyn an unexpected jolt of relief and energy. She took deep breaths, savouring the breeze on her skin. The urge to do *something* hit her again, stronger than it had since she'd woken. A few glances came her way, then shifted away when she caught them.

"You sure the guards said nothing when they brought me into your hut?"

"I've told you everything I know." Kaeri lost patience quickly, and Talyn's repeated questions often made the young woman snappy. "And before you ask, no, they haven't asked after you apart from nagging me to get you on your feet to work."

"Sorry." She frowned, catching on to the fact more and more slaves were staring at her. "What is everyone looking at? Is it because I'm new?"

"It's because you're a terrible sight."

Talyn winced. "That bad huh?"

"You're sure you want to know? Most women wouldn't."

Talyn gave her a look.

Kaeri shrugged. "You're painfully thin, your skin has this horrible sickly hue, and you have purple shadows that look like bruises under your eyes. Don't get me started on the state of your hair. Then there's the mass of scar tissue visible at the top of your shirt and the healing scar along the left side of your forehead. It clashes nicely with the blue slave tattoo on your left cheek."

"Blue." She frowned. Registered for the first time the colour of the tattoos on faces around her. "Aren't they usually green?"

Kaeri gave her an odd look. "Green tattoos are for household slaves. Blue for labour camp workers. You don't seem bothered by my accounting of your appearance."

"Appearances aren't important." How she looked had never mattered much to Talyn. And on the scale of things causing her anxiety at the moment, her appearance was pretty low down the list. She was lucky to have survived, no matter the scars. "Thank you for what you did for me," she added.

"It was nothing."

"It wasn't nothing," Talyn said firmly. "I'm alive today because you wouldn't let me die. I want you to know I'm grateful."

"You have an uncommonly positive attitude for someone who is crippled and trapped in a slave labour camp." Kaeri turned away.

"Now that you put it that way..." Talyn said, mouth twitching in a smile.

Kaeri smiled back. "I'm glad you're okay."

Talyn hesitated a moment, then, "My name is Talyn. I remembered it."

"Oh." Kaeri didn't seem to associate the name with anything in particular, and gave a casual shrug. "Nice to meet you, Talyn. Remember much else?"

"Yes." Talyn almost launched into it right there. Maybe knowing who she was would make Kaeri more willing to talk about what had happened, what she knew—Talyn's desperation to know was eating at her. But they were surrounded by listening ears, and by now she was satisfied the camp guards either didn't know or didn't care who she was. Best not to risk changing that. "I'd rather talk about it in private."

Kaeri's eyes narrowed, but she said nothing further.

Talyn looked around her as they walked, taking everything in. The hut she'd been recovering in was one amongst hundreds of others, all grouped close together in the southwestern corner of the camp. Dirt pathways wove between and around them, and a latrine pit ran along the northern edge of the area, its purpose unmistakable from the nauseating smell drifting from that direction.

She glanced at Kaeri—the woman had been carrying a pot with Talyn's waste to that pit every single day. Gratitude filled her again. Along with a hint of discomfort.

"Don't thank me again," Kaeri said gruffly, catching the direction of Talyn's gaze. "And don't think I'll be doing it anymore. You can take yourself from now on."

On the other side of the latrine pits was more housing stretching towards the northern fence line. Over there, lines of male slaves were weaving through similar pathways and heading in the same direction as Kaeri and Talyn.

"Those huts house the male slaves," Kaeri confirmed before Talyn could ask. "They keep us strictly apart when we're not eating or working."

"How many entrances to the camp?" Talyn's gaze roved the area, but she couldn't see any break in the high wired fence surrounding the western edge of the residential area. Her brain, a little rusted over, creaked into use. Started to catalogue options.

"One. On the eastern side of camp. It's heavily guarded in case you were getting ideas."

"I was just asking."

"Guards patrol the entire fence line all day and night, in case a slave took it into their heads to try and climb it."

"Noted."

"They also have dogs to track anyone who happens to make it over the fence and slip by the patrolling guards."

"Right."

"And this camp is in an isolated area. The nearest village—which has its own barracks housing a full division of soldiers—is at least a day's hike away."

"Useful, thank you," Talyn said mildly, carefully noting Kaeri's information, filing it away for later use.

"You're welcome." Bitterness edged Kaeri's voice, and Talyn frowned.

As they approached the edge of the residential area, her scanning gaze snagged on a large field to the northeast. Orderly rows of Montagni soldiers filled the space, sparring in pairs in the morning sun. Each followed a strict drill—making it appear more like they were all participating in an intricate dance—and bellowed loudly with each strike. They were massive men, with broad shoulders and long, bushy beards.

"They look formidable," Talyn commented.

Kaeri said, "They're Berserkers. I certainly wouldn't want to fight one."

Talyn's gaze lingered on them. They fought as if they were completely unaware of the warm sun beating down on them, or the gusting wind tugging at their balance and perfect footwork. Each order shouted by their leader at the edge of the field was obeyed instantly and with enviable skill.

"Is it usual for a labour camp to have its own complement of Berserkers?" Talyn asked.

Kaeri nodded. "Every camp has a company of soldiers and a detachment of Berserkers. If conflict broke out—anything from invasion to a slave revolt or local unrest—they could be quickly deployed."

"How many in a company?"

"Five hundred. And fifty in a Berserker detachment."

"Five hundred and fifty soldiers holding us in this camp. Got it." The Berserkers didn't look much different to the Firthlander Bearmen in size and fierceness. A shudder rippled down her spine in memory, a visceral response that couldn't be fabricated.

"I don't think I imagined it, Sari. There were Bearmen in that tunnel."

"Then maybe something else is going on."

"Five hundred and fifty is a lot."

"We've faced more and won."

Talyn almost laughed aloud. *"No we haven't."*

The lines of men and women coming out of the residential area crossed an open piece of ground towards a massive single-story rectangular building.

Talyn and Kaeri followed their line inside. The room was filled wall-to-wall with long tables and benches where slaves already sat eating. Tables were separated down the middle of the room between men and women. After getting her tray of food handed to her, Talyn lowered herself cautiously onto a bench beside Kaeri, slowly enough not to pull her scars.

"Why don't the others talk to us?" Talyn murmured so only Kaeri could hear. The women at their table had glanced at them, but those glances slid away before Talyn could catch their eyes to even say hello.

Now most of them were looking down at their food. At other tables the slaves spoke quietly, a soft hum permeating the room.

A sour look flashed over Kaeri's face. "They've been slaves their whole lives, and we haven't. It makes them uneasy, afraid we might do something to upset the balance of their routine here. Especially you, given the state you ended up in."

"Why would we do that?"

"People who haven't been slaves their whole lives don't tend to adapt well to the experience." Kaeri shrugged. "Whereas those born to it know their existence only gets worse when someone upsets the routine or does something to annoy the masters."

"Nobody should have to adapt well to the experience," Talyn snapped.

Kaeri gave her a look. "Where did that come from?"

The anger faded as quickly as it had come. "One of my dearest friends, a man I would trust with my life, wears a slave tattoo. It brings me no shame to wear the same tattoo on my cheek that he wears on his." The words spilled out, and with them a sigh of relief at finally understanding her tangled emotions on the subject. "But slavery is an abomination. There is no other way to put it."

A few of the women sitting close enough to hear Talyn's words looked her way, but only briefly, before turning back to their food. Silence reigned at their table.

"What do you remember?" Kaeri murmured between spoons of watery oatmeal.

"A lot," Talyn said.

"Were you married? Children? Managing a home for your husband? Spending your days embroidering with other wives?"

Talyn snorted, almost dropping her spoon. A smile tugged at the corners of her mouth.

"I didn't think so." A matching smile crossed Kaeri's face. "You have too much spirit for that."

"Later." Talyn kept her voice low.

Kaeri let it go without another word.

When a bell sounded, the slaves rose without being told by the guards, and formed lines to leave through the opposite doorway from the one they'd entered through. Talyn joined the line from her table.

Glances continued to come her way, some edged with curiosity, some with unease, a couple even with fear. The staring irritated her, and she began returning the looks with scowls. She looked awful, so what?

The exit led out to another patch of open ground. Immediately ahead was a multi-storied stone building, to her left the training fields she'd seen earlier. A well-worn and wide path led away to their right.

"Barracks," Kaeri murmured, pointing discreetly to the stone building. "Stables too. Beyond them, the road leading out to the front gate."

"To the right?" Talyn asked.

"The working section of the camp. It's normally where we'd go, but the guards must be bored today."

The lines of slaves were being shepherded to the left, gathering at the southern edge of the training field. A large group of guards stood not far off, passing money to another soldier—a Berserker—walking between them. Two others stood off to the side, a male slave standing silent between them. Those passing money to the Berserker took a long look at the slave before doing so.

"What's going on?" Talyn asked.

"Montagni love gambling. When the guards get bored, they make the male slaves fight and bet on the outcome." She gestured to the slave. "He's new. All the new slaves eventually get picked to fight against the camp's best slave fighter, just to get their mettle." Kaeri shrugged. "The soldiers have their fun, but they also learn how much trouble the new slave could be. It's smart."

"Who's the champion?" Talyn asked.

Kaeri pointed to a tall, well-muscled slave moving through the crowd and onto the field. "They call him Bear. I've heard that he's gone undefeated since he came here. He works in one of the smithies."

Talyn's gaze shifted to the new slave as the guards pushed him forward onto the field. He was small compared to the giant that awaited him. A murmur went through the slaves and guards surrounding the field.

She stared.

It couldn't be.

It was hard to make out the slave's features from a distance, but the way he walked... with the grace of a Callanan. Cropped blond hair, wiry body, constantly shifting gaze.

"This could be interesting."

Kaeri's words crashed dimly against her, ignored. That was Zamaril walking across the field. She was sure of it. That hint of cockiness in his walk. Deviousness, even. She would know that wariness of his anywhere.

"Talyn?"

Relief swept through her so powerfully that she swayed, one hand reaching out to grab Kaeri's arm to stop herself from falling.

"Are you feeling ill?" Kaeri steadied her, gaze flicking between Talyn and the nearest guard. "Talyn, are you okay?"

Talyn managed to find her voice. "When did he arrive in the camp?"

"I don't know—maybe a month or so ago, that's when the last fight was. Why do you..." Kaeri trailed off, her voice dropping. "You know him?"

Talyn nodded, fingers still clenched fiercely in the sleeve of Kaeri's shirt. Zamaril was okay. He was here, with her. Hope flared.

Kaeri shifted, placing herself in front of Talyn and cutting off her line of sight to Zamaril. "Talyn, do not betray your recognition, do you hear me? Pretend you've never seen him before. Talyn!"

"I hear you." Talyn gathered herself, released Kaeri's arm, and forced her cool mask to settle over her features. Kaeri was right. "Thank you."

Kaeri gave a little nod then shifted away, looking faintly bored.

A nearby guard speaking to a comrade caught her attention. "Watch how the new slave walks, how his gaze is studying his opponent. This one's a fighter."

"He looks more like a criminal to me." His companion snorted. "Like he's going to pick my pockets the moment my back is turned."

Talyn shifted, her back beginning to ache from standing still so long. Already weariness tugged at her muscles, and she wondered how she was going to be able to remain on her feet the entire day. But the sight of Zamaril had buoyed her. She felt like anything might be possible now.

A soldier entered the field and tossed a wooden sword to the champion. Bear caught it easily, spinning it in his grasp as if it weighed nothing. Zamaril's eyes narrowed, taking that quick movement in, assessing. Then the Montagni threw a sword to him. He took a step backwards so that it landed in the grass, and crossed his arms.

"I won't fight for your pleasure," he said loudly.

Talyn bit back a smile. Bear eyed him with a measuring gaze, but said nothing.

The soldier barked something at Zamaril, presumably an order to pick up the sword. A quick gust of wind carried his voice away. His scowl deepened.

"If you're afraid, don't be. I won't hurt you." This from Bear.

Zamaril gave him a scornful look. "I can fight. I just don't do it on command."

"Why not?" Bear looked puzzled. "You have to learn the way things work here, or you won't survive long. You do what our owners tell us to do. No matter what."

"Have you ever had to fight like this?" Talyn asked Kaeri.

She laughed. "No. Female slaves are expected to fight if there's war, but nobody actually teaches them how."

The soldier barked at Zamaril again. Zamaril simply settled his insolent gaze on the guard. A surge of affection rose in Talyn's chest, bringing with it a spark of warmth she held onto.

"Do what he says." Bear spoke, an edge to his voice now. "Refuse, and they'll start beating other slaves until you comply."

Before he'd even finished speaking, two guards on the edge of the field grabbed the nearest male slave and backhanded him across the face. The slave cried out and fell to the ground. As he lay there, moaning in pain, the soldier drew his sword and placed it at the man's neck.

Helpless anger rippled across Zamaril's face. He hesitated a moment longer, then bent to pick up the sword lying in the mud in a quick, angry movement. Despite herself, Talyn limped closer to the edge of the field so she could see and hear the fight better.

"They said you're the champion here?" Zamaril asked Bear.

"I haven't lost a fight since I arrived." Bear spoke without a trace of arrogance or cockiness.

"And when was that?"

"Just on two years ago." He glanced at the guards, who looked ready to start the fight. "My name is Jord, but they call me Bear. I'll win this fight because they demand it, and to prevent them hurting other slaves, but know that I don't enjoy it."

"You can call me Amar, and don't worry, you're not going to win this fight." A flash of a cocky grin.

One of the guards ran over, a white handkerchief raised in his left hand. He gestured so that the new slave understood that when he dropped the handkerchief the fight would start. Most of the soldiers started calling out to each other, egging the fighters on.

The slaves stayed silent.

Zamaril's gaze was not on the flag in the guard's hands, but on his opponent's brown eyes. A little thrill went through Talyn at the sight.

The white handkerchief dropped with a flutter. Bear seemed to want to finish the fight quickly, because he leapt straight at Zamaril with a deadly-fast thrust.

Zamaril spun his own blade, clearly enjoying the feel of it whispering through the air despite the circumstances. It came down over Bear's, sending the big man's sword veering to the left. Bear corrected himself with admirable speed and followed with a sweeping thrust to Zamaril's ribs.

As the wooden edge whistled towards his stomach, Zamaril took a step back and once again countered, Bear's blade cracking against his own. Bear disengaged instantly and backed off, surprise burgeoning on his previously calm face. Zamaril had anticipated both moves with ease.

Pride flickered in Talyn.

The guards shouted, taunting Zamaril, who was making no effort to put on a show for them. Zamaril didn't appear to have heard them. His mind and focus were entirely concentrated on Bear.

"He's good," Kaeri murmured. "He wields his blade like an extension of his arm and he sees the fight several steps ahead."

"I taught him that," Talyn couldn't help saying under her breath.

Kaeri's gaze whipped to hers, calculating, but she said nothing.

Bear went at Zamaril again, lightning fast and with a series of complex moves. Zamaril sent each sliding along his blade, one, two, three, then gathered himself and leapt forward into the attack.

Bear scrambled backwards, sword raised to counter. Zamaril thrust straight for his stomach, saw the counter coming and reversed, sweeping his blade at Bear's head. Bear ducked, raising his blade, but Zamaril was already inside his guard, sliding his blade along Bear's and then flicking his wrist in a violent motion.

Bear's blade flew out of his hands, spinning end over end to land in the mud some distance off. Zamaril's own blade was levelled at Bear's throat. "Do you concede?"

And just like that, in the space of two minutes, the fight was over.

Bear nodded, his face wearing a stunned expression. The soldiers muttered, unhappy with being robbed of a competitive fight.

Zamaril held out his free hand. "Nice to meet you, Jord."

Bear took the hand in a strong grip. "And you, Amar."

Zamaril turned on his heel and strode across the field to where he'd been standing amongst the other male slaves before being dragged out. They were all staring at him. Talyn noted the same unease she'd seen in the women earlier, but not in all of them. Some of the slaves crowded around Zamaril, murmuring to him. He acknowledged their words, but none of his reserve faded.

Talyn had to fight down the urge to run over there and talk to him. It took several deep breaths, and even then she couldn't quell the desire completely.

"Come on." Kaeri tugged at Talyn's arm. "Best move before the guards make us."

Talyn turned away from the gaggle around Zamaril and followed Kaeri as quickly as she could as they joined the line of women being led away.

IT RAINED AGAIN THAT NIGHT, providing nice cover as Talyn and Kaeri sat side by side on her pallet and had a whispered conversation. Talyn was swaying with exhaustion from her first day of work, and her back throbbed with a relentless ache, but urgency thrilled inside her. Zamaril's appearance had changed everything.

"Is his name really Amar?" Kaeri asked first.

"No. It's Zamaril. Zamaril Lightfinger." Talyn hesitated, lowered her voice further. "And I know who you are, Kaeri Venador."

Kaeri's indrawn breath was audible, and shock spread over her face. "How do you—"

"I'm Talyn Ciantar."

The woman's shock deepened and for a moment she didn't seem to know what to say. Then her green eyes sparked. "We heard rumours... you're the captain of Prince Cuinn Acondor's guard detail. What happened to you, how did you get here?"

"I was betrayed," Talyn said quickly, tripping over words in her haste. "But I need to know, did Montagn invade Mithranar? How did *you* end up in here?"

Kaeri's jaw tightened and she looked away. For a moment Talyn thought she wasn't going to answer. "Please, Kaeri. You have no idea what it's like to wake up hurt, a slave, and have no idea what happened. I have to know."

She swallowed, nodded. But even then it took her a few moments to speak. Talyn tried to wait patiently, but couldn't stop her fingers tapping a fast rhythm against her leg. Sweat broke out on her skin, fear and hope both lurching within her.

"House Manunin started a spill in Arataire. They removed my father and installed Azrilan Acondor as the new ahara. I was dumped here soon after that, but my understanding is that Azrilan left soon after to take the Mithranan throne as well—his mother was on her deathbed, days away from dying."

"*Azrilan!*" Sari breathed in shock.

"Azrilan..." Talyn said slowly, her mind furiously putting the pieces together. She turned away, hands rubbing her temples. "*He* took your father's throne?"

How had she not seen that coming? And Savin... Savin must have been working for Azrilan, not the ahara. He'd lured her into the tunnels to clear the path for Azrilan to take out Cuinn. And she'd let him. Guilt twisted through her, sharp and unbearable.

She swallowed, forced the words out. "Did you hear... when he took the throne. What happened to Cuinn?"

Kaeri looked away. "I don't know."

Silence hung heavy in the room, their shared pain a palpable weight. Kaeri took a steadying breath. "I only saw you once or twice during Prince Cuinn's courting visit, and always at a distance. When you came here you were so badly hurt, scarred, I didn't recognise you."

"I remember you clearly." Talyn stared into the distance, her thoughts still on Azrilan. The prince of games as ahara? How had she not seen that coming? "So when Azrilan and his family forced the spill, they made you a slave rather than kill you?"

"That's usual practice here for women and unimportant men. Slaves are more useful than dead people," Kaeri said dully.

"What about your father?"

"Dead along with my brothers." Kaeri's eyes were shadowed. "During the spill my guards betrayed me—they'd been bribed by House Manunin. They branded the slave tattoo into my cheek and threw me in with other criminals marked to be sent to slave camps. They told the slavemaster that I'd been working illegally as a street-girl."

Talyn's heart lurched, her worry momentarily forgotten. That was awful. "Do you think it's a coincidence we ended up in the same camp?"

"Yes. This is a relatively new camp, set up only a few months ago. They wouldn't have had enough existing slaves to re-locate here and fulfill the manpower requirements, so all newly-made slaves will be sent here until it's full."

Talyn tried not to be disappointed that Kaeri knew so little, but failed miserably. Then her head shot up with sudden hope. "Then you don't know for certain that Azrilan took the Mithranan throne as well?" Maybe Kaeri had just assumed. Maybe Cuinn and the Wolves had somehow been able to fight Azrilan off and defeat him.

"I'm sorry, but... not long after I arrived here, I heard the guards talking of Azrilan being officially crowned in Mithranar. They were bragging of how our new ahara had taken more territory for Montagn."

Talyn's hope died, her head sagging. Silence fell. Both knew exactly how the other felt. Neither knew how to fix it. "I need to find a way to talk to Zamaril," she said eventually.

"That won't be easy," Kaeri warned. "I'm confident none of the guards here know who either of us are. We can't afford to show undue interest in any of the other slaves."

Another silence, even heavier. It was beyond painful, having Zamaril so close but not being able to reach out, to talk to him.

"I liked you," Talyn said eventually, trying to shake off her misery. "You seemed tough, even though your father and his lords behaved as if you were nothing more than an ornament. But I didn't want you to marry Cuinn."

Kaeri huffed a laugh. "Why not?"

"Because *I* wanted him." She bit her lip at the memory of him.

"You're kidding me?" Kaeri's voice was rich with astonished amusement. "You wanted that pretty, womanizing, lazy prince?"

Cuinn. His face flashed into Talyn's mind and she held it there, taking what comfort she could from the memory of his smile and his laugh. Then she opened her eyes and looked at Kaeri. "He's not really like that."

"Talyn..." Kaeri hesitated. "If Azrilan took Mithranar too... you should prepare yourself for the likelihood that Cuinn is dead."

Talyn shivered and curled tightly into herself. "He's not dead. He can't be."

Kaeri started in shock at the depth of misery in Talyn's voice. She said nothing, just nodded and allowed her gaze to drift into the fire.

"*Sari?*"

"*I'm here.*"

"*Do you think he's dead? The Wolves too?*"

"*I have a feeling I would be sharing a room with Cuinn in your head if he were dead,*" Sari said. "*And your Wolves were trained by you. Don't lose faith in them, in what they're capable of.*"

"*I won't.*" Talyn grabbed hold of those words, clung to them as fiercely as she could. "*Not ever.*"

A brief silence fell then.

"*Sari, I have to get out.*"

CHAPTER 11

*Q*uinn shivered, bracing himself as another gust of mountain air sent icy tendrils creeping through gaps in the thick clothes he wore to dance like sharp needles over his skin. He'd lost feeling in his nose much earlier and was starting to worry about his fingertips and toes.

At night he dreamed of humid air so thick you could almost see it, full of the scent of flowers and kahvi spices. Of sweat dripping down his spine and slicking his skin. Of the warm thermals sliding through his feathers. He woke from those dreams longing for home so badly it brought tears to his eyes.

For a moment he rested his forehead against the icy rock and closed his eyes. He was so far from home that going back was starting to feel impossible. It felt like he'd achieved nothing beyond keeping himself alive. And all the while the WingGuard and Armun would be hunting his Wolves, his network, Saniya. Not to mention what was happening to Talyn after *another* month missing—

He shook his head, dispelling the wandering thoughts brought about by cold and fatigue.

Before he could do anything about any of that, he needed to win the Dumnorix as allies. One step at a time, as Talyn always said.

Thinking of her saying those words brought a brief smile to his face.

He took a deep, steadying breath. There was a plan. A crazy, half-brained, foolish plan, but it was all he had. It was going to take time. He just had to keep putting one foot in front of the other.

Once the gust faded, readying itself for another onslaught, Cuinn began climbing again, gloved hands gripping rock firmly before pushing upwards in a slow, cautious climb. The light grew dimmer as the dying sun dipped behind the tallest peaks. Days were much shorter in the Twin Thrones, and the nights somehow felt darker too.

Still, the climb wasn't overly difficult. His shoulders and upper back had always been strong—the muscles there necessarily powerful to maintain flight—and new, wiry muscle filled out his arms from the long days he'd spent over the past month firing arrows into targets from every distance and angle imaginable.

Entrenched as he had been in lessons and archery practice, Cuinn wasn't fully informed about how the wider battle was going—but all SkyRiders at Mothduriem were kept abreast of major developments. The Firthlanders hadn't breached the foothills of the Ayrlemyre range to the north. Yet.

But the mountains stretched the entire width of the Calumnia-Conmor landmass from east to west, covering hundreds of miles of territory. The SkyRiders were stretched thin, even with Aimsir and Callanan help. More Firthlander troops made landfall every week, in coves and well-hidden beaches along the rugged mountain coastline. Soar estimated the SkyRider legions were able to detect and hit roughly one out of every three ships, and they took losses each time from the niever-flyers flying in protection of those ships.

And although they were training as many new initiates as they could, the numbers of young men and women in the Twin Thrones with the required agility and fearlessness to become SkyRiders were few.

Both the Conmoran and Calumnian Lords' councils had sent reserves of cavalry, longbowmen and Greencloaks—the Calumnian infantry—marching north and south, prepared to defend in case the invaders broke out of the mountains. But the main strength of the army had to be held in readiness to protect Ryathl, Port Lachley and the other large cities in preparation for when the Montagni attacked.

It seemed inevitable that the Firthlanders would eventually break through. Unease curled through Cuinn. Soon he was going to have to join those battles. Try to kill others to save himself or those flying with him. He thought it might be possible... if he kept his magic tightly controlled and maintained his focus on flying, on shooting accurately, and not on what those around him were feeling. The distance would help too.

Despite his fear of real battle, of having to kill, the slow pace of his training chafed. He'd tried to be patient, to grit his teeth and focus on learning the SkyRider hand signals and flight paths, how the flight harness worked and the various formations SkyRiders flew in for scouting, travel and battle. Every bit of frustration he felt he'd chan- neled into firing arrow after arrow into targets, long after the other initiates had gone to rest or eat, over and over until his aim was subconscious.

But eventually it had become unbearable. Not only did he yearn to fly again, to feel the wind on his skin and ruffling his hair, to see the ground far below as he dipped and soared... he'd been away from home too long.

Usually SkyRider initiates trained for at least six months, usually longer, before being allowed to find and bond with an eagle—a rite of passage for all SkyRiders. Cuinn had begun asking for permission two weeks into his training, ignoring the incredulous looks and irritation at what was considered an impertinent, if not outright rude, request.

Eventually, fed up by the constant questioning, and helped along by a touch of song magic, Cuinn's flight trainer had sent a message to Soar. The Sky Chieftain had written back within days giving his permission for Cuinn to find an eagle.

He'd started the climb earlier in the morning, after choosing this nesting area weeks earlier following a conversation with Soar discussing the process of claiming an eagle.

"That eagle convocation is one of the most aggressive we've ever come across." A faint smile crossed Soar's face. "That's where I found Hunter."

Cuinn had decided then and there that he would find his eagle from amongst the same convocation. He couldn't afford to be the *slightest* inch weaker or less impressive than any of his Dumnorix relatives. No matter how he felt on the inside—how doubtful, how nervous, how desperately afraid for Talyn and Mithranar—he would show strength. Only strength would win them to Mithranar's side.

Now he scrambled up onto the ledge he'd been heading for, rolling over and lying there for a moment to catch his breath. His chest burned—the air was so thin up amongst these enormous peaks. It reminded him of skimming in the SkyReach. An ache of memory tightened his stomach and he breathed slowly through it.

The view, once he pushed himself to his feet, was breathtaking, and for a moment he forgot all about his aching arms and burning lungs.

Heavy snow clouds had cleared just enough to reveal the glow of the setting sun over the western ranges. Cuinn's gaze narrowed. West —where Firthland lay. Where Tarcos Hadvezer was. His mouth tightened, fingers curling into fists at his sides.

Impatience resurged with a vengeance.

The cry of an eagle broke him from his descent into bitter anger, and he glanced up at the sight of a full-grown male circling a nearby peak before settling into his nest, the sunset giving him a bright orange halo. Cuinn turned and hiked through the snow, along the ledge he'd found and then higher, clambering up another rock face.

He'd been watching this location the entire previous day. It was a relatively small nest, lower down than those of the full-grown adult eagles of the convocation. Several youngsters had flown in and out throughout the day, but Cuinn's attention had been caught by one particular male. He'd flown in late, carrying a dead mountain goat between his razor sharp talons.

Now, the scent of blood and rotting meat came on the breeze that whipped past Cuinn's face, guiding him straight to the nest. He clambered up onto another ledge and found himself face to face with a messy pile of sticks, tree branches and rocks sitting under an over-hang in the mountainside. The youngster was there, busily devouring the remains of the goat from the previous day. He was bigger than Cuinn had guessed, almost full-grown.

Ready for a rider.

At Cuinn's appearance, the eagle looked up, golden eyes flashing, and screamed a challenge. He was beautiful, all deep brown feathers with hints of bronze in the setting sun and a gaze that warned Cuinn to leave or be ripped apart.

And there, on the underside of his wings, when he spread them threateningly, was what had captured Cuinn's attention. A ripple of midnight-blue so dark it was almost black. Not so different from the flash of dark sapphire in Talyn's eyes when she was angry.

Cuinn smiled, stood to his full height and met the young eagle's gaze without hesitation.

Then he began to sing.

The eagle didn't succumb quickly to Cuinn's magic, nowhere near as quickly as Jasper had. But Cuinn was patient, using the powerful magic he'd been born with—the magic Azrilan would never be able to take away like he had his wings. He ignored the freezing cold creeping into his bones and the growing numbness of the skin on his face. His music kept him warm enough.

And then, over two full-turns later, on that bare, freezing, cliff face, the young eagle lowered his wings and took a single, hopping step towards Cuinn.

Cuinn remained still for a moment, then achingly slowly, he reached out a gloved hand, sliding it gently through the feathers of the eagle's neck. Those golden eyes slid half-closed in reluctant pleasure, and all remaining stiffness in the eagle's bearing faded.

"I'm Cuinn," he murmured, stroking softly. "And I'm going to name you Trystaan."

Trystaan ruffled his wings, tossed his head in one final show of reluctance, then hopped a step closer, wings spreading wide as he let out a soft cry. Smiling, Cuinn drew out the wooden whistle lying against his chest. "You're going to need to learn this sound, my friend."

In that moment, all his doubts about the course of action he'd chosen vanished like they had never been.

He would fly again.

And he would fight.

IT WAS after midnight by the time Cuinn climbed down the mountainside and hiked the distance back to Mothduriem. Finally reaching the relative warmth of one of the entrance tunnels lower down the slope of the massive mountain base, he pulled his gloves and beanie off and made his way to a long, narrow cavern that held a series of hammocks hanging from the roof—the sleeping quarters for SkyRider initiates.

Pride and satisfaction had filled Cuinn on the hike back, despite the cold that ached in his bones and the weariness that dragged at his muscles. But once he was in his hammock, the others sleeping around him, the walls began to close in. It was hard not to feel like he wasn't moving fast enough, that he needed to be doing more, faster.

He tried to stop the spiral of despairing thoughts, to clear his mind so that he could get the rest his body needed, but it proved hard, and he tossed and turned restlessly. The sound of approaching bootsteps was a surprise given the late hour, but Soar's appearance was a welcome distraction.

"Soar!" He rolled off his hammock, keeping his voice low. "I didn't realise you were scheduled for a visit to Mothduriem."

"After Plummet's request came last week, I wanted to come and see how you did." Soar's eyes ran over him, surprise flickering on his face for a moment. "I know it's late, but are you up to a chat?"

"I couldn't sleep anyway," Cuinn admitted, falling in beside Soar as the man led him through a main tunnel winding up through the mountain. He was a little taller than Cuinn, with curling black hair shot through with grey, and luminous Dumnorix eyes a shade deeper than Ariar's sky blue.

Having seen the stars in the night sky from the mountains many times now, he understood why the Twin Thrones folk had likened their Dumnorix monarchs' eyes to them. Bright and luminous indeed.

The Sky Chieftain's quarters were much roomier and more comfortable than anywhere else in the mountain, and Cuinn welcomed the delightful warmth of the crackling fire.

"Have a seat." Soar waved him to a chair by the fire and offered him a glass of wine.

"It's not Montagni?" Never again would he have to pretend to enjoy wine made by slaves. At least there was that. No matter how bad things had gotten, at least he no longer had to pretend to be the indolent prince.

Soar's face darkened momentarily, but then he smiled. "Grown and fermented in Allira's estates—her husband has a fondness for dabbling in wine production. It's actually not bad."

Cuinn took it with a nod of thanks and Soar sat in the chair beside his, stretching long legs out towards the fire. "How did you go?"

A smile spread over Cuinn's face. "I have an eagle."

"A Dumnorix indeed." Soar leaned over and offered his hand. "Congratulations, Cuinn."

"Thank you." Cuinn was surprised by the warmth that shot through him at Soar's regard, his affectionate handshake. It was an odd sensation. Unfamiliar... but welcome.

Though they were relative strangers, Cuinn's song magic felt them relaxing into each other without even thinking, an unconscious familiarity and sense of safety sliding into place. Whatever curious combination of magic underlaid the Dumnorix line, a hint of song magic must be part of it. Did they have a distant winged folk ancestor, or did winged folk magic itself come from somewhere else entirely? The question made him miss Tiercelin fiercely. It was something the healer would have loved to debate.

"I'll make sure Plummet puts you in combat flight training immediately." Soar's voice broke him from his musings. "You don't need to waste your time with the basic teaching all the other initiates go through. You've been flying your whole life."

The depth of his gratitude must have flashed over his face, because Soar gave him a little smile. "I'm sure you miss it terribly. I don't know what I would ever do if I couldn't fly again, and I've never had wings of my own."

That touched on a painful spot, so Cuinn cleared his throat and changed the subject. "Tell me how the fighting is going? Things must be calmer if you've been able to fly back here."

"The Firthlanders made a recent hard push through the northwest foothills, but the Aimsir and SkyRiders helped the Conmoran cavalry hold them back." Soar drained his wine. "Callanan intelligence is keeping our heads above water. They're working furiously with the Aimsir scouts to warn us of Firthlander movements across the mountains, but we're losing numbers we need to niever-flyers."

"You don't sound hopeful." Cuinn felt the waves of worry etched in the man's words.

"My latest SkyRider patrols report that another wave of Firthlander warships is on the move, ferrying troops to the west coast." Soar shook his head. "Tarcos is diverting money and resources to build more ships. And then..."

Cuinn finished the unspoken thought. "Montagn will move soon, won't they?"

"Allowing time for Azrilan to establish his rule in Arataire, muster an invasion force, then start moving warships south?" Soar cocked his head. "A strong leader with skilled commanders could accomplish that in two months."

Neither of them had to say it aloud. Azrilan had taken Mithranar at the end of Elevenmonth. Twomonth had just started. And there was no doubt he had skilled commanders. War with Montagn was imminent.

Soar shifted, glancing at him. "Tell me, Cuinn, I know you aim to get your throne back, but you have to realise how difficult that will be. There *is* a plan, I take it?"

Cuinn huffed a breath, then spoke honestly. "I've got some crazy ideas loosely tied together with a very fragile piece of string."

Soar said nothing to that, seeming to accept it. Cuinn studied the Sky Chieftain's face as he stared at the flames; from their reaction to him when he'd arrived in Port Lachley it had been abundantly clear the Dumnorix would never agree to an alliance, to helping him take back Mithranar. Not as he'd been then, weak and alone. And especially not while they were at war themselves.

If Cuinn wanted the Dumnorix to help, he was going to have to be patient and fearless. And a lot more. He wondered how much it was going to take, how far he would have to go for Mithranar. Would it be enough to become a SkyRider and fight in their battles? He doubted it, even though achieving that would cement his Dumnorix blood in their minds.

He wondered whether Talyn would ever forgive him for what he might have to do.

"How are Alyna and Ariar?" Cuinn asked, shaking away the doubts he felt that he *could* do whatever it took. "Especially Alyna. I can't imagine how she must feel, with Talyn..." He couldn't finish the sentence.

Soar sighed, genuine grief rippling over his face. "They're both as frustrated and upset as I am that the Callanan have found no clue on where she is or what happened to her," Soar said, then looked straight at Cuinn. "How are you doing?"

Cuinn chose to deliberately misunderstand. "I'm working hard here. Now that I have an eagle, I can't wait to fly. You have no idea how badly I need to get into the air again."

Soar smiled. "I wish you luck. I have to fly out again tomorrow, so I probably won't have time to talk with you again."

"I understand."

Soar's grin widened as he reached for the decanter of wine. "Another one?"

That night together, drinking Allira's wine and talking of everything and nothing, served to do more for Cuinn's strength and peace of mind in the space of hours than anything since Talyn's disappearance and the loss of his throne.

When he finally went to his hammock in the small hours of the morning, he slept soundly for the first time since that horrible night, untroubled by nightmares.

· · ·

Soar left orders with Plummet before he departed the next day. Cuinn walked up to the flying platform after a brief sleep, ignoring the bitter cold clawing into his bones the moment he stepped outside.

He was the first of the initiates to arrive, but two of the trainers were already there. A quick use of magic told him they weren't overly pleased by the orders to accelerate Cuinn's training. Conmorans were a prideful lot, he was quickly learning, and they liked their formalities. It was making them intensely uncomfortable that Cuinn was ignoring all the traditions of SkyRider training.

That was fine. The moment he got into the air, he was going to change all their minds about him. There might be nothing else he was certain of anymore, but he was certain of that.

He dug out the whistle from under his shirt and blew on it three times, as loudly as he could. Anticipation curled in his gut, and his hands and arms trembled. He felt simultaneously nauseous and elated.

Moments passed, all three of them staring out into the clouds. And then, a faint speck appeared in the clear blue sky. A distant cry echoed through the peaks. A smile spread across Cuinn's face as the speck grew closer and closer, resolving into a young eagle with a flash of blue on the underside of his wings.

Cold air gusted over their heads as Trystaan swooped low and then landed before Cuinn, his sharp cry of greeting filling the morning air.

"A fine bird," Plummet said with reluctant approval. "What have you named him?"

"Trystaan."

"That's not a sky name."

"It's *his* name," Cuinn said simply.

He stepped forward then, pulling off a glove and running his fingers through Trystaan's feathers in greeting. The eagle accepted the stroking as his due, his golden gaze settling on the watching SkyRiders with a glare reminiscent of Jasper's finest.

Cuinn's heart swelled in his chest. Trystaan was his.

He reached back and unslung the riding harness from his shoulders. The trainers made no move to help him. That was fine. He and Trystaan would work it out together.

He got the harness on, Trystaan standing mostly still. Then, taking a shuddering breath, Cuinn clambered up onto his back the same way he'd watched SkyRiders do it a hundred times before.

It was awkward, and Trystan squawked in annoyance several times, but eventually Cuinn was in place, the harness tight around his back and shoulders. The pit in his stomach opened even further, and when he opened his mouth to speak, his voice came out as a rasp.

"Go, Trystaan," he managed.

Trystaan hopped sideways, tossed his head, then spread his wings. With one giant beat of them he was lifting into the air.

Cuinn's stomach dropped as the eagle dived off the platform, his joyous screech echoing through the mountains.

The icy air rushed by Cuinn's cheeks.

His eyes blurred from the speed.

And he was flying again.

CHAPTER 12

*T*alyn was assigned to the same work group as Kaeri, shoveling coal into the forges of one of the smithies. The work was endless and exhausting, and for the first few days—despite her fierce determination to get strong and escape the camp the moment she could—Talyn simply couldn't keep up.

Without a word, and scowling every time Talyn tried to thank her, Kaeri did her best to manage both of their workloads while Talyn took breaks. Too often, a soldier would walk by and notice her resting. They would force her back to work with a stinging backhand to her cheek or a rough shove and loud, angry shouts. Each time, she would grit her teeth, drag herself back to her feet, and continue.

It was a struggle to stay positive and maintain hope, and sometimes she failed.

But not always.

Days passed, then weeks, and the scars on her back and face healed from a livid red to a healthier pink. Her strength built slowly, until she regained muscle and was able to manage a full day's work without resting.

As her energy returned, enough so that it didn't require everything she had just to put one foot in front of the other, she began playing closer attention to her surroundings.

Their work group laboured in one of three massive smithies in the camp. The buildings took up almost the entire southeastern corner of the fenced compound, and a thick haze of smoke hung constantly over the area. Life in the camp revolved entirely around the smithies. A good portion of the slaves worked inside them, while others laboured outside the fence to cut down trees and chop enough wood to feed the forges, and some worked in the kitchens or laundries responsible for feeding and clothing the workforce. It was a smooth and efficient operation. As far as Talyn could tell it ran without hitch day after day.

"Their battle rage breeds a fearsome strength, and their swords often shatter in battle or training, even when well-made," Kaeri explained one day as they watched Berserker broadswords being made. "So there's a constant need for more."

Talyn nodded and turned to shovel up another load of coal, by now accustomed to the painful tugging of the scars on her back as she moved. She couldn't fully raise her arms above her head, and she walked with a slight limp due to the tightness of the scar tissue. The tide of bitter frustration and anxiety—never far off—surged at the reminder she'd never be able to fight like she once had in this condition.

"Tell me about the colours," she asked, curious and seeking a distraction.

Kaeri shot her a frown of puzzlement.

"That guard over there has cobalt thread sewn into the cuffs and hem of his tunic. But the one by the door has orange. And the guards eating during dinner last night wore green thread. Does it denote rank?"

"No, it tells you which House they're from. Cobalt is Manunin. Orange is Daranin." Kaeri tossed a pile of coal into the forge. "Houses are required to deploy soldiers to labour camps at the direction of the ahara."

"What colour is Venador?"

"Scarlet."

"I haven't seen any guards here with scarlet thread."

"Venador soldiers are cavalry, because our land is mountain territory. Some form part of the ahara's ceremonial guard in Arataire, but you won't find many of us as guards in slave camps."

"I take it someone else will be in charge of your House now that Manunin is in power," she asked quietly.

Kaeri nodded, jaw tight. "My uncle, probably. If he survived."

Talyn wanted to learn more about Kaeri, the only friend she'd found here. There was no softness in her, but no cruelty that Talyn could detect either. But Kaeri wouldn't talk about her past, and Talyn didn't want to cause her any unnecessary pain.

"I can't stay here, Talyn," she said suddenly, grip on the shovel white-knuckled as she kept tossing coal into the forge. Her eyes were downcast, jaw tight. "I can't."

Silence fell. Talyn didn't know how to address the sort of raw desperation she saw on Kaeri's face, especially when it was such a perfect mirror of her own feelings.

"I don't know how much longer I can do this either," she murmured to Sari.

"You'll get there. I know it." Sari was instantly there. *"You'll figure something out. You always do."*

Talyn reached over and touched Kaeri's arm, tried to share some of Sari's optimism. "We'll work it out, I promise."

"Do you ever think about escaping?" Talyn asked later that day as they took a break in the fresh air outside the smithy. The hot summer sun wasn't much better than the heat inside the smithy and sweat slicked her skin. A deep breath of the smoke haze had her coughing so now she was trying shallow breaths through her nose.

Kaeri looked at her. "All the time. But it's impossible. Trust me, I've thought about nothing else since I got here."

At the tone of her friend's voice, Talyn dropped the subject, but spent the next few days studying the layout of the camp and listening more closely to the conversation of the other female slaves. As time passed, and neither Kaeri nor Talyn did anything to upset their fragile standing in the camp, their wariness had mostly faded.

The other two women they shared a hut with introduced themselves—Lia and Roni—and began exchanging the occasional word in the morning or at night. Lia brought Kaeri extra tea one day when she ran out.

Rumour was, nobody had ever escaped a slave camp. Kaeri confirmed she'd never heard of it happening. Talyn wasn't surprised. Even if someone did get away, there was nowhere to run to. Not anywhere close enough to reach before the dogs or soldiers on horses ran you down, anyway.

"The moment anyone shows a hint of rebelliousness, the punishment is sharp and swift," Kaeri had explained. "Slaves are trained, brainwashed even, to behave perfectly."

When Talyn looked unconvinced Kaeri continued. "While you were still unconscious, a female slave was sent to the cells for three days because she forgot she'd been re-assigned to a new work detail and showed up at her old one to begin the day's work."

"The cells?"

"Underground chambers beneath the compound's barracks, where the camp administrator works, and the Berserker and soldier commanders have their quarters," Kaeri said. "And you remember last week when that short, blonde woman who usually sits at our table for breakfast disappeared for almost a week?"

"Right. She reappeared looking half-dead. I didn't dare ask what happened."

"That's what the isolation hut will do to you. No human contact, no comforts like blankets or a bed, barely any food. Word is, she complained to a guard about *her* work detail after spraining a wrist."

Still, Talyn's mind continued to mull on the problem. Searching for something creative, something nobody had thought of. It was a good distraction, and when she wasn't thinking about escape, she was considering the implications of the work being undertaken by the slaves.

The smithy where she worked forged at least twenty blades a day, a chilling number when she calculated that across the other smithies in the camp, not to mention the other camps across Montagn. And Kaeri had said their camp was new, only a few months old.

Montagn was preparing for war.

With the Twin Thrones. There were no other possibilities. If Azrilan had already taken Mithranar, then he could only be planning for war with someone else. Talyn wondered if he intended invasion or was preparing to defend himself against attack from the south.

The thought made her ill with despair. War while she was stuck here, physically limited and unable to do anything about it. Not even Sari could comfort her in her darkest moments—at night when she could think of nothing but what might be happening in the outside world.

She hadn't seen Zamaril again, and as the days passed without even a sighting of him, some of the hope she'd felt at seeing him died too. Her spirits sank even lower at the thought he might have been moved to another camp.

And then, a week after Talyn asked Kaeri about escape, more Montagni soldiers arrived in the camp. A rumour ran through the slaves that the new soldiers were part of a troop buildup in the area.

"They're preparing for war, aren't they?" Talyn asked Kaeri that evening as they ate, keeping her voice low enough that only Kaeri could hear. "I've been taking note. The number of weapons being produced is staggering. And now, more troops arriving? There's a reason for all of it."

"I wondered when you'd mention it."

"War with the Twin Thrones? It has to be."

"I'm not certain." She looked away, spooning up a mouthful of watery gravy and onions. "I was put in here before you, remember."

Talyn frowned. "Any invasion of Montagn would have to come

through the west," she said. "The rest of the country is bordered by rugged mountains. The last thing an invading army would want to do is march through those—you'd be able to pick them off along the way while sustaining limited casualties yourselves, and forget about supply lines. The invader would probably lose their entire force before stepping foot out of the mountains."

Kaeri smiled grimly. "An apt assessment. The only other option would be to invade through Mithranar and the Ice Plains north of the SkyReach. An invading force would still have to come through the mountains, but there are established roads suitable for a large number of invaders, and all they would need is a Venador guide to get them through. Men can be bribed, even loyal ones."

Mithranar.

Her chest squeezed so tightly it was a struggle to breathe. Had Azrilan completely consolidated his rule there? Or was it vulnerable to a Twin Thrones or Firthlander invasion?

Where did Warlord Hadvezer stand in all this? Why had Bearmen and a Shadow ambushed her? She was missing something, she knew it, but couldn't figure out what it was.

Before anything further could be said, the bell by the door rang, signaling the end of eating time. Benches scraped over the floor as slaves rose to their feet and began filing out. Talyn followed the lines until reaching the hut she and Kaeri shared.

As usual, she craned her neck as discreetly as possible, seeking Zamaril's familiar figure in the men standing to file out of the opposite side of the eating hall. Once again, tonight there was no sign of him in the crowd. There were just too many of them.

Frustration burned in her chest.

Back in their hut, Kaeri started a fire and placed a kettle of water over it, her usual nightly routine, and she and Talyn waited silently until their companions fell asleep.

"Want some tea?" Kaeri asked.

She ignored the question. "The options are limited, Kaeri. Either Azrilan is expecting to be invaded, or he's intending to do a little empire expansion," Talyn snapped, unaccountably frustrated. "It will be the Twin Thrones or Firthland—and the difference doesn't really matter given Firthland is ruled by the Dumnorix monarch too."

"I know that." Kaeri shot to her feet, frustration pouring off her. "If Azrilan is picking a fight with the Twin Thrones..." She began pacing, appearing gripped by sudden urgency. "I don't want to see my countrymen killed in a useless war to gain more land that we don't need."

"If you did get out, what *could* you do about it?" Talyn asked carefully.

Kaeri shook her head, made a dismissive gesture with her hand.

Talyn sighed, lying back on her pallet and allowing her aching muscles to stretch out. As desperate as she was, escape continued to elude her. Even her strategic mind had failed to come up with a way of achieving it. *Yet.* She tried to hold on to her determination, to faith in herself and what she could do.

"You'd have a much better chance of getting away without me." Talyn glanced at the sleeping women, hoping neither was awake enough to hear her words.

"I didn't save your life to leave you rotting here," Kaeri said. "And if it came to it, I'm strong enough to get us both away, once we're out."

"That's the problem, isn't it? Getting out."

Kaeri didn't answer. She didn't need to.

Talyn closed her eyes and let her thoughts loose. Maybe she just needed to stop trying so hard and let her brain figure it out instinctively.

A handful of full-turns later, she was still awake. She was exhausted, but too sore and anxious to sleep. And she still hadn't come up with any ideas on how to escape. She shifted, trying to settle into a more comfortable position.

"Your Zamaril is an interesting fellow." Kaeri's voice came from the pallet nearby, seemingly alerted to Talyn's wakefulness by the movement. "I saw him yesterday, when the guards sent me to fetch their lunch."

"You did!" Talyn sat up, excitement thrilling through her. "Why didn't you tell me?"

"I'm telling you now. In private. When nobody can hear."

Talyn sighed and settled back down, some of the anxiety in her chest easing. "Was he okay?"

"He looked fine. They were making him fight again, this time against one of the guards. He beat him inside two seconds—I would have liked to stay and watch him beat the next guy too."

"He's a good fighter," Talyn said, shifting in vain to find a warmer spot under the blanket. "One of the best swordsman I've ever seen. Callanan-level good."

"That's not why I think he's interesting."

Talyn sighed, giving up on sleep. At least conversation might distract her from her aching body. "What do you mean?"

Kaeri turned to face her. "You know that he keeps the other slaves in line? Stops them from doing anything that will bring them to the attention of the guards. They look up to him."

"He's smart, Kaeri. He's working those soldiers, keeping them onside." She paused. "Why so much interest in Zamaril?"

"He intrigues me."

Talyn grinned. "In what way?"

Kaeri huffed a sigh. "Don't be stupid. He's not even close to my type."

"Oh really?" she teased. "He not brawny enough for you?"

"He's shorter than me, for a start. And while I don't mind taking the occasional man to my bed when they're particularly handsome, I generally prefer women."

"Oh." Talyn sighed as the opportunity to needle Kaeri about Zamaril vanished, then shifted, wincing as her back flared in pain. "I'm pretty sure you're not Zamaril's type either."

"I wouldn't have picked the pretty Prince Cuinn as your type." Kaeri snorted.

Talyn grinned, for once not crushed by the pain of missing him, of not knowing if he was okay. "He's far from it. I normally go for the brawny sort. But when he sings, he has the most beautiful voice... I think that's how he got me, at least to start with."

"And then?"

106

"And then... he's the best person I know. He makes *me* want to be better."

"Excuse me while I be sick." Kaeri rolled over, making coughing noises.

One of the other women stirred on her pallet, and Kaeri clapped a hand over her mouth. Talyn sniggered. "Why so cynical?"

"Love is the most ridiculous notion I've ever encountered. Especially in our world. There's no place for it."

"I used to think that," Talyn mused. "I was absolutely certain of it."

"And what changed?" Kaeri didn't sound particularly interested in her answer, but wanted to keep the conversation going because she didn't want to lie there in silence either.

"I lost my Callanan partner a few years ago," Talyn said quietly. The words had become so much easier to say, but there was still a twinge deep inside each time she did. "I don't know if I can convey with words how much I loved being Callanan with her, the happiness I felt. And when I lost her I broke apart. Worse, I felt like it was my fault, like my life was over."

"I'm sorry."

"For a long time I lived in a fog of misery and grief and guilt. But then I was sent to Mithranar. Working with the Wolves there, achieving what we did, it taught me that I could live again. That I could find satisfaction, purpose, contentment even. It saved me."

"But?"

Talyn bit her lip, tears flooding her eyes as some of the pain and worry came tearing back. "With Cuinn I learned that I could be happy again. As happy as I'd been before."

A brief pause, then, "I still want to vomit."

Talyn laughed, the pain clearing and amusement spreading through her. "Okay, okay, fine."

Silence fell then. A warm, comfortable silence. Talyn's eyes slid closed, the sheer exhaustion in her muscles slowly tugging her down into restless sleep.

"*Sari?*"

"*Mmmm?*"

"*Getting out of here… it's going to take time. The only way I can think to cope, to not lose my mind, is to distract myself. To plan.*"

"*For what comes next.* After *you get out.*"

"*Exactly.*"

Sari's anticipation curled around her thoughts like a warm blanket. "*Then let's start planning.*"

CHAPTER 13

*H*is stomach churned from nerves and fear both, and he had to take several deep breaths just to stop himself emptying the contents of his stomach into the dark sky around him.

He tried to focus, to pay attention to his position within the legion as it dropped towards the battle below, to keep an eye out for Swift's hand signals. Shit, what if he couldn't remember them? What if he did something enormously stupid and got himself, or others, killed?

Trystaan banked under him, instinctively following the other eagles, utterly calm where Cuinn was a mess. He'd joined this combat legion two days earlier after completion of training. Had participated in two training sessions with them.

And then it had come a half-turn earlier.

An urgent call from one of the SkyRider patrols; Bearmen and niever-flyers were making a push across the Thalion river and the Aimsir and cavalry were falling back, losing ground. Cuinn's legion was next up on the combat roster.

What was he doing?

He was no fighter. He was a winged prince who could hide in the shadows and sing a pretty song every now and then. He curled his hands tightly in Trystaan's feathers, feeling off balance and vulnerable.

His eyes flicked to Swift in the front, who was making the hand signal for shifting into fighting position. Around him his legion mates smoothly unclipped their harnesses, moved into a seated position, and re-clipped themselves in. Clumsily, awkward with nerves, Cuinn did the same.

His song magic picked up the fear and unease of the flyers closest to him, though this was an experienced legion, and those emotions were well controlled under a layer of calm focus.

Okay. He could do that too.

He sucked in a breath, settled himself more comfortably on Trystaan's back. Reached up to touch the quiver of arrows strapped to his back. He'd come too far to turn around now. Whether he could actually do it or not was a moot point. He was about to fly into a battle.

Swift made another hand gesture, deliberately exaggerated so the riders furthest away could see, then made it again.

Before Cuinn was ready, the legion veered into a sharp dive. The bottom fell out of his stomach, and his gaze tuned in on the glitter of moonlight off the river's surface below.

And the flaming arrows arcing through the night sky from each army's rear lines.

In between, on the muddy banks, soldiers fought fiercely. It was hard to tell who was who, apart from the galloping Aimsir horses. They were everywhere, but steadily being pushed back from the northern banks of the Thalion as screeching nievers swooped down on them. Arrows flew, hundreds of them, falling amongst the infantry. Though too distant to hit his song magic, he still winced at the sight of falling soldiers.

"Cuinn!" A sharp call from the flyer nearest him, Drift, drew Cuinn's attention to Swift, who was issuing more orders.

Shit. He had to pay attention. Fear opened a hole in his stomach. His heart thundered rapidly.

For a moment his mind went utterly blank and he forgot everything he'd memorised in the past weeks about what the signals meant. Panic set in. His breaths came in gasps. Trystaan rocked back and forth under him, as if sensing his distress. It was just enough to clear his mind.

Swift wanted them to make a strafing run—hit the archers in the Firthlander lines and then draw the nievers into the sky after them. The sense of that plan was obvious; it would immediately reduce the pressure on the Conmoran defensive lines.

The eagles dropped lower and lower, wingtips almost brushing the treetops, coming in as low as they could to avoid being spotted by the Firthlanders until it was too late.

Cuinn unhooked his bow. Drew an arrow. Wind rushed by his face, bringing with it the screams and chaos of fighting. He drew in his magic as tightly as he possibly could, then focused his mind, forcing himself to concentrate only on picking a target and hitting it.

Fifty eagles arrowed in on the rear of the Firthlander lines, deadly and silent, Cuinn somewhere near the back of the legion.

Swift lifted a hand. Dropped it.

And then they were in range.

Cuinn's sharp winged folk gaze scanned the ground, saw the archers firing on the Aimsir and cavalry. He lifted his bow. Hesitated for one breath.

Then he fired.

Trystaan was moving fast, so he had only a microsecond to see the arrow strike home. To see the archer topple backwards. And then he was drawing another. Firing again. Passing them too quickly to feel their pain. Too quickly to think about anything but finding and hitting another target.

Before he knew it they were past the lines and Trystaan was streaking back into the sky behind the other eagles.

Cuinn let out a gasping breath. Lowered his bow. His hands trembled and nausea surged.

He'd killed. And he hadn't felt it because it had happened too quickly and too far away. But he'd killed. Men were dead because of him. Their lives ripped away.

He swallowed, trying to keep his stomach from emptying. Sweat slicked his skin.

And then something hissed by his face.

His legion began shouting warnings. He reached up with a gloved hand, felt a stinging line along his cheek.

"Nievers!" Swift bellowed. "Take them out. Take them all out."

Chaos.

It was the only word Cuinn could think of to describe it.

Trystaan screamed a challenge as a niever came too close, the eagle banking sharply so he could lash out with a taloned foot. The niever jerked away, but its rider got off another shot at Cuinn beforehand that caught the side of his arm.

Momentarily made angry by the pain, Cuinn swung his bow around, nocked an arrow, and fired at the turning niever. It hit the rider in her eye and she fell with a scream.

"Nice shot!" Drift bellowed as he passed by Cuinn's left side.

Cuinn stared after the woman as she spiraled toward the ground.

A scream nearby yanked him from his daze. Drift had been surrounded by three nievers in the sky below, one of their arrows embedding itself in his shoulder.

Cuinn didn't think. He urged Trystaan into a sharp dive, firing another arrow. A second was loosing as Trystaan crashed into the niever closest to Drift. His eagle's talons tore through the niever's wing and both creature and rider fell from the skies.

Cuinn turned, craned his neck up, then reached for another arrow. It took Drift's third attacker in the chest, giving his eagle the opening to attack.

"Thanks!" Drift panted as Cuinn brought Trystaan up beside him. His face was tight with pain but he looked alert.

"You okay?"

"Fine." Drift looked around. "I think we're good."

Eagles were circling, screaming their triumph, and the handful of nievers that remained in the sky were fleeing. Swift brought his eagle into the centre, his hand gestures ordering the legion to fall in behind him.

Two more strafing runs on the Firthlander archers and Bearmen and then they sounded the retreat. Cuinn stared at the beautiful

Aimsir horses as their riders, whooping and screaming the whole time, chased down the fleeing soldiers.

Dead bodies lay sprawled on the riverbanks. If it were light, no doubt they'd see the river waters turned temporarily red.

The nausea from before rose again, threatening to swallow him whole.

So this was war.

CHAPTER 14

*W*hen the alarm bells started ringing, her body reacted without thought. She rolled from the pallet and leapt to her feet in one movement, reaching to the small of her back for the daggers that were no longer there. A heartbeat later sharp pain tore through her scars and she dropped to her knees, gasping.

"Talyn?" Kaeri was on her feet too, surprise and concern rippling over her face.

"I'm okay," she gasped. "Just moved too fast."

Kaeri opened her mouth as if to say something else, then closed it, frowning. Over the sound of the bells came the distant shouting of guards.

"What's going on?" She kept her voice low, glanced at the two sleeping women. "And how are they not wide awake from that awful clamour?"

"They're used to it." Eagerness edged Kaeri's whisper. "Shall we find out what's going on?"

They'd never left their hut after curfew. Had never even considered it. But instinct shivered through Talyn. If they wanted to escape, then they needed to start taking some risks.

Talyn glanced at Lia and Roni, assured herself they were sleeping, then reached for her boots. "I'm right behind you." She bit her lip as her aching back protested her bending over. Kaeri moved to the door, taking a careful glance outside before stepping out.

The immediate area was dark, only a handful of flickering torches lighting the path through the huts that led to the latrine pits. But to the east an orange glow lit up the night.

"Something is on fire," Kaeri breathed in excitement. "The eating hall, I think."

The rhythmic thudding of marching feet approached, and Kaeri and Talyn pressed themselves into the wall of their hut moments before a row of soldiers came into sight, moving past them in the direction of the eating hall. The captain shouted an order, and the row of soldiers moved into a jog.

"Let's follow them." Kaeri hissed.

Talyn reached out to catch Kaeri's arm before she ran off. "If it's just a fire, we should stay put. We'll end up in the cells if we get caught outside after curfew."

Kaeri's green eyes glimmered. "What if it's not just a fire?"

Talyn hesitated, but the same instinct from before nudged at her, refusing to let go. "All right."

She limped after Kaeri, shadowing her carefully between the patches of darkness around the torches. Her back stung, already sore from her too-quick movements earlier, but she ignored it. Adrenalin hummed through her veins, dousing the pain, bringing the sweet taste of anticipation instead.

Occasionally they were forced to stop and crouch in the shadows as more soldiers ran past. The bells were still ringing, a steady pattern Talyn didn't recognise but assumed was summoning more soldiers from barracks.

Eventually they reached the eastern edge of the female housing area. A breeze from the north carried the stench from the latrine pits mixed with the acrid odour of smoke.

"It *is* the eating hall." Kaeri stopped in the shadows along the side of a hut. Ahead was the wide clearing which surrounded the long building where the slaves ate their meals every day.

Kaeri crouched, hiding deeper in the darkness, and Talyn bit down on a wince as she followed suit. Flames licked up the southern side of the hall and onto the roof while a group of soldiers battled it with buckets of water from a nearby well. It was a losing battle. A thick haze of smoke drifted on the breeze.

Another group of soldiers came running past, their captain shouting at them to hurry. Talyn frowned as they ran past those fighting the blaze and continued north. "Where are they going?" she asked.

Kaeri glanced at her. "What if the fire was a distraction?"

The adrenalin running through Talyn's blood spiked. "For an escape attempt?"

"Come on." Kaeri rose to her feet.

"Where are we going?"

"To find out where those soldiers are headed. If there's an escape attempt in progress, maybe we can—"

"We can see what's happening from here," Talyn said, trying to be sensible even though part of her wanted to follow Kaeri without question. They were well hidden, but if they broke cover, the chances of being spotted rose exponentially.

"Just a little bit closer."

Kaeri moved before Talyn could stop her. Sticking to the shadows of the huts, she moved north towards the latrine pits, the burning mess hall to their right. Once they reached the last hut before the pits, both women crouched down again, keeping to the darkness.

They'd just settled in position when more shouts sounded. A handful of men burst into sight, seven at a quick count, illuminated by the flames as they sprinted into the open space before the eating hall. They were coming from the men's huts.

Slaves.

All of them carried makeshift weapons. They clustered together for a moment, then one of them pointed, and they veered off—away from the burning building and in the direction of the front gates. Some of the guards fighting the blaze ran to cut them off, and the two groups hit each other with cries and thuds and the clashing of weapons.

Kaeri's eyes lit up. "It *is* an escape attempt!"

But Talyn's excitement died as quickly as it had come. "They're not going to make it. There are too many Montagni soldiers and the slaves don't have proper weapons."

"They can win if we help them," Kaeri urged. "There are only ten or so guards, no Berserkers, maybe we can turn the fight in their favour!"

"We'd just get ourselves killed," Talyn hissed. "The alarm is raised and the soldiers are swarming—where do you think they've all gone? To cut off the exit."

Kaeri's body thrummed with tension. She was clearly torn. Talyn's desire to escape beat incessantly at her too, but there was no point risking certain capture. It took everything she had to battle Kaeri, hold herself back, and even then she kept fighting the urge to simply run.

Together they watched the fighting rage over the cleared ground. They should leave, return to their hut before the situation got worse, but Talyn couldn't help but stay and watch it all play out. Hope refused to die, even though she knew how this was going to end.

"All those soldiers we saw can't just have been to man the front gates and cut off escape," Kaeri murmured at one point, frustration filling her voice. "There must be more groups of escapees."

"Dividing the guards' attention, a good strategy," Talyn said. "But before you say it, we don't know where they are or if they've been successful. They might all be bailed up like this group."

As Talyn had expected, the Montagni were quickly gaining the upper hand. The wind changed, fading to almost nothing, and thick smoke from the fire began filling the open space. The flames licked hungrily over half the building now.

"There must be more escapees." Kaeri saw it too, and frustration filled her voice. "Or there would be far more soldiers here fighting that fire."

Just as she finished speaking, more soldiers appeared from the east carrying buckets of water to attack the flames. The remaining escapees were being slowly forced back towards the open drill field north of the hall, their numbers rapidly dwindling.

More shouts echoed over the noise of the fighting and the fire, and a line of twelve marching slaves came into sight, watched over by four soldiers holding drawn swords. In the distance Talyn spotted more lines of slaves, but they were too far away to make out any detail. Soon smoke obscured them completely.

At Talyn's side, Kaeri's shoulders slumped. "That's why we saw the guards running towards the men's residential area."

"What is it?"

"They're rousing the male slaves to do a head count and make sure no more of them try anything," Kaeri said dully. "But they're keeping them in small, controllable groups. The guards are regaining control."

Talyn hesitated. They should go back to their hut. It was the only safe thing to do—the guards might look to do a headcount of the female slaves too—but she still couldn't tear herself away from what was happening.

One of the slaves being marched towards the dining hall stumbled and fell. A guard tried to drag him to his feet, but he'd sprained an ankle, and cried out in pain, falling again. When the guard tried to heave him back up, the slave slapped his hands away. The guard gave a growl of anger and drove his sword through the slave's chest.

Talyn stared, transfixed, as the slave went still, blood spreading in a pool around him. The other slaves froze too, staring in horror at the body.

The slave hadn't been trying to escape. He'd simply fallen and turned his ankle.

And now he was dead.

Slaves weren't human to these soldiers. Talyn had intellectually known that. Had known she was a slave too. But she hadn't felt it, not truly understood it, until now.

The flame inside her flickered back to life. A steady, rising rage.

Smoke filled the open space, cutting off the guards fighting the fire on the south side from the handful of battling escapees still alive, and the slaves being marched down for a head count.

The different groups of guards couldn't see each other—the smoke was too thick. And none of the soldiers were Berserkers; just infantry. Maybe...

Kaeri's hand settled on her arm, cutting off Talyn's thoughts. "Come on, we should get—"

A howl of fury broke through the frozen tableau and one of the slaves broke ranks, running at the murderous guard and slamming into him, sending them both flying to the ground. Before the Montagni even realised what was happening, the slave had yanked the knife from his belt and slit his throat with it.

Talyn froze with recognition at the quick, efficient kill. It was Zamaril.

The other three guards shouted a challenge, drawing their weapons and closing in on him. Zamaril grabbed the dead soldier's sword and leapt to his feet. The smoke, billowing from the fire, swept into the open space with a strong gust of wind, temporarily obscuring him from Talyn's sight.

The escaping slaves were down to three now, their comrades lying dead on the ground. Talyn counted eight soldiers surrounding them, slowly closing in, the intent to kill rather than capture clear in the way they held their swords.

Eleven soldiers total in sight. And Zamaril had a weapon. Still, they probably had minutes before more soldiers appeared or the smoke cleared enough for those fighting the fire to see what was going on.

But Zamaril had killed a soldier... they wouldn't let him live if he was caught.

Talyn glanced at Kaeri, then rose to her feet. "We have to help him."

"Wait! Talyn, you were right." Kaeri swore and came after her. "It's too late, we won't get out now."

They'd already broken the cover of darkness by the huts, though nobody had seen them yet, the smoke helping to hide them. Talyn glanced at Kaeri. "I won't leave him."

"What are you planning on doing? Watching while *I* help Zamaril?" Kaeri demanded.

Talyn tossed her a grin. "I'm not entirely useless. We help Zamaril, then we kill the rest of the guards so that none of them live to identify us. And we do it before any more guards come."

"Solid plan," Kaeri muttered, but her green eyes were bright. "Not at all reckless and dangerous."

They ran across the open ground, limited to Talyn's limping speed. Abruptly they emerged into a space cleared of smoke where Zamaril was trying to hold off three soldiers while the other slaves watched in mingled fear and horror. Two soldiers already lay dead at Zamaril's feet.

Shit. Some of those fighting the escaping slaves had come to help contain Zamaril.

Talyn came to a halt to assess the situation, but Kaeri didn't. She ran towards the nearest guard, leapt onto his back and forced him to the ground. Once there, before he could even begin to struggle, she reached around and snapped his neck in one movement.

Talyn stared.

A guard shouted and the smoke shifted briefly—there was only one escapee still alive, and he was swaying on his feet, bleeding from numerous wounds, a hopeless expression settling on his face as the guards closed on him.

Kaeri's sudden attack drew one of the guards facing Zamaril towards her. The Wolf held his ground, blood and soot covering his face, daring the remaining soldier to come closer.

A cry of pain echoed through the night. The final escapee was down. A soldier drove a blade into his chest, ensuring he was dead, and then the remaining guards came to deal with Kaeri and Zamaril.

Eight soldiers to deal with. None of them Berserkers.

Talyn glanced back; the smoke still concealed them from the soldiers fighting the burning hall. But that cover could vanish in seconds if the wind picked up again. It would surely only be moments before reinforcements came—and once any of them were spotted they'd be dead. They had to kill these men and disappear before that happened.

Talyn shifted her glance to Kaeri, who was facing down a single Montagni circling her. All the others had converged on Zamaril. Seven on one.

Zamaril whirled, only his sublime footwork holding the soldiers back. But he couldn't attack when he had to focus so furiously on defence, and eventually he'd begin to tire. The slaves from his group were huddled together nearby. Their expressions were rigid with terror.

The sharp scent of smoke and blood filled the air, assaulting Talyn from all angles. Turning, she scanned the area, looking for.... her gaze landed on a knife, fallen in the mud near the guard Kaeri had killed.

She moved for the knife, bending to yank it off the ground, sliding her palm around the leather-bound hilt. Then, she hefted it, lined up one of the Montagni facing Zamaril, and threw.

The knife took the guard high in the back, piercing his heart. As his body toppled lifeless to the ground, the soldier nearest him spun to see what had happened. When he saw the unarmed slave woman facing them, he laughed.

He barked an order to two soldiers and they broke away to come at her, leaving the rest to deal with Zamaril. He took advantage of their momentary distraction and leapt at one of the guards, running his blade into the man's chest before darting back and blocking another attack a second before it would have sliced across his throat.

Talyn stood, feet apart, hands loose at her sides, as the two soldiers approached her, swords drawn.

A deep, steadying breath.

She had limited range of movement, but her body knew what to do. So she let go of conscious thought and *trusted.*

Talyn waited until they were almost on her before bending her knees and *leaping* into the air. She flipped, landed lightly in the mud behind them, and in the same graceful movement reached forward to yank out the knife sheathed at the waist of the nearest soldier.

She gripped the hilt, ducked under his sword as he spun around, and rose up to slam the knife between his ribs. He dropped, breath gargling as his lungs filled with blood, and she grabbed his body, spinning around so that he took the sword strike of the second guard. He stumbled. Talyn stepped in and slammed her knee into his face so that he fell backwards, before taking his sword and burying it in his throat.

Then came the pain.

She dropped to the ground, gasping, body arching as agony screamed through her back. A flood of warm dampness warned her that she'd torn open her scars. She took deep, gulping breaths to control the pain, and looked over towards where Zamaril and Kaeri had been last.

Kaeri straddled her opponent, halfway through withdrawing a blade from his chest. Zamaril was rising from killing the last of the soldiers around him, his attention shifting to Talyn across the open space. When he saw her, his eyes widened with utter shock.

She lifted a hand, dragged herself to her feet, and began limping towards him. When they met she threw her arms around him, ignoring the pain in her back. He hugged her fiercely before stepping away. "Ciantar. I've been... you're here," He breathed, eyes alight despite the soot and blood streaking his face. "You're hurt?"

"I'm fine." She wanted to sink down to the ground and let all the words she wanted to say out, to tell him everything that had happened, find out what he knew, come up with an escape plan together. But it was impossible. She firmed her shoulders. "We're about to have soldiers all over this area and they can't find us like this."

His gaze shifted around, pausing briefly on Kaeri as she approached, then moving to the dead bodies of the escaping slaves. "We can move Rila's body over with those, that way it just looks like he was escaping with them."

"Do it," Talyn ordered. Thick smoke still wreathed the clearing but too much time had passed. More soldiers had to be on their way. They had seconds, maybe a minute if they were lucky.

Zamaril and Kaeri hefted the body and began carrying it over to the others lying in the mud. "Can you trust the rest of your group to stay quiet about what happened?" Talyn paced alongside them, eyes up and watching for guards.

"I'll talk to them. They won't say a thing." Zamaril sounded confident.

"You all need to go straight back to your huts and stay there. When more guards come looking you tell them nobody came for you," Talyn said. "And make sure you wash that blood and soot off."

"What about you?" he asked.

Talyn was cut off by the sound of running feet and the sharp command of a captain. Kaeri tugged at her arm. She met Zamaril's gaze. "I'll be fine. Go, get out of here."

"Ciantar." He hesitated, glancing between her and the smoky haze that obscured the oncoming guards. "We have to talk."

"We'll figure out a way. But right now you have to take your slaves and run!"

Without another word Talyn and Kaeri turned and ran back towards the female huts, as fast as Talyn could go given the slicing pain in her back.

She hoped Zamaril made it back safely. She didn't know what she'd do if he was caught and killed.

She would just have to trust that he could keep the slaves quiet.

A DAZE SETTLED over Talyn as she stumbled along behind Kaeri. Part of her felt alive, vital. The rest felt like dissolving into furious, aching tears at the pain throbbing through her after the fight. Would she ever be whole again?

Lia was awake, eyes widening when Kaeri and Talyn stumbled in. Her gaze took in the blood splattered on their clothes and Talyn's limping movement. All three froze.

Silence held, long and thick.

And then the ringing of the alarm bells changed rhythm, presumably sending new orders to the camp soldiers.

Kaeri spun into movement, dragging her bloodied clothes off

before throwing fresh clothes at Talyn and bundling her dirty ones into a ball she hid under her pallet. "You tell the guards about this, they'll kill us all," she said to Lia, voice ice cold.

"Kaeri, enough." Talyn didn't miss the flash of fear rippling over Lia's face. There had been something else there when Kaeri and Talyn had first come in, though. Talyn thought it might have been hope.

"She needs to know the consequences if she rats us out." Kaeri finished dressing in clean attire and set to work washing her face and hands in their shared bowl of water.

"I think she already knows." Talyn undressed more slowly, wincing with every movement.

Shouts echoed through the night, orders. More marching feet sounded in the distance, thankfully not yet coming anywhere near them.

"There was an escape attempt?"

Lia's voice was so quiet Talyn barely heard it. She paused in pulling on clean pants. "Multiple groups of men tried to escape. They set a fire as a diversion. The ones we saw were all killed," she said.

Lia said nothing to that. She held Talyn's gaze for a moment, then turned away and curled up on her pallet, as if to go back to sleep.

"Hurry," Kaeri told Talyn. "Once they find those bodies they might decide to turn out the female slaves too."

Getting back to her feet. Walking normally. It seemed impossible —she couldn't even reach up high enough to get her bloodied shirt off without crippling pain. Exhaustion washed over her in a wave. "I think my scars have opened up." It was all she could think to say. Her teeth were chattering and she trembled from a combination of shock and fading adrenaline.

"I'm not surprised." Kaeri stared at her. "Do you know what you just did?"

"I was there, thank you," Talyn snapped.

"You killed two highly trained Montagni soldiers without even breaking a sweat. In, like, seconds." Kaeri seemed to have forgotten her urgency. "I've been going on about how good Zamaril is, but you..."

Talyn glanced down at the drying blood on her hands. "I am Callanan trained, Kaeri."

"Here, let me look at your back. Wash that blood off your hands and face while I do."

Kaeri crouched down behind her. Talyn winced as her friend gently pulled away her shirt from her back. She scrubbed her hands as best she could in the now red water.

"It's sticking," Kaeri murmured. "Wait a second."

She dipped a worn rag into the water before dampening Talyn's back until the shirt came away easily. By then her trembling had turned to shivering, caused by a combination of pain and the cold night air.

"Your scars have opened up at the top here." Kaeri touched the spot softly. "I'll bind them as best I can with an old shirt, but you'll need to restrict your movement until they close up."

"I'm never going to be whole again, am I?" Talyn asked bitterly.

"Probably not, no," Kaeri said, quietly.

"Do what you need to do. I appreciate it."

Silence fell for a few moments as Kaeri cleaned out the wounds on her back before binding them. Once she was done she handed Talyn a clean shirt then tossed out the blooded water.

"It's not like you were a slouch." Talyn turned to her, wincing as her back pulled. "And you don't have a scratch on you."

"I had the element of surprise, and then you and Zamaril drawing most of their attention away from me," Kaeri said dismissively.

Talyn sighed. All the fire inside her had died away to ashes. "Do you think the guards will come for us?"

"I hope not. Between the three of us, we managed to kill all the soldiers in sight." Kaeri sighed. "The only thing that could betray us is the slaves with Zamaril. They saw everything."

"Zamaril can handle them. I know he can." Talyn wouldn't doubt him.

Kaeri rose to her feet. "If you say so. Come on, let's get some rest. If the guards come to turn us out, best make it appear like we're sleeping peacefully."

"Kaeri? We're going to get out of here."

She stopped, turned back to Talyn, steel in her gaze. "Yes, we will."

No guards came. For once the Montagni attitudes towards women fighting worked in their favour—presumably the soldiers had assumed that no female slave could have killed so many trained soldiers so quickly. She could only hope Zamaril escaped their inspection unscathed too.

Talyn fell into a fitful sleep that slowly deepened. She had no idea how long she slept before the nightmare came.

The pain hit first, tearing through her side with an agony so powerful that it stole the breath she needed to scream. A blade was buried deep in muscle and bone. Another voice shouted nearby; was it Zamaril? Blood poured down her side... too much blood. She was dying. Strength leeched out of her, but she had to fight, she had to help them, she had to... but the Bearmen were too strong. She couldn't fight them off, couldn't get to Zamaril, couldn't—

Talyn came awake with a gasp. Sweat slicked her skin and she was tangled so tightly in her blanket that she had to fight to be free of it. Gasping, she scrabbled backwards until she was pressed against the wall—needing the solidity of it despite the pain in her back. Her breath came in great heaving sobs and the nightmare was still wrapped around her so that she couldn't breathe, couldn't think.

Trapped. Trapped. Trapped.

A scream threatened to escape her and only the sound of Kaeri's voice prevented it. "Talyn!" It was sharp, cutting through the fog of the nightmare.

Reality began setting in around her. The cold air. The pain in her body. The always-there edge of hunger and weariness. The faint blue light of pre-dawn outside the door.

She was in the slave labour camp. In the hut she shared with Kaeri. She was fine. She wasn't trapped. Lia and Roni had wakened, and Lia stared at Talyn with the same wide-eyed stare she had the night before.

"I'm okay," she gasped, trying to reassure them. "Just let me... catch my breath. Go back to sleep."

Kaeri looked at her. "Another nightmare." It wasn't a question.

Talyn nodded anyway, shivering. She closed her eyes, biting her lip to hold back her tears. She wished Cuinn were there with everything she had. There to sing to her and take away the fear that she'd never be whole again. That she'd never get home.

Where was he?

CHAPTER 15

The silence of the mountain was abruptly broken by the harsh and penetrating clang of bells. Cuinn's eyes flew open. He was already pushing off his blankets and swinging off the hammock when Swift strode into the sleeping cavern Cuinn shared with his fellow flyers. Their legion captain was dressed in flying gear, beanie hanging from his hand.

"We're on!" Swift called out. "Up to the flight platform now."

They moved.

Cuinn and his legion mates stepped agilely around each other as they dressed in woolen breeches, undershirts, shirts, then the wool-lined SkyRider tunic over all of it. He yanked his beanie from the table beside his hammock and made it out the door third, pausing only for a breath to run his fingers over the crossed swords etched from tens of little amber stars over his heart.

Swift waited for them as they filed into the cavern—its walls lined with flying gear and weapons—that opened up to the flight platform. Quickly, efficiently, they tugged on their beanies, slung harnesses over their shoulders, then reached for bows and quivers. While they loaded up, Swift briefed them.

"SkyRider scouts report two Firthlander warships a half-day's sail from the east coast just north of the Ayrlemyre range. They've got nievers on board."

"How many?" Cuinn asked, steadfastly ignoring the anxiety already building in the pit of his stomach. While they couldn't fly as high or as fast as the mountain eagles SkyRiders rode, nievers were strong, vicious creatures, and could inflict serious damage on a SkyRider legion.

"It's unclear. Two ships could fit a legion, depending how many soldiers are packed on board. But we've got helpful weather today—snow and rain moving in from the southeast, which means we can approach above cloud cover. Hopefully we'll be on them before they know we're coming," Swift replied.

In the beginning, these briefings had exhausted Cuinn—the waves of fear and anticipation from his fellow SkyRiders washing over him in a tide, draining his energy and will.

But it had been a month now since that first chaotic battle.

A full month of combat with Swift's legion—flying in support of Aimsir missions pushing back incursions along where the northern foothills of the Ayrlemyre range ran into ocean and Conmoran farming land.

Long hours in the air, little sleep, rough conditions. He'd learned the taste of battle, the fear that came with it, the exhilaration too.

He'd killed.

It would never be easy, never *not* make him sick to his stomach, never not be the last thing he ever wanted to do. But in the chaos of fighting, when nievers were screaming through the air around him and only his focus and Trystaan's ability to swoop and dodge were what kept him alive, firing those arrows was second nature, a defence mechanism. The only way to keep himself and his legion mates alive. There was no time or concentration left over to feel the pain of a dying niever or its rider.

That didn't mean it wasn't hard. That it didn't leave him far more exhausted than any other SkyRider after a fight. That he didn't want to throw up the moment he got back from a mission and the realisation he'd killed again flooded him. But he needed this. Needed to grow strong. Tempered. Hardened.

"Wolf, you'll take Feather and Drift in first. Use the sun to hide your approach, then make a rapid descent and circle the ships—your purpose is to draw out any niever-flyers on board and lead them away. Once they're clear of the ships, the rest of us will break cloud cover and drop on top of them." Swift's gaze landed on Cuinn. "A clean ambush. Take out the nievers, then the ships are vulnerable."

"Sir." He nodded, shoulders straight.

Nobody looked surprised Swift had chosen Cuinn for this task, even though he was by far the most junior member of the legion. A month of fighting and he'd already made a name for himself. The foreign prince who flew like an eagle, whose sharp winged folk eyes could pick out an approaching attack before anyone else, whose arrows rarely missed.

They'd given him the sky name Wolf. A hunter in the air. Ruthless. But one who always looked out for his pack before anything else.

It was a name he carried with fierce pride.

"Let's go!" Swift ordered.

Cuinn's heart thudded with a now-familiar mixture of fear and anticipation as he strode out to the landing platform, the cold mountain air instantly gusting around him, tugging at his clothes. His whistle sounded amongst fifty others, snatched up and carried away on the wind. The prince he'd once been, the one who'd hidden in the shadows of the night as the Shadowhawk, could never have faced open battle like this. Couldn't have even contemplated it.

He wasn't that man anymore.

And then Trystaan swooped out of the sky along with tens of other magnificent mountain eagles, and the fear faded, anticipation surging in its place. Cuinn had the harness on in moments, two quivers bristling with arrows hanging heavy down his back, his bow firmly attached to them.

He stretched out, settling himself onto the eagle's back, then reached down to stroke silky feathers. "Let's go, Trystaan."

. . .

THEY FLEW through thick grey cloud, ice and rain pelting at every inch of exposed skin. The SkyRiders either side and ahead of Cuinn were barely visible. They'd practiced flying in these conditions over and over, Swift in the lead, those behind him flying close enough to see him, those behind them the same, and back through the column. Now it was second nature.

It took over a full-turn to reach the coastline, and then Swift took them higher, until the air was so thin it was hard to breathe, so cold Cuinn shivered even with his layers of clothing.

But the cloud would hide them.

They angled northwest, and then after another half-turn of flight, a hand signal passed down through the legion.

Swift ordering a halt.

The eagles shifted into a circling pattern, bunching close enough they could just make out their captain in the centre. A shrieking wind tore at them, ice and rain soaking through their clothes. The eagles rose and dropped with the thermals. Once they were gathered, Swift made a series of exaggerated signals.

Cuinn focused hard—he hadn't had the months of training in signaling that other SkyRiders got, and it had taken several long nights of study for him to catch up. Even so he still had to pay careful attention to understand the orders given. Making a mistake could mean the death or injury of a legion-mate, or himself.

They were above the area where the scouts had spotted the ships. Swift pointed at Cuinn, then pointed directly below them. Cuinn lifted a hand to say he'd acknowledged, then sought out Feather's eager gaze and Drift's nod.

He settled into the harness, then shifted his body weight forward, giving Trystaan the signal to dive. His eagle gave a screech of excitement, then furled his wings and dove downwards.

Icy cloud rushed past Cuinn's face, blurring his vision and numbing his skin.

In that moment he was flying again. Nothing but air rushing by him and that familiar swoop in his stomach. Azrilan had never taken his wings. In that moment was peace.

With peace came a slowly realised acceptance. He had lost his wings, but he had Trystaan now. And a path back from where Azrilan had tossed him.

And then, abruptly, they burst from the cloudbank and into a clear day with the blue ocean beneath them. Cuinn immediately sent Trystaan banking until their approach was framed by the sun directly behind. His eyes scanned the surface, looking for... there! Two ships, sails billowing, making for the Conmoran coastline.

A quick glance back assured him Feather and Drift were close behind, so he shifted his body again, sending Trystaan swooping down towards the ships. Wind rushed past, the exhilaration of flying at such speed sweeping through him, exuberance and joy all at once.

The ships grew closer and closer, until he could make out the snarling bear of the Firthlander sigil on the sails and the running figures of the crew as they finally noticed the SkyRiders dropping on them. He brought Trystaan in low, giving both ships a good look at the three eagles, before banking east and circling back around.

A high-pitched scream sounded faintly on the wind, soon joined by others. Dark shapes lifted off the closest ship, wings flapping powerfully, one after the other. Niever-flyers.

Cuinn's gaze roved the deck as Trystaan flew by—he counted twenty nievers in the process of becoming airborne, and at least that many more being harnessed by their riders. He made a quick series of gestures to Drift and Feather. They signaled back an acknowledgement of his orders.

"Time to fight, Trystaan," he murmured. Taking a breath, he unclipped his harness so that he could sit up, then clipped it back on. He reached back for his bow, made sure it was firmly in his grasp, then shifted his hips forward. "Now."

The eagle flapped his wings, screaming out in challenge as he swooped on the nievers lifting into the air—the time when they were at their most vulnerable. Cuinn reached for an arrow, nocked, fired. A niever-flyer toppled into the ocean. A second followed, a third. Then Trystaan was past and banking for another run.

Return arrows flew towards him as niever-flyers got into the air and began closing the distance. Trystaan flipped sideways, then straightened. Cuinn got off two more shots as they flew back over the nievers and headed east.

"Up!" Cuinn called to Trystaan, the harness digging into him as the eagle began a rapid upward ascent. Feather and Drift had followed suit, and niever-flyers streamed after them.

Cuinn banked Trystaan left, then urged him back into a dive, attacking from above, firing arrow after arrow at the pursuing nievers. A return arrow flew past his ear, another almost caught Trystaan's wingtip.

The two of them flew right through the pack of niever-flyers for a chaotic few moments of screeching and slashing talons and shouts of the flyers. Then they were through and dropping towards the surface of the ocean, drawing the niever-riders further away from their ships.

New screaming cries echoed from above. Cuinn glanced up. SkyRiders boiled out of the clouds, Swift leading the rest of the legion to spring the trap and surround the niever-flyers now cut off from their ships.

Cuinn fired until he had only a handful of arrows left, killing a niever or its rider with almost every shot he took. Trystaan weaved and banked and swooped, filling gaps, covering the backs of Cuinn's legion mates, killing nievers before they could kill SkyRiders. Even so, two SkyRiders fell from the sky. Cuinn flinched with each hit—the fear and grief of those alive mixing with the emotions of those falling to make it too hard to ignore completely—and fought bitterly not to let it break his concentration.

Eventually, there were only a handful of niever-flyers remaining aloft. They broke away, winging east back towards Firthland. The distance was too great and they probably wouldn't make it. Cuinn did his best not to imagine the despair of that.

He didn't succeed.

His stomach knotted with nausea and the fallout of so many intense emotions as Swift gathered the legion with a series of sweeping hand gestures.

Cuinn took a deep, steadying breath, focused his mind, then joined his legion as together they wheeled around and bore down on the Firthlander ships. He reached inside his tunic and curled his fingers around the flint stored there. He drew an arrow, shielding it from the wind with his body as he used the flint to ignite the prepared arrowhead. It flared into flame, the sweet scent of izerdia filling his senses.

They were almost on the ships now. He nocked the arrow, drew, and fired into the nearest sail. It hit and the flame caught, flared bright orange, then began spreading. Trystaan soared past with a cry, angling back up into the sky. After him, each remaining SkyRider fired their flaming arrows into the ships.

Swift called the retreat. Cuinn lingered a moment before following, watching the ships begin to burn. He didn't allow himself to think about the soldiers on those ships, or the niever-flyers he'd killed. Instead he thought about the fact they were Tarcos's ships. Tarcos's nievers. And instead of pain and tiredness, he felt satisfaction.

Under him, Trystaan screamed triumph.

Cuinn shifted his weight, sent Trystan circling higher after the others. At a safe height, the legion formed up and headed back to Mothduriem, leaving two burning ships drifting on the ocean behind them.

CHAPTER 16

*T*hey landed back at Mothduriem, a legion of forty-four SkyRiders now instead of their original fifty—they'd lost six legion mates in the past month—weary and heartsick but also pleased with their success.

Cuinn unbuckled his harness and spent a moment running his hands through Trystaan's feathers in gratitude, before letting the eagle go to find food and rest. He joined his fellow riders as they ate their fill in the mess and had a cup of ale to celebrate the mission. Then two more cups to honour their fallen.

This was the hardest part of the day. Their shared grief was too much like the grief he still felt for Halun, for Tiercelin and his fallen Wolves. Not to mention he'd grown to respect and care about his legion too. He couldn't stop the tears welling in his eyes or the fierce ache in his chest that made it hard to breathe.

Once the cups had been drunk, silence fell and they all turned to him expectantly. He closed his eyes then and began to sing, a soft melody that gathered up his grief and regret and used it to honour those that had fallen.

His song wrapped them all in comfort, in reassurance, in hope.

Shoulders relaxed, tears slid down cheeks. And for a few moments Cuinn allowed himself to escape into music.

Nobody said anything once his song trailed off into silence. But as each of them rose to head to their hammocks and get some rest, they all had a word for him, or a pat on the back or a quick squeeze of his shoulder. Their appreciation warmed him.

Once they were all gone, Cuinn didn't follow. As weary as he was, as much as he knew he should let his body and magic rest, he was too anxious.

And troubled.

It was getting easier to fight, to kill, there was no denying it. He'd come here to grow strong, to learn to be harder. He should be pleased at his success. Instead he felt doubt. Was learning to bury his compassion, to accept death and violence around him, really the right thing to do?

Unable to rest with these thoughts swirling in his head, he made his usual daily visit to the tiny cavern where any messages delivered to the SkyRider base were held and processed by a single old man with a shock of white hair and bright blue eyes.

"Nothing here, Wolf, sorry," he said with an apologetic look. "I promise I'll come and deliver it myself if something comes for you."

"Thanks, Terra."

His shoulders slumped as he walked away. He couldn't escape the growing certainty that he'd been away from home too long. The entire flight back it had been nagging at him—they'd destroyed two ships and killed nievers. But soon Azrilan was going to add Montagn's ships to Tarcos's.

And they were barely holding the lines now.

He knew he had only had one chance to win the Dumnorix, that if he tried too early, before he was ready, they'd refuse and he'd have nothing. He needed to convince them he was strong, yes, a worthy ally. But more than that, he had to give them a reason to ally with him. He needed leverage.

But it wasn't just that anymore.

He had to leave before he started wanting to stay. Before the exhilaration of SkyRiding took over and distracted him from his true purpose.

He should sleep. Try and shut off his circling thoughts for a few full-turns at least.

One of the servants that lived amongst the SkyRiders in Mothduriem hovered at the door to his legion's sleeping cavern, clearly waiting for him. "Wolf. You've got a visitor."

"Really?" His eyebrows shot skywards. Who would be visiting him in the middle of the Ayrlemyre Mountains?

"It's all a bit mysterious. He wouldn't give a name. He's waiting at the entrance. The guards on shift there are keeping an eye on him, just in case."

Fear shuddered through him. He'd felt safe in Mothduriem, even without his Wolf guards. Now he wondered if Azrilan's hounds had finally learned where he was. But simply walking up to the SkyRider base and asking for him seemed a foolish move for a trained Shadow. Surely they could have just used the darkness to creep inside and get to him?

Cuinn let out an internal sigh. The entry cavern was a long walk down. "Thanks. I'll go now."

So much for sleep.

THE ENTRANCE to Mothduriem for non-SkyRiders was located near the base of the mountain and almost impossible to find unless you knew where you were going. Which made the fact he had a visitor even more intriguing. As he approached, he readied his song magic, just in case it was an ambush. He'd read the emotions of the visitor before whoever it was even knew Cuinn was approaching.

A man waited in the small entry area, the two guards at the narrow cavern opening keeping one eye on him and one on the path leading up to the entry. He was tall, broad-shouldered, with neatly trimmed brown hair and beard and wearing a simple brown cloak.

Hope and delight flashed through Cuinn all at once, and all the weariness lifted from his shoulders. He'd been expecting a written message once Leviana and Cynia had done what he'd asked them to do, not a personal visit. He stopped dead, a smile stretching across his face. "So *you're* what an Armun looks like."

The man flashed him an irritated glance, looking pointedly towards the guards.

"Right, sorry." Cuinn cleared his throat. "Come with me. We can talk somewhere nobody will see us."

He led the Armun back along the tunnel to a food storage area that held emergency supplies and therefore was rarely visited.

"You're Cuinn Acondor," the man said once he'd shut the door. He'd barely looked at their surroundings, but Cuinn got the distinct impression he could recite exactly how many sacks of flour were in the far corner if asked.

"And you're Saundin, I take it?"

The Armun nodded. "I received a message from Warriors Leed and Seinn that you wanted to see me urgently."

And he'd respected both Callanan enough to come all this way to see Cuinn, despite the war between their two countries. Hope flared even brighter in Cuinn's chest. Could this crazy plan possibly work? He almost swayed on his feet at the rush of relief that thought roused.

"You worked with Talyn Dynan and Sari Astley," Cuinn said, settling back against the door. While he talked, he wrapped the man in his song magic. Saundin was a master at shielding his emotions, and the only things Cuinn caught were wariness and calm focus. He wouldn't be surprised if the man was aware of how song magic worked and had come prepared for Cuinn.

"I did. Who are you to them? Warrior Astley died years ago."

Cuinn relaxed further as he caught the hint of old grief that escaped Saundin's control—so he was still sad enough over Sari's death that he couldn't completely hide it. That, in addition to the fact Talyn, Leviana and Cynia trusted him, was enough for Cuinn.

"Talyn is my betrothed."

Saundin snorted, genuine amusement flashing over his unremark-able features. "Sure she is."

"It's true. Do you think Leviana and Cynia would have asked you to meet me if they didn't trust me like they clearly trust you?"

A moment's silence, then, "What do you want?"

"I want to find a way to stop this war." Cuinn pinned him with a look. "Do you?"

"I am a Firthlander Armun. You're a deposed Mithranan prince who has strangely decided to become a SkyRider. You don't think it's a little odd for us to be having this conversation?"

"That's exactly why we're having this conversation. This war isn't any better for Firthland than it is for the Twin Thrones or Mithranar, and it's come about purely because of the arrogant ambition of two men. I'd like to end it with as little bloodshed as possible, and I need your help to do it."

A very long silence filled the space then. Cuinn waited him out, comfortable to let Saundin think it through however long he needed to.

"She agreed to marry you, huh?" Saundin scratched idly at his beard. "Never would have seen that coming."

A smile curled at Cuinn's mouth. "What can I say, I'm handsome and charming."

The Armun pierced him with a look. "What exactly do you want me to do, Cuinn Acondor?"

Cuinn pushed off the door. "Shall we go somewhere more comfortable, and I can explain that over an ale?"

"Hot cider would be better. It's bloody freezing out there."

The hope flared brighter again.

THEY SPOKE for over two full-turns. Saundin didn't give away much of what he thought, was laid back and relaxed when he spoke, but had a mind like a steel trap. Together they hammered out the next part of Cuinn's plan. Well... Saundin's sharp mind picked out all the holes in Cuinn's crazy plan and tried to make it slightly *less* full of holes, anyway.

Once they were done, and Saundin moved to leave, Cuinn reached out to stop him. "I have a question for you, something that's been nagging at me."

Saundin lifted an eyebrow. "What is it?"

"For months before Azrilan made his move, the Callanan were receiving information from an informant they'd recruited in Montagn, someone the Armun helped them recruit. This informant told them that Ahara Venador was planning to invade Mithranar, and that he'd recruited Vengeance to create instability there ahead of the invasion." Cuinn paused, but nothing flickered in Saundin's expression. Damn, the man was good. His song magic didn't pick up anything either. "But now I know that Vengeance was actually working for a rogue Shadow loyal to Tarcos and Azrilan. And Ahara Venador wasn't the one planning war, was he?"

Saundin slowly ran a hand over his beard, still betraying nothing of his reaction to Cuinn's question. "I wouldn't be in a position to know anything about a highly sensitive source being run by the Callanan. But your account is very interesting. If I were to guess, I'd say your rogue Shadow created the informant—if he wasn't the informant himself—to shift Callanan attention away from Azrilan and House Manunin. Have them focus on the threat of a fake invasion of Mithranar rather than Azrilan's secret preparations to invoke the spill in Montagn and Tarcos's actual invasion of the Twin Thrones."

"Is that something you can confirm? I'd like to know for certain. I'd also really like to know where the rogue Shadow is right now and what he's up to."

"Your faith in my abilities is disconcertingly high." Saundin sighed when Cuinn simply shrugged. "What's the Shadow's name?"

"Savin." Cuinn paused. "But he goes by Navis, too." Something did flicker across Saundin's face then, though Cuinn couldn't read the emotion. "You know him?"

"I do." Saundin rose to his feet. "He was posted to the court in Samatia at the same time Tarcos lived there with his uncle. The two were close. He was a bit of a legend amongst the Armun and Shadows, for his shadow skill and ability to plan complex kills. His posting to a relative backwater in Mithranar was a surprise... but it happened about the same time Tarcos was sent to the Twin Thrones to be the hostage for King Aethain."

It all made grim sense. "Thank you, Saundin."

"I'll be in touch, Prince Cuinn."

And he was gone.

CUINN WENT straight to Swift's personal cavern. Excitement bubbled in his chest. Finally! Finally he could take the next step.

"Wolf." Swift looked groggy with sleep when Cuinn knocked on his door. "You should be getting some rest."

"Sorry for waking you, sir. I needed to talk to you, and it couldn't wait."

"Come in." Swift held the door open with a resigned sigh.

The cavern inside was toasty warm from a fire, the blankets on the hammock rumpled, and Cuinn felt a moment's guilt for rousing his captain from much-needed rest.

"Is something wrong?" Swift prompted when he didn't immediately say anything.

"No. But it's time for me to leave."

The fire crackled into the silence that followed his words. Eventually Swift dropped into his chair and ran a hand through his short-cropped hair. "I suppose I was expecting this. None of us thought you would stay long—we know your home isn't here."

"I know that it seems like I'm abandoning you, but—"

Swift cut him off. "You saved multiple SkyRider lives today, don't think I didn't notice. And it's not the first time. Of course I would like you here permanently—you're a crucial member of the legion—but I don't resent you for wanting to go home, Wolf."

Cuinn wasn't sure what to say to that. "Thank you, sir."

Swift chuckled and rose to his feet. "No more of that. You're not a SkyRider under my command anymore, Prince Cuinn."

"I will always be Wolf to you, and any other SkyRider," Cuinn said with quiet determination. "Just like Soar."

Approval glimmered in Swift's yes. "Very well. You'll be missed, Wolf."

Cuinn nodded, opened the door, then paused. "I'll do everything I can to end this war, I promise you."

"As will I." Swift spoke just as fiercely.

Cuinn walked away before the desire to stay kept him in that room.

CHAPTER 17

*T*he sharp crack of chopping wood reverberated through the afternoon. Teams of male slaves sawed through thick trees, while others were busy chopping the fallen trunks into smaller pieces.

Talyn and Kaeri had been re-assigned to a logging work group. Their job was to pile the chopped wood into carts which were then ferried back to the labour camp to feed the forges in the smithies.

Taking a moment's break, Talyn stretched—barely managing to get her arms above shoulder height before the scars on her back pulled painfully—then wiped the sweat from her face with a corner of her grimy shirt.

"Okay?" Kaeri glanced over at her.

Talyn bent to pick up another piece of wood. "Just taking a breather."

"Are you sure?"

"I am." And she meant it. The fresh air and exercise of her new work detail had restored Talyn from the lingering lethargy of her long recovery. Her range of movement was still limited, but she'd adapted the way she moved to the scars and her body finally felt strong again. Hungry. Increasingly trapped and burning with frustration over it. But stronger.

"This would be a good place to escape from," Kaeri commented.

Talyn shot her a look. "Would you like to say that a little louder? I don't think those guards over there heard you. It's been a whole month since the last attempt, I'm sure they've relaxed their vigilance by now."

"How many horses are tethered over by the cart?"

"Six saddled for the guards and two spares in case one of the horses leading the carts goes lame."

"And how many guards watching us work?"

"Twelve in total."

"Any slaves out of the eyesight of a guard?"

"None, as far as I can tell. Except those sent for water."

Kaeri snorted. "Not a single hesitation. And you want to tell me you haven't been thinking about escape?"

Talyn grinned, tossed her wood in, then walked back to the pile. "I didn't say I hadn't been thinking about it."

"Then you've noticed that we've been placed on one of the few work details that operates outside the compound walls, and one of the few where the male and female slaves work together." Kaeri spoke in an undertone. "It's the best chance we'll ever have if we want to escape."

"In that case, why don't we make a run for it right now?" Talyn said dryly, trying not to be drawn in by Kaeri's eagerness. A better chance didn't mean it was a good one. "If we make the cover of those trees, they'll never catch us."

"Such a cynic," Kaeri murmured.

"I think the word you're looking for is 'sensible.'"

Silence fell between them as they continued working. As much as she'd teased, Kaeri had a good point, and her words kept turning through Talyn's mind.

She estimated forty to fifty slaves on their detail. If they all broke at once, the guards wouldn't be able to stop all of them. But they'd kill many. And the alarm would be raised instantly. Talyn had seen the ruthless efficiency of the Montagni soldiers. Mounted guards would be after those that got away in a heartbeat—men who knew the forest surrounding the camp and had tracker dogs to help hunt them down.

For all her burning desire to get out, Kaeri knew it too. It was why she hadn't done anything more than make the odd comment about escaping.

Talyn turned her focus back to lifting wood. If it looked like she was slacking off, the guards would be on her, and so far she'd managed to cultivate the image of a model slave. They barely looked at her most days.

The afternoon trailed on. Kaeri seemed edgy—she worked as hard as the others, but kept glancing off into the trees, as if looking for something. Talyn frowned and started paying closer attention. When she caught a male slave working nearby give Kaeri a slight nod, her shoulders tensed.

"What are you doing?"

"Working." Kaeri grunted and dumped an armload of wood into the cart.

"So you think I'm a cynic *and* a fool?" Talyn dumped her load too, brushing the dirt from her calloused hands. Their loads filled the cart and one of the guards came over to instruct the driver to take it back to the compound.

"Do you mind if we go for water until he comes back?" Kaeri asked the guard casually.

The bearded guard glanced over at the empty water pails and nodded. "Be quick about it. If you're not back before the cart is, I'll come looking, with my truncheon."

"We'll be fast." Kaeri grabbed Talyn's arm and pulled her over to the empty water pails. She shoved two into Talyn's arms and set off into the trees carrying four.

While the guards didn't particularly care about feeding their workers beyond basic sustenance, they didn't want them dropping from dehydration in the middle of a work day. That might affect productivity.

Her anger, usually banked, rose higher, beyond her control for a moment. She'd hated the idea of slavery her entire life, but to actually *be* in a camp, to witness how slaves were treated... it wasn't just endless servitude, it was being made less than human. It was far worse than the ignorance and intolerance with which the winged Mithranans treated their human countrymen. She couldn't wrap her mind around how treating someone like that became possible.

Their worksite wasn't far from a swiftly flowing stream. Talyn stomped after Kaeri, waiting until they were out of hearing range of anyone else before hissing, "What are we doing?"

"Getting water."

Talyn stopped in the middle of the faint path, forcing the other woman to stop too. "Stop treating me like I'm stupid."

"Trust me," Kaeri said. "Come on, we haven't much time."

"Time for what? You're not really trying to escape, are you?" Talyn grumbled, following her reluctantly.

"Not yet, no."

They reached the small clearing in front of the creek. Talyn's boots sank into the mud around the riverbank as she squatted, wincing, to begin filling her pails with water, but she stopped when she realised Kaeri wasn't following. Instead she was scanning the hillside of trees around them.

Shit.

"You're meeting someone here." Talyn straightened in realisation.

"You're the one who's been so desperate to talk to Zamaril." Kaeri glanced back at her. "Apparently he's been asking about you too. Discreetly, thank goodness."

Hope leapt in her chest then, all her worry over getting caught vanishing in a heartbeat. A moment later, rustling sounded in the trees above them—someone was coming down the hillside.

"Why didn't you tell me?" Talyn shifted from foot to foot in nervous anticipation.

"I figured it was safer with fewer people knowing."

They fell silent as the footsteps grew closer and then Zamaril became visible through the trees. Moments later he dropped lightly into the clearing by the stream. He wore the same work clothes they did, and he carried two water pails in each hand. He had the watchful manner of someone who feared being followed.

That watchful gaze went straight to Talyn. The same look settled on his face that she remembered from the night of the failed escape: part stunned astonishment, part grief, part disbelief.

He took a half-step forward. Stopped.

"Ciantar?" He spoke her name quietly, as if it couldn't possibly be her, as if he were dreaming.

"It's me." Tears filled Talyn's eyes as she began walking, meeting him halfway across the clearing to throw herself into his arms and clutch him so tightly neither of them could breathe.

She pulled back from the hug. "Cuinn?" she whispered.

Zamaril's face fell. "I don't know. I was brought here with you. I don't know."

Talyn closed her eyes, her nails digging into her palms as she clenched her fists so tightly they drew blood.

"Talyn." Kaeri's voice broke the emotion-laden silence in the clearing. "We haven't got long, a few more minutes at most before the guards come looking."

"She's right." Zamaril glanced around. "We need to talk. Quickly."

Talyn nodded. Her heart was racing, adrenalin flooding her body and making it *impossible* to stand still. All at once all her hard-won control vanished and all the desperation and panic that had been building in her since getting her memories back burst out like a river flooding its banks. "We have to get out of here, go back to Mithranar. Six thrices, it's been months already."

"Talyn, stop! You're starting to panic."

"I know. I can't..." She couldn't stay here. She couldn't. She couldn't. She had to go, get out, get home. She was breathing too fast, her head swimming.

"Ciantar!" Zamaril's sharp voice drew her back.

She forced herself to take a deep breath, to swallow some of the panic, try and focus on the Wolf standing in front of her. "Have you... have you identified any options for escape?"

"I'm working on it, but haven't come up with anything that gives us good odds of success, except..." He hesitated.

"What?" Her voice came out sharper than she'd intended.

"We're not the only ones who were brought here from Mithranar." Zamaril seemed to realise they didn't have time for dithering, because he came right out with it. "Mithanis is here too."

Talyn reeled, the shock of that revelation enough to banish the remnants of the panic attack that had been descending. "What? Does he know you're here?"

"Yes. We're both on this work detail. He wants to work together to escape—he's too afraid to try it on his own. He hasn't the faintest clue how to track, or forage for food or water, or find shelter." Zamaril scowled. "He'd barely last a half-turn alone if the tracker dogs didn't catch him."

"Are we talking about Mithanis Acondor?" Kaeri snapped.

Still reeling, Talyn's mind went to the random. "Why wasn't he made to fight like all the new slaves?"

"He was hurt when he first got here. His back. Azrilan tore out his wings."

Kaeri's eyes widened. Talyn stared.

Recognising the lack of time, Zamaril forged on. "You've seen how skilled a fighter he is, Ciantar. He was a challenge for you in that duel, not to mention his song and warrior magics. Together, we all might have a chance of getting out."

"*He's right.*"

"I think we can at least trust that he has the same goal as we do, and that's getting out of here," Zamaril added.

"And once we're out, then what?" Talyn asked. "He tries to kill us the moment we're over the fence?"

"I'm with her." Kaeri jabbed a thumb in Talyn's direction. "And I'm worried about your sanity."

The thief's mouth tightened. "We need to actually get out first, before worrying about what comes after. He can help us do that. I'm not suggesting we trust him, just that we use him."

Zamaril was right... objectively. But Mithanis Acondor would be a dangerous weapon to use, posing as much risk to them as anyone they tried to use him against. "I need to think about it," she said, fighting to keep her calm. "And we need to get back. Can you organise this again? Meeting here?"

"Not frequently, but yes. I've been on this detail for months, so I'm often sent to fetch the water."

"Good. In three days' time we meet. Okay?"

He grinned, moved to the stream to begin filling his pails. "I'll be here."

HOURS LATER, Talyn sat on her pallet, back to the wall, arms wrapped around her knees. Seeing Zamaril, *speaking* to him, had cut through all of the numbness she'd built up over days of endless labour without seeing any obvious way out.

She felt as fragile as cracked glass, as if at any moment she could splinter into a thousand pieces. Her heart raced in her chest, too fast, and her throat was dry, making it hard to swallow.

She needed to go. Get out. Tears threatened and she held them back with an effort. She needed to know that Cuinn was okay, that her Wolves were.

Kaeri sat opposite, watching her carefully. She'd so far left Talyn alone to process everything, but her burning curiosity was evident in her frequent glances, each time she opened her mouth to ask something, then thought better and closed it.

Eventually she looked at Kaeri. "This is how you've felt, the whole time?"

"In some part." Sadness rippled briefly over Kaeri's face and she looked away. "But I've got nobody out there to worry about the way you do. I only have myself to look out for."

"You've got me, now," Talyn said softly, meaning it.

"Are you suggesting that Kaeri Venador and Talyn Ciantar-Dumnorix should be friends?"

Talyn reached out, took her hand. "I'm suggesting that we *are* friends, Kaeri Venador."

CHAPTER 18

a familiar thrill shot through Cuinn as Trystaan banked before dropping rapidly through a layer of cloud. Cold air streamed past his face, so bitter that the tip of his nose had gone numb.

When they were clear of cover, his gaze picked out the myriad tiny lights of a city below, situated around a rugged harbour basking in the silver glow of the full moon. He brought Trystaan in low over Port Lachley, circling the night sky above the castle fortress.

A memory came to him unbidden, of a conversation with Talyn after he'd formally turned down the ahara's offer of marriage to his daughter, Kaeri Venador. They'd both been worried about what might have been happening in Mithranar during their absence.

They'd talked about his bloodline, the fact that he had a stronger claim to the Twins Thrones than any other Dumnorix family member alive. She'd been so afraid Mithanis would learn of it and move against Cuinn, nullifying the threat he posed to Mithanis's power.

Cuinn had laughed incredulously at the idea of him being worthy of ruling the Twin Thrones *and* Mithranar. She'd met his gaze, and the resolve in her sapphire eyes had killed his laughter and left him with emotion in his chest so powerful he'd found it difficult to draw breath.

"I couldn't think of anyone better," she'd told him softly.

The words resounded in him now, and the thought of her sliced through him like a knife, leaving pain so deep he almost cried out. Slowly, he took deep breaths, calming himself.

Where was she?

Months had passed and still there was no word. He had no doubt if Saniya had found her, she would have found some way to let him know. Each day Talyn remained gone chipped away at his certainty that she was alive.

It didn't matter. His hands curled into fists. She wasn't with him, but he was determined that he was going to be worthy of the words she'd spoken.

Cuinn finally took Trystaan lower—heading for the rooftop landing at the castle fortress rather than the SkyRider base on the opposite headland—and brought the eagle down in a gust of air. Once Cuinn slid from his back and unbuckled the harness, Trystaan took back to the skies with a cry.

He lifted a hand in greeting to the SkyRider guards watching curiously. "I'm Wolf. I've just come in from Mothduriem."

Both straightened, clearly having heard of him. "What brings you to Port Lachley? Nothing is wrong?"

"No, not at all," he reassured them. "I just need to speak with the Dumnorix. Are they here?"

"All of them." One waved to the door leading down into the castle. "When your eagle returns from hunting, we'll make sure he's nested in nice and warm for the night."

"I appreciate it." Cuinn gave them a warm smile and headed inside.

INSIDE THE CASTLE PROPER, Cuinn found a Kingshield guard and asked him to take a message to Alyna or Ariar, whoever was closest. The guard, recognising him, smiled a warm welcome and showed Cuinn to one of the chambers that the family used for informal meetings.

"Shall I ask a servant to bring you some food or drink, Your Highness?"

"No thank you." Cuinn paused. "I'm sorry, I don't know your name."

"It's Adel." He straightened. "I trained with Captain Dynan in the Kingshield. We joined at the same time."

"Then it's a pleasure to meet you." Cuinn hesitated. "If you don't mind, Adel, keep it to yourself that I'm here. Last time—"

"I remember the attack, Your Highness. Nobody but Lady Alyna and my captain will hear from me that you're in the castle. I believe Lord Ariar is out for a ride," Adel promised.

Once the door closed, Cuinn moved further into the room, catching his reflection in the mirrored surface of one of the windows. It made him start in surprise.

Since shaving his hair for the journey to Port Lachley, he hadn't really paid attention to it as it grew back out—amidst SkyRider training, then flying in battle and trying to manage how badly he missed home, his appearance had been the least of his concerns. And there certainly weren't all that many mirrors in Mothduriem.

But something had changed in him—whether it was all that had happened back in Mithranar, losing his wings, or being closer to the Dumnorix. What had once been fine, silver-blonde hair now grew out in darker gold curls, not too different from Ariar's.

And it wasn't just his hair.

His features had hardened, losing some of their winged folk beauty, and his Dumnorix green eyes held a touch of something in them he couldn't quite recognise. Maybe it was a reflection of the tough scar tissue that had formed around his pain and grief. Steel where there'd once been softness.

Still, he grimaced at the sight. His SkyRider gear was rumpled and worn and it was obvious he hadn't shaved in a couple of days. His impatience hadn't allowed him to consider preparing before facing the family.

Idiot. After waiting so long, being so patient, he couldn't afford to ruin his chance now because he didn't look the part. He considered, then quickly discarded, the idea of using glamour. He didn't want to trick the Dumnorix into anything.

Sighing, he dismissed his appearance, and turned his attention to the room. Detailed tapestries covered most of the stone walls, many depicting battle scenes.

One depicted Alendor Dumnorix, Talyn's ancestor, sitting on a throne, newly crowned after the defeat of Firthland. A dark-haired woman with a fierce expression stood at his right, and a man with flaming red hair at his left.

There was no obvious depiction of Alendor's elder sister—Cuinn's ancestor—in any of the tapestries. But there was one image, this one of the same fierce woman at Alendor's side, riding across an open plain with another. The second woman rode a silver white mare at full gallop, raven black hair flying free behind her. A pair of sharp blue eyes were turned towards the artist, impressive in their strength and confidence.

Something told him it was Rianna. Clearly nobody knew that, or the tapestry wouldn't be hanging from the wall. Cuinn paused there for a long while. Whoever his father was, he had been Rianna's grandson. Had *he* had that impressive strength in his look? That same imperious confidence? If he had, he hadn't passed any of it to Cuinn.

He couldn't imagine someone like that not sticking out in the Acondor court. But maybe that was why his mother had kept the identity of Cuinn's father such a secret. Maybe she'd kept him away from court before he'd died.

Eventually he moved on, running his eyes over the other tapestries depicting Aimsir and SkyRiders in battle, then successive Dumnorix rulers.

It was a rich history, one to be proud of. And he wouldn't deny that he felt a connection with these people, that they steadied him. But he was a Mithranan prince. Mithranar was his home. He belonged to them and they to him.

He wondered what Talyn would think of what he might have to do here. He hoped it wouldn't come to it, hoped it wouldn't be necessary. But he had to be willing, or it would never work. He had to find that strength somewhere.

Footsteps outside alerted him, and he spun to face the doorway as

Alyna entered. She was a striking woman, her raven hair threaded with grey and bound neatly in a bun at her neck. Her violet eyes were sharp as daggers, with the same flinty aspect to them that Soar and Talyn's gazes sometimes held but that Cuinn had never seen in Ariar.

His magic told him Alyna was taken aback by his appearance, but she masked it quickly, and he wasn't sure whether she'd been startled by his rugged clothes and unshaven roughness or something else. "Prince Cuinn. We weren't expecting you."

"That's my fault," he said. "I didn't warn you. I thought it safest given Azrilan's hounds."

She studied him for a long moment. "Soar says you're quickly becoming one of the finest SkyRiders in his legions." She hesitated. "He holds you in high regard."

"As I do him," Cuinn said. "Shall we sit?"

"I'm comfortable standing."

Interesting. His presence was making her uneasy, and by refusing to sit, she was trying to maintain control of the situation until she could work out how best to handle it. Fine. He remained standing as well. "How have you been, Alyna? Is Ariar well?"

Her mouth tightened at his polite attempt at small talk. "May I ask what brings you back to Port Lachley?"

Cuinn frowned. He kept his discomfort well-hidden, but he wished Ariar had been the available one, not Alyna. She wasn't giving him an inch to move. "I'd thought it would be obvious that I wouldn't stay in the mountains forever. I told you before I left that my people need help."

"Your people?" she asked. "You're referring to Mithranar, of course."

"I am. I don't know how much Talyn told you about my brothers, but neither hold anything but contempt for the human folk. And both like to rule by fear. I cannot imagine life there under Azrilan is any better than it was under my mother, if not worse."

"And you think you can offer them something better? From what Talyn told us, you're rather less impressive than either of your brothers, or your mother." Those violet eyes locked on his, ruthless. "A wastrel, she said, a man who refuses to take responsibility for anything, who did nothing but take a new lover every week and drink himself insensible on every other night."

He took a steadying breath. Alyna's accusations were unexpected, but not undeserved. He tried his best to ignore their sting and his dropping stomach. This was going to be even harder than he'd thought. "That was an image I cultivated to keep myself safe from my eldest brother. But it's not who I am."

"Are you sure about that?" She stepped closer. "Dumnorix children are precocious, and willful; they need to be raised by their own blood or they don't mature properly. You retreated into the mask of a playboy because you weren't strong enough for anything else. You were too weak, your feelings of inadequacy too strong, for you to make a stand against your brothers. Isn't *that* the truth?"

"If you truly believed that, you would never have agreed to the formal alliance between our two countries." Cuinn forced the words out, ignoring the part of himself that thought Alyna's words sounded all too accurate. That realised he might never win her over if this was what she truly thought of him.

Alyna pierced him with her violet gaze. "I agreed because I had no choice. It was an alliance I didn't want. It was an alliance that killed my daughter, Cuinn Acondor."

He sucked in a breath, losing hold of his calm mask at those cutting words. "I told you, she's not dead."

"If she were alive, she'd be home by now," Alyna said bitterly. "To believe anything else is merely holding onto false hope."

Her grief was raw and unending, and, unrealising of his magic, she made no effort to hold it back. Cuinn had to hold onto his sense of self with a white-knuckled grip to avoid being sucked into it. Swallowing, he summoned his magic, used it to steady himself and understand her. She was grieving still, terrified that she might be right, that Talyn might truly be dead, and it was making her harsh and angry with him. He was an easy target to lash out at, and she felt so deeply that she needed to lash out at *something* or she'd explode.

"If you truly believe she's alive, then why aren't you out there looking for her?" Alyna continued. "That's what you should be doing, not trying to take back a throne you have no hope of keeping. Why aren't you trying to save *her*?"

"Because it's not what she would want," Cuinn said quietly, holding onto his composure with everything he had. Even then, he was sure tears must be glistening in his eyes. Alyna's words had picked at his own doubts, at his fear for Talyn, at the terrible ache of missing her, his guilt for prioritising Mithranar over her.

Alyna froze as if he'd shouted at her, and he took a steadying breath. "She is out there somewhere, Alyna, and I know, I *know*, with every breath I take, with every second that passes, that she will fight her way back. Whether you are willing to admit it or not, she loves Mithranar, and she loves its people. The last thing she would want is me spending time trying to find her rather than trying to find a way to free Mithranar from Azrilan. So as much as I ache for her, as terrified for her as I am, I honour what I know she would tell me to do."

He stumbled to a halt, chest heaving, tears bright in his eyes. "Talyn and I don't save each other, Alyna. We save ourselves. *For* each other."

"I…" Alyna's mouth fell open and she was staring at him like she'd never seen him before. "You love her."

"More than anything else in this world," he said simply.

"I knew that you'd become friends, that she saw enough in you to be willing to marry you to allow her to return to the place she loved, to her Wolves, but I didn't realise…" Alyna trailed off.

"That she loved me too. As deeply as I love her."

The words resounded through the room, even though he'd spoken quietly.

Alyna stepped away, eyes closing for a moment before refocusing on him. "Give up Mithranar, Cuinn, it's lost to you. Come to us. We could use another strong Dumnorix prince to support our hold on power, especially with the Montagni threatening."

A start of surprise went through him. "You'd be willing to officially claim me as a Dumnorix?"

"No, of course not, but that doesn't mean we couldn't use your help. You're clearly one of us—I've been wrong on that score—and from what Soar says you could be an asset."

"I can't leave my people to suffer," he said quietly. "I am a prince of Mithranar. You are my family, but you are not my home."

"Your home is gone," she snapped. "Let it go, or it will ruin you. You are not strong enough to take it back."

"Even if that's true, I won't give up. It's not in me to give up." He swallowed. Alyna was still angry, hurting. He held onto his patience and decided not to push harder, to wait for morning and all the Dumnorix to be present. If he asked for what he'd come for now, she'd turn him down flat. "Now, it was a long flight and I'm tired. I'll talk to you tomorrow."

He walked past her and out the door before either of their emotions could get the best of them, not wanting to say something he'd regret later. She was Talyn's mother, and he understood all too well the root of her despair.

Besides, her biting words had hit him hard, despite the fact he was trying desperately not to let them. He needed a moment to breathe. He needed his Wolves.

To reconsider whether he could do this or not.

THEAC ANSWERED the door after the first knock, surprise and relief filling his face at the sight of Cuinn. "You're back. You... seem different."

"I'm sorry I was away so long, Theac," he said quietly.

The Wolf shook his head and stepped aside. "Come in. Who knows you're here?"

"Alyna and a single Kingshield. He promised to keep my return a secret." The moment Cuinn stepped inside he already felt better.

He and Theac settled themselves by the fire and Theac offered him a glass of spirits. "Errana and the girls are asleep, but I don't do much of that these days."

"Neither do I." Cuinn sighed and tossed back the drink.

"You've been fighting." It wasn't a question. Theac seemed to just know.

"I've been flying combat missions with a SkyRider legion for the past month." Cuinn nodded. He stared at his hands—even though they looked clean he felt like they were covered in blood. "I learned to fly again, Theac, and I learned to fight."

"Is that what's troubling you?"

He stared at his glass. "I just had a difficult conversation with Alyna. I came here with a plan, and now I'm starting to think it was a really stupid idea. After talking to her, there's no way…"

"Tell me." Theac's voice brooked no argument.

So Cuinn did. He'd seen how these Wolves had healed Talyn when she'd let them in, had seen how much stronger she was when she allowed herself to rely on them, let them—let *him*—help her.

There was a brief silence after he'd finished, then, "She said those actual words to you?" Theac growled.

"Word for word." Cuinn couldn't look at him.

"You believe them?"

"I know, logically, that not all of it was right. But she isn't entirely wrong either. I've Dumnorix blood yet I was raised without a Dumnorix relative. I felt the truth in her words. Talyn has even spoken of it." It was an effort to admit these things aloud but Theac deserved the truth. "All those years, when I didn't have the strength to face my brothers, when I snuck around as the Shadowhawk instead. Was it truly because I'm flawed, scarred from being raised without a Dumnorix influence? It makes an uncomfortable amount of sense."

And if it was true, did he have any hope at all of winning the family to his side? It seemed unlikely.

Cuinn risked a glance at Theac. The man was scowling furiously into the flames. He was angry. "Prince Cuinn, ever since you were born, I've heard folk say that you're the strongest song mage of your generation."

"So?" Cuinn said quietly.

"So tell me this. When Lady Alyna spoke those words to you, where did they come from? What was she feeling?"

Cuinn stilled, his chest constricting almost painfully.

"Laddie?"

"I..." Cuinn had to force the words out, each one hurting more than the last. "She blames me for Talyn's disappearance. In her eyes, I was the reason Talyn stayed in Mithranar."

"You know that's not true."

"Isn't it?" His voice broke on the words. The guilt he'd been burying, trying not to face, came pouring out. "Whatever happened to her, it was because of me, Theac. Because my brother stole the throne from me and I didn't see it coming. I'm trying to do the right thing by her, but she's out there and I just want to find her. What if it's a mistake that I'm here instead of searching for her?"

"Your Highness... Cuinn." Theac cleared his throat, as if made awkward by what he was about to say. "The Ciantar... I imagine, with your magic, you could feel what she felt for you."

"Yes, of course."

"Did she think you weak? Inadequate? Any of the things Lady Alyna accused you of?"

Cuinn leaned back against the chair and closed his eyes, allowing himself to remember. A slight smile teased his lips as he gave his answer. "She loved me. I could feel it, every time we were together. She thought I was strong and beautiful and good."

"Not scarred or weak?"

"No," he admitted softly. "She could not have hidden that from me. She hid nothing from me." She hadn't even hidden her fear over her feelings for Cuinn, her worry about the consequences of their relationship, none of it.

"Do you imagine that Lady Alyna knows you better than the Ciantar does?"

Cuinn smiled at the truth Theac had made him realise. "Never. Nobody will ever know me like she does. Like you Wolves do."

"She had faith in you, lad." Theac reached out to grasp his shoulder. "Your Wolves respect and love you. You must trust in that and trust in yourself."

Cuinn nodded slowly and sat back. He took a deep breath and

simply allowed his pain and grief to be part of him. Theac's question had made him remember what Talyn had brought to his life. The strength and confidence she'd given him didn't have to vanish just because she was gone.

He was going to be okay.

He needed to talk to the family tomorrow. It was time.

"All right, Theac. I came back here to win the Dumnorix to me, to win an alliance to help us get Mithranar back."

"Figured as much." Theac nodded.

Cuinn turned, met his Wolf's eyes. "If you're going to be there at my side tomorrow, then there's something you need to know. About my father. About who I am."

CHAPTER 19

The door to Theac's quarters swung shut behind them and Cuinn paused, looking at the Wolf. "Do I look all right?"

He'd checked his appearance a hundred times already, but this had to be right. He had to win this today, or he would be nowhere. His plan would be over before it had properly begun.

He wore a fine wool tunic and breeches of royal blue, with a linen ivory shirt underneath. He was clean shaven, his curling golden hair trimmed short and neat thanks to Errana. And on his chest he wore the sigil the Wolves had chosen for him—the Acondor outstretched wings with a lightning strike right down the middle. Stitched in bright emerald.

"A Dumnorix," Theac breathed. The man's look of stunned shock still hadn't worn off. When Cuinn had told him the night before, he'd gone silent for a full three minutes, eyes wide as saucers. Even now he gave himself a little shake at the words. "I should have seen it. You look just like them."

Cuinn straightened his shoulders. "Let's do this."

Those passing through the corridors of the fortress glanced at both men in passing, most frowning in brief puzzlement, then staring harder in surprise. Some of them might have glimpsed Cuinn before, especially when he'd been here with Talyn, but he wasn't the same winged prince they'd seen then. Now the resemblance to the Dumnorix family was clear in his features and bearing.

He and Theac crossed an open courtyard linking the guest quarters to the rest of the castle and strode up to the main entry doors. Six Kingshield in formal dress guarded the entrance. All were heavily armed, and their hands hovered close to their weapons.

Their captain was clearly taken aback by Cuinn's appearance, but this didn't deter her from her duty. "Your Highness. Can we help you?"

"I'd like to see the family. I was told they'd be meeting this morning?"

"They are, Your Highness, but Lady Alyna left strict orders not to be interrupted."

Cuinn smiled, used a touch of magic. "I don't think she meant me."

The captain hesitated a moment, but Cuinn had been granted audience with the family previously, and Alyna presumably hadn't left specific orders for him to be excluded. "One of my guards will escort you through."

"Thank you, Captain."

"With your permission, Your Highness, I'll speak to the First Shield about having a guard on you at all times." She cleared her throat. "While you're here, that is. Those Shadows won't get at you again."

It was a surprising offer, given Kingshield protected only the Dumnorix. Cuinn smiled at her, wrapped her in a hint of gratitude. "I would be honoured, Captain."

The doors were opened, and Cuinn felt all five pairs of eyes on his back as he strode through. The Kingshield guard led him inside the castle before transferring him to another two guards stationed in the entrance foyer. They asked him to wait while one went ahead to announce Cuinn's arrival.

"More guards than usual?" Cuinn asked Theac in an undertone.

The man nodded. "There was a noticeable increase after the attack on you."

It wasn't long before a well-dressed servant appeared, conducting a whispered conversation with the remaining Kingshield before approaching Cuinn.

"Come with us, please, Prince Acondor." The older guard gestured.

Cuinn nodded and strode through with Theac at his side. With one fierce look from the Wolf, both Kingshield dropped back a few paces behind them.

"Suddenly I feel like I need a full Wolf detail helping me," Theac muttered.

Cuinn flashed him a smile. "I am confident that you can handle anything that comes up."

"Is this going to be like the time that you went to risk mortally offending the ahara of Montagn by refusing his daughter and didn't tell me beforehand?" Theac enquired.

"This may be similar in scale to that time." Cuinn shrugged, then shot another smile at him. "You know I did that because Talyn asked me to. She snuck into my room the night before."

Red flooded Theac's cheeks and Cuinn looked away from him in delight, the task of distracting the concerned man achieved.

Their boots echoed on the stone floors as they followed the guards down a long, wide hallway towards a pair of arched oak doors. The wood was too dark to ever be used in the citadel or Summer Palace, but the doors were a beautiful piece of work, engraved with epic battle scenes rich in detail.

"They await you inside, Prince Acondor." The servant bowed slightly.

Both Kingshield turned to the Wolf as he moved to follow Cuinn, offence creeping over their faces.

"The Ciantar would not want you out of sight of a Wolf, Your Highness," Theac said for their benefit, no deference at all in his tone. "Especially knowing a pack of Shadows is hunting you."

Affront seethed from the older Kingshield. Cuinn tried not to wince as the man barely held himself back from snapping at Theac. "You will not be attacked inside the palace."

Theac squared his shoulders. "It already happened once."

Cuinn smiled slightly; truly, it felt good to have someone he could trust absolutely at his back. "Talon Parksin comes with me."

The Kingshield didn't look happy, but one reached for the doors, and neither stopped Theac as he followed Cuinn inside, a single pace behind.

Several people waited inside the room: Ariar, Alyna and Soar. Lark Ceannar was there too, and Cuinn started in surprise. He hadn't seen the First Shield since first arriving in Port Lachley. Ceannar offered him a little nod, but said nothing.

When he scanned the room and saw nobody else, his shoulders relaxed fractionally. He would have had to make a very difficult choice, risking far greater consequences, if the First Blade or any of the other Twin Thrones' commanders or lords had been present.

Alyna watched him approach with an expressionless mask, something close to Talyn's habitual cool demeanour. Wariness and unease flickered underneath her self-control. After their encounter last night, she likely had no idea what to expect from him.

"Cuinn, you're back." Ariar came forward to greet him, offering a warm handshake. The man's bright blue eyes were dimmed, and some of his ebullient manner was missing. Cuinn frowned as he shook hands, using a quick tap of magic to study his cousin.

Ariar was tired from long days and nights. So, the Dumnorix were in trouble. Well, that was going to make this either easier or harder. He'd soon find out which.

"You've left your legion?" Soar asked.

Cuinn nodded. "It was time."

Alyna's sharp voice cut through the room then. "I thought I made it clear where things stood, Cuinn. You turned me down. Why are you still here?"

Ariar frowned. "What are you talking about?"

"I offered him our protection and a home in return for his help." She did not look away from Cuinn. "He refused, said his duty was to Mithranar, and that he would be returning there."

Sitting in a chair off to the side, Soar stirred in surprise. Ariar's frown of confusion deepened. Ceannar remained expressionless—Cuinn almost smiled at a brief memory of Talyn complaining about how good his game face was. He made a note never to play cards with the man.

He glanced at Theac, standing calm and ready behind him. Then he pushed aside his instinct to trust these people, to let them comfort him, and allowed his resolve to seep through instead. He thought of Talyn, of what she'd said, of how she'd believed in him.

"Actually, Alyna, that's not what I said." As he spoke, Cuinn injected his voice with a thread of steel. "I didn't accept your protection because I will not abandon my home in order to receive it. But I am not leaving to return to Mithranar, not yet. I came here for a reason."

"Then maybe you'd like to fill us in," she said sharply.

"I came here to reclaim our alliance," he said evenly. "To help you throw back Firthland and regain stability so that you will come to *my* aid and help me regain the throne of Mithranar."

"We have no alliance." Alyna seemed shocked he'd even brought it up. "The agreement was that you and Talyn would marry and we would put you on your mother's throne. None of that happened."

"Yet." The single word rippled through the room and Cuinn let it sink in. "None of it has happened, *yet*. Talyn and I will still marry. I will still take my throne. Our agreement still holds."

"Cuinn, you are family, but we are in the middle of a war," Ariar said soberly. "We don't have the resources to come to your aid, to fight another war. Our first responsibility has to be to our people, our country."

"I'm not asking you to come to my aid now," Cuinn said, infusing his voice with sincerity. "I know that I need to hold to our alliance first. If you agree to ally with me, I will help you, and then, once Firthland is defeated, we will take Mithranar and push back Montagn. Together."

Soar and Alyna shared a glance, but it was Alyna who spoke. "We cannot tie our fate so strongly to you. When Talyn lived and would have been at your side... that was a different matter. We knew her, her skills, her strength. It was her we trusted, and she was the only reason we agreed to the marriage and the alliance."

Cuinn settled his gaze on Talyn's mother. The Dumnorix had not yet officially chosen a regent from amongst themselves, but it had steadily become clear to him that Alyna Dumnorix was the one the other two looked to. She would decide this.

"I am not who you think I am, Alyna."

Her mouth tightened. "Be that as it may, you are not someone I would risk our kingdom for. That is final, Cuinn, I'm sorry."

Ceannar cleared his throat to speak. "Your Highness, if I might—"

"This is a family matter, and therefore not your place to comment, First Shield," Alyna snapped.

Ceannar nodded and sank back into his seat, giving Cuinn a little shrug, as if to say, 'I tried'.

He'd expected it would come to this. He'd hoped it wouldn't, but... holding them to the alliance was a shaky proposition at best, particularly in Talyn's absence. And deep down, he understood their reluctance. He would probably make the same choice if it were put before him.

That didn't make what he had to do next any easier. But there was no choice. Because Mithranar deserved it of him.

Forgive me, Talyn.

"Alyna. Ariar. Aerin." He met each of their gazes in turn, using Soar's Dumnorix name for the first time. At his side, Theac stiffened, as if preparing for what was coming. "I am a legitimate Dumnorix heir. More, I am descended from Rianna Dumnorix, and in Aeris Dumnorix's absence, I hold the strongest claim to the Twin Thrones of all Dumnorix alive."

The room turned deadly quiet. Soar stilled in his chair, staring at Cuinn in shock, while Ariar's mouth had fallen open. His bright blue eyes were dark with an emotion Cuinn couldn't quite untangle. Alyna stood, holding herself still, fear leaking from beneath her self-control.

"To protect my home, I will need the strength of arms that the Twin Thrones can give me," he said. "So if you will not uphold our alliance, I demand the regency. I will take the Twin Thrones by right of succession."

"You will never get it," Alyna snapped. "You may have Dumnorix blood, but you will not have the support of the people or the lords. They don't know you."

"Do you think that will remain true when I tell them my lineage? When your First Shield confirms it? When all you need do is look at me now and know that I am Dumnorix?" Cuinn refused to look away from her. "We are at war, Alyna, and your lords and your people want someone who will deliver leadership and victory." He took a breath. His shoulders had straightened and fire burned through his veins. "I am the most powerful song mage of my generation. All I have to do is open my mouth, speak to the Conmoran and Calumnian Lords' councils, and they will choose me."

"You do not have the backing to take the Twin Thrones, and you are foolish in the extreme if you think so," she said.

Cuinn stepped closer to Alyna, hardened his expression to match hers. "You don't think so? Why don't you ask Soar? The SkyRiders are with me already, and I spent only a few months with them. Do you really think it will take me long to win your lords too? Especially when I tell them I have a way to end this war? What do you have to give them, Alyna? Nothing."

"You cannot do this," Alyna whispered.

"I can," Cuinn said bluntly. "And you know it. Hold to the terms of our alliance agreement, or I will take this kingdom out from under you."

A heavy silence fell. Cuinn did not look away from Alyna, refusing to be the first to buckle. His claims were largely bluff... but she had to think he could do it, or this was going to fail. This was the leverage he needed to force an alliance and he couldn't show weakness now. Not in front of this family. Mithranar needed Cuinn to win them.

"There has to be a middle ground." Ariar finally spoke. He looked haggard, as if this dispute tore at him. "A compromise."

Cuinn turned, gentling his voice but keeping it brisk. "What do you see happening here, Ariar? You can't rule by committee forever—

you can't hold your lords that way and once Montagn properly joins this war you won't defeat them alone. You need allies. I can be a strong ally for you."

Soar rose to his feet. "And what? The answer to that is us crowning you? Help you start building your own empire like Tarcos and your brother?"

Cuinn shook his head. "I have no desire to be king of the Twin Thrones. But if the only way I can secure your help is to claim the regency until my home is free, then that's what I will do."

"You can't become regent without announcing publicly who you are," Alyna said. "I know you understand why we can't do that. Talyn understood it. Knowledge of your bloodline is a threat to the Twin Thrones' stability."

Cuinn had been counting on that. If Alyna and the others were too afraid of his identity being revealed, they would surely agree to what he was asking, if only to keep such an explosive secret.

"I respectfully disagree." Ceannar rose from his chair and completely ignored the look Alyna sent him. Cuinn blinked in surprise. "We have kept this secret for generations, holding onto it with fear of what the consequences could be if people knew. I say that fear is unwarranted. It cannot be held as leverage over us if it is no longer a secret. Your family has ruled and coexisted without conflict for those same generations. Trust yourselves. Trust that Cuinn and Talyn's children and grandchildren will work *with* yours, not against them. Stop fearing what *might* happen." He paused. "Burn bright and true."

A heavy silence fell. Emotions lurched all around Cuinn. Ceannar's sincerity and impatience. Soar and Ariar's consideration of his words. Alyna's weariness and fear for her daughter. Cuinn stared at Ceannar... was he suggesting—

Soar's voice drew all their attention, but he was looking straight at Cuinn. "If we agree to uphold the alliance, you'll withdraw your claim to the regency, keep your lineage a secret?"

The hope in him soared bright, and his heart began thudding in his chest so hard he was glad there were no other song mages in the room to pick up on it. Somehow he managed to keep his expression calm and voice steady as he responded. "If you agree to uphold the alliance, then so will I. I'll remain here and help in whatever way I can—in whatever capacity you demand—until Firthland is defeated. At which point you will come to my aid."

Soar gave Alyna a little nod, leaving her the decision, but making it clear he was comfortable with the agreement.

"I disagree. I say we make Cuinn regent," Ariar said unexpectedly.

Stunned silence filled the open space as his words echoed around them.

Cuinn wasn't sure he'd heard his cousin correctly, but he must have, judging from the way Soar and Alyna spun to look at Ariar in shock. The Horselord gave a little shrug. "Aethain was killed seven months ago. We've been at war for over five months, and yet not one of us has had the fortitude to step forward and claim the regency. He's right, we can't keep ruling by committee and we all know it. Yet none of us have been willing to claim it, not even you, Alyna."

Another silence fell.

"And Ceannar is right too," Ariar added. "We are a family. We will continue to respect, trust and protect each other as we always have. Whether here in the Twin Thrones, or in Mithranar. If problems develop in the future, I choose to trust that our family will manage them successfully."

Cuinn suddenly felt as if the floor had vanished from beneath his feet and he was in free fall with no safety net to catch him.

But maybe he never had to hit the ground.

Maybe he could be a king.

Soar turned to Cuinn, piercing him with a hard look. "Cuinn, you will agree to relinquish the regency the moment the war is over and you take the crown of Mithranar. You give us your word here and now."

Shock and astonishment poured through Cuinn. They were truly going to make him regent?

Shit.

Theac gave him a sharp nudge, snapping him back into focus. He turned to look at his Wolf; the man's grizzled features were fierce, and he held Cuinn's look without hesitation. In that look was all the confidence Cuinn needed.

He straightened his shoulders, looked each of them in the eyes again. "I give you my word that the moment I assume the throne of Mithranar I will relinquish any claim to the Twin Thrones."

Ariar stepped forward, bowed his head. Soar followed suit. Cuinn started to wonder if he was dreaming. Internally he was shaking—with joy, with triumph, with terror that he might fail. Alyna was slower than the rest, but as she came to stand before him, her gaze was scrutinising, not hostile.

"I begin to understand, Cuinn Acondor-Dumnorix, what my daughter sees in you." She bowed her head. "Regent it is."

And just like that Cuinn Acondor had the Twin Thrones at his side.

He wanted to throw his head back and howl like a wolf.

Instead, he glanced up to where the Dumnorix banner hung from the wall, the crossed swords still wreathed in Aethain's amber. "Then I will issue my first order as regent. I want the sigil changed to silver-grey, in anticipation of Prince Aeris returning safely to us."

Ceannar stepped forward, saluted sharply. "With your leave, I'll go and send those orders now, Your Grace."

"Please do." Cuinn held his gaze. "I'm also going to require a full Kingshield detail at all times, but Theac will be in overall command of organising my protection."

Ceannar saluted and left.

Cuinn looked at his family. "And we'd better discuss how we're going to announce this to your lords."

"They're your lords now, Cuinn." Ariar grinned with a touch of his old fire.

Cuinn opened his mouth to respond, but was forestalled by the opening of the doors. Ceannar, who'd almost reached them, stood back to allow the First Blade through. Despite her small stature, the fierce head of the Callanan order immediately drew the attention of the room.

She held up a small piece of unrolled parchment. "This just arrived by bird from Warrior Seinn. A fleet of four warships departed from Acleu three days ago."

Cuinn took a breath, turned to his family. "Montagn has joined the war."

"You said you had a way to end it?" Ariar asked. "Or were you just bluffing?"

Cuinn smiled. "I wasn't bluffing."

CHAPTER 20

*T*alyn hunched over her bowl. The watery stew was hardly appetizing, but she tried to force herself to eat it. Her body needed the fuel.

"I can't stay here, Sari."

To her credit, Sari didn't point out that Talyn had already said that. Many times. *"You can't just get up and walk out either. Patience, Tal."*

She squeezed the wooden spoon in her hand until it carved gouges into her skin. It had been months and she didn't know what was happening in Mithranar, where her Wolves were, where Cuinn… she stopped that thought in its tracks.

She took a breath, refocused her thoughts on something more productive than wallowing. *"What do I do about Mithanis?"* She'd searched for him amongst the male slaves eating on the opposite side of the room but had failed to spot him. The mess had been rebuilt in a week following the fire thanks to slave labour, and sawdust still littered the floor and drifted in the air.

The thought that the prince of night was nearby was unsettling, but she had to admit Zamaril had made some good points about including him in their escape attempt.

"*Use him.*" The response was quick and decided. "*And focus on the positives. There's a way out, and I know you can find it.*"

Right. Not only was Zamaril here, but a powerful song mage and warrior too. As much as she hated to admit it, Mithanis was the strongest asset they had, especially since her ability to fight was limited by her scarring.

"*We could sneak out like we did the night of the escape attempt, meet Zamaril and Mithanis somewhere. Find some horses. Mithanis and I could use our magic to break through the front gates to get out.*"

"*There are about a million steps before there where you could be seen and stopped,*" Sari said.

Talyn shook her head. "*I've memorised the guard shifts and rotations. We'll wait for a night when the laziest guards are on duty, and move during a gap in their patrols. There'll be guards on the front gates, of course, but they'll be taken by surprise and we should be able to manage them between the four of us.*"

"*Except if you're stopping to get horses on the way, you risk being seen and heard before you even reach the gates. And if you don't stop for horses and go on foot, then the guards and their tracking dogs will catch up to you quickly.*"

Talyn paused, considered that.

"*And say you make it through the gates, where do you go next? Even if you managed to get horses, you'll have the whole garrison combing the forest for you. You don't have anywhere to go, or a safe place to bed down.*"

Talyn took a deep, shuddering breath. Beside her, Kaeri glanced over in concern. She managed a smile. "*I'll make it work.*"

"*Talyn, you know I have absolute faith in you, but no slave has escaped a labour camp before—you need to keep that in mind. The difficulty in pulling it off is not inconsiderable,*" Sari counselled. "*Run it by Zamaril when you see him next. He can help.*"

A gust of air blew through the hall as a fresh contingent of guards entered, laughing and joking amongst themselves.

Time for shift change.

Unfortunately, tonight Talyn and Kaeri were seated at the end of one of the long tables, only a short distance from where the guards monitoring them were eating their dinner. The heady scent of their roasted meat and vegetables had been wafting over the entire time they sat eating their stew.

"You'd think they could eat in their own barracks," Kaeri muttered, not for the first time.

A bout of raucous laughter came from a table of guards, distracting her from her thoughts. She glanced at them, wondering what was so funny.

"Died like rabbits in a hole, didn't they, Goran?" the soldier closest to her joked. He was bearded, like all of them, but Talyn had already marked him as the most senior officer at the table judging from how they all deferred to him. He was a new face too, having arrived only a few days earlier from Arataire.

A soldier at the end of the table leaned forward in his chair and looked down towards him with an eager expression. "I heard you were part of the ahara's force when he went to take the Mithranan throne, Captain Daranin. Did you have to fight to put them down?"

Talyn's heart thudded.

"The fighting was disappointingly brief," Daranin said dismissively. "The pretty Falcons came running to their new master once we showed our faces. They were too scared to do anything else."

Talyn's fists clenched. Sapphire light shone from her palms and she ruthlessly crushed her magic. She had to keep control of herself.

"What about their human warriors, the Wolves, Captain?" another man piped up, as eager as the first. "I saw them in Arataire before I was posted out here—they looked like they could fight if it came to it."

"A unit went in early with the Shadow and the Firthlander Bearmen." Daranin shuddered, distaste rippling across his face. "He gave me the creeps, and I don't mind admitting it—all sly and devious. He was good, though, he got the Ciantar down into that tunnel without a fuss, walked her right into our trap. Without her leading them, those Wolves of hers tried putting up a fight, but they were essentially useless. We dealt with them easily enough."

Six thrices, they were talking about her.

By now all the soldiers at the table were listening to Daranin, enthralled. Stationed in the middle of nowhere at a labour camp, he was the closest to action they were likely to get unless war broke out. Even the slaves within earshot seemed to be paying attention.

Talyn began looking about for the guard who rang the bell when dinner was over; she couldn't leave until that bell sounded. But he'd stepped closer to the table too, listening to Daranin as keenly as the others. Kaeri shot a warning look in her direction.

"Was the Ciantar killed?" a man asked.

"She looked pretty dead to me when the Bearmen carried her off, her and the Wolf with her. I heard she got to the Shadow before they could stop her, though, buried her dagger in his heart. No great loss there." Daranin shrugged.

Talyn went rigid. Kaeri flinched when she got a look at Talyn's face. "Talyn, he might recognise you. You can't let him see you, do you understand? Do not get his attention," she hissed.

Talyn pressed her palms into the table, struggling against the waves of horror and anger sweeping up inside her.

"What about the pretty boy prince? How did he die?"

"No, no, oh please no."

"Talyn, I'm here. Focus on me." Sari was there then, solid and strong.

Talyn tried not to listen, tried to block the sounds of the soldiers' voices out, but they were so close and it was impossible not to hear.

"The way I heard it from my boys, the ahara cut into him while he screamed."

A shuddering, rasping sob escaped her. *"No..."*

"Talyn, please. Just breathe. I'm here. I'm here with you."

Talyn tried to focus on Sari. Tried to stay in control despite the way those casually uttered words tore at her soul. Her knuckles had gone white, and a sheen of sweat slicked her skin.

She could still feel Kaeri's eyes on her, but couldn't afford to lose concentration by shifting to meet the woman's gaze to try and reassure her. Everything she had was focused on staring blankly at the wooden tabletop, wrestling with her anger and hurt and fear.

Daranin's voice was infused with respect as he talked about his new ahara. "He groveled at Ahara Manunin's knee, begging not to be killed, practically kissing his feet. And then he screamed."

And she snapped.

Shouting incoherently, Talyn leapt to her feet, the force of it sending her chair flying backwards. Bitter despair and anger claimed her, throwing aside any rational thought, roping through her in an unstoppable force.

She crossed the space to the guards' table in two strides and leapt at Daranin, grabbing up his eating knife and plunging it straight into the man's eye before he even knew what was coming.

Hands grabbed at her, trying to pull her off, but such a rage had consumed her that she brushed them away like flies. She sent one man slamming back into a wall, grabbed the knife from his belt, and hurled it at a guard a few seats away. It went straight into his throat and he fell backwards from his chair, gurgling. Blood sprayed, warm droplets spattering over her cheek. The guard beside him went for his sword.

Talyn caught the movement and scrambled across the table, slamming into him before he could use it against her, and sending them both crashing to the floor. A red mist of rage filled her vision, and her heart pounded, adrenalin flooding her body. Sapphire magic sparked in her palms but the final shred of self-preservation she had remaining stopped her from using it and revealing herself to those gathered.

Instinctively, she shifted to balance herself, but her scars pulled painfully and she stumbled.

The soldier rolled on top of her, trying to pin her to the floor. Talyn let out another roar and hurled the man off her with a practiced *sabai* move. As soon as the weight was gone, she staggered to her feet, again off balance. Three Montagni circled her with swords drawn, forcing her back to the wall.

Breathing harshly, Talyn feinted towards one of them, but was stopped by a heavy weight crashing down on her head. She dropped to her knees, blackness spotting her vision.

Her limbs felt suddenly heavy, and moving was an effort. A few seconds later, she toppled over, struggling uselessly against the grogginess sliding down over her mind. Hands grabbed her from behind, pulling her arms painfully behind her body. A burly guard appeared in front of Talyn, slamming a fist into her stomach.

The air shot out of her chest, and Talyn doubled up, tears in her eyes from the pain. That fist was quickly followed up by another, and then another, until she was hanging in their grasp, dazed and bleeding. Even then she struggled, ignoring the pain in her body, her flagging strength.

They laughed at her weakening struggles, dropping her to the ground and finishing her off with a final blow to the head that sent the blackness rushing in to claim her.

WHEN TALYN FLOATED BACK to consciousness, she was sprawled face down on a hard, earthen floor. She shifted slightly, wincing when stabbing pain shot through her body. Slowly, breathing through the agony, she tested her arms and legs, then carefully reviewed the rest of her body.

Nothing seemed broken but her chest and stomach were a mass of tender, purple bruising, visible even in the dim light of a lantern hanging outside what she assumed was her cell door. Not to mention the sticky feeling of drying blood down her back—the scars had broken open again.

Finally, she ran her fingers lightly over her face. There was a sore, swollen spot on her left jaw, and dried blood crusted on her right cheekbone. They'd really worked her over.

She sank back to the ground, fingers curling in the dirt. Daranin's words echoed over and over through her thoughts.

Azrilan had cut into him as he screamed.

If Cuinn was dead... she forced herself to take a deep, steadying breath around an agony that was sharper than any pain her body could throw at her.

"*You don't know he's dead.*"

"*I know that.*" Talyn grabbed tight to her partner. "*I know that.*"

"*You've kinda made a big mess of things though.*"

Talyn smiled at the affectionate exasperation in her partner's voice. *"Yeah. I know that too."*

She'd clearly been put in the cells under the barracks. But for how long? Would the guards kill her for what she'd done, or just leave her locked up indefinitely? No, she'd murdered a captain and at least one other soldier. Surely she'd be executed for that. Her head pounded as she tried to think, and eventually she gave up, slumping down in the dirt. Sari went too.

She wanted to cry so badly that the tears welled in her eyes and trickled down her cheeks, but she forced herself to breathe through it. She had to keep herself together, had to be strong. If she let go now, she'd break.

And if Cuinn was still alive, then he would be waiting for her. He would know she would fight her way back.

So that's what she would do.

CHAPTER 21

Talyn had no idea how much time passed as she continued to drift in and out of consciousness, but she finally swam back to hazy clarity when the sound of voices drifted in from outside her cell. Shortly after, the door creaked open and a man's voice told somebody to hurry up. Footsteps approached and then someone kneeled beside her and fingers brushed her forehead.

"Talyn?"

She risked the pain to open her eyes and squint upwards, her voice only a faint rasp when she spoke. "Kaeri? What are you doing here?"

"I seem to be the person designated to look after you every time you get yourself beaten up," she said dryly.

Talyn blinked, forced herself into a sitting position. It hurt. "If they sent you to clean me up, they must not be planning on killing me right away."

Relief flashed over Kaeri's face at the evidence of Talyn's lucidity, and she nodded. "Let me take a look at you."

Water splashed in a bowl, and then a soft cloth wiped gently at the wound on her cheek. Talyn bit her lip, forcing herself not to flinch away. "Why *aren't* they going to kill me?"

"Your little outburst has them suspicious about you," Kaeri said in a murmur, clearly not wanting the guards to hear. "They saw how you fought, and they're putting that together with the dead soldiers they found after the attempted escape last month. They want to learn more about you before killing you outright."

Talyn frowned. "At least now we know for sure they didn't know who I was when I was brought here."

Kaeri agreed. "I'm guessing whoever handed you and Zamaril over to the slave master that sent you here didn't tell them who you were. They just threw you in with the latest intake of slaves—probably thinking you were going to die from your wounds."

Tossed away with contempt, uncaring whether she lived or died. That sounded like Azrilan.

Although she didn't understand why he hadn't just killed her outright. The prince of games had made the wrong gamble there. The fool.

"This is only a reprieve. A slave killing a guard has to be dealt with harshly," Kaeri continued. "They'll kill Zamaril and Mithanis too if they work out the link between you."

"I won't tell them a thing," she muttered. "Shit, Kaeri, that hurts!"

Kaeri didn't let up, and fell silent for a few minutes as she continued to clean Talyn's cuts and scrapes. Eventually she sighed. "If they're following protocol, then the Montagni commander in charge of the camp has probably sent for a higher officer to interrogate you. They'll keep you alive until he arrives."

Talyn nodded. "Kaeri, we both know I'm not going anywhere."

"Talyn—"

"I'm hurt and my scars have broken open," Talyn said as firmly as she could. "I barely have the strength to walk, let alone run or ride, and I'm not going to improve enough in a day or two to make an escape attempt."

"What are you trying to get at?"

Talyn gasped as she shifted and pain tore through her. She ignored it, reached out to take Kaeri's hand. "You need to go back and keep your head down. Wait until all this blows over, then you and Zamaril find a way to get out—use Mithanis if you have to. The two of you can pull it off, I know you can."

"Even if you're right, that will take weeks to plan, if not months. You'll be dead by then."

"Forget about me. Kaeri, you've saved my life twice over. It's time to look out for yourself. You are a Venador princess. Bide your time, work with Zamaril, and get out of here." Talyn refused to let Kaeri escape her gaze.

A door clanged at the end of the hallway and the guard's boot steps sounded as he returned for Kaeri. Talyn grabbed her arm, leaned forward to murmur in her ear so the guard couldn't hear. "When you get out, find your way to my family. Tell them I sent you, what you did for me, and they'll protect you. Zamaril too. And never trust Mithanis. Not for a second."

"Talyn..." Kaeri wavered, torn.

"Go," Talyn hissed.

Kaeri hesitated again, then nodded and stood abruptly to move to the door. The guard swung it open and she stepped out, giving Talyn one last look before the door shut behind them.

Once both Kaeri and the guard had gone, Talyn settled back on her stomach on the hard floor, the least uncomfortable position she could find. Her mind spun, studying her situation, and despite her words to Kaeri, trying to find some hope.

She had a day at the very least to regain some strength, hopefully longer. Everything she'd said to Kaeri was true. She was in no condition to escape. But that didn't mean she wasn't going to try.

She was Dumnorix and Ciantar. She was Aimsir and Callanan and Kingshield.

She was a Wolf.

If they wanted to take her down, it was going to cost them.

WHEN SHE AWOKE AGAIN, neck prickling from a spider crawling across her skin, she was still in pain, but there was more strength in her limbs than there had been before.

It was impossible to keep track of time in the dark cell. Twice a guard brought her a tray with a mug of water and bowl of slop. Her muscles stiffened further but none of her wounds seemed to get worse—Kaeri had done a good job cleaning and binding them.

More time passed.

The distant sound of bells—the pattern used to announce arrivals to the main camp entrance—woke her from a fitful doze.

Perhaps her interrogator had arrived.

It didn't take long for them to come for her. Voices sounded further along the corridor and then several soldiers came to a halt outside her cell. One guard unlocked her door and swung it open to allow the entrance of a tall, broad-shouldered Montagni. Two Berserkers stepped into the cell, flanking him protectively.

This man was important, then.

He hunkered down in front of her, studying her with a hard, unrelenting look. "Who are you?"

She'd had time to think about what to say, what would keep Kaeri and Zamaril safe. In the end, she'd decided to stick with the simplest answer, and one that had been true when she first arrived in the camp. "I don't remember."

He cocked his head, giving her a nice view of his perfectly groomed beard. "The guards tell me the same thing, but I don't believe that's true."

"I don't remember anything from before I woke up here months ago," she said calmly. "I was hit in the head, hard. I think that's how I lost my memory."

He smiled, but there was no warmth in it. "You take me for a fool? A slave with no memories does not suddenly attack her guards in the middle of dinner."

"I've been... muddled... since I woke up. My mind isn't always right." She tried to force sincerity into her voice, but even to her the excuse sounded flat. She wasn't strong enough to pull off the act.

The Montagni lashed out with his fist so quickly she didn't even see it coming. Talyn's head snapped sideways with the force of the blow, and she tasted blood on her lip. The pain was sharp and it took her a few moments to breathe through it. By then, the Montagni had risen to his feet.

"Put her in the isolation hut and give her no more food," he said to the guards. "Let's see how willful she is after a few days of cold and hunger."

Two guards stepped forward to take an arm each and haul Talyn to her feet. The rough movement tore at the opened scars on her back, and she cried out in pain. They ignored her, dragging her battered body down the hall outside her cell.

She thought briefly about fighting, discarded the idea just as quickly. In her state she had no hope against two Berserkers. She'd have to bide her time and wait for a better opportunity.

Outside, she was thrown unceremoniously into a cart caged in wood—the usual method of transporting slaves. Landing hard, she cried out again from the pain, and managed to roll onto her stomach. She felt fresh blood trickling down her back, and every bruise she'd sustained protested loudly.

She slammed a palm against the floor of the cart in frustrated anger, a snarl escaping her at the same time.

She would not allow these men to see her beaten.

They laughed at her show of defiance. The general said something to the Berserker at his side, then turned and strode away. A guard swung himself up onto a seat in front of her and picked up the reins of the horse driving the cart. He made a clicking sound and they jerked into movement, again jarring Talyn's wounds.

Shit.

"The isolation hut sounds bad." Sari couldn't conceal the worry in her voice.

Relief flooded Talyn at the return of her partner. *"They use it on particularly willful slaves to force them into submission. It's a tiny wooden hut in a corner of the compound with no heating and dirt floors. Guards surround it at all times."*

"That's not entirely bad news." Sari brightened. *"Isolated means far away from any guards but the ones assigned to watching it. If you could get out and deal with them…"*

"I'll have a straight run to the boundary fence—it's not far away."

"How many guards?"

Talyn paused. *"The last time I passed the hut when a slave was being held inside there were seven. None of them were Berserkers though. I'm guessing babysitting duty is beneath them."*

"Okay. You can take down seven Montagni soldiers easy."

"Not hurt like this I can't." Talyn pressed her face into the wood of the cart as another jolt sent her back into agony. The despair was gone now, oddly enough, in its place only determination. She'd made the decision to fight no matter what, and that eased the trapped feeling she'd been wrestling with for weeks. *"But I'm going to try anyway."*

"If I was there I'd tear them all to pieces." Sari uttered the words with such fury that it gave Talyn strength. And made her smile.

Soon after, they stopped. The cart had turned off one of the main paths through the compound and was travelling along a narrow, bumpy trail to where the isolation hut stood. There was nothing around it but cleared earth in all directions, giving the guards posted outside a clear view if she tried to make a run for it.

The southeastern corner of the boundary fence wasn't far off—maybe twenty or thirty strides at a full sprint. Across open ground. And there were guards constantly patrolling the fence lines too. Their visibility would be limited at night, though, and the nearest backup guards were a longer distance away.

"Don't forget the tracker dogs and the fact any pursuing guards will be mounted," Sari said quietly.

"One step at a time," Talyn said just as quietly.

The cart stopped with a jolt, and Talyn was dragged out and onto her feet. One of the waiting guards opened the creaking door to the hut and she was shoved inside.

The door slammed behind her, leaving her in quiet. Once her eyes adjusted to the dim light—there were no windows—she could make out the hardpacked dirt of the floor and nothing else. Draughts of cool air came through cracks in the wooden walls, and there were no blankets or sleeping pallet. A particularly putrid stench emanated from a hole dug into the corner of the floor.

Refusing to despair at the situation, she did a quick inventory of her physical condition. Apart from the new bruise on her cheek, nothing seemed terribly worse. The scrapes and cuts were healing over, and she couldn't feel any fresh bleeding down her back.

Infection was a concern if those torn scars weren't cleaned out though. She'd have to make her move quickly. Before hunger and cold stole her energy too.

She forced herself to her feet and spent a few moments gathering her balance and allowing her sore muscles to stop protesting. Once she could walk, she paced out the interior of the hut. There was only one door, and none of the cracks in the walls were significant enough that she could leverage one to make an escape route—not without making too much noise and alerting the guards outside.

No. It didn't take long for her inspection to reveal that there was no viable way of escaping easily or discreetly. Sitting again to conserve her strength, she considered her options.

"What do you think, Sari?"

"You need to even up the odds. Can you lure one of the guards inside, take him down first?"

Talyn nodded. *"I could feign illness, or a seizure of some sort? That might even bring two of them in."*

"That's a start."

Neither mentioned how difficult it was going to be to overwhelm two guards in her condition, let alone then face the five others that would converge on her the moment she stepped outside.

Talyn sighed, rubbing a hand over her face.

It didn't matter how hard it was going to be. She was still alive. She had a responsibility to her people to try and help them. To do that, she needed to get out, no matter the odds.

One step at a time. She would get out of this, and she would go back and help them.

"You'll need to wait for nightfall." Sari's mental voice wrapped Talyn in strength and reassurance. *"And hope it's a cloudy night. That will be your best shot of getting to the fence and over it without been seen."*

If she managed to take down seven Montagni soldiers when she couldn't even lift her arms over her head. Not to mention how impossible it would be to get away from the inevitable pursuit in her condition. *"It will have to be tonight. Wait too long and hunger will drain my strength."* She closed her eyes, the ache of grief for her lost partner stronger than it had been in a very long time. Tears threatened. *"I wish you were here."*

"You know I'm always with you."

TALYN WAS DOZING when a faint sound woke her. She sat up, trying to work out what she'd heard. Night had fallen and the interior of the hut was almost completely dark. Thin shafts of watery moonlight pierced the cracks in the wooden walls.

Silence reigned, but she was sure she'd heard something. It had been like a soft sigh, an exhalation of air. From close by, just beyond the wall she'd been leaning against. Odd enough to wake her trained senses.

She rose to her knees, listening intently. If a guard was coming to check on her, this would be an opportunity to surprise him. But several moments passed and everything remained deathly quiet. She wondered if she'd imagined it, but her instincts told her to be alert.

A soft thud came from behind the hut.

Talyn rose to her feet, heartbeat quickening. A muffled call from a guard drifted through the night air outside; it had a questioning note, like he was asking someone what was going on.

Then a soft exclamation of surprise, and another thud, this one a little louder. Talyn's ears strained as she tried to follow what was happening. Bootsteps sounded as a guard from the front of the hut walked briskly around the side.

Then there was silence.

Talyn's fingers curled. The silence lengthened. It was anticipatory, expectant. It thrilled through her.

Another voice called. This one a different guard, again from the front of the hut. When it went unanswered, he called again, louder. Talyn shifted on her feet, instinct telling her she needed to be ready to take advantage of what was coming. Her fingers clenched and unclenched at her sides, ready to hold a weapon.

Silence. The silence of the calm before a storm. Or the expectant hush before battle.

Something was out there.

The ring of steel cut through the quiet. The remaining guard out the front had drawn his sword. Even though she had no explanation for what was going on, anticipation flowed like wine through Talyn's veins. A moment later the lock on her door rattled. Talyn tensed, ready to leap on the guard the moment he walked inside.

The door swung open and a shaft of moonlight fell across the floor. The guard's face was suspicious, tense, his sword raised and ready.

Before Talyn could move, before she could even take another breath, a dark shape leapt out of the night, crashing into the guard and slamming him down to the ground. The guard's cry of fear turned into a horrific gargling sound as his throat was torn open.

What...

A soft snarl sounded, then a tawncat prowled through the doorway, green eyes glimmering, tail waving back and forth. Blood dripped from his muzzle and claws.

Talyn couldn't breathe. "Jasper?"

His ears twitched, then he turned and padded out, pausing in the doorway as if to say, "Are you coming?"

"Don't hesitate."

Sari's words galvanized her and Talyn moved.

Jasper headed directly for the compound fence line. The ground around the hut was littered with bodies lying prone in pools of blood.

Jasper had taken the guards out one by one without making a sound.

Hope, wild and furious, flooded through Talyn, giving her a strength she hadn't had in months.

Jasper had come for her. Which meant Cuinn had sent him.

He was alive. Her steps staggered, then she forced herself to calm, to focus.

More surprises waited. Jasper led her unerringly to the boundary fence, where a neat hole had been sliced at the bottom—just large enough for the tawncat and her to wriggle through.

Jasper wasn't alone.

The tawncat waited patiently as Talyn scrambled through, then the moment she was on her feet he was off again, leading her to the cover of the forest.

So far no alarm bells had rung. Nobody had seen them.

Had the tawncat killed the guards patrolling the fence without detection too? An almost hysterical urge filled her to lean down and hug the tawncat fiercely.

They reached the trees and again Jasper seemed to know where he was going. They began moving up a slight incline, Talyn forcing her battered body to keep up. She didn't think to try and stop him, to try and figure out where he was going. She trusted him implicitly.

Eventually they reached the top of an incline and entered a small clearing. Jasper came to a stop and let out a questioning yowl. Talyn stopped too, dropping instantly to her knees beside the tawncat to wrap her arms around his neck, silent tears soaking into his dark fur.

His head turned slightly, bumping his bloodied nose against her ear, then he wriggled out of her hold.

When a shadowy figure stepped out from the trees on the other side of the clearing, Talyn started violently, hand unconsciously scrabbling for a weapon she didn't have.

"Fancy meeting you here." The voice was familiar, female, sardonic, but she couldn't quite place it.

"Who are you?" Talyn backed up a step. Jasper turned to watch her, as if making sure she was okay. The fact he wasn't already tearing this person's throat out had her relaxing.

"You don't recognise my voice? I'm offended." The woman stepped closer, the light of the moon revealing her dark skin and faded sapphire eyes. "We are family, after all."

Talyn stared. "Saniya?"

"That's right."

"What are you doing here?" Maybe she was hallucinating. Maybe infection had already set in and this was some kind of fever dream. How else to explain the leader of Vengeance working with Jasper to help her escape?

"Getting you out." Saniya's voice turned brisk. "I know you've probably got a hundred questions, but they have to wait. It's imperative we get out of the guards' search zone as soon as possible, so for now I just need you to trust me and follow. Okay?"

"I..." Talyn glanced back toward the camp, where Kaeri and Zamaril were. "I've got friends back there. I can't abandon them."

"Then go back. But I'm leaving now and this is your one opportunity to get away clean." Saniya's voice was ruthless, but when Talyn still hesitated she let out an annoyed sigh. "We're just going to a safehouse a short distance away. That's all for now."

"Use Saniya's expertise to get clear of the search and then work out what comes next," Sari urged. *"You can't do anything for Kaeri or Zamaril right now."*

Talyn took one look at Jasper and nodded. "Okay."

"Good. Can you run unaided?"

"Not fast and not far." Admitting that was torturous, but it wasn't going to help any of them if she lied.

"You don't have to go far. We've got horses waiting." Saniya was already turning. "Let's go, hurry!"

Talyn didn't have to be told twice. She followed.

Her limping run had become a stumbling walk when the scent of horses hit her on the night breeze. The familiarity of it steadied her, gave her the strength she needed to cover the final distance.

Two others—a young man and older woman—waited with four horses. None of the animals looked pleased by Jasper's presence. The man led a horse to Talyn. "I'm Colm. That's Tari. You good?"

She nodded, placed her palm against the horse's warm neck for a long moment, then summoned the strength to swing into the saddle. A grunt of pain escaped her, but she made it, and settled into her seat, adjusting to the unfamiliar saddle.

"We need to ride fast." Saniya gathered her reins. "Let's go."

As they rode away, Talyn glanced back. Jasper followed, far enough not to panic the horses but close enough to get to her if he needed to.

Cuinn was alive. And he'd sent Jasper for her.

She was going to be fine.

Azrilan was a fool—and a walking dead man.

CHAPTER 22

*D*awn was a faint pink glow on the horizon as they skirted a small town then emerged from thick forest into the tilled fields of an isolated farmhouse. As the light grew, Saniya began casting anxious glances around—likely worried that someone would spot them.

Their approach was clearly expected. Two lanterns burned either side of the farmhouse door, and the horses' hooves had barely sounded on the paved drive when the door swung open and a middle-aged woman stepped out.

"Take the horses straight around to the stables," she told Colm and Tari in a brisk voice. "Saniya, bring her in. Dastril's waiting below."

By then Talyn was trembling with pain and exhaustion—the horseback ride at a gallop had not been kind to her injuries and only gritty determination and her Aimsir skill had kept her in the saddle.

She managed to half-dismount, half-fall from the saddle, only Saniya's quick steadying hand keeping her on her feet.

"Can Dastril come up and help get her downstairs, Daya?" Saniya asked the woman.

"I'm fine," Talyn gritted out. "Just show me the way."

Daya searched her face for a moment, then nodded. "Best he not be seen up here. Hurry now, it's getting light."

The farmhouse door was closed as soon as they were inside, and while Talyn propped herself against a wall, Saniya and Daya bent to quickly unroll a rug back from the wooden floorboards of the main room. Daya hauled up the trapdoor that was revealed while Saniya waved Talyn over. "Down here."

Talyn somehow managed to get down a steep set of narrow stairs to an underground room, Saniya and Jasper hovering close behind. They'd clearly been prepared for her to be hurt because a healer—presumably Dastril—waited in the warm and well-lit space beside a small table covered in healing supplies.

"I'll go and make sure Colm and Tari are settled," Daya called down before closing the trapdoor. "Don't come back up until I tell you it's clear."

Saniya and Jasper then looked on while Dastril—an older, stick-thin man with a snowy white Montagni beard—painstakingly cleaned and dressed Talyn's wounds. Jasper refused to take his eyes off the man, clearly not impressed about the pain he was causing her, but somehow understanding that it was necessary.

Every time she looked at the tawncat, she wanted to cry.

Judging by the occasional tensing of Saniya's jaw, the bruises and broken scars must look bad. Talyn tried not to think about it. By the time Dastril had finished and she'd drunk the herbal tea he gave her, she was utterly exhausted from the pain. He pushed her gently down onto the soft bed and told her to rest.

"Wait..." She forced her eyes to stay open, to focus blurrily on Saniya, to ask the question she was terrified to ask, even though Jasper's appearance had eased her fear somewhat. "Cuinn. The Wolves?"

"Cuinn was safe last time I saw him, as were most of your Wolves," Saniya said. "Now rest. I'll explain everything when you wake."

Tears slid down her face unchecked, but she allowed herself to close her eyes and sink into the softness. The last thing she remembered was the sight of Jasper leaping onto the blankets to curl up at her feet, his fierce glare daring anyone to come near her.

"*Sari?*"

"*I'm here. Rest, Talyn.*"

WHEN SHE WOKE, she was curled on her side, warmth and softness surrounding her. Someone had dressed her in clean clothes, and her raven hair was damp, as if it had been washed. Jasper remained at her feet, fast asleep and snoring softly.

Talyn's gaze went straight from him to where Saniya sat on a chair at the bottom of the stairs. Dastril was gone. Wincing, she gingerly uncurled and pulled herself up, resting on a forearm. "How did you find me?"

"He did." Saniya jerked a thumb towards the tawncat. "Don't ask me how. I've been searching everywhere, using every contact in my network. It didn't even occur to me that you'd been made a slave. But after finding no trace in Mithranar, we crossed the channel. The only thing I could think was that maybe Azrilan had brought you to Arataire as a prisoner. Jasper disappeared the night we arrived in Acleu." Saniya let out a sigh that was a mix of annoyed and impressed. "He reappeared nearly two weeks later, by which time I was at my wits' end trying to find trace of you. The beast would not let up snarling, or glaring at me like he was going to eat me, until I started following him."

"You were both searching for me?" Talyn stared wonderingly at the sleeping tawncat.

Saniya nodded. "The creature has somehow decided I can be trusted—he even came to fetch me to help Cuinn and your Wolves flee Dock City after Azrilan's coup. I heard tawncats are uncannily smart, but—"

Talyn froze. "You said they're okay... they escaped? Where?"

"There were casualties, and Cuinn was hurt, but I got them out. They're hiding in the north, at a hidden location some Falcon by the name of Windsong organised." Saniya's words were brusque, simple. She clearly had no idea what they meant to Talyn.

Emotion flooded her so strongly the tears began streaming unchecked down her face. Her fingers curled in the bedsheet and a shuddering breath escaped her.

"When did you see them last?" she managed.

Saniya's hard face softened slightly, but her tone remained brisk. "Months ago. I've been gone, working with my people and the Shadowhawk's. Trying to find you."

"And you're sure Cuinn was okay?"

"He was on his feet and planning his next move." Saniya nodded. "He sent Jasper with me to find you while he concentrated on figuring out a way to take his throne back."

Talyn swallowed. He was all right. Well enough to plan how to fight back. The relief was endless and she couldn't stop the tears no matter how hard she tried.

There were more questions to ask, truths to understand. Saniya had mentioned casualties. But Talyn feared she might not be strong enough to bear some of those answers. Not yet. She told herself she would face them soon, but for now she held on to the fact that Cuinn was alive. That many of her Wolves were alive.

And she focused on Saniya instead.

"Why did you do it?" Talyn said bluntly. Saniya was the leader of Vengeance, a group Talyn and the Wolves had hunted down. A group whose members she'd killed. A group who'd tried to kill both her and Cuinn more than once. "Help them escape. Search for me."

"You spared my life twice, Cousin. I owed you."

Saniya's tone and voice indicated she had no desire to discuss that topic further. So Talyn dropped it for the moment, instead lifting a hand to her face, palpating her bruised jaw and the sore spot over her cheek. "What was Dastril's assessment?"

"You're pretty banged up, but you'll live." Saniya's eyes narrowed. "I've seen worse, actually, amongst slaves we've gotten out before. Your back is a mess, but those are older wounds."

Talyn nodded, bit her lip.

"We'll lay low here until the search for you is over, then we'll leave. It should take a week or so."

"In the camp." Talyn cleared her throat when it rasped. "They say no slave has ever escaped."

Saniya's expression turned grim. "It's true that most of our rescue missions are of household slaves; they're easier to get out. But occasionally we can spring someone free from a labour camp. And when we do, the guards tell the rest of the slaves in the camp that the escaped slave is dead."

"They can't afford any of them knowing that someone got out," Talyn said quietly.

"Exactly." Saniya stood. "We'll get you out of Montagn, across the channel and to the SkyReach without too much trouble—that's where your Wolves are hiding."

The SkyReach. Her Wolves. *Cuinn.* Home. She swallowed, head bowing with the weight of how badly she wanted to be there as fast as was humanly possible. But she couldn't do that. Not yet.

She pushed off the blankets and swung her legs over the side of the bed. "I can't leave yet. Zamaril is in that camp. And a friend who saved my life is there. I'm not leaving without them."

"If you think I'm risking my people to go back to that camp, you're crazy," Saniya said flatly. "I'm here for you, that's it."

"Then I'll go by myself." As exhausted and sore as she was, Talyn's voice was iron-hard. She wasn't leaving Zamaril and Kaeri behind.

Saniya huffed out an impatient breath. "Talyn, that camp will be like a hornet's nest right now. Reinforcements will have been called in to help with searching for you. Even if I was willing to help, there is no way my people can extract two more slaves without us all getting caught and killed."

"I know a way," Talyn said eagerly, feeling better than she had in months. Freedom, treatment, but most of all the knowledge Cuinn was alive and well, had restored her. "Zamaril and Kaeri are both assigned to a work crew outside the camp." Or they had been before Talyn's escape. If that had changed, her chances of getting them out without an army at her back were slim to none.

"You want to snatch them while they're working?" Saniya shook her head. "I don't have the resources for an ambush on a work crew. I won't risk my people for it."

"You don't need to. You've seen Zamaril fight, and Kaeri can handle herself, not to mention Jasper. We surprise the guards, toss Kaeri and Zamaril weapons, and that's two extra fighters. We use your horses too, get clear before the pursuit comes."

"Work crews outside labour camps are watched over by at least twelve guards, and since your escape, I won't be surprised if they've doubled that number. We *might* be able to overwhelm twelve guards, but not twenty, and even if we could, we wouldn't be able to do it before reinforcements arrived from the camp."

"I can—"

"Don't even try and tell me you can fight effectively right now."

Talyn hesitated. Saniya was right. But there was something that would tip the balance in their favour. "What if I told you there was someone else who could help us? A skilled warrior with both warrior and song magic?"

Confusion flooded Saniya's face. "Who—"

"Mithanis is in the camp too. He's on Zamaril's work detail."

"No way," she said flatly.

"With his help, we could take out the guards and be away before reinforcements get there," Talyn said stubbornly. She couldn't believe she was arguing on Mithanis's behalf, but she wasn't leaving Zamaril and Kaeri behind. Not for anything.

"And then what? We exchange murderous soldiers for a murderous prince of night?"

"He knows we're his only chance of escape. For now our goals align. He won't act against us."

Saniya was still shaking her head. "We wouldn't be able to return here. We'd have to ride straight for the coast and hope to lose those pursuing us along the way. That isn't likely—the soldiers at the camps know the terrain. With superior numbers and fresher horses, they'll catch up. Even if they didn't, we'd have to contend with reinforcements drawn from other camps in the region to help search for us."

Saniya was right. It still didn't matter. "Then I'll do it alone and take my chances. I know Zamaril and Kaeri would make the same choice for me."

Saniya's jaw clenched, the finger of one hand tapping out a furious rhythm on her knee.

"I know that you don't want to endanger your people, and I'm grateful for what you've already done for me," Talyn said. "All I ask is that you leave me the horses."

A silence fell. Eventually Saniya expelled a frustrated breath. "I'll help you, but my crew stays out of it."

"Thank you," Talyn said, voice full of feeling. It was more than she had any right to expect.

"Don't. We're more than likely about to end up right back in that slave camp, only together this time." Saniya rose to her feet and took a step up the stairs. "I'll go and tell Colm and Tari of the change in plans."

"Saniya?" Talyn stopped her. "Tawncats live and hunt in family groups. There's no hierarchy, but they all have an innate sense of each other—developed as a way to hunt more effectively but also keep each other safe," Talyn said. "At least, that's what Tiercelin read somewhere. Jasper came to you because you're family. His and mine."

Saniya started at that, her sapphire eyes turning back to Talyn. "I sometimes used to think, in moments of ridiculous weakness, that it would be nice if a time came when we weren't enemies."

Talyn smiled. "So did I."

Saniya hesitated again. "I made an agreement with Cuinn before I left, to ally our networks. We won't fight for him… but I agreed that our people should work together to continue undermining Azrilan and his court every opportunity we get."

Talyn's smile widened. "Like you and the Shadowhawk used to do."

"Exactly." Saniya's eyes met hers unflinchingly. "I made no promises about what happens after Azrilan is taken down. I don't want another Acondor on the throne, Talyn."

But Cuinn wasn't like his family. Talyn didn't point that out, figured Saniya already knew it deep down. A logistical alliance was more than they could have imagined anyway. "Understood," she said. "And thank you."

"*Talyn, we could use that. When we get back,*" Sari breathed.

"*Yes. Yes we can.*"

They wouldn't be starting from scratch after all.

SANIYA SENT Colm and Tari to ride on ahead to Acleu to organise passage across the channel for Talyn and the escaped slaves.

"We'll be riding into Acleu with half an army on our heels," she warned Talyn. "But if we can get to Toscal, we should be fine. He's one of our people in Acleu. A fisherman who's happy to sneak passengers up the coast and across the channel to Darmour for the right amount of coin."

They waited three days, until the search teams from the camp had passed through the district without finding Talyn. There was a tense full-turn or two while dogs searched the nearby area, but Saniya remained confident the horseback ride would have confused their scent.

"We've done this many times before," she said.

"The people who own this place are part of your network?" Talyn asked.

"Not technically. But they help us where they can," Saniya said. "Their son was caught stealing—a drunken prank with his friends— when he was seventeen. He was sent to the slave camps to work off a ten-year sentence. That was four years ago."

"Ten years for stealing?" Talyn asked incredulously. "Not everyone in Montagn approves of slavery then."

Saniya shot her an incredulous look. "The only people who approve of it are those who are from rich and powerful families like yours whose wealth comes from the work of slaves."

"Save the preaching," Talyn snapped, irritated by her cousin's accusatory tone. "The Dumnorix abhor slavery and you know it."

"Abhor it all you like, but what are you actually doing about it?"

Saniya shot back. "Refusing to send a liaison to Montagn to register your displeasure? Please!"

"Oh, I suppose you think we should use our military might to invade other countries and take their sovereignty just because we don't like the way they run things?" Talyn lifted an eyebrow. "Throw away the lives of our citizens in doing so?"

"Why not? You did that to Firthland, didn't you?" Before Talyn could respond to that, Saniya waved a dismissive hand. "War isn't the answer to problems. There are other ways."

"Such as?"

A knock at the trapdoor above interrupted the heated conversation. It was Daya coming to let Saniya know the searchers had left the area. Throwing a look at Talyn, Saniya muttered something about getting food, and disappeared up the stairs.

Talyn sighed and looked at Jasper. "She's really annoying."

Jasper blinked. Waved his tail.

"I'm glad you agree."

CHAPTER 23

*T*he air was still, almost as if it was waiting, holding its breath. Talyn dismissed that fanciful thought with a huff. She rode behind Saniya, two more horses on a lead rope following, Jasper padding along enough distance away to not entirely spook the horses.

The labour camp wasn't far off now, despite the thick forest around them giving the illusion of being a long way from anywhere civilized. The horses picked their way through brush, Saniya deliberately choosing the most difficult approach. "When we leave we'll be following forest trails so the horses can move quickly. Approaching via a different route *might* confuse the Montagni trackers and their dogs for a short time."

Any Aimsir worth their horse would be able to tell the difference by simply looking at the tracks, so Talyn held little hope that would be the case. But even if it delayed pursuit by a quarter-turn and no more, it would be something. And Talyn had made a career of leveraging small somethings into success.

"*You* are *feeling better*," Sari commented.

She was. Despite the limitations forced on her by her scarred back, her bruises were fading and the cuts were healing over. The trapped panic that had been building inside her while she remained a slave in the camp had vanished—fading to a noticeable but dull ache of memory. Even though she was attempting something with impossible odds. Even though the way ahead was going to be difficult and dangerous. It didn't matter.

She was free. She knew Cuinn and her Wolves were alive, and where they might be—or at least somewhere to start looking. Now all she had to do was get Zamaril and Kaeri and she could go home.

"And Mithanis."

"Sure." She winced. Wished she could think of a way of accomplishing this without needing to include the prince of night.

"What are you going to do with him once you've helped him escape?"

"We'll need his help to get clear, particularly if pursuers catch up to us."

"Noted. And then what? Once you're safely away, I mean?"

"I'm taking this one step at a time."

"So basically you have no idea."

Talyn shifted uncomfortably in the saddle. *"I will."*

They timed their approach to the outskirts of the camp for late afternoon. The work crews would be taken inside before nightfall, but Talyn wanted darkness to cover their escape as quickly as possible.

Eventually the horses approached the opposite side of the riverbank where slaves were sent to fetch water for the work crews. The water rushed by, dark and green, but shallow enough here for the horses to cross. Saniya and Talyn brought their horses to a halt behind the tree line and out of sight of anyone approaching the banks.

"I'm not sure we should separate." Saniya hesitated. Jasper padded ahead, glancing back when they didn't follow, annoyance flashing in his eyes.

"Zamaril and Mithanis will be working in a different area to Kaeri." Talyn tried not to be irritated about having to explain this again. She'd already drawn a detailed map of the work area and its surrounds for Saniya back at the farmhouse. The forest would give them some cover on approach, but things would turn chaotic the moment they broke from cover. "We have to split up, or by the time we both go for Kaeri, then get to Zamaril, the guards in the compound will have been alerted. You're the one who said that the faster we get clear, the more chance we have of evading pursuit."

"Your back," Saniya said eventually. "I'm worried you can't fight—"

"I have other advantages." Talyn cut her off, impatience making her sharp. "And I'll take Jasper with me. The plan is sound, Saniya. We grab them, meet in the middle, then ride east as fast as we possibly can."

A breeze kicked up then, suddenly scattering leaves across the forest floor. Talyn's horse shied, stamping its foot. Saniya gave a single nod, then handed Talyn the reins of her spare horse before urging her mount into the water.

Talyn loosely tied the reins of both spare horses to a nearby tree before leaving them and kicking her gelding after Saniya. Water splashed around them, and she hoped the noise didn't carry on the breeze.

On the other side, Saniya rode up the embankment, angling north-east to circle the work area to where the male slaves worked. Talyn broke away, heading west along the riverbank towards where the carts and female slaves would be. Jasper padded behind.

The remembered thrill of battle heated Talyn's blood. She refused to let herself think about her new limitations. Or what they'd do if Kaeri or Zamaril weren't still assigned to this work detail.

"Sari?"

"I'm here. You'll be fine." There was no doubt in her partner's voice.

Her mount's hindquarters bunched as she pushed him up the incline above the riverbank, then reined him in. The sound of chopping wood drifted on the breeze, along with the occasional snippet of an order being given.

Talyn's hand curled around the reins and she settled herself in the saddle. She sent a glance at Jasper, who was already looking at her with impatience in his gaze, and then lifted her head, pursed her lips, and sent a shrill whistle reverberating through the forest—the signal to go.

Then she dug her heels in.

The horse launched into a gallop through the trees, making for where the transport carts sat ready to be filled with chopped wood. Moments later they burst onto open ground, her horse half-rearing with a protesting whinny at how suddenly she reined him in.

The slaves in the vicinity froze in the middle of whatever they were doing, faces utterly bewildered by the sudden appearance of a rider in their midst.

Talyn's gaze scanned every slave carrying the chopped wood to the carts. When she spotted Kaeri, relief relaxed her tense shoulders. The woman had already seen her, shock flashing over her face before being replaced by a growing smile.

"Ha!" Talyn urged the horse. "Ha!"

He lurched back into a gallop, weaving through slaves and piles of cut wood alike, and Talyn leaned down out of the saddle, arm extended.

The Venador princess didn't hesitate. She tossed her armload of wood aside and ran towards the galloping horse without a trace of fear. As the two collided, Kaeri's arm gripped hers firmly and she swung herself up behind Talyn.

Grunting with the effort, ignoring the tug of sharp pain from her back, Talyn turned the horse to gauge where the guards were. Those nearest—she counted five—were drawing weapons. She was about to ride at them when Kaeri tugged on her arm.

"The guard's horses!" she shouted, then pointed. "That way."

Brilliant idea—she should have thought of it herself.

Talyn twitched the reins, sending the horse in the direction Kaeri had pointed. Two soldiers came sprinting after them, while the others —having heard Kaeri's shout—ran to cut them off before they could reach their goal.

But then Jasper exploded from the trees, long strides carrying him across the clearing in front of their horse with a speed that belied belief. The guards barely had time to see him coming before he was on them, claws extended, a snarl ripping through the clearing. He tore the first man's throat out, then leapt at the next.

Moments later Talyn and Kaeri reached the guards' horses.

Drawing a knife, Talyn leaned down and sliced through the rope tethering them to a sturdy tree. "Jasper!" she bellowed.

The tawncat had been poised over the third dead guard, blood spattering his nose and claws, but at her shout he turned and ran towards them. Another snarl ripped from his throat, striking terror into the already uneasy horses. All but two of them bolted. Talyn swore as her horse reared too, as panicked as the others, and it took a precious few seconds to get him back under control.

"You right back there?" she asked Kaeri.

"Fine."

"Good. I have an idea."

Kaeri's weight at her back made movement more limited than she preferred, but she still managed to lean out and grab the reins of the two horses that hadn't bolted. Bucking, snorting, they fought her hold, almost dragging her from the saddle until Kaeri reached out and grabbed on too, adding her strength.

Eventually they calmed, snorting their displeasure but willing to be led. Now they had two spare horses in case any of theirs were lamed in the escape.

Without needing to be told, Kaeri swung out of the saddle behind Talyn and clambered onto one of the spares. Once settled, she grabbed the reins of the other one, freeing Talyn's hands.

Shouts broke out in the distance, and Talyn's head whipped around. There was a flash of dark light, a sharp crackle like lightning on a stormy day.

Saniya had reached Mithanis and Zamaril.

Talyn was turning her horse to head back to the meeting location at the riverbank when a hissing sound thrummed into a break between shouts.

"Duck!" Kaeri shouted.

A second later, arrows whistled through the air around them. Cursing, Talyn turned the horse sharply to the left, taking them away from the point of attack before reining in at a grunt of pain from Kaeri. "You okay?"

"It's a scratch. I'm fine." Blunt, annoyed words.

Talyn looked properly at her friend. The arrow hadn't nicked her arm. It was lodged in her shoulder. Anger snapped through her. "Tell me the truth."

"I can't move my shoulder, but the bleeding isn't bad. I'll be fine." Kaeri sounded confident, despite her skin having gone several shades paler than usual. "We need to move. There will be more where that came from."

"Jasper, run!" Talyn bellowed. The tawncat was vicious and deadly, but as vulnerable to an arrow as anyone else, and his size made him a good target. He hissed, but did as she asked, racing for the cover of trees.

The archers had cut them off from the approach to the river. They could circle around, but that would take time she didn't want to waste. Hopefully Saniya had already gotten Zamaril and Mithanis clear.

Another arrow whistled by—they'd been found. Talyn made up her mind.

"We're going to take out the archers and ride through the work area. Stay close behind!" she told Kaeri.

Her gaze searched for her archer, catching sight of him just as she had to duck to avoid another arrow. Lifting her arm, she summoned her winged folk magic and sent a sapphire bolt of energy flying at him. It exploded into the ground at his feet in a flash of electrical light and he screamed in pain.

Digging her heels in, Talyn galloped at the second archer, flinging another bolt before he could get a shot off. Gasping, she fought not to sway in the saddle from the energy drain. Back by the cleared area around the carts, the only guards she could see were all dead. The rest had probably gone to deal with Saniya.

Now they just needed to get to the riverbank and—

"Talyn, look!" Kaeri warned.

She was pointing to the road leading back to the camp's front gates. Mounted soldiers boiled out of the gates at a gallop—at least ten at a quick count—and Berserkers swarmed the compound grounds, clearly preparing to come after them. It looked like the full company had been roused.

Shit. They'd been even faster to organise than she'd thought.

"Talyn!" Saniya's voice.

Her cousin was galloping toward them from the trees on the northern side of the work area. Zamaril clung to her back. A man ran several paces behind. He had no wings and he was pale, gaunt, like all slaves. But there would never be a place or a time when Talyn would not recognise Mithanis Acondor. His dark eyes glowered at her.

"Soldiers?" Talyn snapped out, tearing her gaze from Mithanis to Saniya and Zamaril.

"All dead from our area," Zamaril replied, sending a grudging look of approval at Mithanis. "Seven down."

That made twelve. That was all of them.

Talyn switched her gaze to Mithanis, hesitating. His dark eyes bore into hers, almost challenging. "Get on the spare horse. Quick!"

"Let's go!" Saniya shouted once Kaeri had relinquished the reins of the spare mount to Mithanis. The prince of night clambered awkwardly into the saddle and then perched there even more awkwardly. Shit. She hadn't thought of the fact he wouldn't know how to ride.

"Let your horse follow ours, don't worry about trying to steer it. But you stay in the saddle or you get left behind," she told him sharply.

He scowled, but determination hardened his face and he gripped tightly to the reins.

Kaeri pointed down the road with her good arm, where the reinforcements were rapidly approaching. "That lot will be on us in a heartbeat."

Talyn scanned the riders, trying to figure out the best option. Part of her marked the slaves huddling around the trees, clearly terrified and not knowing what to do. She squashed the guilt before it could form. None of them had been hurt, and she could only hope they wouldn't be punished once it was clear they'd done nothing but stay where they were during the escape of others.

The rest of her planned, thoughts racing. If they fled now, the pursuit would likely catch them—they were too close. Her horse sensed her nervousness and backed up, snorting. She tightened her hold on the reins.

"Why aren't we riding?" Saniya had her horse on such a tight rein he was dancing in anxiety underneath her. Zamaril clung to her.

"I need them to get a little closer," Talyn murmured. "Kaeri, how are you doing?"

"Quit asking me that, I'm fine."

"Talyn!" Saniya snapped. "Tell me you have a plan, because we're about to die or be captured."

The first group of galloping soldiers was at the top of the road now, almost on them. Behind them, though, it was taking longer for the Berserkers to sort out horses and get saddled up. No others had left yet.

Good.

She glanced at Mithanis. "Prince of Night, would you like to be of use?"

He tried to kick his horse forward, managed it after a few tries, and came up alongside her. He stared ahead at the guards with a calculating expression, clearly understanding what her plan was without needing to ask. She reminded herself not to underestimate him.

Talyn took a deep breath. Forcing away her awareness of everything but herself, she closed her eyes and summoned focus. She gathered up her fear, her pain, her anger at everything that had been done to her.

Then she lifted both hands in the air.

Opened her eyes.

And threw her magic at the approaching soldiers.

Blue energy flew from her hands, several bolts of sapphire warrior magic. They hit their target in a series of successive blasts, exploding so fiercely the ground rocked beneath their feet.

Mithanis let loose a heartbeat later, his warrior magic far more powerful than hers.

Their sapphire and black magic collided in a storm of energy that had Talyn seeing stars, ears ringing, chest constricting, seconds later.

By the time the light faded and the ground had stilled, not one soldier remained. Instead the ground where they had been was utter carnage, splattered with blood, gore, and bits of clothing.

And then there was a twitch of movement in her peripheral vision. She spun, readying more magic, but it was only one of the slaves.

Running away into the trees.

And then another ran after him. The slaves that had spent their lives being brainwashed to behave. To follow orders. To never even think of escaping.

They scattered and ran.

There was hope in that. And the glimmerings of an idea she couldn't quite grasp. Not yet. Her breath came in harsh gasps, but she wasn't tired, she was exhilarated. Battle rage flooded her system, taking away all the pain.

"Ciantar indeed," Saniya murmured, eyes wide as she stared at the destruction.

Mithanis tossed her a dark look, clearly unhappy at the evidence of Talyn's warrior magic. But he didn't say anything.

Talyn lifted the reins to turn her horse, to make their escape back to where the spare horses were tethered. Where Jasper was hopefully waiting.

But Mithanis reached over and grabbed her wrist in a fierce grip, a murderous light in his eyes. "Them too."

His other hand was pointing at the Berserkers already leaving the compound, at the rest milling about by the main gates readying to leave. Before Talyn could say anything Mithanis let out a roar, hands raised, flinging his magic farther than she could have achieved.

Burst after burst after burst, his towering rage on full display, powering his magic, until he slumped, spent, in the saddle.

The main gates and anything near it had been completely obliterated.

"*Are we sure breaking Mithanis out was a good idea?*" Sari asked after one, awestruck moment.

"*On the bright side, he's just won us some time to get clear,*" Talyn managed. *"On the significantly darker side, he just destroyed steel gates and about fifteen-odd elite warriors in under a minute."*

"Why didn't he just do that weeks ago?" Sari still sounded awed.

"Questions can come later."

"There are hundreds more soldiers in that camp." Saniya spoke coolly into the thick silence that had fallen. "Let's go before they can organise themselves."

They rode.

CHAPTER 24

*T*rystaan landed at the Port Lachley castle fortress amidst a strong gust of wind, wings flaring at the last moment to balance himself. The SkyRider members of Cuinn's new Kingshield detail circled above in a ruckus of screeching and shouted farewells until he was safely down, and then they banked away, heading for the SkyRider base to the east.

Cuinn's heart sank at the sight of Ariar waiting for him. Theac and Evani stood at guard position by the doors leading into the fortress, and he gave them a wave of greeting before going over to where Ariar stood at the battlements along the edge of the roof.

"I prefer the fresh air," he explained when Cuinn joined him, palms resting on cool stone. The east of Conmor sprawled out before them, fields and forest, and Mount Fanar and its watchtower in the short distance. "I hate staying inside these walls too long."

"Is it going to cheer up that woeful expression of yours if I tell you Soar's legion just wiped out the Montagni fleet heading our way?"

Ariar did brighten for a moment. "No casualties?"

"None."

The Callanan warning from Acleu had been a saviour. The Conmoran navy had deployed in a search pattern as soon as they received the message, and a patrol had spotted the ships two days' sail from the north coast.

Four warships packed with Berserkers and infantry and two smaller vessels escorting them, their small size and maneuverability indicating their purpose was likely to identify landing spots for the warships to ferry in their troops.

Cuinn didn't give them the opportunity.

He'd sent Soar and one of his legions to intercept the fleet the moment they'd come within SkyRider range of the coast. Without nievers to defend them, the ships had gone down quickly. Anxious about the outcome, Cuinn had flown out the previous night to check in on his cousin, then returned immediately with the good news, leaving the SkyRiders patrolling the coast on the off chance they'd missed a ship.

Finally, they'd had a win. He couldn't deny it felt good. That a decision he'd made had led to a small but decisive victory for the Twin Thrones. But Ariar's glum mood was quickly souring that triumph.

"If those ships had finished what they came to do, we'd be in trouble," Ariar said. "Imagine hundreds of soldiers spreading through the undefended fields of north Conmor?"

"Your Aimsir and the Conmoran cavalry would have helped the army destroy them before they got far."

"Maybe," Ariar said grimly. "But how many more would follow?"

"The ahara doesn't have an endless supply of ships." Cuinn strove for optimism, but Ariar was right. Azrilan would take this loss and learn for next time.

"They'll adapt, and quickly." Ariar echoed his thoughts. "I don't know your brother well, but Tarcos is a smart man and experienced warrior, for all his pride and youth. Azrilan won't send any more unguarded ships. At least not in small numbers."

"I certainly wouldn't," Cuinn mused, his good mood fading entirely. He *did* know Azrilan. More ships wouldn't be his response. No, he'd have something else up his sleeve, something cleverer. Ariar's grim mood settled like a heavy weight against Cuinn's song magic.

There was more going on. He'd been waiting out here for Cuinn for a reason. "Are you going to tell me what's going on?"

Ariar rubbed a hand over his face, then passed Cuinn a folded piece of parchment. "I just got this a full-turn ago. My scouts in the mountains report movements of Firthlander troops south."

"Shit." Cuinn sucked in a shocked breath. "Towards the Calumnian border?"

"That's my guess. They're pushing hard in the northern foothills, trying to break into Conmor, but my scouts think they have enough numbers now to make a similar push south into Calumnia."

Cuinn rubbed a hand over his eyes. "The fleet was a feint."

"Maybe. Even if not, it was timed well to draw our attention away from the mountains." Ariar let out a breath. "We need those SkyRiders back there right away, working in tandem with my scouts. We'll be fighting on two fronts soon."

Frustration flared. Azrilan and Tarcos seemed to always be a step ahead somehow. Cuinn wished Talyn was here. She was their best chance of outwitting both men. "I'll send a SkyRider to recall them as soon as we go inside." And then they'd have to hope no other Montagni ships were on their way. "What does Alyna have to say?"

"She's closeted with Shia and Ceannar. They're waiting for you before making any final decisions."

"What do you think we should do?"

"We can't let them get out of the mountains. Once they do, we don't have the numbers to cover the open territory they'll be marching through, not to mention the troops we'll need to commit to the north to deal with Montagn's next move."

"What will we need to hold them in the mountains?" He was glad Ariar had met him out here. Glad for the opportunity to talk freely with a cousin he trusted before running the gauntlet of Alyna and the military commanders.

Even though they'd accepted him as regent, he was on unsteady footing. Nobody knew him yet, not properly. One misstep and he'd lose everything he'd gained.

And that was out of the question.

"All the Greencloaks currently stationed in reserve in the north of Calumnia, plus a legion of SkyRiders." Ariar made a frustrated face. "My Aimsir—although they're already spread thin holding the northern foothills."

"We can't afford to thin the defensive lines in Conmor much more." They were already unsteady. "Not to mention we'll have fewer SkyRiders to defend the eastern coastline and pick off Firthlander ships if we have to divert a legion south."

"The Greencloaks already there can't defend such wide territory alone, not against Bearmen and niever-flyers. And we can't call up more from Ryathl—putting aside how vulnerable that leaves our capital, they wouldn't get there in time."

Cuinn thought on that a moment. "What about the Callanan?"

"Shia might be able to spare a few, but again, it's a numbers game. We're talking about miles and miles of rugged terrain."

There was no good way out of it. No obvious solution.

"Preventing a push south into Calumnia is the priority," Cuinn said eventually. With the resources they had, they could hold the Conmoran border, harry Firthlander ships and prepare for attack from the north. A new front opening up in Calumnia would break them. "So we do whatever we have to do to push them back."

"Attack them in the mountains before they hit the border, hit them hard enough to discourage any further attempts to move south?" Ariar cocked his head. "The forces we'd need for that will thin our northern lines, but hopefully only for a short time. It might work."

"Then that's what we'll do." Cuinn infused his voice with magic, confidence and surety. He and Ariar would walk down to the council room where Alyna and his commanders would have already come to the same conclusion. But he would use that same magic when he agreed with them. And it would give them hope, prevent them from falling into despair.

The Twin Thrones needed the Dumnorix. And Cuinn would keep them strong.

"I'll fly south to Ryathl tonight," he told Ariar as they headed downstairs. "The Calumnian Lords' Council should hear from me directly. I'll do my best to reassure them and work out a way to get more forces north in a hurry in case they make another push after we stymie this one."

Ariar nodded. "You can carry the orders for Soar and my Aimsir too."

"The Twin Thrones will hold, Cousin. We'll make sure of it."

THE COMMANDERS' meeting was quick and decisive. As Cuinn expected, Alyna and her commanders had come to the same conclusion as he and Ariar. He signed the orders to deploy SkyRiders and the Aimsir as part of a concentrated offensive to hit the Firthlanders moving south and disrupt them entirely.

And they would hope it would be enough.

He asked Shia and Ceannar to travel to Ryathl with him—it would be the first time that he was formally introduced to the Lords' Council as regent, and it would help to have the First Blade and First Shield at his side when he addressed them. Never far from his mind was the knowledge that the Twin Thrones had to hold together, or they would lose.

His thoughts were full of what he would say to them as he strode the hallways to his quarters, trailed discreetly by Theac and Evani and several other Kingshield. Theac and Evani followed him through the door—the rest of his detail would array themselves around every conceivable entrance to his quarters, but only his Wolves were allowed inside with him.

He'd only taken two steps before he spotted Saundin sitting in an armchair by the unlit fireplace. Metal rang as his Wolves drew weapons and pushed in front of him.

After a momentary freeze of terror—Azrilan's hounds were never far from his mind, even though he had Kingshield around him at all times now—he snapped, "Stand down. He's a friend."

Theac scowled, but stopped instantly at Cuinn's command. Evani halted too, but stared at the Armun like she wanted him to blink the wrong way so she could teach him a lesson.

Once it was clear Saundin wasn't about to be murdered in front of him, Cuinn took a steadying breath and pretended like he hadn't been momentarily terrified at seeing a strange shadowy man in his rooms. "You couldn't have started a fire?"

"I'd really rather nobody know I was here," Saundin said dryly, apparently unbothered by the fact he'd been seconds away from death. The man hadn't even reached for a weapon.

Hope edged Cuinn's voice before he could hide it. "You've got good news?"

"I've got news."

"My family needs to hear this too." He waved a hand to forestall the inevitable debate. "Theac, please go and invite Ariar up for wine and cards. Invite Alyna too, and have her put her most disapproving face on. The Kingshield guards outside won't see you, Saundin."

"Fine, but I'd appreciate if you were quick about it. I don't have all day."

Cuinn nodded at Theac. He left. Evani took up a watchful position while Cuinn started a fire.

"Tarcos is pushing south for Calumnia." Done with the fire, Cuinn found his saddlebags and began packing the bare necessities.

"I'm aware," Saundin said.

"I'm headed to Ryathl to talk to the Lords' Council."

"A good idea." A pause, then, "I heard you were named regent. A secret Dumnorix… that's quite the revelation."

The door opened before Cuinn could respond, Theac holding it for Ariar and Alyna to enter. He closed it as soon as they were inside and took up a guard position beside Evani.

"Why is a Firthlander Armun hiding out in your quarters, Cuinn?" Ariar held a jug of stoppered wine and three glasses in his hands. Despite his jovial words, his stance had shifted to one of readiness. Alyna looked furious at the sight of Saundin, and her hand unconsciously reached for a weapon before she realised what she was doing.

"His name is Saundin." Cuinn introduced the unsmiling, bearded man. "And he is a man Talyn and Sari trusted. They worked together often."

The Dumnorix visibly relaxed, although Alyna's scowl didn't fade completely. Ariar shrugged and began pouring wine for everyone.

"I requested his assistance several weeks ago," Cuinn added.

"With what?" Alyna demanded. She reluctantly took the glass Ariar offered then sat on a chair opposite Saundin. Ariar sprawled beside the Armun and Cuinn took the fourth chair.

Ariar brightened. "Are you finally going to let us in on your plan?"

Cuinn sat forward, looking at the Armun. "Tell us what you've learned."

"The niever-flyers are unified behind Tarcos, the majority of Bearmen too. The Armun Council is divided, the Shadowlord for now loyal to Tarcos but not happy about his actions. The lords are equally divided—some love Tarcos's territorial ambitions, others see a dangerous war in which lives will be lost for no good purpose." Saundin hesitated, gaze flicking to the Dumnorix. "A good majority hold the middle ground. They don't like war, but they're sympathetic to Tarcos's cause—nobody likes being a vassal of the Twin Thrones."

"But clearly everyone is following their new warlord's orders," Ariar pointed out.

"They are," Saundin confirmed. "And if he continues to win small battles, that will solidify their loyalty. Losses will do the opposite. Having Montagn as an ally helps him too. The more strength Tarcos conveys, the more lords will fall in line with him."

"How do you judge the strength of their forces?" Alyna asked.

"The niever-flyers have been hit hard by your SkyRiders, but more are being trained. And he's building ships too. You're making an impact, and if it were just Firthland in the war, I judge you'd eventually fight them off."

But not if they had to battle the Montagni army too. Saundin didn't need to say it aloud.

Cuinn glanced at his cousin. "You and Tarcos spent a lot of time together when he rode with your Aimsir."

"What of it?" Anger rippled over Ariar's face.

"What did he talk about? Over ales, waiting for battle, that sort of thing."

216

"He was a quiet one." Ariar shrugged. "Didn't like to talk unless he had something worthwhile to say. I liked that about him."

"Did he ever talk about his uncle?"

"Sure. Tarcos wanted to be named heir, that was always obvious." Ariar paused, considering. "But he has a lot of cousins—he used to jokingly talk about how much competition he had."

"But his uncle *did* pick him," Alyna said. "Is there a point to this, Cuinn?"

"He hated one of them!" Ariar said suddenly, straightening in the chair. "Most of the time he spoke about his cousins with a quick joke or polite respect, but he hated Rados. Went on quite the diatribe one night when he drank a little more than he should have."

"Why Rados?" Cuinn asked carefully.

"Called him a daddy's boy. Said he looked for their uncle's respect too much, that he couldn't be his own man. That he valued loyalty over speaking his mind."

Cuinn smiled, a quick thrill of hope running through him, quickly quenched. It was too soon for hope. "Saundin, is Rados still alive?"

"Yes. His father—the previous warlord's younger brother and Tarcos's uncle—has sworn loyalty to Tarcos."

"Even better." Cuinn sat forward. "Do you think you can contact Rados on our behalf? I've got an offer for him."

Saundin made a face. "You don't ask for much, do you?"

CHAPTER 25

Saniya led the way, Talyn and Kaeri directly behind her, with Zamaril and Mithanis bringing up the rear. Cuinn's brother had yet to utter a word, but his angry scowl was reassuringly familiar. Jasper kept pace, almost invisible in the shadows and dim light.

The breeze that had kicked up earlier brought clouds scudding across the darkening horizon, and nightfall arrived with the beginning of a steady, drizzling rain.

It felt good to be on horseback again, and though they weren't Aimsir, the Montagni horses were strong and fleet, bred for the hardy terrain. Saniya forced a hard pace, wanting to make as much ground as possible before stopping to rest.

"How are you doing back there?" Talyn asked Kaeri.

"It damn well hurts, but I'm not dying. Focus your worry on more important things, like how we're going to deal with the inevitable pursuit."

"Fine. I'll stop asking on the condition you agree to tell me when the blood loss approaches fatal."

Kaeri snorted. "Agreed."

Zamaril spoke up. "How quickly do you think they rallied to come after us?"

"Between the magical theatrics and the pet tawncat, I wouldn't be surprised if the remaining soldiers at the camp are more cautious than usual in pursuing. That will help," Saniya responded.

"They might be a little slower, but they'll be coming after us with everything they have," Kaeri countered. "Their commanders won't tolerate losing us. Already messenger birds will be flying to every garrison in this region and soldiers will be riding out to try and cut us off."

Saniya turned to glance at Kaeri, but didn't disagree. Her expression was grim.

Talyn looked ahead, refusing to worry. They were free. They'd figure it out.

THEY PUSHED until the horses began to slow with exhaustion. Not long after midnight, Saniya called a halt by a fast-flowing stream. They dismounted and left the horses to drink and graze.

Talyn glanced at Kaeri, who was biting her lip with pain. Fresh blood seeped through the makeshift bandage she'd wrapped around the arrow still embedded in her shoulder. "We need to take a look at Kaeri's shoulder."

"We can't afford a fire." Saniya glanced around. The rain had cleared a short while ago and faint moonlight shone from above. "Come over here where the light is a little better."

Kaeri propped against a large boulder near the water. Saniya gently peeled away the torn parts of the woman's shirt. "I'll have to take the arrow out so it doesn't fester. Lucky for you it missed bone and went all the way through."

"Do it," Kaeri said tersely.

"Zamaril, go and find something to bind the wound with—we packed healing supplies in the saddlebags of my horse," Talyn ordered. "And if your friend decides to try and murder us while I'm not looking, I'll tear you limb from limb. *After* I'm done with him."

To his credit, Zamaril didn't point out that it had been her decision as much as his to bring Mithanis along on their escape, and obeyed her instructions without a word. Mithanis perched a distance off, gaze hooded, remaining silent.

With a quick, practiced movement Saniya snapped the shaft of the arrow, then gently but firmly drew the arrowhead from Kaeri's shoulder. Throughout, the Montagni princess gritted her teeth and made no complaint. Her skin turned from fair to white in the moonlight though and her hands trembled where they rested at her sides.

"Who are you, anyway?" Kaeri grunted as the last part of the shaft slid from her shoulder with a nauseating sucking sound.

"Saniya Ciantar." She tossed the arrow away and Talyn leaned over to study the wound it had left. Blood seeped from the area, but it wasn't flowing rapidly—a good sign. "You?"

"Kaeri Venador."

Saniya rocked back. "Seriously?"

"Indeed."

Saniya spun to Talyn, eyes flashing. "We broke a Venador out?"

"One who saved my life," Talyn said.

"One who can look after herself." Saniya lifted her hands in the air and stalked off without another word.

Zamaril reappeared, offering bandages and a tiny pot of healing paste. Talyn took them, then glanced at Kaeri. "She doesn't like slavery."

"Ah." An infectious energy vibrated off Kaeri despite the pain she must be in, her bright eyes almost feverish against the paleness of her skin. Talyn knew the feeling—Kaeri had found captivity as difficult as she had. "I assume the anti-slavery lady was the one who got you out? I couldn't believe it when I heard you'd escaped isolation."

"It was Jasper who got me out, but Saniya helped, yes."

"What were you thinking, coming back for me? You should have run and never looked back," she said pointedly.

"I was thinking I wasn't going to escape and leave you and Zamaril behind."

Kaeri scowled, but didn't protest that further. "What about your wounds? How are you doing?"

"I'm stiff and store, but I'll be fine." Talyn briskly smeared paste over Kaeri's wound and then began bandaging her shoulder. "You'll have to keep your arm still to slow the blood flow—the wound needs stitches, but tight bandaging will have to do for now. Zamaril, can you fashion a sling? Use your shirt, there should be a spare one in the saddlebags."

"Your back?" Kaeri's gaze pierced Talyn's.

Talyn looked away. "It's fine. Saniya's people cleaned and re-dressed the scars."

"Is there something I should know?" Zamaril paused in tearing the arms from his shirt and looked between them.

"No." Talyn straightened, holding out her hand for the torn strips of cloth.

Kaeri hissed as Talyn wrapped the long strips in a sling that held her right arm to her chest, something Tiercelin had taught them all to do a long time ago. Once she was satisfied the sling was stable enough, she turned to her Wolf, keen to address their next most immediate problem. "What do we do about Mithanis?"

"I *can* hear you," Mithanis drawled. He remained in what might be considered a watchful position staring back the way they'd come. Or he may have just decided they weren't worth his attention. Jasper lay a short distance away, unblinking green stare focused on the prince of night.

"He speaks," Saniya muttered.

Talyn looked at Mithanis, wondering if he'd heard Saniya give her name earlier. What he thought about it if he had. Despite her confidence that he was an ally, at least for now, she wanted to be sure. "Why did you escape with us? I know you're not a stupid man—aren't you worried we'll kill you and leave your body for the crows?"

He smiled without warmth. "I just blew up a gate and at least twenty soldiers. You're smarter than to think you can kill me in your condition."

It was a good point, but begged the obvious question. "Why didn't you do that months ago when you first arrived in the camp? Why wait to try and plan an escape with Zamaril?"

Mithanis looked away, jaw tight, and Zamaril sniggered, voice full of derision when he spoke. "It's like I said. He's powerful, but the spoiled prince who's never had to do a day's work in his life doesn't know the first thing about navigation or fending for himself. He could have blown himself out, but he'd have been re-captured and likely killed within days."

Again, Mithanis said nothing, but the way he stiffened told Talyn everything she needed to know about the truth in Zamaril's words. The prince of night was an angry, powerful man. But he wasn't a courageous one. He'd never had to be self-sufficient in his life and probably didn't even know where to begin now that he found himself completely alone and cut off from his friends and influence and wealth.

"We can help each other, which makes us allies for now," Talyn said eventually. "But you have to know that if you stay with us, I'm not letting you walk away at the end of this."

"I'm aware," Mithanis said simply. "We escape clean, then you do what you need to do, and I'll do what I need to do."

"*Reassuring.*" Sari sighed.

"*Very.*" Talyn heaved a matching sigh.

"Why didn't Azrilan kill you?" Saniya demanded, staring at Mithanis.

"He loves me." Mithanis barked a contempt-filled laugh. "In some twisted way at least."

"Explain," Talyn snapped when he didn't seem to be planning on elaborating any further.

He scowled. "In case you don't recall, you and my *other* loving brother locked me away after you beat me in the duel. Next thing I know Brightwing and some hulking Firthlander warriors are dragging me out and dumping me in a heap in front of Azrilan. He demanded my allegiance, threatened to cut my wings out if I didn't give it, then proceeded to do exactly that when I refused."

"That doesn't sound like love," Talyn said, refusing to allow herself to feel any sympathy for Mithanis.

"He wanted me with him, at his side. But when I refused, he

couldn't bring himself to kill me. So he removed the one thing that makes me a threat to him, then tossed me away."

Mithanis had song magic. What he claimed might actually be true. And it might explain why Cuinn was alive too. Maybe Azrilan had hesitated in killing him and it had given the Wolves time to get him out.

"His story tracks." Saniya glanced at Talyn. "It's the same thing Azrilan did to Cuinn."

Everything froze.

Talyn sucked in a breath, the words slamming into her midsection like a blow, and she barely noticed as Zamaril went utterly still. "What?"

"Azrilan demanded Cuinn swear allegiance, threatened his wings if he didn't. Your lover gave the same response that Mithanis here did and had his wings mostly butchered before your Wolves could get him out."

"You said he was all right!" Talyn roared the words at her cousin, fists clenched at her sides.

Saniya seemed to finally register the expression on Talyn and Zamaril's faces, and her voice gentled. "He is. Jystar couldn't save the wings, but the last time I saw Cuinn he was fully healed."

Cuinn had lost his wings.

She couldn't even begin to imagine how devastating that must be for him. She wanted to burst into tears, but that wasn't helpful for anyone. Instead she let anger take over. Anger at Azrilan and what he'd done. She swore to herself she'd make him pay for all of it.

"Why didn't you just give Azrilan your allegiance and save yourself?" She rounded on Mithanis, voice coming out as a rasp as she fought to hold back her emotion. His face had gone taut with some undefinable feeling at Saniya's revelation. Her eyes welled, and she furiously scrubbed at them, not wanting him to see.

"The Mithranan crown is mine, Captain Dynan. Nobody else's."

"What a touching sentiment," Saniya said icily.

A silence fell, one which Zamaril broke, his characteristic sneer firmly in place. "Ciantar, now we've sorted the Mithanis issue out, can

I ask why we're trusting the leader of a murderous group who tried to kill us multiple times?"

"What are you talking about?" A dangerous note filled Mithanis's voice.

"Who else do you see helping you escape?" Saniya snapped before Talyn could respond and ignoring Mithanis completely. "It's not like there's a long line of people waiting for the opportunity. A little gratitude would be nice."

"Bickering can wait until we're clear of pursuit." Kaeri strode into the clearing and headed for the horses. "We should keep going."

"She's right," Mithanis grunted, rising to his feet and following her. "You can explain what you meant while we ride."

Talyn stared at him as he passed. Even though it had been her decision, and Zamaril's suggestion, it still seemed impossible they were allied with Mithanis Acondor. The thief gave her a little shrug, then followed the others to the horses.

"It's a shame she's a Venador," Saniya said as Talyn passed. "I can already tell she's far more sensible than you. No ridiculous sentiment, just straight practicality."

"Thanks," Talyn muttered.

"Want me to kill him?"

Talyn paused mid-step. "No. Not yet. You saw what he did back there—we might need that again before this is done."

"I don't want to agree with you." Saniya turned away. "But I do."

THEY RODE on and on and on. Zamaril took obvious delight in filling Mithanis in on who exactly had helped rescue him from a slave camp—the prince of night was predictably furious but seemed to realise he could do little about it—but soon conversation died. The drizzle started up again, turning the ground muddy and slippery and making their tracks far too obvious for comfort. Exhaustion set in, the opened scars in Talyn's back tugging in pain with every movement of the horse under her.

Kaeri's shoulders slowly slumped, a clear sign she was beginning to struggle too. As dawn approached, Saniya slowed their pace, looking for somewhere to stop. Eventually she found a small clearing, surrounded on three sides by a rocky outcrop. Not too far in the distance, the river they'd been following rushed by, heading east.

Zamaril dismounted first before coming over to help Kaeri out of the saddle. She scowled at the offer of assistance, but didn't push him away, an indication she truly was hurting. Talyn swung a leg over the saddle and dropped to the mud. A hiss of pain escaped her despite her best efforts. Jasper padded over, winding around her legs as if to offer comfort.

"How are you going?" she asked Kaeri to mask her own pain. The woman's face was pale and drawn.

"It hurts, but I'll be fine." She spoke through gritted teeth, voice weaker than the last time she'd spoken. Talyn stepped closer, studying the sling and bandage. Fresh blood seeped through, but not an alarming amount.

"The movement on horseback isn't helping," Zamaril offered.

Saniya cast a glance between Talyn and Kaeri that was almost concerned. Almost. "It's not helping Talyn either. We don't have a choice though."

"I'll be fine."

Both Talyn and Kaeri spoke at the same moment, then glanced at each other and smiled wearily.

"We should get a fire going." Mithanis spoke unexpectedly. "Heat water to clean the wounds properly and re-apply clean bandages and paste. The last thing you can afford is infection setting in."

Saniya rounded on him. "Since when do you care, princeling?"

"I care very much about escaping this blasted hole of a country, and my chances of doing that drop rapidly if you all start keeling over from your injuries." Mithanis's temper flashed in his dark eyes. Talyn shivered.

"We're being tracked. If the pursuit is close enough, a fire could reveal our position," Zamaril warned.

"We'll risk it," Talyn said decidedly. She didn't want to take any chances with Kaeri's life. "It's daylight. That will reduce the chances of a fire being spotted."

"No." Saniya's mouth was set in a straight line. "Even if we can't see or hear anything, the pursuit will be closer than you realise. Neither of you are critically wounded, you can hold on till we're clear of Montagn."

Kaeri gave Saniya a pleased look. Zamaril scowled at her tone.

Talyn sided with her Wolf. "You're not in charge here."

"You better believe I am," Saniya snapped. "Who's the one who's done this successfully multiple times before? Who knows about being chased by Montagni soldiers better than any of you?"

Talyn tried to put a lid on her growing temper. Yelling at Saniya would only make the woman angrier. "I respect your knowledge, Cousin, but our pace is going to be a lot flea-shitting slower if Kaeri succumbs to infection or falls off her horse from blood loss. We'll be quick. But we're making a fire."

Saniya stared. "When did I enter the upside-down world of breaking dangerous enemies out of camps and babying slave masters with barely a scratch on their shoulder?"

"You can dispute it if you like," Zamaril cut in, insolent look firmly in place, arms crossed over his chest. "But all three of us—prince of night included—follow what the Ciantar says."

Mithanis opened his mouth as if to protest this, but at a pointed look from Zamaril, he closed his mouth and glowered instead.

Saniya's face hardened, but she capitulated with a terse nod. "I'll see to the horses."

Talyn stepped over to her Wolf, lowering her voice. "I understand your feelings towards Saniya, but she has spent the last months trying to find us, then risking her life, twice, to get us both out of that camp. Drop the attitude. We need her to get home. Am I clear?"

He took a breath, clearly conflicted. "What happened to Prince Cuinn in that rockfall... that's because of her. It's hard for me to let that go."

"For me too. But people aren't all one thing. And they can change."

"I trust you, Ciantar."

She softened, letting out a small sigh. "I'm glad you're here, Zamaril."

He smirked. "I'm glad I'm here too."

She laughed.

SOON THEY HAD a small fire going. Zamaril took Mithanis's offer to fetch fresh water. Once the water heated in a small pan they'd found in one of the spare horse's saddlebags, Zamaril pulled it off the fire, then crouched before Kaeri.

Talyn watched, mesmerized by his steady, rhythmic movements as he thoroughly cleaned Kaeri's shoulder before wrapping it in clean bandages and re-applying the sling.

"You look like you know what you're doing," Saniya commented.

Zamaril smiled, but there was an edge of sadness to it. "Tiercelin made sure we knew how to treat field wounds; he was always nagging us about proper procedures. It was irritating. Jystar was the same. The Stormflight brothers took their duty as our wing's healer very seriously."

Jystar's name rang in the clearing for a moment, both Talyn and Zamaril stiffening slightly. Talyn swallowed, looked at Saniya. "Jystar, did he..."

"Yes," Saniya said immediately. "He was amongst those that got clear of Dock City."

"Will she be all right?" Talyn turned her attention back to Kaeri, her courage failing her when she thought about asking more questions about the Wolves. She cursed herself for the weakness. Eventually she had to ask. The sooner the better. Zamaril shot her a look that indicated he felt the same fear.

"Stop worrying," Kaeri snapped.

"The arrow went clean through, but there is risk of infection." Zamaril finished his work and stepped away. "The sooner we get her to a winged healer, the better."

"Jystar will be where you're going," Saniya said.

"I can wait that long." Kaeri's voice was sharp with irritation. "Quit coddling the slave master and take a look at Talyn's back."

"Kaeri—"

"Stop pretending you're fine." Kaeri barreled right through Talyn's warning tone. "I can tell how much pain you're in from how carefully you're holding yourself. We both know what happened to you."

"Ciantar?" Zamaril looked at her, concern creeping over his face.

Talyn glared at Kaeri for a long moment, jaw clenched.

"Don't be an idiot," Sari said primly. *"Let him take a look. Mithanis was right before, you won't do anyone any good if you keel over before you get home."*

"Fine." She turned around and gingerly began unbuttoning her shirt, holding it to her chest for modesty but revealing her back to him.

"Six thrices!" Zamaril sounded like he was torn between crying and throttling someone. "They did this to you?"

"Yes."

She flinched as Zamaril gently touched her back. "Your scars have been bleeding. I don't know how you stayed on a horse all day."

"Just clean it up as best you can. I'll be fine."

He did as she bade, and Talyn gritted her teeth as he cleaned out the opened scars and then bound them gently. Once he was done, she gratefully pulled her shirt and jacket back on and sat in front of the fire.

Her gaze fell on Mithanis. Shifted away. Went back. She huffed an annoyed sigh. "What about your back?"

"No whipping for me," he said morosely, biting pain in his voice. "The scars from my wing removal healed within weeks of arriving at the camp."

Zamaril settled beside her and Talyn leaned into him. She closed her eyes, taking warmth and comfort from the presence of such a trusted friend. She was gladder than she could ever say that he was there.

"That's it for the bandages and herbal paste," he said to nobody in particular. "What I've done will have to hold until we make it to Acleu."

"It's another two days' hard ride," Saniya said. "Providing our pursuers don't catch up before then, we should be fine. We can get more supplies there."

"We should leave now." Kaeri made as if to rise but Saniya stopped her with a look.

"The horses need to drink and graze or we'll lose them. Another full-turn at least."

"We should kill the fire though," Zamaril said with a little smile for Saniya. "Mithanis, be a good prince and go fetch some water to throw on it."

Mithanis scowled and opened his mouth for what would no doubt be a furious retort, but when all gazes swung expectantly to him, he stood and stalked off. Saniya tipped her head in Zamaril's direction.

Silence fell. It was too loud, full of the questions Talyn hadn't asked yet and the answers she was terrified to hear. She told herself to summon her courage and get it done. The anxiety and fear would only wear on her strength otherwise.

"Saniya." Talyn hesitated. "We need to know what happened. Everything. You said the Wolves managed to get Cuinn out of the citadel and flee Dock City. Did they have to fight their way out?"

Her cousin turned towards them, tone brisk. "Yes. Azrilan allied himself with some Firthlander prince who'd brought a force of Bearmen with him to help Azrilan take the citadel from Cuinn. The Wolves had to fight through—"

"Firthlander prince?" Talyn interrupted.

"Tarcos Hadvezer."

The world went still. Talyn sat up, shoulders turning rigid, almost knocking Zamaril over in the process. "What are you talking about?"

Sari said nothing, but her shock and horror rippled through Talyn's mind.

"I don't know the whole story." Saniya seemed to be making an effort to hold back her impatience. "But Hadvezer used his ships and Bearmen to help Azrilan take the Mithranan crown." Saniya glanced up as Mithanis stalked back into the clearing and tossed a pan of water on the fire. "And when Cuinn refused to swear loyalty to Azrilan, well... I told you what happened. Your Wolves intervened and got him out of the palace and down to Dock City."

Horror crawled up Talyn's throat and soured her stomach. "I brought Tarcos to Mithranar with me. I thought he was my friend, my... why would he...?" How could she have gotten it so wrong? *Tarcos?* It didn't make sense.

"As far as I understand it, Tarcos and Azrilan had an alliance. Tarcos helped Azrilan take both Montagni and Mithranan thrones, and Azrilan agreed to help Tarcos take the Twin Thrones in return," Saniya said.

She felt ill.

Now that the entire puzzle was in front of her, Talyn put the pieces together in seconds. Vengeance, the Shadows and niever-flyers. There was never a Montagni invasion, only a cleverly laid trap by Firthland, by Tarcos and his Shadow, Savin. To de-stabilise Mithranar for Azrilan to step in and take over, to have them all looking at Montagn while Firthland crept into the Twin Thrones. Only by concentrating fiercely could she stop her entire body from visibly shaking. She bit her lip hard enough to draw blood.

She'd missed it. She'd taken Tarcos as a lover and hunted Vengeance and missed what was really going on right in front of her.

"*Talyn, you can't—*"

"*Don't,*" she cut Sari off savagely. "*Just don't.*"

Zamaril spoke into the heavy silence. "How did they even know each other?"

"Az travelled to Firthland with Tarich Swiftwing when we were younger." Mithanis spoke unexpectedly, bitterness making his voice shake. "He would have been eighteen or so. They must have met then. Seems both my brothers have been lying and manipulating me their entire lives."

"You can't seriously expect us to feel sorry for you?" Kaeri asked scornfully. "From what I know, you spent your whole life terrorising them both. You did this to yourself."

"You need to tell us..." Zamaril hesitated, visibly gathered himself. "The Wolves. Who made it, Saniya?"

Talyn's eyes squeezed shut, desperately needing to hear the answer but utterly terrified of it at the same time. The Tarcos revelation already had her raw, off balance, but part of her knew this was going to be worse. Glancing down, she became aware of Jasper lying across her feet, green eyes fixed on her face. His nose nudged her ankle, offering silent comfort.

"I'm here," Sari whispered.

Saniya glanced between Talyn and Zamaril, looking uncomfortable at the depth of their emotion. "When we were fleeing the citadel, Cuinn sent Theac and Corrin to get their family and escape the blockade—he wanted them to get to the Twin Thrones for safety but also to warn the Dumnorix about Tarcos. I don't know if they made it out. Of your other talons, Andres, Liadin and Lyra made it safely north."

Talyn's indrawn breath resonated through the morning and Zamaril's arm resting against hers turned rigid. Tears spilled down her cheeks. "Halun?" she managed.

Saniya shook her head. "He took on several Bearmen so that Cuinn and the others could get clear. He didn't make it. I'm sorry."

She couldn't breathe. The grief was a live creature inside her, thrashing and kicking. A sob escaped her, and another one, until she was hunched over, head in her hands, mortified but unable to stop crying. Zamaril's arm came around her and she turned to bury her head in his chest as his tears soaked the skin of her neck. They clung to each other, sobbing.

Halun. Not Halun.

"I'm so sorry, Talyn," Sari whispered.

"This is my fault."

"No, it's not." The words were like a slap, they were spoken with such force.

"I trusted Tarcos."

"And Cuinn trusted Azrilan. There's no blame in trusting someone you care about."

Eventually the sobs faded in intensity and she was able to wrangle them under control. Sniffing, she pulled away from Zamaril. His face was streaked with tears, but as his blue eyes met hers she saw only strength written in them. Determination. The unflagging support of a friend who would always have her back, no matter what. She nodded acknowledgement of that and he managed a little smile.

"I will destroy Tarcos."

"And I will help." Sari's voice was as cold as hers.

THEY SET out again when Kaeri's impatience won over Saniya's insistence they let the horses rest. Mithanis had become even more withdrawn. Talyn guessed that the raw grief still resonating through both her and Zamaril was testing his song magic. He probably didn't know what to do with an emotion like love, like grieving someone so much it was hard to draw breath.

Saniya took the lead again, with Talyn behind, burying her pain in rage, using the heat of it to stay in the saddle despite exhaustion. Zamaril and Mithanis brought up the rear. The terrain was rough, and most of the time the best they could do was keep the horses at a fast walk. By nightfall, the exhausted animals were stumbling with nearly every step, and it was clear Kaeri was struggling with the pain in her shoulder.

Saniya called a halt in another sheltered clearing, and there was no fire this time as they huddled together out of the stiff breeze.

"They'll have picked up our trail by now." Kaeri sat hunched over, face deathly pale in the faint moonlight. "And there will be Berserkers and soldiers from every barracks between our camp and the east coast out searching for us."

"I wish we could work out how close they are," Talyn said.

Kaeri shook her head. "Birds fly faster than we've been moving. They could be ahead of us by now. We have to hope they haven't guessed where we're heading."

"How long to Acleu?" Zamaril asked Saniya.

"Another day at least. The forest clears up soon—there is a lot of farming land between us and the port. That means we'll be able to move faster, but we'll also be more visible."

"You don't think we'll make it to Acleu without being spotted." Talyn heard it in her cousin's voice.

"We've never hit a camp so openly before. The Montagni will be furious, and they won't let something like that go. Even if they don't know exactly where we're going, the terrain between here and Acleu will be crawling with soldiers and Berserkers."

Talyn thought about that for a moment. "What if we don't go to Acleu, veer north instead? Try and find passage from a smaller port on the coast."

"There isn't one. Three days' ride north of Acleu, the mountains start. The only harbour between is Mandau. It's primarily a fishing village and it's small. We'll be noticed the moment we step foot there, and there's a Berserker barracks on the north side of the town." Saniya ran a hand through her hair. "I have a contact there, but we wouldn't reach him before getting caught, and we'd blow his identity in the process."

Kaeri huffed in annoyance. "You shouldn't have come back for us, Talyn."

"Well, she did, so how about showing a little gratitude," Saniya snapped.

Surprisingly, Kaeri smiled. "Fair point. I'm hurting and grouchy because of it. And like you, Saniya, I know how the Montagni operate. I know how small our chances of getting out of this place are."

Talyn expected a snarky comment along the lines of Kaeri being one of the people now hunting them, but Saniya accepted her comment with a little nod.

"You're planning on leaving Montagn with us?" Mithanis enquired of Kaeri, speaking for the first time. He looked menacing in the firelight with his pale skin and dark eyes, but the words were oddly mild.

"As a slave, there is nowhere safe for me here now," Kaeri said. There was bitterness in her words, as much as she tried to hide it.

"We should get some rest." Saniya stood and wrapped her thin blanket around herself. "I'll take first watch, Mithanis you're next. Zamaril after that. Five full-turns and we're on the move again."

"I'm not sleeping while the prince of night is on watch," Zamaril grumbled.

Talyn couldn't help but agree.

"And I'm not a fragile flower," Kaeri added. "I'll take Mithanis's watch."

Mithanis gave them all a scornful look, and wrapped himself in a blanket before closing his eyes. "Suits me just fine."

Talyn curled up on the ground, trying to get comfortable and failing, before closing her eyes. Her body shivered with cold, but just as she'd decided there was no way she'd be able to sleep, a warm body pressed against hers.

Jasper.

Once again swallowing back tears, Talyn turned towards the tawn-cat, one hand reaching out to press gently against his side.

And then she slept.

"Noooooooooooooooooo!" Talyn came awake screaming, horror gripping her down to her very bones. Her body was stiff with cold, the blanket half-off. Jasper was gone.

"Talyn!" Kaeri called out to her, but Zamaril reached her first, closing a palm over her mouth.

"Shush," he murmured in her ear. "You're fine, you're safe."

She shoved him off, unable to bear the feeling of being held down. She couldn't even remember what the nightmare had been about, she just knew she had to get free, to escape, to not be where she was.

"Keep her quiet!" Saniya hissed.

A moment later magic wrapped around her emotions, a soothing calm, trying to draw away her panic. Revulsion surged through her as she instantly recognised its source.

"Stay away from me!" Talyn launched herself at Mithanis, crashing into him and sending them both rolling over the ground. Zamaril's arms wrapped around her, pulling her off, while Saniya stepped into the space between them.

"Do you *want* to call down any searcher in the area on us?" she demanded.

"I was just trying to help." Mithanis spat blood from a newly split lip.

"Keep your magic away from me." Talyn had calmed enough to keep her voice low, even though it shook with anger. "Do you hear me? Never touch me again."

"Fine." Mithanis lifted his hands in the air in scornful surrender.

"Where's Jasper?" Talyn asked.

"Gone hunting," Zamaril said. "Or scouting our back trail. The tawncat is creepily intelligent."

Kaeri appeared at her shoulder. "Nightmare?"

Talyn looked away. "I'm sorry."

"Don't be. Just get back to sleep." Saniya strode back to her blankets. "You go near her again, prince of night, and I'll skewer you myself."

Talyn didn't stop shaking for hours. She certainly didn't sleep again.

And in the full-turn before dawn, when Zamaril roused them to start moving, a dog howled in the distance.

The pursuit had found them.

CHAPTER 26

*J*asper reappeared as the morning sun rose toward the centre of the sky, dried blood spattering his muzzle and paws. The howls and barking of the tracking dogs had been growing closer and closer before stopping suddenly a half-turn earlier—it seemed Jasper had found them.

"Now they're on us, they'll still be able to follow our tracks in this muddy ground," Saniya said tersely. "And they'll be on fresh horses. We need to move faster."

But the horses were floundering, and they couldn't get more than a brief canter out of them before they sagged back to a trot and then a fast walk. By mid-morning, the trees began to thin, and then a quarter-turn later ended completely.

Rolling farmland spread away to the north and east. Workers dotted the fields. A wide road snaked down from the north until hitting a crossroads where several buildings sat. More roads diverged from it.

"From here to Acleu it's a ride of two full-turns at a gallop. At least three full-turns at a pace these horses can manage. And villages or towns everywhere," Saniya said.

"*I don't like it, Sari.*" It was too open. They'd be horribly vulnerable on their weary horses.

"*Neither do I.*"

"Not to mention barracks," Kaeri added. "By now the soldiers in Acleu would have been warned to look out for our arrival. We'll be stuck between them and the soldiers behind us. We should veer north, away from Acleu. Bide our time, come back when the search dies down."

"We have no healing supplies left and limited food. When they don't find us, they'll increase the search zone, not reduce it. We might stay ahead of them for a while, but then what?" Zamaril shook his head. "We need to get out now, or we never will."

"He's right," Mithanis said. "We have to go now."

Saniya looked over at Talyn. "There might be another way."

"Tell us."

"This forest stretches south for several miles, then curves around and back up the coastline, almost to the southern edge of Acleu. It'll add at least a half day to our journey, but it forces our pursuit to move as slowly as us."

"Adding a half day to our journey also increases the chances they catch up to us," Zamaril pointed out.

Saniya nodded. "But it's also the path they'll least expect us to take. And we'll be hidden within thick forest."

"I know the route you're talking about, and we'll be lucky if it only adds a half day to our journey. The forest runs a good distance south before curving back up towards Acleu." Kaeri sounded uncertain. "But I don't think we'll make it if we take the direct route. Even staying off the roads."

"How are we getting into Acleu?" Talyn asked. "I assume there will be soldiers posted on the main entries?"

"We have to expect that, yes. But I can sneak us into Acleu without going through the main gates—it's the access we always use, and it's through the south city wall," Saniya said.

"Then we keep to the forest," Talyn said decidedly.

"Do you have a plan for when we're inside the city? Because they will hunt the streets for us. Our soldiers are disciplined, methodical and determined," Kaeri pushed. "We won't be able to hide long in Acleu."

"We won't need to. We'll be out and across the channel within a day or two," Saniya assured her.

Talyn glanced back, her hearing catching on something. She could see nothing through the unending line of trees, but in the faint distance the thud of hoofbeats was just audible.

"And if we can't sneak in unnoticed?" Zamaril asked the obvious question.

"Then we fight our way in and lose them in the streets. We'll have a fighting chance once we're in. My people will be waiting for us and they'll help." Saniya glanced up again. "It's going to be dark in a full-turn or so. That will help too."

DARKNESS SETTLED OVER THE FOREST, and with it a steadily increasing tension. Every step the horses took south was a step further away from Acleu, another layer of anxiety to add to the tension.

It only relaxed slightly once they were finally able to veer east. The closer they came to Acleu, the louder the sounds of pursuit behind them grew. When the moon appeared briefly from behind a cloud, Talyn could just make out the glitter of moonlight on dark ocean through a gap in the trees to their right.

They'd crossed a main road leading to the port city a full-turn earlier, creeping across with their horses one by one in between passing traffic.

"That road is the quickest way in, but they'll be watching it," Saniya explained in an undertone while she and Talyn waited for the others to cross first. "They might have lookouts on the walls too, which is why I want to follow the coastline in—it's forest all the way."

"Won't watchers on the walls still spot us once we break the tree line?"

Saniya shook her head. "The southern edge of the city is the slums —the wall there is crumbling and broken in several places and parts of it are patched up with rotting wood. Patrols are sporadic. My people will be watching the entry and waiting to get us through to a safe-house. We'll hunker down there, wait for the search to move on, then we'll head for the docks and get on a boat."

It sounded simple. Well-practiced. And Saniya's team were experienced. But Talyn worried anyway.

The sound of galloping hoofbeats grew to a steady rumble behind them—Talyn guessed at least thirty riders by the level of noise, maybe more. That was a lot more than she'd hoped for. More than she and Mithanis could deal with given how weary and hungry they both were.

A wind whipped up from the north, bringing with it the salty smell of the ocean mixed with the less desirable smells of a packed and poor living area—the slums of Acleu. Hope stirred in her chest. Maybe they would make it.

All of them were constantly glancing back now, even Jasper. Tension hummed in the air, anxiety filling the empty spaces, compounding the emotion. Talyn's horse stumbled in the darkness, almost going down. The sound of approaching riders grew louder.

"Nearly there," Saniya said tersely.

Less than a minute later, excited cries broke out behind them, frighteningly close. A glance back showed riders visible through the darkness—the fastest of their pursuers. They'd been spotted.

Talyn swore under her breath, digging her heels into her horse's side, trying to urge him into a final gallop.

And then they broke out of the trees. A stretch of flat, grassy ground stood between them and the southern wall of Acleu.

Their horses were lathered in sweat, chests heaving, barely able to manage a canter despite their riders' urging. Saniya steered her horse to the right, heading towards a section of stone wall. It wasn't until they were much closer that Talyn made out a wooden plank set in a narrow gap between two crumbling sections of wall. It had been painted the same grey colour as the stone, and was barely noticeable. Talyn had no idea how Saniya had even seen the gate in the dim light.

The excited shouts behind them grew louder and riders boiled out of the trees in pursuit, eagerly spurring their mounts on. Arrows whistled through the night air towards them.

Talyn swore, spun, lifted her hand and summoned her bright sapphire Callanan shield. It leapt into existence between the arrows and Zamaril's lagging horse. Arrows rained down into it and she grunted, slumping with the effort of keeping such a large shield aloft.

"Drop it!" Mithanis bellowed.

He was turned on his horse too, one hand holding white-knuckled to his pommel, the other raised and wreathed in black light. Talyn dropped the shield, waited until Mithanis had sent three bursts of warrior magic at the pursuers, then raised it again.

Saniya's horse reached the gate first. She reined in, kicked out with her foot to send the gate slamming open, then urged the exhausted animal through. Kaeri went through after, glancing back to gauge where the others were.

Talyn's chest heaved as she reined in by the gate. What seemed to be a full unit of mounted cavalry bore down on them—Mithanis and Zamaril were barely ahead. The lead riders had replaced bows with drawn swords, and she dropped her shield.

"Go!" Zamaril bellowed at her. "GO!"

She kicked her horse into reluctant movement, urging him through the narrow gap, knowing she had to get clear so Zamaril and Mithanis could come through behind her.

Her horse stumbled into a narrow alleyway lined with brick build- ings. The alley widened just past the gate, wide enough to bring her horse up beside Kaeri. Saniya waited just ahead. Several hundred meters away, another street crossed the end of the alley, but it was equally dark, so not a main thoroughfare. All three of them turned back to watch the narrow opening in the wall. By tacit agreement they refused to move until Mithanis and Zamaril made it safely through.

The stench of sewerage mixed with seaweed hung thick in the alley. Talyn coughed and switched to breathing through her mouth. Shouts and hoofbeats filled the night air, the ground rumbling under their feet.

Moments later, Zamaril and Mithanis clattered through the gate.

The prince of night tried to kick it shut behind them, but it was slammed back open by the first Montagni through.

Shit.

An axe cracked into wood, splintering the makeshift wooden wall around the gate so that more riders could get through.

"Talyn, come on!" Saniya shouted, urging her horse forward.

She hesitated, breath catching as the lead Montagni swung his sword at Zamaril's head. The thief ducked. An arrow whistled from beyond the gate, thudding into the wall near Mithanis's arm.

Talyn waited until Zamaril reached her, then dug her heels in to force her floundering horse after Saniya. They needed to get clear of the archers, lose the horses in the street. They...

A strangled cry sounded behind.

Talyn spun back, eyes widening as the lead Montagni fell backwards out of the saddle, an arrow embedded in his throat. More arrows fired in quick succession and took down the three riders behind him. She looked up, where a hooded archer perched on the nearest roof, firing in an unbelievably quick rhythm.

Another hooded figure dropped from the opposite roof, landing right beside Talyn's horse and flashing her a bright grin. "Time to move on foot. Let the horses clog up the alley."

Talyn stared, unbelieving. She'd know that voice anywhere. "Levs!"

The Callanan warrior stared back, astonishment widening her eyes an almost comical amount.

Leviana was the first to regain her senses. "Talyn." Leviana reached up, squeezed her hand. "You have no idea how good it is to see you, friend, but no time for chatter. Let's move."

Reason reasserted itself. "Kaeri, go, you first," she ordered, ducking as a stray arrow whistled through the air.

At the tone of her voice, Kaeri didn't argue.

Zamaril was already dismounting. "Is that Cynia up there on the roof?" he asked.

Leviana nodded. "She'll keep them at bay till I get you clear."

"You were waiting for us." Talyn smothered a wince as she

dropped to the ground and they began moving. Ahead, Saniya was dismounting too.

"It's a long story, but we've been working with the Shadowhawk's network here in Acleu. Word came from one of their contacts that some escaped slaves were coming this way and might have half the army on their heels." Leviana reached Saniya, looked at her. "Who are you?"

"Saniya. That's *my* people you're talking about." Saniya sounded snappish.

"Colm's one of yours?" Leviana waited for the nod. "All right, get out of here. They've got the Lister Street safehouse set up and waiting —you know where it is. I'm going to join Cynia. We'll lead them a merry chase away from Lister Street then double back to meet you there."

Saniya moved off without another word, turning left onto the street ahead. Zamaril, Mithanis and Kaeri followed. Talyn stopped Leviana, drawing her into a brief hug. "Thank you."

Leviana hugged her back fiercely. "I had no idea it was you. You okay, Tal?"

She nodded. "I will be."

And she would. She was free. She had her friends with her now.

And soon she'd see Cuinn and her Wolves.

CHAPTER 27

hey reached the safehouse within a quarter-turn. Several blocks from where they'd left their pursuers, it was in a quiet, rundown area. A baby cried nearby and chickens clucked in the neighbour's tiny yard. Saniya lingered briefly out front to speak with Colm and Tari while Talyn and the others headed inside.

Talyn dropped into a chair, a gasp of pain escaping her. The journey had taken six days and all of them were exhausted, hungry and hurting.

Mithanis took one look at the sleeping pallets and blankets on the floor and went straight over to drop onto one. Zamaril shared a look with Talyn and then walked over to keep a close eye on the prince of night.

"Get some sleep," Saniya said as she entered and closed the door. "You'll be safe—Colm and Tari will warn us if the search for you gets too close. There are food supplies in the next room when you wake, and I'll get more healing supplies here as soon as I can."

Talyn stared for a moment. After so long running and hiding, it was strange to suddenly be able to relax. "Are you sure?"

Saniya smiled suddenly, her whole face lighting up. "That look right there. The one slaves get when we tell them they're safe. That's why I do this."

"I'm sorry Savin twisted that," Talyn said quietly.

"I let him do it, because I was angry and felt hopeless. The blame is mine, and I accept it." Guilt and bitterness warred in her eyes. "Now rest, please. I need you strong for when it comes time to leave."

"She's an interesting person," Kaeri murmured as she and Talyn curled up beside each other as far from Mithanis they could get, Jasper on Talyn's other side. "She's impressively practical and tough, doesn't take nonsense from anyone. But she uses those attributes to help slaves, of all things."

"You think there's something wrong with that?" Talyn asked, an edge to her voice.

"It's not that. I just... I never thought about slaves as needing help."

"Until you became one?" Talyn didn't want to be angry at her friend, but that level of ignorance was astounding.

Kaeri didn't answer. She turned away and closed her eyes. Soon her breathing sounded the regular rhythm of sleep.

Talyn closed her eyes, reached out to press her hand against Jasper's side, and joined Kaeri in sleep.

FEELING MARGINALLY BETTER when she woke, she looked for Zamaril. He was nearby, sitting with his back against the wall, keeping an eye on her. Kaeri and Mithanis slept on. Jasper too.

"Did you sleep?" she whispered.

"A half-turn or so, that's all I needed. You've been out for two full-turns." He answered her next question before she had to ask it. He glanced over at Mithanis, mouth tightening. "He slept the whole time too."

"We can't take him back with us." Talyn kept her voice low in case the prince of night was faking sleep.

"I..." Zamaril made a frustrated noise. "Maybe we should."

"Take a murderous heir to the throne back to Mithranar? How is that a good idea?"

"What if he's not?"

"What?" Her tired thoughts were easily confused.

"He's angry all the time, and he's obsessed with being king... and he ordered the execution of Falcons for treason." Zamaril winced as the words came out, presumably hearing how they sounded. "But is he a murderer? We've assumed it all this time, but who do you *really* think killed Raya or set off the explosion in our barracks?"

"I think it doesn't matter," Talyn said wearily. "I think he remains a threat to Cuinn, and we're fools if we take him back with us."

"Maybe we could use him. He hates Azrilan as much as we do."

"*He might have a point,*" Sari murmured.

"*I doubt it.*"

The front door opened, and Talyn clambered gingerly to her feet when Leviana and Cynia walked through, both their faces creasing into grins when they saw her.

"You have no idea how good it is to see you." She hugged Cynia fiercely. "Thank you for saving us back there."

"Tal, to see your face back in that alley... it was beyond surprising. We've been worried sick." Leviana sounded tired, some of her usual ebullience gone.

"I barely believed it when Levs told me." Cynia squeezed her hand. "We feared the worst."

"Your face... they made you a slave?" Leviana's eyes turned dark with smoldering fury. "The Dumnorix are going to raze Montagn to the ground."

Talyn smiled gently. "The tattoo doesn't bother me, not at all."

"What happened, Tal?" Cynia searched her face, clearly still worried and upset.

"I'm sorry. It's a long tale to tell, probably best for once we're safely out of here and have the time," Talyn said. It was an excuse, a stalling tactic. She didn't have the strength to go through it right now. "What are you both doing in Acleu?"

"Another long tale to tell." The partners shared a glance. "But one you should hear now."

Glancing at Mithanis's sleeping form, Talyn gestured towards the other room. They filed in there, Zamaril too, and closed the adjoining door, leaving only a narrow gap through which they could keep an eye on the prince of night. This room had supplies stacked haphazardly along the far wall, and Zamaril immediately began foraging.

Talyn settled with her friends and Zamaril joined them shortly after, handing out cheese, bread and a flagon of water. They both dove in hungrily while the Callanan told their tale.

"Cuinn's in the Twin Thrones, that's the first thing you should know," Cynia said bluntly.

Talyn stilled in shock. "He's *what?*"

"We saw him with our own eyes." Cynia shared a glance with her partner. "It was his idea to send us here with a small group of Callanan warriors."

"To provide early warning of Montagni naval ships departing south towards the Twin Thrones," Leviana added.

"The first lot of six ships set out just under a month ago. Two days back we got word that they were destroyed by SkyRiders," Cynia finished.

"That's a smart move," Talyn said, thinking quickly. "But it won't work forever. Azrilan will work out you're here and—"

"Already happening. This city is crawling with Armun and Shadows—two Callanan were killed last week along with three members of the Shadowhawk network, which has merged with Vengeance. Saniya told you about that?" Leviana paused, and Talyn nodded. "They're good, Tal. Really good. We wouldn't have gotten half the information we have without them."

Talyn shook her head, trying to process all of that. Cuinn was in the Twin Thrones? Bitter disappointment filled her at the realisation he wasn't in the SkyReach with her Wolves. But she pushed that aside —he was clearly helping her family in some way. But why had he gone there?

Cynia's next words drew her back to the present. "We're seeing troop buildups outside the city—I was out scouting the other day and watched rows and rows of soldiers marching into a temporary camp. Wilin and Tapper are in Darinoue and they report the same. We suspect the new ahara is planning on sending a larger fleet next time… one big enough to overwhelm any defence the Twin Thrones tries to put up."

"Not to mention we're hearing whispers that Tarcos has agreed to send some of his niever-flyers to help protect the next war fleet," Leviana said.

Talyn lifted a hand to her forehead, rubbed absently at the ache building there. "If that's what eventuates, you can do some damage before the ships leave port, right?"

"You bet. That kind of war fleet will take weeks to prepare—some of the ships are still being built, we think, so we have time to plan," Leviana said enthusiastically.

"It won't be easy. You know how good the Armun are, Tal. We have to keep moving around to avoid being caught, and once they catch our trail, those Shadows are damned hard to lose," Cynia pointed out. "Levs and I almost got cornered by one last week."

Talyn nodded. "How have you been getting messages south? Birds?"

"Mostly," Leviana said. "But doing it that way is risky—we have no way of verifying whether the birds reach Port Lachley safely, not to mention we don't have an infinite supply. When we can, we sneak someone onto a merchant ship heading south—there's still a little bit of trade but it's drying up—and then the First Blade tries to get someone on a ship back. It's not perfect."

"Can you get a message to Cuinn and my family that I'm alive?" she asked.

Leviana smiled, reached across to wrap an arm around her shoulder. "Absolutely. If it's possible to be even more worried and heartsick than Cynia and I were, then that's how to describe your family."

She bit her lip. "And Cuinn was okay?"

The partners shared a glance and it was Cynia who answered, gently, "You know he lost his wings?"

Talyn nodded, unable to say anything around the lump in her throat.

"He was clearly badly shaken by what had happened, and probably finding it hard to put one foot in front of the other, but he was upright and clear-headed." Cynia shared another look with her partner. "There's something else you should know. He was attacked by a Shadow—Azrilan has apparently sent a group of them hunting Cuinn. Calls them his hounds. Another lovely gift from Tarcos."

A cold shudder swept through Talyn, and not just because of the stark danger Cuinn was in. "Tarcos has given him so much. There's no way Azrilan backs out of this war."

"No," Cynia said quietly.

Leviana straightened suddenly, excitement in her brown eyes. "I'm so sorry, Tal, we should have told you straight up—Corrin and Theac and their family were there too, safe and sound. Cuinn sent Corrin back to Mithranar, but Theac stayed with him. And we've had word that Corrin made it to Darmour safely."

Talyn and Zamaril looked at each other, Zamaril's pale blue eyes shining. He bit his lip, turned away. She reached out to squeeze his arm.

Thank everything. Theac and Corrin were okay. She could breathe.

"What were Cuinn's plans?" she asked her friends.

"We don't know. He wouldn't tell us—he figured the fewer people who knew, the better, given the Armun on his tail," Cynia said, then glanced at Leviana. "But we suspect it has something to do with his... connection... to your family."

Talyn frowned. Had he gone to her family for protection, hoping they'd see it as their obligation? No, Cuinn wasn't the type to hide out somewhere while Mithranar was in danger. He'd gone there for a reason. She wondered... Her heart thudded.

Did he have it in him? Of course he did, though he might not realise it himself.

"What am I missing?" Zamaril asked, eyes narrowing in suspicion.

The front door creaked open and then closed, saving Talyn from figuring out how to answer. A moment later the interior door opened and Saniya ducked her head in before pushing it open. In the room beyond, the sound had woken Kaeri and Mithanis, and they pushed off their blankets, looking expectantly at Talyn and Saniya.

Talyn gathered some of the bread and cheese she and Zamaril hadn't eaten and carried it through to the others.

"Everything is ready—your boat is being prepared as we speak," Saniya explained. She placed a leather satchel on the nearby table and began unpacking bandages and small jars of ointment and paste. "Even better, soldiers are searching the city for us, but it doesn't seem like they have any idea where we are."

Zamaril immediately took some of the supplies and gestured to Talyn's back. Making sure she was out of the Callanan's eyeline, she lifted her shirt so he could work on her scars. "When do we leave?"

"At dawn." Saniya glanced between Talyn and Kaeri. "That's when the fishing boats leave, and Toscal can hide amongst them. Make sure you tend those wounds properly. We need you up for a solid hike once we reach the Mithranan coast."

"What's wrong with you?" Leviana asked, gaze fierce on Talyn's.

"I'm fine. Just an old injury that opened up in the escape." She dismissed her friend's concern.

"Sure," Cynia said, clearly not believing a word. "Saniya, we'll be going with you. I assume you can make room?"

"You can't," Saniya said flatly. "The work you're doing here is too valuable for you to leave, especially now the Armun are hunting us. My people are good, but they need your protection to be able to oper-ate. I'll make sure Talyn stays safe."

"There are six other warrior pairs in Montagn, and Talyn is a Dumnorix who has been gone for months. We're not letting her out of our sight," Cynia said cheerfully. "So we'll be coming with you."

Talyn opened her mouth. "I don't really need you to—"

Leviana speared her with a look. "Talyn, sometimes I think you imagine you're the only one who lost Sari. Cynia and I have no inten-tion of losing another dear friend, especially when we've been franti-cally worried about you for months and feared we had lost you."

Mithanis snorted in disgust and turned his attention back to his food. Saniya and Kaeri shared rolled eyes. Zamaril smiled to himself, gathering up bandages and paste and moving over to look at Kaeri's shoulder.

Trying not to wince, Talyn stepped closer to her friends, lowering her voice. "I'm sorry, I don't mean to be so cavalier. But Saniya says what she means. If she says your work here is invaluable, then you have to stay. I love you both, but I'm going back to my Wolves. I'll be safe with them."

Cynia glanced at her partner. "Do we really want to trust Durran and Teer with sabotaging a Montagni war fleet?"

Leviana shuddered. "No. But I don't want to leave Tal again either."

"We do what we have to," Talyn said quietly. "And we'll see each other again, I promise."

"Not to mention being able to keep in regular contact via our network," Saniya pointed out in irritation.

"Cheer up, Levs." Cynia nudged her partner with a smile. "You didn't really want to miss out on the opportunity to sabotage a bunch of stuff, did you?"

Saniya cleared her throat, looked at the Callanan. "Will you two go on ahead and make sure no surprises are waiting for us at the usual spot on the docks? We'll be right behind."

Leviana and Cynia nodded, winked at Talyn, and slipped out the door.

"What are you going to do about him?" Saniya jerked a thumb at Mithanis.

Talyn glanced at Zamaril, then went over to stand before the prince of night. The thief followed, hovering protectively at her shoulder. Mithanis's jaw tightened as he glanced between them. "What?"

"You've got two choices," she said calmly. "One, you leave us now, and try to survive on the streets of Acleu while Armun, Shadows and Berserkers hunt you. I won't ask the Callanan to help or protect you, and I wouldn't count on Saniya's people doing it either. Still, I will let you walk if that's your choice."

"And my second choice?" he snarled.

"We take you to Mithranar with us, and you go back to being a prisoner. We'll keep you comfortable, and we won't touch you, but you'll be locked up."

Fury tightened his features to the murderous expression of the dangerous man she remembered. "Until?"

"Until Cuinn decides what to do with you. As was always the plan."

"That's all you offer, after I helped you escape that camp, helped save your life?" he snarled.

"That's all I offer the man who executed innocent Falcons and treated the humans of Mithranar like they were nothing more than dirt under his shoe," she said coolly. "You should count yourself lucky. I could do a lot worse."

His entire body tensed as he clearly wrestled with what was the best choice, his pride struggling to accept it. "Then I go back to being a prisoner," he said eventually, gritting the words out.

She hunkered down, meeting his dark eyes. "Let me be clear on something, Mithanis. I saw your power back at the camp. I know you could use it to try and break free once we reach Mithranar. But if you harm a single Wolf, I will kill you this time. Don't doubt me on that."

He sneered, but didn't protest. She was sure his song magic read the honesty of her words.

"Don't worry." Talyn flashed a smile as she stood up. "We won't make you chop wood and live in a muddy hut."

He didn't look appeased.

DESPITE THE CONSTANT pain tugging at her body and the weariness sucking every bit of strength from her, anticipation began curling in Talyn as Saniya took them through the slums and out to the docks.

She was almost off Montagni soil.

Almost home.

Her eyes closed at the thought, and she staggered a step. Zamaril reached out a hand to steady her. She ignored his concerned glance and focused on the path ahead.

Several times on the way they had to stop suddenly, or duck into a dark alley while a patrolling unit of soldiers marched by. They were everywhere, but Saniya and her people knew the back streets better than they did.

When they reached the docks, the Callanan appeared from the shadows to report all was quiet. A mid-sized fishing boat rocked gently at anchor, one of several moored along the jetty, nothing remarkable about it at all.

A thin, rangy man with a scraggly beard jumped across to the wooden boards and leaned down to work the knots on the ropes mooring his boat, but he didn't say much apart from a quick exchange of words with Saniya. Or maybe it was just Leviana's fierce glare that kept him quiet. Or Jasper's soft snarl when he stepped too close to Talyn.

She assumed it was Toscal, the man sailing them to Mithranar.

Talyn was the last to board, lingering to hug both Callanan fiercely. "You both be safe, you hear me?"

"It's those Montagni ships and crew that have to worry, not us." Leviana grinned. "We'll see you soon, Tal."

"I'll make sure of it," she promised, then stepped onto the boat.

Leviana waved madly until they drifted out of sight.

They moved slowly through the port, Toscal joining the myriad other fishing boats heading out to sea to fish for the day's catch. Once they were out on open ocean, he unfurled his second and third sails and a stiff breeze filled them with a snap.

The boat listed sharply as it hit a swell, and Talyn's back tugged painfully when she reached out to brace herself against the railing. She swore under her breath.

"I'm never going to be whole again," she confided to Sari, saying the words for the first time.

"You don't know that."

"I'm warrior born, Sari. It's everything I am. If I can't fight anymore..."

"I'll never believe that, Talyn. Right now you're exhausted, heartsick and in pain. But you're going home. Jystar will do wonders for you. You're going to be fine."

"What will I do if I'm not?"

"You will."

Talyn wished she could believe her partner.

CHAPTER 28

*T*alyn woke from a restless sleep when Toscal called out softly. Dawn had come and gone, but a thick mist surrounded them, making it impossible to see anything further than a stone's throw away. The water was calm, the sails of the fishing vessel barely filled. Jasper lay across her legs, his unblinking stare on Mithanis.

"We're almost there," Saniya murmured.

At the opposite end of the boat, Mithanis shifted too, dark eyes scanning the mist as if he could penetrate it to see what was ahead. Wingless, gaunt, and with the lingering pallor to his skin from his time as a slave, the prince of night looked nothing like the darkly beautiful winged man he'd once been. But Talyn sometimes thought she saw the same longing in his eyes that had been tugging at her the closer they came to Mithranar.

She pushed away the empathy before it could take hold. Mithanis Acondor was not a man to feel sorry for.

Zamaril and Kaeri were awake too, watching the water as it lapped against the hull. Talyn sat up, ignoring her stiffness—easy given the excitement that was uncurling in her stomach.

"Colm sent word on ahead." Saniya offered a hand to help Talyn to her feet. "Your Wolves will be waiting for you."

"Where exactly will we be making landfall?" Zamaril asked.

"Right where the coastal road north hits the Ice Plains. There's a small jetty there used sporadically to deliver supplies to the waystations along the road. It's proved useful for us too."

"The Wolves are hiding in the mountains?" Talyn asked. She hadn't asked too many questions before now, satisfied just to know they'd escaped Dock City and were safe.

"I don't know exactly," Saniya said. "The exact location is kept a strict secret from any but those who need to go there. All my people in Acleu were told is that we should head for the jetty and we'd be met there."

Good. Talyn's shoulders relaxed slightly. Since Tarcos had clearly left Shadows and Armun behind to help Azrilan, they were no doubt being used to track down any resistance to his rule. It had been worrying at her ever since she'd learned the Wolves had fled into hiding.

"You said Windsong organised the hiding place?" Zamaril queried.

Saniya nodded. "That's what I was told."

"Is there a problem?" Talyn could always tell when something was gnawing at her thief.

"Something about him…" Zamaril frowned. "I feel like I've seen Windsong before, but I just can't place it."

"Before what?"

"Before he took over as flight-leader after Iceflight's murder."

"That's impossible." Talyn frowned. "He was stationed in the Summer Palace for well over a decade before Mithanis brought him back to take over for Iceflight."

"I know, and I'd never left Dock City before becoming a Wolf." Zamaril's frown deepened. "But there's something nagging—"

A sound came from Mithanis, dragging Talyn's attention away from Zamaril. His shoulders were stiff as he stared ahead to where the mist was beginning to clear, revealing what lay beyond.

Talyn sucked in a breath at the sight of mountains rearing high above—much closer than she'd imagined despite Toscal's warning that they were close to shore. Warmth began unfolding in her chest, spreading through her and dispelling any pain or stiffness.

Home.

She shifted her gaze downwards, searching the rugged shoreline until she spotted the ramshackle jetty poking out from a pebbled shore.

A handful of figures stood at the end of it, with more waiting back on the shoreline, their white and grey clothing blending seamlessly with their surroundings. Around them was nothing but rocks and ocean and the occasional gull soaring the thermals.

It took a moment for them to notice the boat through the lifting fog, but the moment they did, flashes of emerald and sky blue caught the morning light as two winged folk leapt into the air.

Moments later and Liadin was dropping into the boat, heedless of how he made it rock or how his outstretched wings almost sent Saniya flying over the side. Lyra was only a heartbeat behind him, equally uncaring of Toscal's shout of annoyance. Jasper yowled in protest.

"Ciantar," Liadin breathed.

They stared at each other. The talons' gazes flicked to the tattoo on Talyn's cheek, then back to her eyes. For a long moment Talyn didn't know what to say. Gladness rushed up from the depths of her soul. Words. She needed words. Finally she found some, though she had to clear her throat before she could speak. "You have no idea how good it is to see you both."

Eyes shining, they bowed abruptly, wings half-furled, while Kaeri and Saniya scrambled out of the way, cursing. Zamaril lightly stepped around them both and slapped Lyra in the shoulder while slinging an arm around Liadin. "I've missed you!"

"Zamaril." Liadin hugged him back, beaming, half his attention still on Talyn.

Lyra's eyes were bright as a summer sky. "Can we take you in?" Her wings flared as she stepped forward eagerly. All four Wolves had forgotten everyone else on the boat.

"Please!" Talyn stepped into the woman's arms without hesitation, desperate to get off the boat and be back on land. With a few strong wing beats Lyra soared into the air. Talyn craned her head back to see Zamaril firmly in Liadin's grip. Toscal returned to steering the boat, bringing it towards the jetty.

Lyra flew with dizzying speed, dropping out of the air and landing gracefully, jolting Talyn's back in the process.

She barely noticed.

Because Corrin was standing there, his face so much older, more *harrowed*, than she remembered. But his green eyes were clear and he radiated a calm assurance she'd only ever seen glimpses of before.

They stilled, staring at each other.

Until Zamaril broke the moment. He burst forward, past Talyn, and ran to throw himself at Corrin. The Wolf staggered back a step, face twisting with emotion as he returned Zamaril's hug and the two men rocked together, saying nothing for a long moment.

"Go to them, you idiot."

Letting out a sobbing laugh, Talyn strode forward, breaking into a run, then joining the hug and wrapping her arms around both talons.

"Is it really you?" Corrin breathed, eventually pulling away and staring at them with unbelieving hope. She could tell the moment he processed the slave tattoos. The colour drained from his face and he looked suddenly heartbroken, tears springing to his eyes. "They didn't."

"They did," Zamaril said quietly. "But we're here and alive, Corrin. That's all that matters."

Talyn nodded, scrubbing at her wet cheeks. "I'm sorry it took me so long to get back to you."

"You've been missed, Ciantar." Corrin swallowed, that calm assurance returning to his features. "But Prince Cuinn said you would come. And we would have waited forever for you."

Zamaril stilled and Talyn reached out for Corrin's arm, needing to steady herself. "Have you heard from him?"

"Not recently. But he's safe in Conmor," Corrin said quickly. "With your family. Theac's there too. They're all okay."

Relief flooded her—she wished Cuinn was here too, wanted so desperately to see him. But at least he was safe. Then Zamaril reached out to Corrin, pressing a palm to his heart. "Saniya told us about Halun."

Corrin rocked, tears sheening his eyes as his hand curled around Zamaril's. "He died saving Prince Cuinn. I miss him every day."

Zamaril moved closer to him, and the three of them stood in silence, allowing themselves a moment to grieve together.

Eventually, Corrin shook himself and stepped away, glancing behind him at another winged man Talyn hadn't even noticed in the flurry of reuniting with Corrin. "Colm's message said you were hurt. Jystar came with us."

The healer was as sober as Talyn remembered, but the softening of his face when she smiled at him betrayed his joy in seeing her. His delight quickly faded as his eyes roamed her, his magic likely sensing her pain, then landed on the slave tattoo. A muscle ticked in his jaw. "Ciantar. Welcome home. Are you or Talon Lightfinger hurt?"

"My friend Kaeri took an arrow to the shoulder that needs looking at." Talyn waved to where the boat was just now pulling up against the jetty. "I have some... older wounds that need treating, but it's not urgent."

"It's worse than she makes it sound," Zamaril said sharply, command echoing in his voice. "You'll look at her immediately, Jystar."

"After Kaeri," Talyn said firmly, searching for a subject change and finding one. "Oh, and Corrin, we brought you a present."

Corrin's face darkened when he spotted Mithanis clambering onto the jetty, and his entire body turned rigid. "What is he doing here?"

"It's a long story, but I doubt we would have gotten home without his help." She sighed, still hating the fact that was true. "Right now, he's our prisoner. Can we get out of the cold before explanations so Jystar can have a look at us?"

"Where do we put him?" Liadin asked, voice thrumming with restrained anger. Lyra's wings furled and unfurled in agitation. The song mages were probably being doused in anger at Mithanis from all of them.

"You and Lyra escort him to one of the storage rooms and lock him in," Corrin said crisply. "We'll work out what to do about him later once we've talked."

Both winged Wolves saluted and headed away to deal with Mithanis. Jasper prowled over then, bumping his head against Corrin's leg before continuing along the jetty.

"We can fly you and your friend up, Ciantar, if—" Jystar started.

"I'll be walking, thank you very much," Kaeri snapped, stepping forward. Saniya was with her, her expression indicating she had absolutely no intention of being flown anywhere either.

Talyn smothered a smile. "I'd prefer to walk too. Is it far?"

"About a full-turn or so, but the trail isn't easy," Corrin said.

"Let's get to it then." Saniya pushed past, heading for a path leading up into the mountainside. "It will be dark soon."

"She found you at the labour camp?" Corrin asked quietly as they began walking, Jasper padding at her side. "Colm's message said you'd escaped from one, but didn't have much more detail."

"He found me." Talyn pointed to the tawncat. "But they were both searching for me. The two of them got me out, then we went back for Zamaril and Kaeri."

"It's Kaeri Venador, isn't it?" Corrin asked. "She looks different than I remember from Arataire, but that air of superiority is familiar."

Talyn nodded. "She saved my life, in the camp." She shook her head, dispelling the dark memories. "Is Andres here too?"

"He's in Dock City right now—he's running our network there along with Saniya's people, helping to recruit, as well as move people and messages between Mithranar and Acleu."

"Recruit?"

"Yes. Volunteers willing to train to fight for us. For Prince Cuinn."

"Captain Dariel is in charge of the Wolves now." Jystar spoke into the brief silence that fell. "He was appointed by the Falcon."

Talyn stared at them both. "Ravinire is here?"

"No, he's still missing," Corrin said. "Before he left, Prince Cuinn named Anrun Windsong as Falcon until your return, Ciantar. We owe him our lives—I don't know where the Wolves would have gone if he hadn't prepared this hideout for us. It's an old WingGuard outpost, of all things, abandoned decades ago when the Falcons grew lax about watching for threats from the north."

"We owe him and Saniya both, the way I understand it," she murmured.

Corrin glanced at her. "Yes."

Silence fell as all their energy was needed for clambering up a particularly steep section of trail made dangerous by the ice and snow covering the ground. Talyn's muscles began trembling, the pain in her back resurging with a vengeance. She swore inwardly and hoped they reached their destination soon.

Eventually they reached the top of the path, where it widened into a flat area before a heavy wooden door set into rocky cliff face. Two Wolves stood guard at the entrance, both human, both shooting wide-eyed gazes at Jasper. Talyn didn't recognise either of them but they seemed delighted to see her, saluting sharply.

"Welcome home, Ciantar," one said as she pulled open the heavy door.

Talyn acknowledged them both with a smile and a nod as they passed by, before turning a questioning gaze on Corrin. "Who are they?"

"Torini and Jorjen joined us two months ago from Dock City—sent by Andres. They finished basic training just last week," Corrin explained as they began walking down a corridor ending in a wide stairwell. "We currently number just under three hundred strong."

"Three hundred?" Zamaril stopped in his tracks, astonishment colouring his voice.

"Two hundred and eighty-three, to be exact." Corrin nodded. "With another twelve recruits on their way or already here to begin training."

The pain in Talyn's back and weariness in her muscles fought with astonishment over Corrin's revelation as they started up a set of stone steps. Eventually they reached the top. Here was an open foyer, with typically cavernous winged folk walkways, stairs and corridors leading off in all directions.

"When Prince Cuinn left, he told us to wait here and grow strong. That you would come back," Jystar said somberly, picking up the thread of the conversation.

"We began recruiting as soon as I returned," Corrin added. "I felt the Wolves needed to be more than just a protective guard if we're going to win Prince Cuinn his throne back. So now we train for combat as well as protection."

"As impressive as all that is, could we perhaps wait on a full accounting of everything you've been doing until your healer has looked at Talyn." Kaeri spoke sharply into the silence. "She's pretending she's fine, but she's not."

Despite Talyn's protests, and a furious scowl directed at Kaeri, her words promptly put an end to all discussion.

"*I like her,*" Sari announced.

"*That's just because she nags like you,*" Talyn shot back grumpily.

"*I do not nag!*" Sari's indignance almost made Talyn chuckle. Almost.

"Are you up for visiting the Wolves first?" Corrin asked quietly. "They've been waiting since we got news of your coming."

"I don't care if I'm bleeding out on this floor!" Talyn rounded furiously on Kaeri as she opened her mouth. "I will see my Wolves before I do anything else."

"Perhaps I could look at your shoulder in the meantime, Lady Venador?" Jystar asked smoothly, his years of courtly politeness taking over. "Captain Dariel will bring the Ciantar to my healing room once she has greeted the Wolves."

"Fine," Kaeri said with ill grace, stalking after Jystar when he set off down the corridor.

"She's a delight, isn't she?" Saniya remarked. "I'm exhausted and touching reunions aren't my thing. I'll find you all later."

"It's not far," Corrin explained as they started walking again. "They're gathered in the mess hall. It's getting tight in there with our increasing numbers, but I suppose that's a good problem to have."

"How do you feed everyone?" Talyn wondered.

"Our people in Darmour smuggle food in through the tunnels—it's a difficult, tiring trip for them each time, and there are only a select few trusted enough to know our location, but we wouldn't be able to do any of this without them."

Talyn shot a considering glance back at a quickly-disappearing Saniya. Cuinn's agreement to ally his Shadowhawk network with hers had been the right decision. Vengeance had proven crucial to the ongoing survival of Cuinn's forces. She wondered if there was more at work than simply Saniya's hatred of Azrilan. She hoped there was.

A loud hum of conversation drifted down the hall as they approached the opened double doors, the notes of it washing over her and sliding into her bones.

Her Wolves.

Time seemed to slow a little as she, Corrin, and Zamaril walked side by side towards those open doors, Jasper padding behind them. Soon she could see the long tables lined up inside, the grey and white of the Wolves uniforms, the striking teal and scarlet of Falcons. Hear the clatter of cutlery and breathe in the scent of freshly baked bread.

And then they were walking through.

A few Wolves caught her entrance immediately, and they began rising to their feet. Conversation died and a heady energy filled the room. And it wasn't just the Wolves. Falcons rose to their feet as well, wings rustling in excitement.

Talyn came to a halt. Zamaril and Corrin remained a step behind at either shoulder.

At the back of the room, one of the winged Wolves tossed back her head and howled. Several more followed suit until the enormous hall was a cacophony of triumphant howling.

Talyn let it wash over her, hold her up despite her weariness, heal some of the tears in her spirit that had opened in the past months. They loved her. They always had. This was her home.

She waited until the howls died away, until there was only three hundred Wolves and Falcons staring at her with shining eyes, then she smiled and said simply, "I'm back."

A raucous cheering let loose, feet stamping and hands banging on the tables.

When it finally died down, she took a breath. "I'm sorry it took me so long. Let me tell you what happened."

THERE WAS NO AVOIDING Jystar once Talyn had spoken to the Wolves. Corrin and Zamaril escorted her to a warm room on one of the higher levels. Large arched windows gave an impressive view of mountains and ocean. On the other side of the glass, a gentle flurry of snow drifted by.

Jystar was just putting the finishing touches on a clean bandage around Kaeri's shoulder when they entered. Already the woman looked better than she had in weeks, with colour restored to her face and that indefinable energy she carried with her almost back to normal.

"I knew about your healing magic, but didn't really understand." Kaeri hopped down off the bench. "It's a wonder."

"Jystar is very good," Talyn said, then hesitated.

"We'll wait out here." Corrin stepped back for Kaeri and Zamaril to leave, then closed the door behind him. She didn't move. Jasper refused to follow the others out and waited for the door to close before promptly lying down in front of it.

Fear enveloped her, freezing her to the spot. What if he couldn't fix it? What if she was always like this, unable to fight properly, to move, to... She swallowed, trying to get control of herself.

"You realise that I am a healer with decades of experience," Jystar said dryly. When she still hesitated, he frowned. "I also have some understanding of what happens to slaves in Montagni labour camps. Whatever it is, we can manage it. Trust me, Ciantar."

Talyn forced herself to walk over to the examining bench and sit down. Her hands reached for the hem of her shirt, and she paused again, hands trembling. "They whipped me within an inch of my life, beat me too. My head was injured and I had temporary memory loss. The whip scars healed badly without proper treatment and I don't have full range of movement anymore." Her voice lowered to a whisper. "I can't fight without the scars tearing."

Jystar reached out, gently tugging the shirt from her shaking hands then lifting it over her head. "Did you know that I was considered the strongest healing mage in the citadel?"

She nodded. "You were placed at the head of the healing guild after Tabatha Flightbreeze's murder."

"Indeed." Jystar hummed as he traced his fingers lightly over her back. From there, he examined her ribs, the old stab wounds, and finally her head. His magic flowed through her the whole time, filling her with strength and renewed vitality. Despite that, she had to fight the urge to cry from terror of what he might say.

Eventually he slid her shirt back on and walked around to face her. "The scarring is bad, Ciantar, but I believe I can fix some of it. It will take time, and I'll need to use some of your magical strength to do it. It won't remove the scars entirely, but I can restore your freedom of movement."

She bit her lip. "Truly?"

A little smile crossed his face. "Truly."

She nodded, scrubbing at the tears wanting to spill down her face. The relief was so crushing she couldn't speak for a moment. "Thank you."

"Your older wounds have healed well enough, and I can't detect any ongoing damage from the head wound that led to your memory loss," he said briskly. "I'm going to clean and rebandage your back for now. The talons will be waiting impatiently with a million questions for you, no doubt. Once you've all talked, we'll discuss treatment for your back."

"That sounds good, Jystar. Can I ask—" She hesitated, worrying briefly that if she asked her question, he might think her head injury worse than he'd diagnosed.

"Ask me anything."

"I almost died," she said simply. "I think I would have, except..." She met his eyes. "The place with green fields and blue sky. Do you know what I mean?"

He stilled. "Very few do outside the most experienced healers in the guild, Ciantar."

"So it was real? I wasn't hallucinating."

"You must have been very close to death." The horror of that flickered in his eyes.

Talyn bit her lip. Her father. Sari. She'd really seen them. Her father had saved her life, he and Tiercelin had. And Jystar deserved to know that.

"My father came to me there, did enough to save my life— Tiercelin taught him how, Jystar. He's happy, wherever that place is beyond the field, your brother is happy."

Jystar swallowed. Tears sheened his eyes and he looked away.

Talyn slid off the table, paused briefly before passing him to lay a hand on his arm. "I suspect a large part of that happiness lies in knowing the choices his brother made after his death."

The healer took a shuddering breath. Swallowed. "Thank you, Ciantar."

TALYN STEPPED out of the healing room with Jasper to find Anrun Windsong waiting alone in the corridor outside. At the sight of her, he bowed low, sea-green wings half-furled. "Ciantar. I apologise I wasn't here when you arrived; I was supervising a scouting patrol over the northern road."

"Falcon." She smiled in delight. "It's good to see you."

"And you." He straightened, a similar smile spreading over his face.

Talyn opened her mouth to speak, but the words froze in her throat as Jasper went over to the man and bumped his head repeatedly against his leg until Windsong warily reached down to stroke his ears. Satisfied, Jasper returned to Talyn, tail waving.

"He's never, *ever*, done that before," she managed.

"It's better than him trying to eat me, I suppose," Windsong said cheerfully.

She cleared her throat, switching her attention from the tawncat to the Falcon. "I hear you've been holding down the fort admirably in my absence?" When he shook his head, opened his mouth to demur, she cut him off. "I will never forget what you did for us, Anrun Windsong. Not for one single second."

"You are my Ciantar, and he is my king," Windsong said simply. "The talons are waiting to speak with you if you're up for it? I'll show you the way."

"I'd like that, thank you."

CHAPTER 29

Windsong brought Talyn and Jasper to a firelit sitting room. Corrin and Zamaril were already there, along with Kaeri and Saniya. After a session of Jystar's healing magic, Talyn felt stronger and more alert than she could remember being since waking in the slave camp, and the pain in her back was blessedly gone too, if only for a short time.

Jasper went straight over to the hearth, where he sprawled out and closed his eyes.

For a moment they all looked at each other, none of them knowing where to begin. Then Corrin offered a crooked smile and passed Talyn a mug of steaming liquid. "Zamaril and Lady Kaeri filled us in on what happened at the camp while you were with Jystar. Where do you want to start?"

She took a deep breath, the spiced scent of kahvi hitting her nose and almost making her cry right there. "I missed this." She savoured a long sip, then gave Corrin a considering glance. "You've been hiding out there, building an army. Vengeance and the Shadowhawk's networks have merged and are now active in Dock City, Darmour and Acleu?"

Corrin ran a hand through his hair. "Yes, but it hasn't been without difficulty. Azrilan uses Armun and Shadows to hunt them. Several have been killed. I worry that it's only a matter of time before they find us here."

"Not to mention that it's been more than four months since Azrilan took power. He will have used that time to consolidate his hold on both thrones," Saniya said. "We were briefed in Acleu that Azrilan is gathering large numbers of troops together and building new ships to hold them. We assume he's preparing a war fleet to send against the Twin Thrones."

"What's the latest news from the Twin Thrones?" Talyn braced herself for the answer. "We heard in Acleu they fought back the initial exploratory fleet from Montagn, but that's all I know."

"It's unclear. The blockade remains in place in Feather Bay—only approved naval and merchant vessels are allowed through," Windsong said. "So we're reliant on any messages getting to Acleu, and from there to Darmour via our network. As you can imagine, that takes time, and not all messages get through."

"Our only other source of information are the rumours and gossip we pick up on the docks," Corrin added. "Last week we heard the Firthlanders had overrun Conmor and were marching south on Calumnia. The day after that whispers came that the Twin Thrones had routed Firthland and were massing ships to start an invasion of Montagn."

"In short, you have no idea what the current situation is," Kaeri said flatly.

Saniya glanced at her, gave her a little shrug. "Pretty much."

Silence descended on the room, thick and heavy.

Talyn asked, because she couldn't *not* ask. "Corrin, how was Cuinn, when you saw him?" Levs and Cynia had said he was all right. But he'd lost his wings. And she hadn't been there. She'd been gone, unable to help, to comfort, nothing.

"He showed such courage," Corrin murmured. "He sent me back here to lead the Wolves. To wait for you. He was fierce on that, Ciantar, that you were alive and would come back."

Her chest constricted so tightly it hurt. She swallowed, but that was difficult around the lump in her throat. She needed to see him, to make sure with her own eyes that he was okay. But he was so far away. Zamaril glanced over at Talyn, read her expression, then changed the subject. "You were right before, Corrin. We have to assume the WingGuard or Armun will find us here eventually and prepare for that happening."

Talyn cleared her throat, sat up straighter, and forced herself to pay attention to the conversation.

Windsong nodded. "We've got measures in place so that we're warned if the WingGuard move on this location, but yes, our army is growing larger. It can't stay hidden forever."

"You should diversify. Split your Wolves and Falcons between multiple safe locations," Kaeri said. "Otherwise you risk your entire force being taken out in one hit."

Three set of eyes turned towards the Venador princess. She met their looks with a raised eyebrow.

"She's got a point." Talyn stifled a smile. "But I have a better idea."

Talyn didn't have to be a song mage to pick up the excitement that flashed through the room at her words. Even Jasper cracked an eye open.

Corrin bowed slightly. "We've been waiting for you to come back and lead us, Ciantar."

"Maybe you could let her get a good night's sleep before asking her to plan an insurgency against the king of Mithranar and Montagn," Kaeri said sharply.

Kaeri was right. She'd barely arrived home. Hadn't had any time to think in the chaos of escaping the slave camp. Had only just learned Jystar might be able to fix her. It didn't matter.

Talyn knew exactly what came next.

"It's all right." Talyn sent a grateful glance at her friend, then turned to Corrin. "First, a question. You say our network has been recruiting, smuggling supplies in, helping move people and messages back and forth. What else?"

"That's all," Corrin said. "The priority has been achieving those things while remaining safe."

In her absence, it had been a smart move. But she was back now. "Fair enough. But we're going to change that."

Saniya lifted an eyebrow. "How so?"

"Sometimes the best defence is a good offence." Talyn allowed some of the anger that she'd been smothering for weeks to edge her voice. "We're going to start making things very difficult for Azrilan and his Kingcouncil, and we're going to soften them up for Cuinn's return in the process. If we do it right, they'll be too busy defending themselves to come looking for us."

"What are you suggesting exactly?" Windsong asked. He looked calm, but a leap of glee flashed through the room, quickly stifled. She was sure it had come from him.

"For a start—how are the Montagni building new ships for his massive war fleet?"

"With wood, obviously, from..." Corrin trailed off, light flashing into his eyes. "Wood from Mair-land shipped out of Darmour."

"You've built an army, Corrin. I say we start using it." Excitement thrummed through her. "No more Mithranan wood is leaving Darmour. Azrilan will have to make do with what he has already. Next, the izerdia. Saniya, your people are going to find out where it's being stored in the citadel, and then we're going to steal it. All of it. In stages, if necessary, but we're going to take everything they've got."

"I... actually..." Saniya cocked her head. "Really like that plan."

"All the supplies coming into Feather Bay for the citadel, I want to hit them. I want to disrupt the movement of goods between Dock City and Darmour," Talyn said. "I want the Kingcouncil to start feeling the pinch. Unhappy winged folk nobles will be an annoyance for Azrilan at worst, a serious distraction at best."

"You're talking about starting a civil war," Windsong said quietly.

Talyn rose from her chair, meeting his gaze. "There will be conditions. Any Armun, Shadow or Bearman we encounter, we kill without hesitation. Falcons or City Patrolmen we don't attack unless in self defence, and if we have the opportunity to do so without putting ourselves at risk, we give them the opportunity to stand down."

"And if they don't?" Windsong pushed.

"Then we fight. We're already in a war, Falcon, and if we want to come out on the right side of it, people will be hurt. People will die. I don't like it any more than you do, but it's necessary."

He bowed his head.

"They've been coming at us, Windsong. Killing us. Hunting us." She reinforced her voice with the anger that had been stewing inside her for months. "I am Ciantar and I won't stand for that any longer. It's time we hit back."

"I agree." Corrin spoke into the silence that followed. "What are *your* plans, Ciantar?"

"I'll stay here for a short time," she said. "Jystar needs to do some work on me, and I want to be here to help kick things off. Then I will go south to Cuinn."

Because she had to see him, see with her own eyes that he was okay. To have his arms around her, his voice in her ear, his magic entwining with hers. But also because she suspected she knew why he'd gone to the Twin Thrones. And if she was right... then she needed to talk to him once she'd set things in motion in Mithranar.

Saniya let out an irritated breath.

Talyn stood. "Saniya, you'll head south to run the operations to steal izerdia and mess with the supply runs coming into Feather Bay. Anrun, you and Corrin will begin preparing small strike teams of Wolves—we'll meet here with the other talons first thing tomorrow and start planning where and how to deploy them. I have another idea too, but that will take some time to prepare."

Saniya predictably bristled. "I don't take orders from you. I agreed to merge our networks, provide you support, not to be part of your army. I won't ask my people to die for an Acondor prince."

Talyn crossed the room, sapphire gaze meeting sapphire gaze. "It's time to decide which side of this fight you stand on, Cousin. You saved my life, the debt between us is cleared. But you claim Vengeance was always about trying to help the human folk of Mithranar. Well, now *all* of Mithranar needs help. You know where I stand in the fight to come. And you know where Azrilan stands."

"Our group is about freedom," Saniya said quietly. "From oppression, from poverty, from winged folk ignorance."

"All those things are what I stand for too. They're what Cuinn stands for. You know it. There can only be one overall leader here until Cuinn returns, and that is me."

Saniya's mouth tightened. "Our problems haven't gone away. Our grievances haven't vanished just because a tyrant winged man sits the throne."

"You know Cuinn is different," Talyn said softly. "And I give you my word now. If you fight with us, stand at our side, we will listen to what you and your people have to say. We will give you a voice."

Zamaril broke into the heavy silence. "Are you forgetting they almost killed Prince Cuinn twice? That they hunted us for months? They murdered the same humans she claims to be protecting from oppression."

"We made mistakes. I admit that here and now. But you murdered scores of ours too." Saniya turned on him with a snarl.

"Prince Cuinn accepted Saniya's help. It was his decision to merge our networks." Windsong spoke into the tense silence. "Talon Lightfinger, Captain Dariel, consider that before refusing someone who has been an invaluable ally these past months despite what happened in the past."

Talyn offered a hand to her cousin. "I am willing to forgive. Are you?"

Saniya glanced at the hand, then back up at Talyn's face. "Your word. That we will have a voice?"

"I swear it." She knew without doubt Cuinn would support her in this.

Saniya hesitated for a long moment, gaze shifting back to Talyn's outstretched hand, clearly torn.

"Let's make what our fathers worked for, what your father *died* for—what Tiercelin and Halun and Ronisin Nightdrift died for—happen in Mithranar," Talyn urged. "Let's do that together."

"All right, Cousin." Saniya's hand lifted and slid into Talyn's. "Let's do what our fathers could not."

Zamaril and Corrin shared a glance, little smiles creeping across their faces despite their lingering resentment. Kaeri, silent for a while now, looked intrigued. Light flashed in Windsong's eyes.

A grin—not a full one, but an echo of the old reckless one—flashed over Talyn's face as she stepped away. "Good. Then let's take the fight to Azrilan."

TALYN LEFT THE ROOM, Jasper at her heels, and went back to Jystar. He left instructions not to be interrupted, and Liadin and Lyra, who'd been waiting, took up guard positions outside the door.

She laid down on a comfortable pallet, warm blankets covering everything but her back, and rested her head on folded arms.

"This is going to take some time, several full-turns probably," Jystar warned after another close inspection of her back. "These scars are old, and they've broken open and re-scarred in several places. I'll have to slough away some of the scar tissue and encourage healthy skin to grow."

"Will it hurt?" she asked warily.

"It will be uncomfortable, but I'm going to use my magic to relax you." He smiled slightly. "It won't be anywhere near as bad as when you sustained the injuries."

She hesitated a moment, then, "My wing buds?"

"Still there." He rested a palm on her upper shoulder. "Do you want me to..."

"No." She closed her eyes. "Not now."

"I need you to relax. Don't fight what I'm doing," he murmured. "Try and think of this as time to properly rest. Your body has been running on nothing but reserves and not enough food for months and it needs a break. Meditate, if you can."

Sari snorted with laughter inside her head. "*Meditate? Has he met you?*"

"I'll try," she promised. "*Shut up. I can meditate.*"

Sari laughed uproariously.

"I might need to draw upon some of the raw strength in your

magic," he said. "If you feel that, don't resist me. I promise I won't drain enough to hurt you."

She forced herself to relax into the soft pallet, settling until she was comfortable. Jystar's hands touched her skin, and a moment later his magic seeped through into her. She didn't fight him, instead allowing him to lull her into a near-sleeping state.

It was restful, and for a long time she just drifted. Relaxing wasn't always easy—every now and then there would be a sharp pulling sensation on her back that edged close to pain. Each time a touch more healing power flooded her and the sensation would fade.

Cuinn.

Without even thinking about what she was doing, she gave in to her yearning for him. Ever since her memories had flooded back she'd avoided thinking too much of him—the emotions he'd roused had been too sharp, too painful, too terrified. But now that she was finally safe, that Jystar was healing her, that she was home, she wrapped herself in Cuinn and memories of their time together.

And then she slept.

TALYN WOKE to the sunlight of early morning streaming through the windows above the bed she laid in. A warm fire burned in the grate, and she could smell the fresh kahvi in a steaming cup Corrin held in his hands. The Wolf captain sat in a chair by her bed.

The new rank suited him. She tried to work out whether she was sad that captain of the Wolves wasn't her title anymore, and couldn't really decide. It didn't feel wrong, though.

"Thought you might enjoy this." He smiled, passing the kahvi to her when he saw she was awake.

"You're wonderful." She sat up and took the drink, sipping it with delight. Such a simple thing to miss so much, but she had. Kahvi was everything that she loved about Mithranar in one small drink. Sweet and potent with a magical rush of energy and spice.

"How are you feeling?" Corrin asked.

Talyn thought about it for a second. Nothing hurt, and her body had that languor she got when she was well rested and content. "I feel good, actually."

Both looked up as the door opened and Jystar and Zamaril entered.

"I did the best I could," Jystar said immediately. "I couldn't remove the scars entirely, but you will have your full range of movement back."

She put down the mug and swung her legs over the side of the bed. There was no pain, not even a twinge from her back. From there she stood, slowly stretched her arms above her head.

Nothing.

She swung them out to the sides. Bent over to touch her toes.

No pain. No restriction.

And she started to cry.

The three men stood in awkward silence for the mortifying few moments it took her to calm herself and scrub away the tears.

"*I never used to cry like this,*" she grumbled in furious annoyance.

"*Yeah, well, you've been through a lot in the past few months. Maybe try giving yourself a break.*" Sari was unsympathetic.

"Your council of war awaits, Ciantar." Corrin smiled a little.

"We'll let you dress," Jystar said, ushering the others out.

Once the three men had filed out, Talyn stripped off the robe she was wearing and crossed to a mirror, eager to see what Jystar had done with her.

Turning gracefully before it, she gasped in surprise.

She still had scars crisscrossing her back, but they were faded and thin compared to what they'd been—there was no red, angry tissue, just healthy skin around the pale scars. Spinning, she leapt up, twisting mid-air and kicking out in a traditional *sabai* move. No pain.

Laughing, Talyn tried another move. She hadn't realised what sheer pleasure it would be simply to be able to move without restriction again. Still smiling, she stepped back to the mirror, this time studying her face.

The scar from her head wound had been worked on too. Jystar had healed it to a narrow white line running from her forehead over her left eyebrow and stopping just above her left cheekbone. She still looked too thin, but otherwise colour and health had returned to her skin.

She almost looked like the Talyn she'd been before. Only the shadows lurking in her sapphire eyes were any indication of how much she'd suffered—that and the blue tattoo on her left cheek.

"I'm glad I have it," she admitted to Sari. *"In some strange way I feel like I honour Halun's sacrifice by wearing it."*

"It's not strange. It's perfect."

Talyn straightened her shoulders, let her newfound strength wash through her, then reached for the clothes.

She had an insurgency to plan.

CHAPTER 30

*C*uinn brought Trystaan in low over Mothduriem. It was an uncharacteristically clear day over the highest peaks of the Ayrlemyre Mountains, and the skies were crowded with legions of SkyRiders practicing maneuvers.

The message in his pocket weighed on him, anxiety spiking in his chest each time he thought of its contents. Trying to forget his worries for a few moments, he pushed all thoughts of it out of his head, and reached back to un-sling the bow from his back. Then he brought Trystaan swooping up underneath the SkyRiders under-taking target practice, weaving through another legion at flight prac-tice as he did so.

The SkyRiders recognised him immediately from the blue sheen on the underside of Trystaan's wings and shouted greetings. The words were lost in the wind gusting around them, but he lifted a hand in response.

Once he was in position above the group undertaking target prac-tice, Cuinn unbuckled his harness and dived off Trystaan's back. Icy air swept past his face and body and he closed his eyes for a moment at the sheer bliss of flying again.

Cries of surprise and encouragement resounded through the sky.

Smiling, he angled his body mid-air, bringing his bow up as he swept past the target, and firing three arrows towards it. All three thumped into the centre. Cuinn slung the bow over his back and rolled again, falling spread-eagled.

Trystaan came in underneath him, and he landed on the eagle's back gracefully, one hand raised in triumph. The SkyRiders cheered loudly, several following him in a long line as he soared down to the landing platform.

The first SkyRider to land after him grinned as he undid his harness and dropped to the ground. "That was insane. How do you do that?"

Cuinn smiled. "Easy. Trystaan always knows where to catch me."

"Nice one, Wolf!" More SkyRiders were landing now, unbuckling and dropping to the ground. Cuinn slowed his pace to allow them to catch up to him. Like the Aimsir, SkyRiders put little stock in rankings and title—apart from their commanding officers. To them, Cuinn was a fellow SkyRider, not a prince or a regent. It made being around them the most relaxed he'd ever felt in the Twin Thrones.

"Nice to have you back." Drift clapped him on the back.

"Teach me how to do that, yeah?"

"I don't think so, Feather." Cuinn's smile widened. "You'd have to learn how to fly without your eyes shut first."

Laughter drifted around him.

"You've come from Ryathl?" Dive asked, and the laughter faded, their attention on him turning serious.

The contents of the note in his pocket hit him, and his smile faded, even though he tried to hide his unease. "I have, but I need to speak with the Sky Chieftain." He paused at the entrance to the caverns. "That was some nice work I saw up there."

"Thanks, Wolf." Their pride washed over him.

CUINN'S THOUGHTS WERE BUSY, distracted, as he walked through the tunnels to Soar's quarters. He'd remained in Ryathl almost three weeks, giving the lords the attention they needed, talking through options for deploying more of the army north without leaving the southern cities vulnerable.

Dealing with them hadn't been easy, but aided by his song magic and Shia and Ceannar's support, he'd calmed most of their fears and their uncertainty about him as regent. News that Ariar and Soar had halted the southern push through the mountains with a furious onslaught of Aimsir and SkyRiders had been the win Cuinn had needed to reassure them.

Now a full division of Greencloaks was marching north from Ryathl. Once they arrived, the Aimsir would be able to return to their positions along the northern Conmoran lines.

But then had come word from one of Soar's commanders that four Firthlander ships had gotten troops ashore in the mountains under the cover of night. In the process, they'd established a beachhead in a defensible cove, a secure spot to land more ships that slipped through the SkyRider patrols. Cuinn left Ryathl that night to return to the Dumnorix and plan their next move.

Thoughts of war strategy immediately brought Talyn to the surface of his thoughts, like it always did. What would she think of him now?

Where was she? He'd been so certain she was alive, still was. But why hadn't she come back? And he was so far away, busying himself with running a kingdom at war instead of looking for her. Familiar guilt soured his stomach.

He shook his head. He'd come here for a reason. He straightened his shoulders, summoned a hint of magic that emanated strength and confidence, and knocked on Soar's door. The Sky Chieftain looked up with a smile when Cuinn entered. "You must have been flying a while to get here so quickly."

"I have, and the windstorm over the southern foothills wasn't a picnic." Cuinn grimaced, dropping into the other chair by the fire. "Ceannar and Shia left with me, but their escorts diverted around the storm to head straight to Port Lachley."

Soar matched his grimace. "You should have too. Those storms are dangerous, even for the most experienced SkyRiders."

"I was fine." Cuinn waved a hand. "And besides, I didn't want to detour around. I came to get you. We need you back at Port Lachley. Ariar is already riding north from the Thalion."

"Problems?" Soar frowned. "More than the beachhead on the east coast?"

Cuinn nodded. "Just before I left Ryathl, Shia received a message from her people in Acleu—reports of troop movements in south-western Montagn, clustering together in three of their port cities."

"Damn." Soar rubbed a hand over his face. "We'll leave as soon as that windstorm has passed over. In the meantime, fancy a drink?"

"Let me go and visit the mess first, say hello to the riders." Cuinn rose to his feet. "But dinner together after?"

"You put me to shame, Cousin." Soar rose too, a little smile on his face. "Let's both go and talk to our SkyRiders. They've been working hard these past months."

"We hit the first wave of ships out of Acleu," Cuinn said as they walked; he could feel Soar's weariness, his grim outlook, and sought to cheer him. "They didn't get anywhere near our coast. We held back the southward push in the mountains."

"And had to divert two precious legions of SkyRiders and too many Aimsir to do it. Firthlander ships established a beachhead while they were away," Soar said. "And it sounds like Azrilan is preparing to send a much larger force at us. We're on the back foot, Cuinn, and falling further behind each day."

"I'll never count against the Callanan in Acleu," Cuinn said, meaning it. He didn't know Cynia or Leviana very well, didn't know the other Callanan with them at all, but he knew what Talyn thought of them.

"Tarcos and Azrilan will quickly work out what we're doing, if they haven't already, and when they do, Tarcos will send Armun and Shadows to Acleu. They'll have one purpose. Taking out our early warning system."

Soar was right. But Cuinn stopped a few paces away from the eating cavern. The conversation of SkyRiders floated out, comforting in its own way. "For now, we're holding the line. Tarcos will run out of ships sooner rather than later."

Soar nodded slowly. "And it's not forever. Saundin will be doing his work."

"Talyn trusted him. He'll come through for us," Cuinn agreed. "We have to be patient."

He just hoped it wouldn't be too late. They couldn't afford to wait forever.

SOAR AND CUINN landed at Port Lachley three days later amidst a flurry of screaming eagles. Theac waited at the entrance to the stone stairwell leading down into the castle. Evani stood at his side, her demeanour as watchful as his, and she wore two daggers at her waist.

"Miss me?" Cuinn asked them with a smile.

"Our days were dark, Prince Cuinn." Theac glowered. The familiar look brought warmth rushing to Cuinn's chest. But also an ache... he wanted to go home.

"I'm glad to hear it." He flashed a smile. "Ariar?"

"The Horselord rode in last night and is waiting with bated breath to see you."

"Evani, ensure you don't allow him to teach you that tone," Cuinn said lightly. "It's rude."

Evani's eyes warmed. "I'm of the understanding that's how Captain Dynan used to speak to you all the time, Your Highness?"

His chest clenched, but he forced a smile. At his side, Theac's shoulders sagged slightly.

"I don't know what Talyn was thinking," Soar said lightly as he caught up and they began making their way down the steps. "A Kingshield would never dare speak to their assigned Dumnorix like that."

Two Kingshield standing guard at the base of the stairwell saluted sharply as Cuinn, Soar and the Wolves clattered down and into the main entrance hall of the castle.

"Cuinn!" Ariar strode through the open front doors. His curls were askew and his bright blue eyes flushed from a ride. Kingshield trailed in his wake. "You're back!"

"I was told you were pining. I thought I'd put you out of your misery." Cuinn shrugged.

"Aren't the Montagni trying to invade or something?" Soar changed the subject.

"Have I missed the meeting?" Alyna walked into the hall, all Callanan grace and sharp authority. Ceannar and Shia were with her, looking none the worse for wear for their flight back from Ryathl.

"Montagni?" Soar said loudly. "Invading?"

"The First Blade has news," Cuinn said, deferring to Shia. "It isn't good."

LATER THAT NIGHT, Cuinn encountered Alyna down in the castle kitchens. He'd been out practicing his archery then sparring with Theac and Evani to keep up his strength and conditioning—though the thought of driving a sword or any sort of blade into another person continued to make him ill—and now sought food and something to pass the time rather than going to bed. He liked the castle kitchens late at night; they were quiet and peaceful in the soft glow of the big ovens.

He still didn't sleep much. Night remained the one time where, without anything to distract him in his silent room, he struggled to forget, to not miss her, to not worry himself sick over his Wolves and the people he'd left behind in Mithranar.

Surprise flickered through him at the sight of Talyn's mother seated at the table running down the middle of the large room. He offered her a nod of welcome before searching out some bread, cheese, and leftover stew.

They hadn't spoken privately since he'd claimed the regency, although she remained unfailingly civil and respectful. He couldn't regret what he'd done by challenging her, it had been necessary, but he did regret that it had caused more pain for her.

He of all people understood her grief at losing Talyn. He'd wanted to try and mend that gap somehow, but it had seemed better to keep out of her way, rather than force her to deal with him.

"Can't sleep?" he asked after a few moments of silence passed.

Alyna raised a shoulder. "I don't sleep much, not since..."

"Talyn's father died," Cuinn finished quietly, understanding Alyna better than she likely realised.

Another few moments of silence passed, and Cuinn ate his way steadily through the stew and bread. He'd left an opening for Alyna to speak, but it would be her choice to use it.

"When Talyn was first assigned to Mithranar, I thought it was a good thing." Alyna eventually spoke, her violet eyes distant as they stared at the tabletop. "She had always been so restless, and after Sari's death... I thought it would do her good, seeing where her father came from, to be away from all the painful memories she had here."

"I understand," Cuinn said quietly. "I know what losing Sari did to her."

Her gaze flicked up to him. "But when she came back, when she resigned from the Kingshield to return to Mithranar, I was afraid. I never told her that, of course, I wanted her to do what would make her happy. And I always thought she would come back, take up her duties as a Dumnorix. It never occurred to me that she wouldn't want to."

"And Trystaan?"

"He was scared for her, but he wouldn't tell either of us why." Alyna looked down again. "It ate at him, being away from Mithranar. He loved me enough to be happy here, but it was like a part of him was always missing."

"Did he ever tell you who he was in Mithranar, who Talyn is?" he asked gently.

"He offered, once." Alyna's gaze was distant as she stared across the kitchen. "He loved me enough to never want to keep secrets from me. But I loved him enough not to want to cause him pain. And talking about it... so much agony in his eyes. I couldn't bear it. So I told him it didn't matter. And it didn't." She paused, swallowed. "Talyn told me

283

some of it though, when she was trying to explain why being in Mithranar was so important to her."

Cuinn met her gaze. "Would you like me to tell you the story, from one who was born and raised in your husband's home?"

Alyna turned to him in a single, graceful movement. "I would, yes."

And so Cuinn told Alyna the tale of the Shadowhawk, how Trystaan had loved both his brother and the human people of Mithranar. How the entire Ciantar family had been executed on the order of Cuinn's mother. How Runye had sacrificed himself so that Trystaan could flee.

Tears sheened Alyna's violet eyes. Halfway through, he reached across the table, touched her hand, and wound soothing magic into his voice.

"Talyn is just like him, just like the both of you. She is our Ciantar." Cuinn paused. "She will be able to do for us what Trystaan and Runye couldn't."

Alyna shook her head a little, withdrew from his touch. "You named your eagle after him."

"I will never forget what he and his brother did for my people."

Alyna lifted a trembling hand to her forehead. Her emotions were a jumble, but he sensed he'd been able to fill in some missing pieces that had long been gnawing at her.

"You're the new Shadowhawk, aren't you?" She shifted her gaze to him, direct. "Talyn found out. That's why her attitude towards you changed."

"Yes."

She turned away, letting out a sharp breath in shock. "That's... you're not anything like she said. Like we believed. Was she deliberately lying to us about you?"

"She understood better than you ever will how dangerous it would have been if anyone learned that I was the Shadowhawk. My mother, my brother, they would have executed me without hesitation."

"She tried to explain." Alyna scrubbed a hand over her face. Her shock still reverberated through the space between them. Cuinn's magic told him she was rapidly reevaluating everything she'd ever thought about him. "I wouldn't listen."

Cuinn smiled a little. "Ah. So that's where Talyn gets her stubbornness from."

Alyna huffed a breath. "I don't know whether I'm relieved or worried that we put a crown on your head, Cuinn."

"I'll do my best for you. I promise."

Alyna hesitated, face taut with emotion. Hope flickered underneath her shock, quickly buried. "How are you so certain she is still alive?"

Cuinn took breath. Let it out. "Did you know that Sari is still with Talyn?"

"What do you mean?" Alyna frowned in confusion.

"A winged healer could explain this better, but because of how close Talyn and Sari were, and how strong Talyn's winged folk magic is, their Callanan magic became intertwined over time. When Sari died so unexpectedly, those bonds were torn apart, which is part of the reason Talyn took her death so hard. But it also meant a part of Sari stayed with Talyn."

"She never said anything about that."

"She hasn't told many people." Cuinn's mouth quirked in a smile. "I think she's afraid they'll think she's crazy. She's not. Sari is still there, with her, talking to her when Talyn needs it."

Understanding spread over Alyna's face. "And you think if Talyn were dead she would be in your head, talking to you?"

"I do." He said it without arrogance. Just with the simple certainty he felt all the way through to his bones.

Alyna rose. "Good night, Cuinn."

She was halfway across the kitchen when running feet—multiple sets—pounded down the staircase leading from the level above. Cuinn stood, curious.

Alyna glanced back at him, eyebrows raised, but he shrugged. "I'm confident you can protect me if we're about to be attacked by very loud running assassins."

She almost smiled. He beamed inwardly.

"Alyna! Cuinn! Are you down here?"

It was Ariar's voice, lifted in a loud bellow. He appeared moments later, leaping down the last few steps, curls ruffled, face alight, clutching a torn and filthy scrap of parchment in his hands. The First Blade appeared a heartbeat later, Ceannar on both their heels.

"You all look very excited," Cuinn drawled, his tone masking how fiercely he was being deluged in their emotions. He almost staggered back a step with the force of it. Something good had happened.

"What is going on!" Alyna snapped.

"Talyn's alive." Ariar brandished the parchment as if it were a victory banner. "She's alive. She's okay."

Cuinn sat down before his legs gave out completely. Alyna turned rigidly still.

"Word from Warriors Leed and Seinn just arrived by bird." Shia spoke briskly. "They saw Talyn in Acleu, on her way to Darmour to re-join the Wolves. She was in a slave camp this whole time but managed to escape. She was a little banged up, but they're confident she's okay."

He couldn't speak. Could barely breathe around the lump in his throat. He lifted one shaking hand to his forehead, the boisterous conversation around him turning to a distant chatter.

She was alive. She was okay. He wasn't sure he remembered how to breathe.

A soft touch on his shoulder broke the daze he'd fallen into. It was Alyna, sitting next to him on the bench. Her violet eyes were bright, sheened with tears.

She gave him a single nod.

He swallowed, smiled, reached out to curl an arm around her shoulders. She clung fiercely to him.

Ariar joined them, sitting on Cuinn's other side, wrapping a long arm around them both. "She's alive."

And the First Blade and First Shield left them there together.

CHAPTER 31

Talyn turned as the door opened after a quick knock. She'd been staring at her fire, but her mind was miles away, thinking over everything that had happened, putting together more pieces of the puzzle. The things she and Cuinn had missed. That the Dumnorix had missed.

If they were going to figure a way out of this mess they were in, she needed to understand what had gone wrong. Ensure she didn't make those mistakes again.

Night had fallen and the only sound was the crackle and pop of the fire in the grate and the wind gusting outside. Jasper was asleep at her feet. "Saniya," she greeted her cousin, pleased by the fortunate coincidence of her appearance. "You're back from Darmour."

"I am," Saniya said warily. "What is it? You look like you're bursting to ask me something."

"I am. Was it Vengeance that assassinated Goldfeather, Iceflight and Flightbreeze?" she asked without preamble. "I'm not looking to lay blame. I just need to know."

"I told you before, we didn't sneak around with tawncats and Shadows. It wasn't us." Saniya hesitated.

"But?"

"You already know that Navis provided us with money, weapons, information?" After Talyn's nod, Saniya moved closer. "We never trusted Navis, and so where possible I had my people doing a little independent investigation. We became fairly certain that the money he was providing us came from one of the winged folk. Someone important. That's when our relationship with Navis started to break down. We didn't want winged folk money."

"Azrilan," Talyn murmured.

"We didn't know it at the time, but it must have been. Goldfeather was the Queencouncil lord responsible for Mithranar's treasury. I think he found out Azrilan was funneling money somewhere he shouldn't."

Talyn frowned, shook her head. "Ravinire was convinced Iceflight was blackmailing Goldfeather about something and that's why they were both killed."

"More likely, Goldfeather sought Iceflight's advice about what to do with the information he'd discovered. After all, Iceflight was Mithanis's man, no?" Saniya pointed out. "I doubt Goldfeather wanted to tell Mithanis himself that his brother was stealing crown money."

"And Savin killed them before they could tell Mithanis anything." It tracked, but not entirely. Talyn frowned. "Then why kill Flightbreeze? Was it because Azrilan saw what a destabilising effect the unsolved murders had on his mother's rule?"

Saniya shrugged. "Makes sense. Nothing better to set terror into the hearts of indolent winged folk than a series of violent, unexplained murders that the WingGuard was helpless to do anything about. Made their queen look weak. Suited us just fine too."

"Then we have to assume that Azrilan was helping Savin with the murders by controlling the tawncat with his song magic? Where is the creature now?"

Saniya shoved her hands in her pockets, impatience lining her voice. "Who cares? We've got bigger problems to deal with."

"No, we don't." Talyn dropped into a chair and motioned for Saniya to do the same. "Azrilan beat us before because we didn't understand what was going on. We allowed him to manipulate all of us. To win now, we have to get ahead of his games. It's the unknowns that could tear us apart again."

It was what she'd been mulling over in this room for the past full-turn, for the past weeks as she healed and returned to combat training. She'd been so confident before, yet she'd had literally no idea what Azrilan and Tarcos were up too. She couldn't afford for that to happen again.

"Fine, but we still have more important things to deal with than figuring out where a murderous tawncat is," Saniya said flatly.

Talyn finally registered the agitation in her cousin's face. "What is it? Something wrong in Darmour?"

"One of my people caught wind of a stockpile of izerdia being shipped into Darmour tomorrow night. Its arrival is being kept really quiet—only the Patrol commander and watch-officer on duty know about it."

In the month since Talyn's return to the SkyReach, their forces had stopped two supply boats full of wood being transported to Acleu and staged a raid on the main stores of copper in the mines ready to be shipped south to Dock City. Three of theirs injured, no Falcons hurt, and two Bearmen killed.

But their sudden activity had drawn the Armun and Shadows to them like flies to honey—for them, this was an opportunity to stalk Talyn's forces to their hideout. But she'd planned for that. "You think it's a trap?"

Saniya gave her a look. "Why in flea-biting shit is the Kingcouncil sending izerdia to Darmour? If it was for the mines, it wouldn't be so much, and it wouldn't be all secretive. They know this will catch our attention."

"It has." The excitement in Talyn's voice caused Jasper to uncurl and blink sleepily. "And we're going to hit it."

Saniya opened her mouth as if to protest, but then sighed. "You were waiting for this."

"I was."

"And you want to walk into an ambush why?"

"Because I want to turn it around on them."

Saniya frowned, her gaze troubled as she stared into the fire.

"You hate the idea that much?" Talyn asked, surprised at Saniya's lack of response. "I honestly thought you'd like it."

"No, I do. It's just… what you said just now, about understanding Azrilan properly." Saniya ran a hand through her hair. "There's something going on."

"Tell me." Talyn leaned forward.

"Len mentioned something else when I spoke to him. Messages being sent back and forth between Acleu and Arataire carried by a single Armun. Nobody seems to know what's in them. One of our people tried following one of the messengers and never returned. It's fragmentary, I know, and normally I'd brush it off, but…"

"It doesn't feel right." Talyn trusted her cousin's instincts.

Saniya shook her head.

Talyn considered it. "Who is sending the messages in Acleu?"

"The city governor. Your Callanan have either tailed or spoken to every servant in his household. None of them know the contents of the messages, or even who they're for, though presumably it's Azrilan." Saniya waved a hand. "And before you ask, it's a different Armun messenger every time."

"I think it's safe to assume Azrilan is up to something that isn't obvious to any of us." Talyn rose. "We need more operating space, here and in Acleu. Force pressure back on him, force him into making a mistake. Come with me? We need to talk to Corrin, Windsong and Zamaril."

"I *do* like your ambush plan." Saniya's shoulders shook a little as she followed Talyn, as if she were trying to shake away her unease. "It feels good to go on the offensive for once."

Talyn smiled, walking with renewed vigour in her steps, anticipatory excitement unfurling in her stomach. She'd spent a month hidden away in the SkyReach, obeying Jystar's instructions to let her back heal properly, resuming her physical training in a graduated way so as to rebuild the strength and muscle tone her body had lost.

But she'd had enough of stamina training and endless drills with her Wolves.

It was time to get into the fight.

FOUR NIGHTS LATER, Talyn and Zamaril stood in an empty street, rain pouring from the sky above, flooding the gaps between the cobble-stones with water and sending it gushing from over-burdened drains.

It felt odd not to have Jasper nearby—she'd grown accustomed to his faithful shadow since breaking out of the camp—but she'd left him behind in the SkyReach with Windsong. Anyone spotting a tawncat on the streets of Darmour would either panic and start a furor, or guess Talyn or Cuinn or the Wolves were nearby. Or all of the above.

They were two blocks back from the northern end of the docks. Across the street stood a two-story warehouse sitting amongst a block of other two-story warehouses. Ramshackle but large, some were in use, while others sat empty. The one they waited across from had been abandoned for months.

Over at the docks, the shipment of izerdia should be arriving.

Talyn and Zamaril were hidden by darkness. There were no lamps to light the streets in this part of town, and rainclouds hid most of the moonlight. Even so, they were pressed against the wall of a shop, hidden deep in the shadow. Neither of them spoke.

She estimated a quarter-turn for the ship to tie up at the jetty and begin unloading. Then her Wolves, led by Corrin, would hit them.

If the trap sprung there, Corrin's handpicked strike team was prepared for it and they would be able to fight their way out. But Talyn was confident it wouldn't happen there. If Armun had planned this, they'd let the Wolves steal the izerdia, then follow them back to their 'hideout,' a much bigger prize.

They had time to wait. She didn't make the mistake of moving, making a sound, or relaxing in any way at all. Neither did Zamaril.

Instead she watched the curtains of falling rain. Concentrated on not moving. She fought down the growing restlessness, the ache of standing so still. Came to the realisation that she could never be a Shadow or Armun.

Sari's chuckle rippled through her mind. *"Me either."*

The first Wolves appeared slightly ahead of schedule, two of them, slinking down the street to Talyn's left, sticking to the shadows where they could, clearly keeping an eye on their surroundings. Each carried a wooden box in their hands—presumably the stolen izerdia. After studying the street for the few moments to make sure it was empty, they entered the warehouse across the street.

Moments later, a faint orange glow kindled in one of the second story windows.

"You don't think that's a bit much?" Zamaril breathed at her side, barely audible over the rain.

It was a fine balance. They didn't want to make it too obvious, but... "A dark and empty building might not convince them we're in there," she murmured.

Zamaril nodded imperceptibly. Fell silent again.

Four more Wolves came sneaking down the road to Talyn's right, crossing the street one by one after making a good show of checking their surroundings. A little shiver of relief went through her at each sighting—they were okay.

Two more groups of Wolves snuck into the warehouse over the next half-turn.

Only one of those two groups had lost their tail.

It was Zamaril who spotted them. After the last group went into the warehouse, he nudged her slightly, his head shifting to the left.

She stared, strained her eyes through the rain and the darkness. For a long moment she couldn't see anything. She was about to turn and ask Zamaril if he was certain when she caught it... and went even more still, if that were possible.

On the same side of the street as they were, but one block to the south. A single blur of movement as someone slid around a corner and out of sight.

"How many?" she breathed.

"Two."

Shit, she'd only seen the one. The second must be a Shadow. Thank the skies she'd brought Zamaril with her.

"Go," she murmured.

They had to move quickly. One of the followers, probably the Shadow, would stay to keep an eye on the warehouse while the other would go back to where the Armun were holed up in Darmour to report in that they'd found the Wolves' hideout.

Exactly what Talyn wanted.

She and Zamaril inched their way to the corner, slowly enough that their movement wouldn't be noticeable in the darkness, then circled the block at a run, pausing to press themselves against the wall of the street corner. The lookout was around to their right. The other was heading away down the street to their left.

"I'll take the lookout." Despite her Callanan training, Talyn wasn't confident she could successfully tail an Armun without being noticed. Zamaril could do it in his sleep.

They moved at the same time.

Talyn dove right, not bothering to try and sneak up on the Shadow. She had to do this quickly enough that Zamaril didn't get too far ahead of her.

She literally couldn't see the Shadow amidst his cloaking magic, but she knew the rough approximation of where he had to be, and increased her pace, drawing a dagger. Rain slicked her skin, splashed up in puddles under her boots.

He stepped out to attack, knife flashing. She dodged aside, slammed her elbow into his jaw, then gripped the wrist holding the knife and twisted sharply. He dropped it with a cry of pain, his hold on the shadows vanishing at the same time.

She brought her knife sliding across his throat, then turned and left him bleeding out in the rain.

Zamaril was just vanishing around a corner two blocks away.

Talyn started running.

The Armun led them on a merry dance across the city, the Firth-lander spies as well-trained and disciplined as their Shadow brethren in keeping themselves hidden and discreet. The only difference was that one could hide in the shadows and was trained to assassinate, while the other had no shadow magic, but was just as deadly in their ability to find secrets and information—or plant it.

Eventually, over a full-turn later, and after a long stop at an inn that had Talyn itching with frustration, Zamaril stopped in an alleyway a block ahead of her and didn't move.

She gave it a quarter-turn, then crept over to join him.

The alley walls were high, closed in by apartment buildings, most of which had lit windows despite the late hour. Zamaril stood in a pool of darkness under one of several rusted stairwells leading to higher levels.

"That one." He pointed to a set of windows three stories up on the eastern side of the alley.

"It's the highest floor." She scanned their surroundings. "Go in via the roof?"

"It's what I would do."

She smirked. "You're the thief. I'll follow you."

He led her around to the other side of the same building, the rain still driving into her face, having long since soaked through her clothing. She barely noticed. Anticipation had kindled a flame of warmth in her chest that wasn't going out anytime soon.

In what she thought was an abundance of caution, Zamaril broke into a building further down the street, crept up to that roof, then made her clamber over the neighbouring rooves.

"This is how I was the best thief in Dock City," he muttered when he caught the look on her face. "By being careful."

"Yeah, yeah," she countered. "You've never been able to explain how the best thief in Dock City got himself caught."

Zamaril was through the lock on the roof access in seconds, and they moved quietly down the interior stairwell. Nothing looked or sounded out of place. Amidst the dull roar of the rain hitting the roof came the usual sounds of a building full of people.

Talyn drew her dagger when Zamaril paused outside a nondescript door that looked identical to the other doors in the hall. A crooked number thirteen hung from the paint-chipped wood. "You sure this is the one?"

He gave her a scornful look.

"Fine." She rolled her eyes. "Remember, go straight for the windows. I'll hold the door. Those should be the only two ways out... I hope."

Another scornful look.

"Attitude, Zamaril," she warned, grinning. "Now do your magic."

Zamaril had the lock picked without a sound in three heartbeats.

He went through the door at a run, Talyn close behind. Down a short, narrow hall and into an open living area lit by the hearth to their left.

Zamaril kept running, leaping up to the couch, across the table, and flipping before landing gracefully by the window. He beat one man there by seconds. "Nope," he said, drawing his sword and holding it ready. "Back you go."

Talyn stopped at the room's entrance, trained gaze taking in the situation in a single sweep.

Three men, two women. A Shadow and four Armun at a guess. All armed, but none holding drawn weapons. Four on the couch—it was the Shadow who'd made a run for the windows. He was only half visible, trying to cloak himself in the shadows from the dim corners.

"How did you find us?" a male Armun asked. He was soaked, his dripping cloak making a puddle on the floor. He'd clearly been so eager to share his news he hadn't bothered to take it off.

"We followed you. Your little ambush at the docks gave us a nice opportunity to turn the tables." She smiled without warmth. "Hate to tell you, but that warehouse you followed us to isn't our hideout."

"We're armed." A female Armun slowly rose to her feet, her calm and confidence indicating she was the leader. "If you attack, we'll defend ourselves."

"I'm sorry," Talyn said, meaning it. "But we can't afford to leave you alive."

The Shadow lunged at Zamaril while the Armun came for Talyn. Armun were elite fighters, almost as good as Callanan, and they could suck at her Callanan magic, draining it in a blink.

So she didn't use it.

Talyn parried the first knife thrust, swung around behind the woman, and buried her dagger in the Armun's back, right through her heart. She ducked the second woman's swing as she yanked the blade out, leaping up onto the back of the couch to avoid being flanked. Sheathing the dagger, she spun into a kick, slamming her boot into the nearest Armun. As he staggered away she jumped at the next, drawing to parry his knife, sweep his foot out from under him, then follow as he fell, sliding her blade into his heart.

She rose, breathing fast, scanning the room. Zamaril had killed the Shadow and remaining Armun and was watching.

"Well," he said, "it's going to be much easier to operate in Darmour now."

Talyn cocked her head. "Until Tarcos sends more."

"*If* he sends more. I doubt he's got an infinite supply lying around, and I imagine your friends are raining merry hell on them in Acleu too." His face darkened as his gaze scanned the room for any other potential threats. "Not to mention the hounds hunting Prince Cuinn."

Zamaril had a point. She forced away the rush of fear that tried to sweep through her at the idea of Shadows on Cuinn's tail. "Let's get out of here."

"Wait." Zamaril moved to the fireplace, quickly stamping out the fire with his boot before reaching in to pull out the remaining scraps of what had been burning in there.

Talyn went to kneel beside him, studying the burned scraps as he laid them out.

"'*Port*'… '*four divisions*'…" He read aloud from one, then, "'*Warlord has approved*'. What do you think it means?"

"No idea. But it confirms Azrilan and Tarcos are working on something together." Impatience surged. She hated not knowing.

Zamaril picked up a larger piece of charred parchment that had been lying under the others. "'*Armun report planned Aimsir redeployment to Conmoran border*'….'*Fivemonth. Week three*'….'*signal to move*.'"

Talyn cursed. "That's a month away."

Urgency thrummed at her. Azrilan and Tarcos were planning

something in the Twin Thrones. It might be nothing. Just a status report.

But her instincts told her it was worse than that. They were planning something in particular. Something the Twin Thrones wouldn't see coming.

She needed to figure out what it was.

CHAPTER 32

$\mathcal{T}$alyn and Zamaril arrived back at the real safehouse not long after midnight.

"A couple full-turns of sleep, then I want to get into the mines while it's still dark," she said as they climbed long narrow steps up to the apartment. Her body ached pleasantly—nothing worse than she'd always felt after a fight. For the hundredth time she sent silent thanks to Jystar for his work.

"I'm as keen to get back as you are," the thief agreed.

Reaching the door, she knocked out the code, waited until a return knock came from inside—signaling all was well—before she opened the door and entered. They often didn't keep a fire going, so it was dim inside and it took her a moment to register the two additional people in the room aside from Saniya.

"Let me guess." Cynia's voice sounded dryly. "Darmour's contingent of Armun and Shadows is no more."

Talyn grinned, crossed the room to hug her friends. "What are you two doing here?"

"It's certainly not for the décor," Leviana grumbled. "A fire would be nice."

"We do our best to make it appear as if nobody lives here full time,"

Saniya said. "Standard practice for keeping an un-discovered safehouse."

"Could we at least have a lamp?" Cynia asked.

Without a word, Talyn and Zamaril went over to pull thick curtains across the room's two windows, and then Saniya struck flint and lit a lantern, placing it on a small table in the centre of the room. "Liadin's team?" Talyn asked Saniya.

"Holed up in the warehouse waiting in case any Armun or Shadows broke free of your trap," Saniya confirmed. "All safe and accounted for."

"None got free," Zamaril said simply. "They're in for a quiet night."

It was only once the lamp's dim glow began to suffuse the room that Talyn noticed the bruising on Leviana's jaw and the bandage wrapping Cynia's left calf. Worry flooded her. "What happened?"

"A run in with a particularly nasty Armun on our way out of Acleu." Leviana shrugged. "He won't be bothering anybody else."

"Something's wrong," Talyn said as they gathered around the table, not framing it as a question. Her friends were tense, standing close together as if for reassurance.

"Azrilan's fleet is ready to go," Cynia said bluntly. "Ten ships are sailing south along the Montagni coast from Darinoue as we speak, where they'll join twenty more waiting at Acleu. Six more are on their way to Feather Bay to pick up every bit of izerdia the Kingcouncil currently has stored at the citadel."

Saniya whistled. "You got all of that? I'm impressed."

"We got more," Leviana continued. "The ships from Darinoue are packed with Berserkers, those in Acleu with cavalry and slave infantrymen. Tarcos is sending two Firthlander ships to meet them halfway with three legions of niever-flyers to protect the fleet."

"Three legions." Talyn frowned, sitting back. "He's been at war for what, five months? And battling SkyRiders that entire time. Three legions has to be a significant percentage of his remaining force."

"He's over-extending," Zamaril said quietly.

"For good reason," Saniya pointed out. "A war fleet that size, protected by over a hundred niever-flyers, has an excellent chance of making it to the northern coastline of Conmor. That's a small army marching inland, a new front for the Dumnorix army to contend with."

Talyn's gaze flicked to Zamaril—could that be what the message they'd recovered had been talking about?

"There's more, we think." Cynia looked grim.

Talyn's heart sank. "What is it?"

"Saniya, one of your people managed to get himself seated near a group of Montagni naval officers drinking together." Leviana took a breath. "They were drunk, and not overly coherent, but they were of the belief that their war fleet is being timed to coincide with something."

"What?" Zamaril demanded.

"It wasn't clear. My guess? An attack Tarcos is planning to launch ahead of the fleet arriving to draw forces away from the Conmoran north coast," Cynia said.

A brief silence fell. Talyn kept pacing. "That fits with something Zamaril and I just learned." She gave them a quick explanation.

"The secret messages to and from Arataire." Saniya was on her feet now too. "It's all connected, surely. But how?"

"To defend against a fleet this size, the Twin Thrones will need to bring the Greencloaks and longbows in from Calumnia." Leviana looked at her partner.

"*If* they can march them over the Ayrlemyre and all the way to northern Conmor before it arrives," Talyn murmured. "Fivemonth is only a few weeks away. And then they'll be vulnerable to a flanking attack from the south—something both Azrilan and Tarcos are clever enough to do. I wouldn't be surprised if that's what Tarcos was planning."

"We've known this was coming," Saniya said sensibly. "Now it's here, so let's deal with it."

"She's right," Zamaril, looking unhappy to be agreeing with her. "The solution is to stop the fleet. That gives the Dumnorix a fighting chance against whatever else Tarcos and Azrilan are planning, right?"

Silence fell.

It wasn't as simple as that. Whatever Tarcos was planning, it would be clever, and unexpected. And if the Twin Thrones didn't know where the threat was coming from, there was no way to properly defend against it.

Talyn halted her pacing. "I have to go to Port Lachley," she said, throwing up a hand to forestall the protests forming on all their faces. "Levs, Cynia, estimated arrival of the ships travelling to Feather Bay for the izerdia?"

"I'd guess two days from now, then a day or two to load up, and two more days to re-join the fleet," Cynia said. "The ships from Dari-noue will have arrived by then, and I imagine they won't linger long before sailing south."

"The ships Tarcos is sending with the nievers—have they set off yet?"

"Don't know."

"Look, Tal, if you're heading home, we're coming with you. That's non-negotiable." Leviana wore her fiercest expression.

Talyn smothered a smile. "Saniya, I need to get to Dock City. Zamaril, myself, the two Callanan and ten of the Wolves that came with us for tonight's ambush."

"You don't ask for much," Saniya said sourly. "But it's doable."

"Good, make room for yourself as well."

"Really?" She brightened.

"Yes, but after we do what we need to in Dock City, you'll be on the first boat across the channel to Acleu to take command of your network and the remaining Callanan there. You're going to do your utmost to take apart that fleet before it leaves. Zamaril, can you go to the warehouse and speak with Liadin? Tell him the plan. He should take the rest of the Wolves back to the outpost tonight and fill Windsong and Corrin in."

He nodded and left, the door clicking soft shut behind him.

"Levs, Cynia, start talking. Saniya needs to know everything you do."

Cynia lifted a hand. "You said *after we do what we need to do.* I take it you have some sort of crazy plan?"

Talyn grinned. "When do I not have a crazy plan?"

"*This is so exciting!*" Sari chirped in then.

"*Isn't it!*"

"*You sure you're not coming up with some crazy plan just so you can go south and see Cuinn?*"

Talyn's smile widened. "*That's the beauty of it. This is my most epic plan ever, and it just so happens carrying it out means I get to go see Cuinn. And my family.*" Finally.

"*In that case, let's get started.*"

CHAPTER 33

*C*uinn bustled out of his room, shirt mostly buttoned, hair damp. The echo of the ringing bells announcing an inbound SkyRider still sounded through the corridors. An eagle landing at the fortress rather than the adjacent SkyRider roost meant an important message for the family, so he'd dressed quickly and bolted out.

Theac waited outside, impeccable in a clean uniform. A quarter-turn earlier, they'd both been sparring in the yard with Evani and other Kingshield.

"How do you do that so fast?" Cuinn asked him as the two began walking for the war room.

"Some of us don't need to preen over our appearance, Your Highness."

"Be grateful there's nothing to be done about that ugly mug of yours, Theac. I am regent, remember. I need to look regal."

"Yes, Your Highness." A smile twitched at Theac's mouth as he cleared his throat. "Do you think it's word from the southeast?"

They'd sent fresh troops to reinforce the lines two weeks ago when the Firthlander forces began pressing so hard there was danger of them breaking through. The diversion of troops to the Calumnian border had cost them. But so far they were still holding the lines.

"I'm hoping it's news telling us the great big Montagni war fleet about to head this way sank in a freak storm." That depressing tidbit of information, from the Callanan in Acleu, had arrived two days earlier.

His boots rapped on the stone floor as he marched into the audience chamber. Alyna would have made herself available the moment the bell sounded, but he was surprised to find Ariar there as well.

"You're usually on a horse this time of day," Cuinn commented.

"The bells intrigued me. Maybe this one is a good message," Ariar said sourly.

Soar came through the doors on the heels of Ariar's comment, and all three Dumnorix straightened. The Sky Chieftain had been away leading the SkyRider hunt for the ships full of nievers Tarcos was sending to meet with the Montagni war fleet.

A quick use of magic told him Soar wasn't bringing good news, though. He sighed. "Lay it on us, Cousin."

"How do you do that?" Ariar complained.

"It's my magic, which I've explained before," Cuinn said dryly.

Soar dragged off his beanie, exhaustion in every line of his body, and dropped into a chair. "We can't find the ships."

Cuinn winced, and he tried to keep the unease that announcement caused from leaking out through his song magic. If Tarcos's legions of niever-flyers successfully joined the Montagni war fleet, they'd have to throw most of their SkyRider force at it to have any chance of stopping them making landfall on the Port Lachley coastline.

And with so many niever-flyers, they'd lose a lot of SkyRiders. SkyRiders that were the main reason ships weren't landing in force on their eastern coast.

"I'm not surprised." Alyna spoke what they were all thinking. "Tarcos probably sent his ships on a heading far to the north before veering west to join the Montagni fleet—he knows the range of our eagles off the coast is limited."

"Then we need to send the navy out there to try and intercept them," Ariar said, pacing the floor by the table. His frustration was visible, and it made Cuinn want to leap out of his chair and start pacing too. Sometimes song magic was as much of a curse as it was a blessing.

"If we do that, they'll be searching miles of ocean with no idea of where to look," Cuinn disagreed. "We need them here to throw at the Montagni fleet when it arrives."

"What if we make a hard push in the mountains—rather than holding the lines in the foothills, we send the army in, try and force the Firthlander forces back to give us a bit of time to redeploy to the north and defend against the fleet?" Alyna suggested.

"It might work," Ariar said. "But having to face such a fleet—we'll take a big hit. We might not have enough to deploy back to the mountains and hold them. And the distances involved… we can't move our army around quickly enough."

"Not to mention sending our infantry into the rugged terrain of the mountains against Bearmen is a recipe for disaster," Soar pointed out. "Your Aimsir could do it on a smaller scale like before, Ariar, but I don't think we can afford to send enough of them into the mountains to do what Alyna is suggesting. It would leave our defensive lines horribly vulnerable."

That was what Cuinn feared too. But he didn't have any better solutions—war strategy wasn't his forte. Anxiety made his chest tight. The situation felt akin to holding onto a precipitous clifftop with aching fingers that were slowly losing their grip. And right now, he didn't have the answers they needed.

The terrible truth was, if the war fleet arrived, the Twin Thrones couldn't defend against it while it was still facing the Firthlander invasion. The Callanan, SkyRiders and Aimsir were elite, but their numbers were limited and they were already stretched too thin. The whole room knew it—the silence was heavy with the weight of that knowledge.

"Dammit, where is Saundin?" Soar slammed a frustrated hand on the table and rose to his feet.

"Even if our plan with him works, it won't be in time to recall those ships full of niever-flyers going to join the Montagni fleet," Ariar pointed out.

The table sank into another bitter silence, all of them mulling over the problem. The sound of the door opening broke it and they watched Theac stride across the stone to Cuinn. The Wolf leaned down to murmur in his ear.

"Saundin is here. In your rooms."

Relief sank through him and Cuinn leapt to his feet. "Soar, it seems like your demand has been met. Lunch in my quarters? We can come back to solving impossible problems after we've had something to eat."

THE ANTICIPATION of the three Dumnorix buzzed around Cuinn like an annoying gnat as they headed up to his rooms. They'd guessed instantly at the reason for his invitation.

"Could you just take a breath? All of you, please," he ended up pleading.

Three surprised looks turned his way. Which just added confusion to the anticipation hitting him. He sighed and did his best to ignore it.

Saundin didn't appear from within Cuinn's bedroom until all of them were inside and Theac and Evani had closed the door. Cuinn's song magic immediately swung from anticipation to dread. The Armun was expressionless as always, but he carried bad news.

"Rados didn't go for it." Cuinn's shoulders slumped. What was he going to do now? He had no other ideas, no solutions.

"It's not that. And I'm sorry I've taken so long. I would have been here a week ago but I heard something odd as I was leaving Samatia and thought it worth the risk to stay and find out more."

Alyna crossed the room and sat on Cuinn's sofa. He took the seat beside her, Soar on the other side. Ariar remained standing by the fireplace.

Saundin dropped smoothly into the remaining chair and clasped his hands. "Rados is open to negotiations with you. It will require you getting him out of Firthland safely, and given what I know of him, I suggest you send someone important to fetch him. You need to make him feel like he's being treated with the right amount of respect."

Cuinn wanted to be happy at this news. Relieved. Grateful that his plan might be bearing fruit. But all that was stifled under dread. "And what's the bad news?"

"I'm sorry I don't have more to give you, but..." Saundin took a breath. "Seven Shadows were dispatched from Samatia over the course of a week just before I left. I spoke to a friend who is one of the Shadowlord's aides—the orders for the Shadows came after a series of highly discreet messages exchanged between Tarcos and Azrilan."

"Messages about what?" Soar demanded.

"They were carried by a single trusted Armun chosen by Tarcos. The way I understand it, not even the Shadowlord knew the contents. The warlord was taking every precaution possible that these messages were not intercepted or read by anyone but Azrilan."

"Where were the seven Shadows going?" Alyna asked.

"I don't know."

A muscle in Ariar's jaw ticked. "They might be coming at us again. We'll have to alert the Kingshield."

"It makes sense. Assassinating Aethain worked for Tarcos before. If he takes us out, worst case there'll be enough turmoil in the kingdom leadership to make full invasion much easier. Best case the Lords' councils just hand the Twin Thrones over to him," Soar said grimly.

Cuinn's eyes shot to Saundin. There'd been *something* in his expression. "You don't agree?"

Saundin lifted a hand to stroke his beard. "I do, actually. But I would advise against assuming you know what Tarcos is up to. The lengths he's gone to in keeping the messages secret are extreme, and that tells me whatever he's planning, it's big. And risky."

"I think we can assume that whatever it is, it'll be timed to coincide with the Montagni fleet's arrival." Alyna stood. "I'll go and brief Ceannar now. We'll make sure the Kingshield are on full alert."

"We'll need to discuss who goes to fetch Rados, too," Cuinn said.

"If you'll loan me a SkyRider, I'll leave for Samatia now and let Rados know you've agreed to extract him to conduct the negotiations here in Port Lachley." Saundin crossed to the desk and quickly scribbled out a note on a blank piece of parchment. "I will meet whoever you send at this location in seven days, and I'll use the time to try and find out more on what Tarcos is planning."

"Thank you." Cuinn shook his hand, hesitating. "I know that by doing this, you're technically betraying your warlord, but—"

"I don't need you to tell me what I'm doing." Saundin said tightly.

Cuinn studied him, sensing only resolve with a hint of regret in the man "All right. Theac, will you ask one of the SkyRider Kingshield to get Saundin back to Firthland as fast as possible? Take one of the naval patrol boats—that's the quickest way to get a SkyRider in range of the Firthlander coast." With that combination, Saundin should be back within three days or so.

Theac saluted, opened the door for Saundin, and the two men left.

"Are we sure we can trust him?" Soar asked once the door closed. "He could be playing us all."

"Talyn does. That's good enough for me." Ariar pushed off the wall. "I'm going to get a ride in before we talk about who goes to fetch Rados."

Once they were both gone, Cuinn sank into a chair by the unlit fire, running a tired hand through his hair. He wished Talyn was there so badly the feeling overwhelmed him. At least he now knew she was alive and safe. Just knowing that... it made him stronger, more confident. Even so, unease thrummed through him.

What was Tarcos planning?

CHAPTER 34

$\mathcal{T}$alyn, Saniya, Zamaril, the two Callanan and ten Wolves travelled down the west coast of Mithranar from Darmour in three separate fishing vessels. They made landfall in the eerie hours before dawn in a remote, forested area on the western peninsula that cradled Feather Bay.

From there, Leviana, Cynia and the Wolves remained hidden while Saniya led Talyn and Zamaril through the trees until the forest thinned and they reached the outskirts of Dock City.

When they stepped out into hot, Mithranan sunlight, the ramshackle city laid out before them, Talyn stopped. Her eyes drank in the beautiful marble wall and gushing waterfall, then swept out over the turquoise bay and the chaotic hustle of the Dock Quarter. A deep breath filled her lungs with spices and thick, soupy air. Sweat already trickled down her back.

"Something wrong?" Saniya asked.

"I'm fine." Talyn took another deep breath. "It's just... it's good to be home."

"Once we enter the city, you can't afford to be spotted or this game is over before it's even begun." Saniya looked at Zamaril too. "Keep those hoods down over your faces and let me do the talking if anyone speaks to us."

"We heard you the first time," Talyn said impatiently.

They mingled with the crowds on the busy streets as Saniya led them through the Wealthy Quarter and into the Dock Quarter. Despite Saniya's caution, Talyn thought it unlikely she or Zamaril would be recognised. Her eyes were admittedly unique, but they were mostly hidden by the hood, and the tattoo and scar on her face would deter people from looking too closely. And Zamaril had always been adept at being innocuous.

The raucous clatter and the myriad scents overlaid with sweat and humidity, after so long gone, were like a balm to her still-healing spirit. Even Zamaril wore a little smile at her side.

Even so, she didn't fail to notice the change in mood since she'd been here last.

Then, cautious hope had pervaded the streets. Mithanis had been defeated and Cuinn was on the verge of taking the throne and marrying a Dumnorix princess in a formal alliance with the Twin Thrones. For the first time ever, the humans looked forward to the possibility of a home that treated them as equals, not inferiors.

How quickly that hope had crumbled.

Now the humans looked cowed and afraid, and there was a visibly stronger presence of WingGuard flying over the streets and standing guard on major corners. City Patrolmen were equally numerous, though from what Talyn could tell the two parties regarded each other with wariness and suspicion.

Talyn sucked in a breath, refusing to let guilt or despair claim her. They would fight on. They would bring that hope back. She would settle for nothing less. And she knew without doubt that Cuinn was doing the exact same thing.

Still... doubt continued to nag at her. Doubt in her ability to counter another move of Tarcos's. She'd failed before so thoroughly, it was hard to be sure she could see whatever they planned next in time to stop it.

She and Zamaril both started when a whoosh of wings rushed

over their heads, feathers almost close enough to touch. Saniya slowed as, just ahead, five Falcons dropped out of the sky, surrounding a man about to enter a shop. Without hesitation, two of the Falcons grabbed the man's arms, while the other three spread out to keep the public from interceding.

The man struggled, but all he earned for his efforts was a hard blow behind the ear. He slumped in his captors' arms, moaning in pain and bleeding.

Without making a conscious decision, Talyn lurched forward, one hand going to the knife hidden in her sleeve. Before she could move two steps, an iron-hard grip closed over her forearm and yanked her back.

"Do nothing or you'll never get out of here!" Saniya hissed in her ear.

"I can't just walk away." *I am their Ciantar,* she wanted to scream.

"You have to." Now Zamaril was at her side too, helping Saniya to shepherd her away as unobtrusively as possible.

Bitterly torn, she reluctantly allowed Saniya and Zamaril to guide her away down a side street. The man's cries of fear followed them, scraping over every nerve she had.

"You used to have better control of yourself," Saniya muttered, finally dropping her arm.

Her mouth tightened in affront, but she didn't deny it. The injuries, the slave camp, the desperate fear for Cuinn and her Wolves, it had left her with mere remnants of her hard-won control. As if she were still a flayed nerve, exposed for all the world to see. She had to re-learn it. Tried not to be afraid that she never would.

"It'll take time. You'll get there," Sari murmured.

As if sensing her distress, Zamaril leaned into her briefly, shoulder to shoulder, before swinging away again. Her emotion settled to a manageable ache.

"Talyn, you know Zamaril—"

"Don't. Just don't, Sari."

Talyn's heart began thudding when they approached their destination, Saniya slowing their pace even further to ensure it didn't seem as if there was any particular purpose to their movements.

A small bell chimed over the café door when Saniya opened it and strolled towards the scruffy young man making kahvi for his customers. Talyn and Zamaril lingered in the corner.

Petro stiffened the moment he saw Saniya, then his eyes immediately roamed the room until they fell on Talyn. He looked away just as quickly, carefully putting down the pot of steaming liquid he was stirring. Then he came out from behind the counter and walked around to unlock a door leading into the back. "Come through here." He waved the three of them over.

Talyn and Zamaril followed Saniya without comment, hoping none of the other customers thought to wonder what two hooded people not obviously carrying anything were doing. Petro came last, closing the door behind them and cutting off the light.

They walked into a storage room lit by a single lamp hanging from the centre of the ceiling. Once they were all crowded inside, Zamaril and Talyn pushed their hoods back and Petro swung to face Talyn. He took a halting step forward, then reached out to take her hand. "Ciantar."

She squeezed it. "It's good to see you, Petro. Thank you for helping us."

A smile flashed over his face. "I hear you have a plan."

A knock sounded at the back door. Petro gestured for them to move into the shadows out of the line of sight of the door, then went to open it. The moment he saw who it was, he stepped back to wave them through.

A small, straight-shouldered man stepped inside, his watchful demeanour indicating he spent a lot of time looking out for danger. He looked different in the motley attire he was wearing, less proper than when he wore his Wolf uniform, his dark hair longer and stubble on his jaw. But he was still the talon Talyn had always been able to rely upon.

His eyes went straight to her. "Ciantar?" he asked tentatively.

"Andres!" She crossed the room and threw her arms around him before he could process what was happening. He hugged her back, then seemed to realise who he was hugging and stepped away, clearing his throat awkwardly.

She smiled, trying to hold back tears. "It's really good to see you, Talon Tye."

"I'm alive too." Zamaril chose that moment to step forward, his characteristic smirk lighting his narrow features.

"Zamaril!" A wide, delighted smile crossed Andres's face. The two men shook hands enthusiastically, beaming at each other.

"My people generally just say hello when we see each other and then get on with things," Saniya muttered. "You lot are positively nauseating."

Talyn chuckled. "Andres, I'm told you've been running our underground network here?"

"Along with Len, her second." Andres cocked an eyebrow Saniya's way. "He would have been here, but he's occupied with a situation that unexpectedly cropped up—six Montagni warships just arrived in the bay."

"Perfect." Talyn smiled.

"Are you finally going to tell us what your plan is?" Saniya asked pointedly.

"I certainly am." Talyn clapped her hands. "First, Saniya, Andres, can you get the Wolves and me up to the citadel without being seen, preferably inside the palace?"

"You don't ask much, do you?" She arched an eyebrow in a perfect imitation of Talyn. "Why?"

A smile curled at Talyn's mouth. "Because we're going to put on a nice display for Dock City. Some entertainment for the humans and a distraction for anyone paying attention to Feather Bay."

"A distraction from what?" Andres asked.

"From Zamaril, Leviana and Cynia doing a stealthy bit of work. And from me getting out of the harbour on a ship south," Talyn said.

Zamaril smirked. "I'm good at stealthy work."

"Love entertaining displays, myself," Andres echoed. "Whatever you're planning, though, I hope it takes into account a larger number of Falcons than usual in the palace."

"Why?" She frowned.

"King Azrilan is here. He arrived a few days ago—word is, he came to check in on how Swiftwing is managing things. The copper production has dropped in the north, the wood shipments to Montagn have stopped, and he doesn't like it."

Grins all round. Azrilan was uncomfortable enough to make a personal trip here. A little bit of Talyn's doubt receded. Maybe she could do this.

Still, the news of his presence was a shock. Talyn had planned her display for Azrilan's Kingcouncil, banking on word of it quickly making its way to Arataire. She hadn't expected to find him here, right in front of her.

But it could work. It could work *really* well.

"Anything on the secret messages the Acleu governor has been sending to Arataire?" Saniya asked quietly.

Andres shook his head. "Len's got one of his best informants coming over for a scheduled meet on the dawn tide tomorrow. We're hoping he's managed to learn something. Azrilan wouldn't be putting so much effort into secrecy unless he was hiding something big. I admit it worries me."

"Us too." Zamaril filled him in on what they'd learned in Darmour.

"Have we considered that the messages are simply passing *through* the governor?" Andres asked them. "What if they're coming from Samatia?"

"From Tarcos." Talyn murmured the words. It made her instincts scream to life. She should have thought of it herself. "Nice, Andres."

"This isn't good," Saniya muttered. "It's making me itch. And things are *never* good when I start to itch."

"One thing at a time." Talyn lifted her hand before they let the cloud of uneasiness that was building drown them completely. "Tomorrow, we're going to bring a bit of hope back to Mithranar and strike a blow against Azrilan while we're at it. Maybe it will be enough to stop whatever he's planning. And if it's not, then we will deal with that too."

"I wish I was there!" Sari said enviously.

"Me too. This is one of those plans you would have loved."

It was time to fight back.

CHAPTER 35

The ringing bells sounded urgently through the pre-dawn hours. Sleeping uneasily—part of him expecting a Shadow attack at any second since hearing Saundin's news, the rest trying to figure out what Tarcos was planning—Cuinn came instantly awake. Shoving the blankets off, he dragged on pants and a shirt, then yanked open his door.

Evani fell in next to him, a quiet but reassuring presence as he walked through the empty corridors. The rest of his detail surrounded him at a distance.

The entrance foyer was dim, only a handful of torches lit, the great double doors closed for the night. Ariar huddled with a SkyRider messenger who'd just come down the stairs from the landing platform. It was Drift, one of Cuinn's old legion mates—whatever news he carried, it must be from Mothduriem.

"What is it?" Their shock and horror was so strong it hit him halfway across the room. He swallowed around the gaping pit opening in his stomach, forced himself to keep walking.

Ariar turned to him, blue eyes dark, face paler than Cuinn had ever seen it. "Tarcos hit Port Lathilly three days ago."

The world went momentarily still.

"That can't..." He stopped, cleared his throat. Before he could manage anything further, footsteps approached.

"What's going on?" Alyna's sharp voice rapped out. Soar was close behind her, hair tousled from sleep.

"Tell us everything, Drift," Cuinn said, using a hint of magic to give the SkyRider confidence in such intimidating company.

Drift straightened his shoulders. "Port Lathilly has been hit. The Firthlanders sent Shadows in to kill the city's garrison commander and officers a few full-turns ahead of the attack. They also took out the skeleton crews onboard all ships in harbour, including our navy boats. They hold the harbour and the land surrounding it. They'd have the city too if it weren't for the Callanan bolstering the division of Greencloaks stationed in the city. They're holding the wall..." He trailed off, cleared his throat. "They *were* holding the city wall when I left."

Cuinn, Soar and Ariar stared at each other as Drift's words faded into horrified silence. The news was like a body blow. Port Lathilly... one of their biggest trading ports. If they lost Port Lathilly...

Alyna turned, summoned the nearest Kingshield with an imperious flick of her wrist. "Wake the First Blade and get her here now."

The woman saluted and left at a run.

"What forces has Tarcos committed to the attack?" Soar asked Drift, seemingly galvanized by Alyna's calm. Cuinn took a breath and let it steady him too.

"Three legions of niever-flyers and close to a thousand Bearmen. They were carried in on three warships that are now blockading the harbour."

Soar looked horrified. "It's a miracle he didn't take the city if those numbers are accurate."

Alyna frowned. "Three legions and that many Bearmen... if you add that to the numbers he's already got pushing through the Ayrlemyre Mountains, then he's over-committed."

Cuinn felt their shock and despair and tried fiercely to separate it from his. Nobody would think clearly if they gave in to it. He was regent. He had to make this right somehow.

"The war fleet is coming," Ariar said, panic tugging at his voice. "We can't fight both off at once. Sending soldiers to help defend Port Lathilly will draw our forces away from the north."

Alyna began to pace. "It's worse than that."

"Alyna, what is it?" Cuinn was fighting a losing battle with his own emotions compounded with those of his family, but he did his best to focus. Bring himself under control. Fill his voice with calm.

"Port Lathilly is one of our main weapons' storehouses. Over half our stocks of izerdia are kept there, and a good percentage of our stores of swords, shields, arrows." Her mouth tightened. "We keep them there because they can be moved quickly anywhere throughout the kingdom from that port."

"Tarcos knows that." Cuinn's stomach sank. "Doesn't he?"

Soar said, "He might be over-committing his forces, but he's also put himself in position to win a massive stockpile of explosives and weaponry to bolster his army."

Ariar's shoulders straightened and a determined look filled his face. "Then we make sure he loses. We do whatever we have to. We win Port Lathilly, then we deal with the fleet."

Nobody pointed out that winning a battle for a port they'd half-lost already seemed impossible to do in a matter of days before the fleet arrived.

Cuinn took a deep, steadying breath. "Soar, you will take a handful of your best SkyRiders and a Callanan warrior pair, and go to Firthland tonight to get Rados and bring him here."

"We need Soar leading the SkyRiders to defend Port Lathilly," Alyna disagreed. "We'll have to send several legions there to have any hope of winning it back."

"No matter what happens in the short term, we will lose this war without Rados," Cuinn said.

"You say that as if Rados is a sure thing. He's not," Soar snapped. "It's a plan with a small chance of success. We can't afford to place all our hope in it."

Cuinn rounded on him. "We have no other choice. Even if we win Port Lathilly, then somehow defeat the war fleet, more will come. We are losing fighters and flyers with every battle we fight. This war has to end before we lose it."

They stared at each other for a long moment. Cuinn forced himself to hold his cousin's gaze, to use the strength he'd learned, that he'd fought bitterly for, to hold his place as regent, as the man making the final decisions.

"I think Soar is right. But you are regent, and we all accept that," Alyna said quietly.

At Alyna's words, Soar nodded and broke Cuinn's gaze.

In that moment, when the Dumnorix submitted completely to him, Cuinn felt the true weight of kingship for the first time. If he chose wrong here, it would ruin them. But it was *his* choice, and he would make it without fear.

"Good," he told them, infusing song magic into his voice, turning it to steel. "Rados is the priority. Soar is a Dumnorix prince, rank enough to give Rados the appropriate respect. *I* will lead the SkyRiders in the fight for Port Lathilly."

Their eyes widened. Drift smiled, realised the company he was in, and dropped his gaze to the floor.

"The legions know and trust me. I can do it. Ariar, you'll come too and help with tactical advice. Alyna, you have my proxy to do whatever is necessary while we're gone."

"The SkyRiders will fly for Wolf." Drift spoke suddenly, unexpectedly, flushing deep red when the Dumnorix turned to stare at him. "And we will win for him."

Ariar almost smiled. "I suggest we deploy SkyRiders and Callanan along with the Greencloaks already stationed at Port Lathilly. We keep the navy in the north, ready to defend against the Montagni fleet."

"Alyna?" Cuinn turned to her.

"Ariar is right. We can't leave ourselves entirely exposed." She looked grim. "We have to gamble on re-taking Port Lathilly without the navy."

"What of the mountain coastline? We'll have to pull troops away from defending the borders," Soar said.

None of them had an answer for that.

"Then that's what we'll do and we'll make it work," Cuinn said, forcing confidence into his voice. "Soar, how many SkyRiders are currently stationed here in Port Lachley?"

"Half a legion. All on rest and recuperation after combat in the mountains."

As if knowing it was her cue, Shia Thorineal appeared on the opposite side of the entry foyer, quick strides carrying her over. Her gaze ran over the grim faces, and she visibly braced herself.

Cuinn looked at her. "First Blade. Can you get your hands on twenty-five Callanan within the full-turn?"

She paused, cocked her head. "I can get twenty."

"Do it. Now. Get yourself and them up to the SkyRider base as quickly as you can. I'll explain what's going on when you get there." Cuinn spun back to the others. "Ariar and I will fly for Mothduriem tonight with Shia and her Callanan to gather the SkyRiders. We'll all be in Port Lathilly in four days."

Soar nodded. "And by the time you win this and return, I'll have Rados safely here and ready to negotiate."

Cuinn met all their gazes in turn. "Burn bright and true."

CHAPTER 36

*a*n early morning mist shrouded the palace like a blanket. Saniya had moved them up there during the early hours, a long walk up from the bottom levels to avoid crossing the guarded bridge over the Rush.

Zamaril and Andres paced just behind Talyn. The mist was a bit of luck. Only human servants and workers moved through the palace at this hour, but Talyn had still been concerned they would be recognised before they could get into position. She tried not to worry about the other ten Wolves, being escorted by Saniya's second, Len.

She didn't want to be seen until they were ready. And then, well... fierce anticipation heated her blood.

"Here's a bit of delicious irony for you," Saniya murmured as she and Talyn waited for the two talons to clamber up a ladder. "This is the route Navis showed us for the night we broke in to try and steal the izerdia."

"He's dead now," Talyn said flatly.

Saniya scowled. "He'd have been dead sooner if you hadn't set him free when we held him prisoner."

"Don't put that on me. You had him for weeks—you weren't planning on killing him." Talyn's counter hid the guilt she still felt. She'd helped Savin escape Vengeance's compound, thinking he was an ally. If she'd just left him there... so many things might be different.

"I was. I just wanted to make sure I couldn't use him first." Saniya shrugged.

The mist slowly lightened, burned away by an already warm sun overhead. Good. The cover had been useful so far, but it wouldn't do for what was about to happen to be obscured by the weather.

They began passing the occasional human servant. Each time, they kept their heads down and stride loose as if they were on an important task. The occasional winged person soared by overheard, but winged folk never paid undue attention to human servants.

The tension ratcheted up sharply as they entered the Falcon barracks area and approached their goal. Talyn glanced back to give both men a warning look—any hint of nervousness, especially around Falcons with song magic—and someone *would* start paying attention. The cloaks wouldn't hold up to more than a passing glance.

It was hard to shake off her own anxiousness as they made for the Kingcouncil chambers near the barracks. The closer they came, the greater the odds of being spotted and stopped.

Talyn took a breath, pushed the nerves deep down inside.

The ring of clashing blades caught her attention, and she slowed. Falcons trained with wooden training weapons. The only people she'd ever seen spar with real blades in Mithranar were...

Going with instinct, she turned, hoping that Saniya and the Wolves behind her did the same. Minutes later she stopped at the railing of a walkway looking down into a Falcon drill yard.

She rested her hands on the cool marble, her heart beginning to thud in her chest.

Azrilan sparred below, fair skin glistening with sweat, charcoal wings catching the glow of morning sun as the last of the fog burned away. His opponent was desperately trying to stay in the fight, wings rustling in agitation, footwork sloppy and panicked. It was only the two of them, with a couple of Falcons from the protective flight hovering nearby. The hour was too early for the wings to have started the day's drill yet.

Fiery rage leapt in her chest, and a blue glow sparked around her hands. For what he'd done to Cuinn, for what he'd done to her Wolves, she thought about killing Azrilan then and there. But reason asserted itself. He was a skilled warrior, and while she could probably best him, it would take time, and by then the WingGuard would be swarming all over her. She wouldn't escape that.

No. She was going to kill the prince of games. Just not today.

"Saniya, go. Get clear before we start this," she said quietly.

"You sure you don't want me to stay and help?" her cousin asked.

"I need you down on the docks." Where Leviana and Cynia would be waiting for Saniya and the signal to move. The enormity of her plan weighed on her for a moment—so many moving parts, so little time to have organised it—until she thought of those who would be carrying it out. And how much faith she had in them.

Saniya left without another word.

"Are you ready?" she asked her talons quietly.

"Always," Zamaril murmured.

A smile curled at Andres' mouth. "This is going to be fun, isn't it?"

"*So much fun*," Sari breathed in excitement.

All three of them shucked their cloaks, letting them fall to the ground at their feet.

Talyn lifted one palm off the railing, summoned her warrior magic, then sent a bright sapphire energy burst flying through the morning air. It exploded above Azrilan's head with a loud *crack*.

The prince of games spun, wings flaring wide, dark eyes flashing straight to hers across the space between them. His gaze flickered briefly to Zamaril and Andres at her side. Shifted back to her.

She lifted a hand. Waved.

Azrilan's lips curled in a snarl and he raised both hands to send his warrior magic flying at her. Talyn ducked and the two black balls of sparking energy flew harmlessly over her head and slammed into the wall behind her. A bellow of rage echoed through the morning as Azrilan spun to the Falcons in the yard with him. "Kill them. NOW!"

Several Falcons lifted into the air, two coming directly for Talyn and the Wolves, the others veering off—no doubt to raise the alarm and summon more Falcons.

Talyn gathered her magic and sent two quick bursts of warrior power at the approaching Falcons, forcing them to veer away, wings flapping madly.

"Time to go." Talyn turned to her Wolves.

"Go safe, Ciantar." Andres saluted.

"And you. Make sure you put on a show while you do," she told them. "Zamaril, your task is the most important."

"No need to remind me." He snorted, then he ran. Andres followed suit, heading in the opposite direction.

Talyn spun back to the railing, offered another wave at a furious-looking Azrilan, then shouted, "Come and get us, Prince of Games!"

Alarm bells began pealing. Bright colours flashed as Falcons shot into the sky from all directions. The two Falcons she'd attacked were righting themselves, swooping back in her direction.

Talyn grinned.

Then she ran.

TALYN SPRINTED along the open-aired walkway Zamaril had disappeared down, glancing back over her shoulder to track the two Falcons in pursuit. Although she'd forced them off-course, they were rapidly catching up, wings spread wide as they prepared to drop on her. Warrior magic flashed, slamming into the ground at her feet. She dodged, judging the distance and their speed finely, and when they were almost on her, she moved.

Veering abruptly to her left, she grabbed the walkway railing and swung herself over the side. Her body dropped two flights before she landed on another walkway below. Magic flashed harmlessly in the air over her head and exploded with three successive *cracks*.

Adrenaline and exhilaration flooded her, making her faster, stronger and more agile.

This was what she was born for.

Only one of the Falcons had been quick enough to swerve after her. She came to her feet, ducked under the downward thrust of his sword, then stepped inside his guard and slammed her knee into his groin.

A grunt of agony escaped him and he staggered away, doubling up. She picked up his fallen sword and took to her heels again.

Her run took her into a covered walkway, but shouts from above warned her that the other Falcon had drawn his companions to where she was. As soon as she emerged back into open air, a cluster of them dropped on her. She spun, swinging the sword in a wide enough arc to keep them from closing in.

A bow twanged above and she dropped to her knees, erecting a sapphire shield over her head. Three arrows ploughed into it.

Interesting. Someone had turned Falcons into archers during her absence.

Well, Azrilan had never been a fool.

Arrows and bursts of warrior magic ploughed into her shield, draining her magical energy. She dropped the shield, then lunged at the Falcons on her left so quickly all they could do was scramble awkwardly away. Talyn took two steps through the opening they made and dived out over the walkway railing.

This time she flung her body outwards, twisting in the air so that instead of landing on the walkway below, she fell past it, reached out to grab its railing and briefly halt her momentum before dropping down to the next level. Here she moved quickly into a closed walkway and started running.

Talyn knew the palace and citadel like the back of her hand, and her moves were planned. Using covered walkways to keep just ahead of pursuers, she got herself across the Rush and into the citadel proper.

Winged folk passing by or coming out of homes, inns or shops stopped in astonishment at the sudden appearance of a Wolf sprinting through one of the main thoroughfares of the citadel. The surprise quickly turned to unease when they spotted the Falcons pouring out of the palace skies in pursuit of her.

She was barely ahead of them.

Talyn paused to judge how close they were, and flashed a grin at those staring. "Remember me, your Ciantar?"

Not waiting for a response, she took off at a run again, weaving her way through the crowd. In such a populated area, the Falcons didn't dare loose their arrows or magic at her, so they had to chase her instead, trying to get close enough so they could surround her and force her to stand and fight.

But she wouldn't let them.

In the crowded and tangled walkways of the citadel, Talyn was faster without wings to drag her down, and she chose her route deliberately to keep the Falcons at bay.

Breath coming fast, sweat slicking her skin, Talyn sprinted out of a walkway lined with cafes and into a wide-open plaza that hosted a market. Loud shouts drifted from somewhere below and she moved to the southern edge of the plaza, leaning to stare over the edge.

Below, Andres' wiry form raced towards her through a wide-open street, several Falcons on his tail. He dodged and weaved, comfortably ahead for the moment.

Smiling, Talyn glanced back to sketch a wave to her own pursuers before leaping out into the open air, arms spread wide. Halfway down, she executed a lazy flip, using the *sabai* move to look behind and catch the wide-spread wings of the WingGuard as they followed her off the edge.

She came out of the flip, controlled her fall and landed on the walkway just ahead of Andres' running form. In a breath she was up and running beside him.

"Seen Zamaril?" she asked.

"Three streets back and heading straight for the wall walk," he said. "He's having way too much fun with this."

"Aren't you?" Talyn shot a look at him.

An uncharacteristic grin lit up Andres' dark face.

Without further ado, she split off from him and dodged onto a narrow bridge stretching between two forested hillsides.

More Falcons massed above, and once again she needed to erect an energy shield to protect herself from a hail of arrows as she crossed

the bridge. The area of the citadel on the other side was less populated, giving the Falcons more opportunity to fire, but she soon
reached another busy plaza and the arrows stopped.

Again, the winged folk in the vicinity stopped to stare at the astonishing sight of a Wolf being pursued through their citadel by a hoard
of increasingly frustrated Falcons. Shouts of consternation from
above warned her, and she looked up.

A grey and white-clad figure with scarlet wings plummeted down
through the massed WingGuard, sword flashing in the morning sun.
The Falcons milled uncertainly, crashing into each other in an attempt
to avoid the swinging blade. The skies were momentary chaos, especially as other winged folk enjoying the morning thermals were
caught up with pursuing Falcons.

"Ciantar!" Tirina dropped to the ground at Talyn's side. "It's a fine
morning for a run through the citadel."

Talyn grinned. "It certainly is. Thanks for the help."

"Anytime."

Tirina grinned back, saluted, then lifted into the sky as Talyn
turned on her heel and sprinted across the plaza. The Falcons were
forced to split up to follow them.

More cries of surprise and alarm drifted towards Talyn as she
approached an intersection of walkways. Seconds later, Nirrin and
Dansia came sprinting across the intersection from her right, a pack
of angry WingGuard in pursuit.

Laughing, Talyn judged her run so that she ducked and weaved
through the Falcons pursuing her Wolves, emerging out the other side
at just the right moment so her pursuers and Nirrin's crashed
together.

"*I wish I was there.*" Sari sighed wistfully.

"*Me too.*"

FOR THE NEXT HALF-TURN, Talyn and her Wolves led the WingGuard
on a merry dance through the citadel. The Falcons were limited by the
covered walkways and their lack of speed on foot compared to their

mostly human quarry. Talyn managed to keep far enough ahead to avoid a stand-up fight.

She could only imagine the thoughts of the winged folk citizens of the citadel, staring at Wolves racing past them with what must seem like hundreds of the WingGuard ineffectually trying to catch them.

Hopefully it made the point that humans were far from useless.

And that Azrilan and his WingGuard were.

Those Talyn passed mostly said nothing, only watched with a mixture of unease and shock on their faces, but none got in her way or made an attempt to stop her.

And the occasional anonymous cheer was exhilarating.

Eventually she put on a burst of speed and wound her way through a series of covered walkways until she emerged at the top of the marble wall dividing the citadel from Dock City—the top of the wall walk was only two strides to her right.

Chest heaving, sweat running in streams down her face and soaking her shirt, she surveyed her surroundings. The shouts and cries of pursuit came from several directions—following the plan, her Wolves were all slowly making their way to this spot.

The skies above the citadel seemed full of Falcons, but it didn't take long to see how chaotic it all was. There were too many of them, and there was obviously no central command hierarchy in place—nobody coordinating the pursuit. Instead Falcons all chased different targets.

Exactly as she'd expected.

Still, some were already dropping out of the sky towards her, finally catching up.

She dropped the sword she'd been carrying and took a deep breath to calm her racing heart. A moment later she sank into her magic, summoning as much of it as she could hold.

Her Callanan energy shield flashed into existence. She fed it with more power, growing the shield, making it brighter and larger.

It was a beacon for miles around.

And a wonderful, perfect distraction.

Once she'd made it as large as she could, teeth gritted with the effort, she shaped the shield, closing it in around her and then spinning it about in the air.

Cries sounded far below as those near the base of the wall caught sight of the bright beacon above them. Every human in Dock City knew what that particular hue of sapphire meant.

One by one, her Wolves appeared, sliding around her to run down the wall walk and into Dock City. As instructed, they'd lost their pursuers before making the final run out to the wall. It wouldn't take long for the Falcons above to catch on, though.

The last was Tirina, soaring over Talyn's head and dropping to the ground beside her.

"Ready, Ciantar?"

Both women looked up, at the tens upon tens of Falcons milling above Talyn, just waiting for her shield to die.

"Ready."

Talyn held the shining sapphire beacon for one more moment, flooding as much power into it as she could, making it high and bright enough for everyone to see. Then, with a gasping breath, she dropped it and stepped into Tirina's arms. The Wolf took them both into a plummeting dive off the wall.

The other Wolves had already scattered into the lanes and alleyways of the Wall Quarter. Tirina landed in the main street at the bottom of the walk, saluted, and sprinted away to the east.

Talyn went south.

If there had been the occasional cheer amongst the winged folk at the citadel at the sight of the Wolves, the Dock City humans were in an uproar. As Talyn ran, the shouts and cheers crashed around her, nearby and in the distance, exuberant and joyful.

For a brief, shining moment, the pall of fear that had hung over the city was lifted.

The Falcons tried to hunt them, of course, but those who got too close to the ground suddenly found themselves under a barrage of stones, fruit, sticks, buckets and anything else the humans had at hand to throw at them. Too many for the Falcons to arrest, too many to even take note of who they were, even if they could afford to waste time catching humans rather than chasing Wolves.

The City Patrol Talyn passed didn't seem to know what to do. Or what was happening. And the Falcons didn't think to try and get them involved in the pursuit.

After a time, Talyn ducked into an empty shopfront and ran through it into a series of back alleys hidden from sight from above by how closely the tall buildings were stacked together. It didn't take long to make her way out of the Market Quarter towards the Dock Quarter.

She lingered on a street corner to look up at the skies. It was hard to see much from her location, but the teal and scarlet clad Falcons were clustered in the sky over the Wall Quarter and parts of the Market Quarter—nowhere near where she was.

She'd done her part. Now she had to hope Zamaril, Saniya and her Callanan friends had done theirs.

Talyn kept going. She had somewhere to be.

SANIYA STOOD WAITING at the rendezvous point, halfway down a narrow lane at the northern edge of the Dock Quarter. Andres and the other Wolves were with her, flushed, sweating, and alight with excitement.

"You lost them?" Disappointment flashed over Saniya's face at the lack of pursuit behind Talyn. Her cousin held a drawn sword and was clearly hoping for a fight.

"For now." Talyn hunched over, catching her breath. Her muscles trembled from weariness—as much as Jystar had done for her, Talyn hadn't exerted herself like this in months. "It will take them some time to sort themselves out, but as soon as they do, they'll rouse the City Patrol and start a methodical search of the city. Any word on Zamaril?"

"No, but I wouldn't expect to hear anything from him unless something went wrong. We need to get moving or we're going to be late for the next part of your insanely genius plan."

Talyn's head shot up. "Insanely genius? I think that's the first nice thing you've ever said to me."

"Credit where credit's due." Saniya sheathed her sword and tossed Talyn a large brown cloak. "Put that on and pull the hood up."

Talyn did as she bade, her breathing slowly coming back under control. The other Wolves did the same. Once Saniya was satisfied with their appearance—they'd turned from a unit of uniformed Wolves to a ragtag bunch in ratty cloaks—she led them towards the opposite end of the alley.

They'd almost reached the turn into a much busier thoroughfare when the ground suddenly rocked under their feet. A heartbeat later an enormous boom sounded, followed by a series of smaller echoing booms.

Saniya's gaze swung to Talyn, alight with hope. Tirina whistled. Andres gasped. Talyn grinned at her cousin, and without a word both women started running. They pushed through the busy street beyond, then rounded a corner and ran onto the main road along the harbour. The Wolves gathered behind them, all staring out at the water.

The six Montagni naval ships that had come to stock up on izerdia supplies before rejoining the war fleet sat anchored together in the turquoise waters of Feather Bay, separated from the merchant shipping. Except one of them was now alight, flames licking up into the morning sky from a massive hole in its stern. A gust of wind carried with it the sweet scent of izerdia.

The quarter seemed to have fallen momentarily silent in shock at the explosion that had torn through the morning.

So the next booming explosion was even louder.

The hull of a second Montagni ship went up in flames. Everywhere along the docks, more and more people were stopping and staring, unable to believe their eyes or understand what was happening. Falcons that had been pursuing Wolves halted mid-air, clustering in a chaotic tangle.

"They did it," Talyn breathed.

"*Of course they did. This is Zamaril, Levs and Cynia we're talking about.*"

When the deck of a third ship exploded, bright flames shooting into blue sky, Saniya straightened, shaking herself from the awed wonder that had taken over them all. "Come on, we have to hurry."

Focused on the destruction happening out in the bay, bystanders barely noticed as their group ran down the road and onto one of the long jetties. The fourth ship exploded—the biggest roar so far—just as Saniya led them to a small fishing boat amongst many tied up at the end. A man was uncoiling the mooring rope and the boat's single sail was already unfurled and filling with the morning breeze.

Petro.

Saniya took a running leap into the boat, Talyn a step behind. The Wolves moved just as quickly. Their weight set the boat rocking violently back and forth. At a look from Talyn they sat down and tried to keep out of Petro's way.

"Everything going to plan?" Saniya asked as the boat edged away from the jetty and the sails caught the wind, Petro's steady hand at the tiller.

"They're on that one." Petro pointed to the Montagni ship on the eastern edge of the group. "It was hard to tell from so far away, but I think everything is fine."

Talyn's gaze scanned the skies. Groups of Falcons were winging their way towards the ships, but the intensity of the fourth explosion had made them hesitate, unwilling to fly lower and potentially get caught up in another blast.

They didn't know what to do.

Anxiety and impatience ate at her in the time it took for Petro to get their boat out to the Montagni ship. She kept glancing at the Falcons—this was their most vulnerable moment. If the Falcons came down to investigate who was on their boat, she had limited magic left to handle so many of them and they would be vulnerable while trapped in such a small space.

But the bay was thronged with fishing boats just like this one, as it was every morning of every day. And there was nothing about Petro's boat to make them stand out.

Then the fifth ship exploded.

Talyn ducked reflexively at the nearness of the blast roaring through her ears. Excited triumph filled her at the same time, making it almost impossible to sit still.

Most other fishing craft in the water were steering away from the still-burning ships, but as Petro brought them closer a thick smoke wreathing the air effectively hid them from the Falcons massing so high above.

Inside a half-turn, Petro brought them bumping up against the side of the remaining Montagni ship. A rope ladder dropped down from above, a clear invitation.

Talyn relaxed as Zamaril's head appeared over the railing. "Come on up." He waved. He was soaked through, blond hair plastered to his head, shirt dripping. Tirina spread her wings and flew up. Talyn gestured for Andres and the human Wolves to climb up first.

While they did, the ladder rocking wildly, Talyn turned to Petro. "Once again, I'm in your debt."

He merely rested his hand over his heart. "Ciantar."

Talyn went to Saniya then. "Thank you, for everything."

"No, it's time for me to thank you, Talyn. What you did today..." Saniya turned to stare over the destruction, smoke and ash drifting on the morning's breeze. "The hope you gave them. I won't forget it."

"I'll be back to finish the job," Talyn promised. "You go and take care of that war fleet for me."

A smile flickered over her serious face. "You know I will. I wish our fathers had been here to see this."

"It's far from over," Talyn warned, but reached out to grip her cousin's shoulder. "I think they'd be proud."

Talyn climbed the rope ladder quickly, despite her increasing exhaustion, eager now to be gone. Zamaril waited for her at the top.

"Levs and Cynia?" she asked immediately.

"Present and accounted for!" Leviana's head popped over the opposite railing, dripping wet, before swinging gracefully onto the deck. Cynia was right behind her.

Relief flooded Talyn and she grinned at them both.

"Five ships down—that was awesome!" Leviana crowed enthusiastically at her partner, and they hugged briefly.

"It was awesome, but—" Cynia was cut off by a loud, booming voice.

"Ciantar!"

Talyn turned to see a surprising figure step out of the wheelhouse. "Mayor Doran," she said, eyes widening at the sight of the bearlike man.

"Ciantar." He placed a hand over his heart. "When I heard about this plan, well... your stolen ship needs a captain and I had a hankering to see the open seas again."

"The ship is ours," Zamaril assured her. "The Montagni crew are dead, the slaves freed overboard in one of the lifeboats. There are over ten crates of izerdia in the hold."

"And the Shadowhawk's Dock Quarter group has taken the place of the crew," Doran said. "We're ready to leave at your order."

"Hold up a moment!" Cynia bellowed.

Everyone turned to stare at her. The excitement that had been on Leviana's face faded to grimness.

"What?" Talyn asked as dread began creeping through her with icy fingers.

"Len got to us just before we swam out to blow up the ships. His informant brought the info we've been waiting on." Cynia spoke quickly. "Tarcos is going to hit Port Lathilly."

The deck fell silent.

"Talyn! Roan and Tarquin." Sari's worried voice crashed into her thoughts.

"I know, I know. Just let me think a second." Talyn tried to push away the panic that wanted to swamp her so she could think clearly. Sari's fear for her family wasn't helping matters. "Does my family know?" she asked Cynia.

"We have to assume not. They'll be preparing to deal with the Montagni fleet we warned them about," Cynia said.

"Which means all their forces will be deploying north, away from Port Lathilly."

Talyn's head spun, her own shock and fear almost overwhelmed by Sari's.

"If Tarcos takes Port Lathilly, the Twin Thrones will be sunk, excuse the pun," Leviana said gloomily.

"Mayor, get us out of here." Talyn spun to him. "I want to be out of flying range before someone finally gets control of the Falcons and they come after us in force. It won't take them long."

"And then?" he wanted to know.

"And then we set course for Port Lathilly," she said.

Herself, eleven Wolves and two Callanan to defend the port alongside whoever was already there. It would have to be enough. There was no other choice. "And you get us there as fast as you possibly can."

"We'll get it done, Ciantar." The mayor turned immediately, long strides carrying him away as he bellowed orders to draw the anchor.

The ship rocked as the anchor was lifted, and Talyn leaned over the railing. Petro and Saniya both lifted a hand to wave as Petro steered the smaller boat away. She waved back until the fishing boat vanished into the smoke.

Wind gusted over her sweat-slicked skin as their ship slowly moved free of the haze and headed steadily towards the point where the two headlands of Feather Bay closed towards each other.

Leviana and Cynia came to stand beside her, dripping everywhere, silently joining her vigil. Andres and Zamaril hovered a short distance off, watchful. Guarding her.

Talyn's hands gripped the railing, white-knuckled, anxiety churning in her gut. She glanced back constantly, waiting for pursuit, hoping against hope they'd get clear. In the moment they cleared the headlands of Feather Bay and the ship tacked into the winds, heading south out into open ocean, the relief was potent but brief.

Port Lathilly was under attack. It would take eight days, maybe less if the winds were good, to get there.

She could only hope it would be fast enough.

CHAPTER 37

*S*moke filled the air, thick and hazy. Cuinn's eyes watered and he blinked, trying to clear his vision. Trystaan coasted under him, riding the thermal, allowing his rider a moment to survey the situation.

Cuinn's reinforcements had arrived to find the defence of Port Lathilly in chaos, the Greencloak commander and his senior officers killed by Shadows, the Firthlander forces in full control of the harbour and the narrow strip of land east of the city walls.

Niever-flyers had done significant damage, swooping unchecked across the city to pick off any defender that left cover and firing flaming arrows into whatever target looked good. The residents were locked down inside their houses, only able to go out to get food or supplies during nighttime when the nievers were grounded.

Tents lined the northeastern shore, protected from the Aimsir by quickly-dug trenches, and housing the thousand-odd Bearmen who filled the shoreline each day to launch attack after attack on the eastern city wall.

Sixteen Callanan had been in Port Lathilly when the attack was launched, having arrived from Callanan Tower the previous day ready to deploy into the mountains in support of the Aimsir. They'd managed to rally the leaderless Greencloaks, their elite fighting skill and strategic training meaning they'd been able to rouse the port's defences quickly enough to hold the walls.

If it hadn't been for that fortuitous stroke of luck... Port Lathilly would have been lost well before reinforcements arrived. His stomach turned every time he thought of it.

And even so, they were still far from out of the woods.

Cuinn's SkyRider reinforcements had been able to do little more than stop the nievers from making forays over the city. The anchored Firthland warships provided roosts for the nievers and protection if anyone tried to attack from the sea. Not that the Conmoran navy was coming. He'd tried to push the SkyRider force forward over the harbour to get to the ships, but the nievers held them off each time.

Ariar and his Aimsir milled inland of the town, their horses useless in the narrow city streets and highly vulnerable to nievers. The best they could do was ensure the Bearmen weren't able to creep further inland and encircle the city.

Three days later and the fight was at a temporary impasse. The Firthlanders were embedded in defensible positions. Callanan and Greencloaks, reinforced by the twenty fresh Callanan warriors from Port Lachley, lined the walls of the town and had so far pushed back any attempt to overrun them, but they were losing fighters to injury and death in every attempt. The SkyRiders and niever-flyers fought their own battle in the air.

So many dead and injured. Cuinn felt sick, exhausted, heartsore.

The setting sun was an orange glow on the horizon and the activity along the eastern walls seemed to have slowed. He wheeled Trystaan around and they spiraled down to where the commanders of the defence of Port Lathilly had taken up residence in a townhouse in the higher area of the city, well away from the fighting.

"Your Grace." The Kingshield on the door saluted as he entered.

He smiled at them both, then walked through to the back of the house, quietly opening the last door on the left. A dark-haired man with paint-stained fingers sat on the couch by the fire, a boy curled sleeping in his lap. He looked up at Cuinn's entrance. "Your Highness."

"I've told you my name is Cuinn." He smiled. "Are you both well?"

"We are. I can't thank you enough for this. If anything happened to Tarquin..." Roan shook his head.

The first thing Cuinn had done on arriving in Port Lathilly was send Kingshield to find Roan and bring him and his son to safety. "I'm glad. Make sure you let me know if there's anything you need."

"We have to be able to do something!" Ariar's furious voice sounded from the main room.

"I'd best go talk to them." Cuinn wrapped Roan in a touch of reassuring song magic. "I'll come and say hello later if I can."

CUINN BRACED HIMSELF BEFORE ENTERING, preparing for the emotion inside. "I think things are winding down for the night," he said as he walked in. "We can expect the attack to resume in the morning."

"The walls aren't high enough to hold them back much longer." Shia spoke. Though she seemed calm, her face and clothes were streaked in dust and blood. "Once they breach, it will become open warfare in the streets."

"How long do you think you can hold the walls?" Cuinn asked her.

"We'll do our best, but I doubt we'll hold them beyond tomorrow," Shia said. "The Greencloaks are no match for the Bearmen coming at us and my Callanan are too few. More are on their way from Callanan Tower but they won't arrive in time."

"I can't spare SkyRiders to fetch them," Cuinn said grimly. As it was he was down to three legions, a hundred and fifty against at least that many nievers. Hope and frustration surged in equal measure. Judging from the numbers, Tarcos had sent most of his entire remaining niever force at Port Lathilly—all he had left were those he'd sent to protect the Montagni war fleet. If they could win here, Tarcos's military might would take a significant hit.

If they could win. It wasn't looking likely.

"At least my Aimsir can be of use if the city falls," Ariar said grimly. "I'll send orders tonight, and we'll be in position to cover the retreat of the civilians if it comes to it."

At least that was something. "Send your fastest rider to Ryathl," Cuinn said. "We need the Lord's Council to send more Greencloaks and longbows north. If Port Lathilly falls, it will be up to them and your Aimsir to hold them from pushing further into Calumnia."

Ariar opened his mouth, closed it. They all knew how difficult that would be, impossible even, with the Firthlanders already pushing south out of the Ayrlemyre Mountains.

"We just have to hold on as long as we can." Cuinn wove determination and reassurance into his voice, filling the room with it, watching it clear the concern from Ariar and Shia's brows. "Don't forget we've got Rados in play. Soar will have him back in Port Lachley soon."

None of them doubted Soar would succeed. And Cuinn was right. All they had to do was hold on.

And hope his plan with Rados worked. And worked fast. Because if it didn't... he shuddered to think what would happen then.

CHAPTER 38

$\mathcal{A}$ ny hopes she had that Len's information was wrong died a quick death as Talyn studied the smoke haze over the city of Port Lathilly.

She crouched on the hillside overlooking the port from the north. Zamaril, Andres and the two Callanan sat with her. The other Wolves waited a short distance off.

Not wanting to sail into the middle of a sea battle in a Montagni ship, Talyn had asked Doran to anchor north of the port and set them ashore. She'd then directed him to sail for Port Lachley and wait for them there—making sure to emphasise the need for him to fly a white flag before approaching the harbour. At least the mayor and his crew would be safe with her family. And hopefully Cuinn was there too. He would recognise Doran and his old Shadowhawk members and ensure they were looked after.

It was mid-morning, and the fighting looked like it had been raging since dawn. Three Firthlander warships were anchored in the harbour, untouched, and from what she could tell, the Firthlander army had taken the docks and any clear space beyond the low city walls as well as the northeastern peninsula.

Greencloaks and Callanan fought on the walls as lines of Bearmen repeatedly tried to breach them. Some of their forays had been successful, and even while Talyn watched, the numbers of Greencloaks dwindled.

And the screams, from eagles and nievers both as they battled in the sky. The SkyRiders were clearly trying to reach the Firthlander ships and provide cover for those fighting on the walls at the same time, but the niever-flyers knew it. All they had to do was keep together and protect the skies above their ships and fighters and they were doing it successfully.

"The fighting hasn't broken through into the city yet. Tarquin and Roan are safe," she said, trying to reassure her partner. Sari's fear had been shivering in her mind since they'd left Mithranar.

"But those nievers hit the city before the SkyRiders got here, you can see the damage to buildings and houses." Sari's voice trembled.

"I'll make sure they're okay, Sari. I swear it," she said. *"The Aimsir are swarming west of the city. The trenches protect the Bearmen camp, but if they tried to leave the safety of the trenches to surround the city and attack, the Aimsir would destroy them."*

"I know." The worry faded, Sari's faith in her absolute.

"Shit," Leviana muttered. Anger had turned her features into a snarl.

"Thoughts, Talyn?" Cynia was calmer.

"Sari?"

"You want to take out their ships like the SkyRiders are trying to do. Make them realise they've got nowhere to run to—that they're essentially trapped between the harbour and the Aimsir arrayed outside the city."

"They'll fight more fiercely if they're trapped, but they'll also be desperate and less clear-headed. And if we hit them at the right time with enough force, we might break them."

"It won't be easy. You'll be vulnerable to nievers. Whoever is commanding the Firthlander forces clearly knows what they're doing. They'll send the nievers at the most immediate threat."

"I'll trust the SkyRiders to take care of the nievers."

Talyn turned to her talons and friends. "We'll hit the ships, take them out, then make a push from the walls at the same time, try and break the back of their assault."

"The same thing we did in Feather Bay," Zamaril said.

"It worked so well there, why not try it again." She smiled. "And we did bring that crate of izerdia with us, after all. It would be a shame to waste it."

"Those walls look close to breaking," Andres said quietly. "And there are only fifteen of us here. If we split our numbers to send some at those ships, that's not a lot of fighters to break the assault."

"Are you saying we Wolves can't push back a few hulking Bearmen, Andres?" she said with a little smile. He was absolutely right. But it did no good to worry over what they didn't have. She would make do with what they *did* have.

Leviana stared at the city, clearly thinking it through. "Some of us sneak down into town to find whoever is commanding the defence of the walls, while the strike team gets out to the ships. We gather what's left of those fighting, then when the first explosion goes off we push hard in an attempt to force the Firthlanders back away from the walls and into the water."

"Exactly." Talyn nodded.

"How many for the ships?" Cynia asked. "It will have to be those that know how to set an izerdia explosion, so myself and Levs with a couple of Wolves for backup?"

"No, I'll need you both with me for the assault on the walls, we'll—"

"I'll do it," Zamaril said quietly.

Talyn swung to face him.

"I can do it, just me. You need all the fighters you can get for the walls." His face was set and determined.

"You want to blow three ships alone?" Leviana gaped at him. "Once the first one blows, the crew on the others will be waiting for you. You'll get yourself killed."

"I'm a thief. I can get on those ships without them seeing me and set off an explosion to blow the hulls. And if I'm seen... well, I can fight too." Zamaril switched his gaze to Talyn. "Let me do this."

Andres reached out, grasped Zamaril's shoulder and squeezed.

"*Bearmen are fierce and skilled, Tal. You need every fighter you can get your hands on,*" Sari said reluctantly. "*And you trained Zamaril.*"

"All right," she said, and they were amongst the hardest words she'd ever spoken. She wasn't even sure *she* could manage to do what he was proposing. And the thought of losing Zamaril...

His eyes glowed and she realised that he hadn't expected her to agree. That he hadn't expected her to trust him enough to do it.

"The best thief in Dock City, right?" She smiled at him. "Sink those ships for me, Zamaril, and we'll save Port Lathilly."

"Consider it done, Ciantar."

Talyn rose to her feet. "Let's fill the Wolves in and get moving. Those walls aren't going to hold much longer."

IT WAS mid-afternoon by the time they moved out of the hills and into the city, through alleys and roads as familiar to Talyn as those of Dock City. She and Sari had ruled these streets once and she was determined to take them back.

The screams of eagles and nievers battling above was louder once they were in the city, sharp and piercing. Sometimes they were challenging, other times triumphant, and occasionally they were screams of pain.

She tried to block out the noise. Her fear for Zamaril. For the Callanan and Wolves trailing behind her. For her countrymen fighting bitterly in the skies and on the walls.

Smoke hit her nose as they approached the fighting. The streets here were empty, the Greencloaks having moved all the residents further back into the city for safety. They passed a hastily-put together medical area bustling with healers and filled with bodies lying on pallets.

Talyn grabbed the first Greencloak she saw. He was bloodied, exhausted looking. He frowned at the white and charcoal Wolf uniforms, but his expression cleared at the sight of two Callanan cloaks.

"Who's commanding the wall defences?" she asked him.

"The First Blade... Ma'am." He didn't seem to know what to call her.

Her heart leapt at that. The First Blade herself was here; that improved their chances significantly. "And where is she stationed?"

"She'll either be up at the command centre on Whaler Street, or down at the wall. Do you know Flotsam Alley?"

"I do."

"The warehouse on the corner is serving as a command post for the wall defenders."

"Thank you." Talyn turned and ran. The Wolves and Callanan streamed behind her.

PARTS of the wall had crumbled—the Bearmen must have had small amounts of izerdia with them—and rubble lined Flotsam Alley. Talyn glimpsed the warriors on the other side through the gaps, and a glance upwards showed chaotic fighting figures on the wall. Steel rang through the afternoon air, mixed with shouts and grunts and the occasional order being shouted.

"Talyn?"

She spun at the familiar voice, gaze landing on the diminutive figure of Shia Thorineal, First Blade of the Callanan. She stood just outside the door of a warehouse, huddled with two Callanan masters. Astonishment filled her face.

"First Blade!" Talyn strode over. "It's good to see you."

"And even better to see you." Shia's eyes were wide, unbelieving.

"I've got a plan, First Blade, a way to win the city. But I'm going to need your help."

Shia didn't hesitate. Didn't bristle. Simply straightened her shoulders. "What do you need?"

"Can you get a message to all the Greencloaks and Callanan on the wall?" Talyn glanced towards the harbour. Zamaril should be approaching the first ship by now. "Within a half-turn or so."

"I can. What's the message?"

"Tell them they only need to hold the walls for a little longer. When they see the signal, we're going to push out, attack the Bearmen and Firthlander infantry, force them away from the wall, and hopefully break the back of their assault."

Shia glanced behind Talyn, where Leviana and Cynia and the Wolves waited patiently. "You bring an army with you?"

"Just what you see behind me." Her smile widened.

"The Firthlanders outnumber us more than five to one, Talyn. If we leave the protection of the walls we risk losing our defending force entirely."

"We're going to lose the walls anyway. And we won't attack until the timing is right." Talyn filled her voice with confidence. "This is going to work, First Blade. Callanan are not going to be bested by Bearmen. Not today."

Shia turned to the two Callanan masters lingering nearby. "Darien, Jora. Send word down the walls. Greencloaks and Callanan to hold until the signal, then go on the offensive."

The two men glanced at each other. "What's the signal?"

"Trust me," Talyn said, a smile spreading over her face. "They'll know."

CHAPTER 39

Cuinn huddled with Ariar, both furiously trying to work out how to break the stalemate with the nievers. If only his SkyRiders could get the upper hand, they might have a chance of holding the walls.

"Could you draw them out over the plains, bring them in range of my Aimsir and their arrows?" Ariar suggested. It was a brave idea to raise. Despite how quick and agile their horses, the Aimsir would come off the worse in that fight.

Cuinn shook his head. "Their only priority is defending their ships and their soldiers attacking the wall. They would be foolish to allow themselves to be drawn away."

Ariar sighed, rubbed his face. "They certainly haven't been foolish so far."

"We might have to summon another legion from Mothduriem," Cuinn said heavily.

"Do that and we'll have nobody left to defend the foothills. The Firthlanders will break out of the mountains into Conmor."

"I—"

The explosion was deafening, roaring through the open windows and shaking the half-drunk glasses of water on a nearby tray.

Ariar and Cuinn stared at each other.

Then they ran for the window.

Smoke plumed into the air from one of the Firthlander ships, flames licking at a massive hole in its hull. As Cuinn watched, it listed slowly to the side. Crew raced around on the deck, running for boats or diving into the ocean.

"What the...?"

"Did they blow up their own ship accidentally?" Ariar stared.

Cuinn's eyes were drawn to the sky, where nievers were already massing to drop down towards the remaining ships, preparing to defend against whatever was attacking.

Frantically, he yanked his whistle from inside his shirt and blew hard. Turning, he ran across the room, grabbing up his bow and two quivers of arrows. Once they were slung over his shoulder, he leapt up onto the window frame, hands braced either side. "Ariar. Get a message to your Aimsir. Make sure they're ready."

"For what?"

"For any Firthlander or niever that tries to escape the city."

Trystaan's scream echoed through the sky and a shadow passed overheard. Cuinn waited a few more heartbeats then dived out the window, arms and legs spread.

Trystaan swooped in underneath him and Cuinn gripped hard to the eagle's feathers until he righted himself. Trying not to fumble, he managed to get the harness on, then he pushed the eagle up into the sky.

As he flew, he made the same hand gesture over and over, so that any SkyRider looking his way would see it.

Re-form. Re-form into legions. Re-form.

The nievers had broken their force in half to protect the burning ship. If Cuinn hit one of the halves with all the SkyRiders at once, maybe, just maybe...

Trystaan flew hard, wings beating into the sky, weaving through nievers and SkyRiders alike, Cuinn flashing his orders over and over. SkyRiders broke off the fighting and came after him and they spiraled down towards the nievers circling the ships.

They'd almost engaged when the second blast went off.

Trystaan screamed, veering away from the wall of heat and smoke that billowed towards them. Sitting up in the harness, Cuinn stared in astonishment.

Someone was attacking the ships.

Something made him turn towards the city. To the walls under attack.

But the Greencloaks and Callanan weren't on the wall anymore. They were leaping off it, pushing forward into the Firthlander warriors, trying to force them back to the ocean.

And then he saw it.

A bright flash of sapphire light. Warrior magic. *Ciantar* magic. Ploughing into a group of Bearmen. A heartbeat later there was another flash of light, this one scarlet, then a purple flash.

Wolves. It had to be.

With Talyn.

He allowed himself a heartbeat. A single moment to close his eyes in joy and relief.

Then Cuinn pushed his hips forward and sent Trystaan soaring high, gesturing his new orders over and over.

He knew what to do.

CHAPTER 40

Talyn waited on the wall, Leviana and Cynia on one side, Andres on the other. Her Wolves were arrayed behind them, and even though she had no song magic she could feel their anticipation.

A sheathed sword hung down her back, a better weapon for the fight to come, and Sari was coiled ready in her mind. Her warrior magic simmered.

And then the first ship blew.

The Wolves behind her howled.

Talyn lifted her hand in the air and sent bright sapphire light flashing into the skies over the wall.

At her signal, the defenders pushed forward.

Talyn leapt from the wall, summoned two bursts of magic, and sent them into the pack of confused soldiers immediately ahead of her. Then she drew her sword and hurled herself into the fight.

Bearmen were big, and powerfully strong, elite swordsman. A match in skill for a Callanan any day. The fighting was hard, and bloody, and before long sweat slicked her skin and her breath rasped in her chest.

Cynia fought on her left side, firing arrow after arrow with dizzying speed until her quiver was empty. Then she slung her bow over her shoulder and drew a sword. Leviana fought like a demon, knives flashing so quickly they were a blur, blood spraying her face and cloak until the stuff was dripping from her.

And Talyn's Wolves.

They howled as they fought in a tight unit, Ehdra and Tirina and Andres, Dansia and Nirrin. Humans and winged alike, covering for each other, holding together, not backing down for a moment.

When the second explosion went off, they were surrounded by fighting bodies and Talyn couldn't see a thing.

"Tirina? Can you get me an overview?" she shouted.

The winged Wolf nodded and leapt into the air. Immediately Ehdra and Dansia's Callanan shields snapped into place around her, protecting her from any stray arrows.

"The Callanan and Greencloaks are fighting in pockets." Tirina dropped back to the ground, wings furling. "There are so many Firth-landers, Ciantar..."

"We need to bring the pockets together, fashion a larger force," Talyn said, ducking a swipe and countering before driving her blade into the soldier's chest. "Where's the nearest pocket?"

"Six Greencloaks just through there." Tirina pointed.

"Cover me!" Talyn snapped to Andres, then sheathed her sword and lifted her palms. The magic was harder to summon this time, the energy drain more noticeable, but she focused hard and sent two more bursts at the Bearmen between her and the Greencloaks.

The moment the light faded, she re-drew her sword and pushed forward, cutting down the injured soldiers and fighting through to the Greencloaks.

"Form up on me!" she shouted. "Form up on me. Stay together."

They solidified into a large group.

"Tirina, next?"

"Three Callanan, just through there!" came the reply.

Tirina's magic joined hers this time, scarlet and sapphire flashing bright into the smoky sky.

Slowly but surely, Talyn began linking all the groups. Once they were large enough, she split them, sending one group under Andres' command to try and flank the Firthlanders. If they could attack from two sides at once, it might buckle their fighting strength.

When the third ship exploded, Talyn stared out over the water, taking a moment to hope that Zamaril got out safely.

That's when she noticed the SkyRiders.

The niever-flyers hadn't troubled them yet, and Talyn had been too focused on the fight to pay much attention to them, hoping the SkyRiders would keep them at bay.

But they were doing more than that. SkyRiders swarmed in three distinct legions. They'd dropped into the sky between the harbour and the ships, cutting off the nievers from flying in support of the Firthlander soldiers.

The fighting was fierce, eagle and niever alike dropping from the sky, but the three legions fought in concert, keeping the niever-flyers contained and engaged, unable to break away to attack the city's defenders. And they flew with purpose and passion, like she often saw in the Wolves.

She wondered if Soar was up there. It must be him, conducting his SkyRiders like an orchestra.

Then a sword came whistling toward her head. She ducked instinctively, almost slipped in the mud, then came up swinging. Before she could counter, a knife flew into the Bearman's eye. He swayed, then collapsed in a heap.

"Thanks!" Talyn panted with a grin at Leviana.

"Any time." Leviana spun away, bloodied knives dripping.

Cynia gave a little wave as she fought at her partner's back. Ehdra backed towards her, barely countering the strikes of a massive Bearman, only his exquisite footwork keeping him alive.

Talyn took two strides towards her Wolf, leapt upwards, and flipped over the Bearman, landing in the muddy sand behind him and driving her sword into his back. He grunted and she drew the blade out with an effort before kicking him forward.

And then they were in clear space.

Her breath rasped, heartbeat thudding in her ears. Her skin was slick with sweat and blood and gore and she stung from several small cuts.

They were winning. The Firthlanders were battling in small pockets now, their fighting strength cracked apart by the Callanan's relentless skill and the Greencloaks' determination.

"I think we have the day."

Talyn turned as Shia appeared at her side. The First Blade was bloodier than Talyn, her face set in fierce lines, every inch the leader of the Callanan.

"Give them the opportunity to surrender," Talyn said.

Shia hesitated, but then nodded. "Aye."

Andres approached her as Shia strode away to begin calling out orders to let the Firthlanders surrender if they chose. Blood trickled from a wound on his forearm, but he looked otherwise fine. "Make sure the Wolves give them the opportunity to stand down," she re-iterated to him.

"Ciantar!" He saluted and left.

Part of her wanted to find somewhere to sit down and take a moment to catch her breath. Another part was still thrumming from adrenalin and the fight. The rest of her scanned the ocean for any sign of Zamaril.

"Looks like the air battle is almost over too." Leviana and Cynia came over, looking as weary as Talyn felt.

The niever-flyers were slowly being pushed east out over the ocean, further away from the port. The SkyRider legions massed together to chase them off, making certain of the retreat.

She turned to her friends, huffing a breath of disbelief. "We did it."

"*You thought you wouldn't?*"

"We did. But there's still a massive Montagni war fleet heading our way," Cynia pointed out.

Leviana rounded on her partner. "Could we just bask in our triumph for like a quarter-turn before you go getting all practical?"

"No, she's right," Talyn said quietly. "We're still a long way from winning this war."

And their forces were depleted.

The shriek of an eagle caught their attention. Two SkyRiders had broken free of the legions chasing the niever-flyers out to sea and were heading back towards the beach.

Talyn watched the two specks as they resolved into the shape of flying eagles, and soon she could even make out the distant shape of the riders perched on their backs. As they approached, one of the SkyRiders circled higher, heading towards somewhere in the town. Her heart lifted in hope—maybe it was Soar, heading back to the command post.

The second came in low and fast, soaring mere inches from the top of the grey ocean before shooting at dizzying speed over the figures standing on the beach. Sapphire glinted in the afternoon sun from the underside of the eagle's wings and he let out a challenging shriek before coming to a graceful landing atop the wall.

The SkyRider rider tore at his harness as if he couldn't get rid of it fast enough, then he was yanking the thick beanie from his golden curls and swinging off his eagle's back, gaze clearly searching for someone.

Her entire world went still.

"Shit," Leviana swore in astonishment. "Is that—"

And then Talyn was running across the sand, weaving between fallen bodies and pools of blood and gore. Someone shouted in warning—maybe a Wolf—but she ignored him.

Cuinn saw her the moment she'd started running. A wondering smile spread over his face as he dropped from the wall in a single jump, long strides carrying him towards her.

And then she was in his arms and he was crushing her against him so tightly she couldn't breathe, but it didn't matter because he was here and he was alive and she could breathe him in again.

It was a long, long time before either of them was able to stop simply rocking back and forth. And then Cuinn's arms loosened, and he drew his hands up to frame her face, pressing his forehead against hers. "You finally came," he murmured. "I've been waiting."

"I'm sorry it took so long." She took a steadying breath, forcing herself to be brave enough to lean back and meet his eyes. "I'm so sorry."

He saw the tattoo straight away, his fingers reaching up to trace gently over it, nothing but relief and joy on his face. "You have nothing to be sorry for. *I'm* sorry. For leaving, for coming here and making you look for me."

She shook her head at the absurdity of that, and tried to think of something to say as he kept staring at her in wonder. "We won."

He laughed, and it brightened her entire world. "We did. Thanks to you."

"No, the SkyRiders..." She stopped, eyes widening as she finally processed the eagle, him on it. "*You* were leading them. You're a SkyRider now."

"I am. After Azrilan took my wings, I wanted to learn to fly again."

"You look amazing on him."

"His name is Trystaan," Cuinn murmured.

Talyn bit her lip, the tears that had already been welling in her eyes spilling down her cheeks.

The sound of a loud, pointed clearing of the throat broke them apart. When Talyn turned to see Zamaril standing there, soaked through and bloodied, but *alive* with that characteristic smirk on his face, she launched herself at him with a cry of relief.

He staggered backwards a few paces, clearly astonished by her reaction. But he'd barely un-entangled himself from Talyn when Cuinn swept in, tears in his eyes, and wrapped him in an even tighter hug. "Zamaril, you're here too!"

"I don't think princes are supposed to hug their bodyguards," Zamaril managed to squawk, going slowly red in the face.

Cuinn let go and turned to her, tears falling down his cheeks too. "I have so many questions, so much to tell you... but Ariar is here too, and he'll want to see you."

Talyn bit her lip. "I want to see him too."

"Oh!" Cuinn's face cleared. "And tell Sari, she must be so worried, Roan and Tarquin are safe. They've been with me, under Kingshield guard the whole time."

Talyn swayed on her feet at the force of Sari's relief thundering through her. *"They're okay."*

"Tell him thank you. Tell him I'll never be able to thank him enough. Oh, Talyn, they're okay."

Talyn took Cuinn's hand. "Thank you."

He squeezed gently. "There's no need for it."

ARIAR PACED outside a townhouse as Cuinn, Talyn and their weary Wolves and Callanan walked down the street towards him.

"Finally!" Ariar shouted when he caught sight of Cuinn. "Your SkyRider told me the battle was won, but I've been worried sick with—"

Then he saw Talyn at Cuinn's side and his eyes turned bright as a summer sky. A moment later Talyn's hand was torn from Cuinn's grip and she found herself being caught in an enormous bear hug and swung up into the air.

"Ariar!" She clung tightly to him as more pieces of herself, ones that had been locked up tight for months, slowly unfurled. "You have no idea how good it is to see you."

"Right back at you," he said in disbelief. "Talyn, he swore you were alive, swore you would come. But it's been so long, and we've been so worried. And you're here! How did you get here? How did you know? That was *you* with the ships, wasn't it?"

"Actually it was Zamaril." She laughed, pointing at the Wolf. "But it was my idea. As to the rest of your questions, well... we stole a ship together. It's full of izerdia. The rest of the crew are from Cuinn's Shadowhawk network—they, along with Saniya, helped us destroy a good portion of Montagn's current izerdia supply on our way out of Dock City."

Cuinn's eyes shone. "I can't wait to hear about it."

"I can't wait to tell you." She meant it. All of the pain and triumph and difficulty of the past months. She wanted him to know all of it.

"Are we going to get a mention at any point?" Leviana called out.

"Or would you like to keep gazing moonily at each other for the rest of eternity?"

Talyn chuckled. "Levs and Cynia might have helped too."

"It's good to see you both," Cuinn said. "And your warning about the fleet was received. Thank you."

The mood turned grim.

"We need to get back to Port Lachley," Talyn said. "Sooner rather than later."

"Not quite yet," Ariar said. "We have prisoners to process and some order to restore."

"Leave Shia in charge of that. We'll fly out as soon as it's light," Cuinn said.

Talyn noted the tone of command. Ariar's easy acceptance. "There's something else going on?"

Cuinn nodded. "Soar isn't here because he was working on something important, but he should be back in Port Lachley by now. I want to return as quickly as possible."

"Cuinn has a plan," Ariar added at Talyn's confused look.

"Which we can discuss later. I'm sure you have just as much to tell us about the situation in Mithranar and Montagn." Cuinn drew her close. "How about a bath, sleep, then a long flight back to Port Lachley. Your mother will be waiting there for you and we can go over everything then."

"Sounds good to me."

BEFORE THE BATH, Talyn went to check on Roan and Tarquin. They sat in the corner of a small room, Roan drawing something while Tarquin played with building blocks.

"Talyn!" Roan breathed, a few steps slower than his son in getting across the room to hug her.

"Steer clear, I'm covered in blood," she said laughingly. "Hugs can come later. You're okay?"

"We are, thanks to Cuinn." Roan's expression turned curious. "The Kingshield watching us say you're betrothed to him?"

356

"It's true." She couldn't hold back the smile.

"I'm really happy for you," he said simply, eyes roving over her in relief. "You look exhausted and filthy, but that empty expression I saw in your eyes when you came to visit… it's gone."

Talyn simply nodded. "I'd best go clean up, but I'll come and say goodbye before I leave again."

Roan's face turned grim. "Are we going to lose, Tal?"

"Not if I can help it." She paused at the door. "And no matter what happens, I'll make sure you and Tarquin are safe."

A HALF-TURN LATER, Talyn climbed out of a bath and roughly dried her hair before shrugging on a clean robe hanging on the back of the bathing room door.

Cuinn was waiting for her when she pushed open the door to his room. He sat on the edge of the bed, hair still damp from a wash, weary but calm.

"You seem very much in command," she murmured, closing the door and leaning back against it. "Tell me, are you king yet?"

He stilled for a moment, green eyes going to the floor before lifting to meet hers. In them she read determination with a hint of doubt. "Regent," he said. "Can you ever forgive me?"

"When they told me you came here, I suspected why. There's nothing to forgive, Cuinn, but we've got a lot to tell each other."

He nodded, gave her a little smile.

She didn't know what to say next. The adrenalin of battle had faded to exhaustion and an odd brittleness, like she might explode into a million pieces at the softest touch. She'd made it home. To Cuinn. And now she had no idea what to say.

From elation to anxiety in the space of an afternoon.

He read it all. Of course he did. Rising from the bed, he crossed to her, pulling her gently away from the door so that he could stand behind her. Warm hands landed on her shoulders, kneading gently. Magic curled around her, soft and soothing. "It's all right," he breathed.

Those words and she was turning in his arms, burying her head in his chest as she began crying in great gulping sobs that shook her body and made her throat hurt. His tears came too then, equally grief-stricken, and they clung to each other in the middle of the room.

She didn't know how long they stood there crying, but eventually the emotional storm calmed. Cuinn pressed a soft kiss against her forehead.

"I love you," she whispered.

"And I you," he said huskily, turning her face up to meet him as he leaned down to kiss her. The kiss was desperate, hungry, the desire between them flaring bright and dispelling any weariness or remaining grief.

He pushed the robe off her shoulders, making her gasp as he ran his hands over bare skin and pulled her body flush with his. She pulled away from his kiss to yank his shirt off, and when his mouth returned to hers, she explored his warm skin as eagerly as he was touching hers.

When her hands dropped to his belt, he picked her up and swung her onto the bed. She sighed as his weight lowered onto her, and pulled his head down to kiss him again.

"I love you," she whispered between kisses. "I love you so much."

"I'M SO SORRY." His fingers traced the scars down her back, a haunted look appearing in his green eyes.

She shifted, rolling onto her side to face him. "I almost died in that camp."

"But you didn't." A strength she'd only ever seen flashes of before glowed in Cuinn's eyes as he regarded her. What had happened to him, to them, could have broken him. Instead it had made him breathtaking. "Azrilan and Tarcos are not going to defeat us, Talyn."

"Never." Talyn snuggled closer. "I missed you like I've never missed anything in my life."

He pressed his face into her shoulder and she could feel the wetness as more tears fell. "I kept telling them that you would find a way, that you would fight and come back, but I was terrified for you."

"You did the right thing," she said. "You came here to help Mithranar."

"I knew that's what you would want."

"And I fought." She caught his face in her hands, forcing him to meet her eyes. "I fought like you knew I would. To come back. I will always fight."

"So will I," he swore. "Always."

CHAPTER 41

Talyn's eyes teared up when Port Lachley came into sight on the horizon, and she cursed herself for being a weepy fool. Cuinn said nothing, but his arms around her tightened a little.

The alert bell rang at their approach and Cuinn brought them down quickly. The eagles carrying the Wolves and Callanan landed with them, the rest of the legion diverting to the SkyRider base to the east. Once Trystaan settled, Cuinn pressed his face into her neck.

"I don't want to let you go," he murmured.

"Me either."

They sat there a moment longer, then Cuinn reached around to unbuckle the harness. He let her down first, and she turned to slide her hand into his as he dismounted after her. Trystaan gave a cry then lifted back into the air.

Two Kingshield appeared at the top of the stairs leading down into the castle, having clearly run the whole way. She figured those inside must be desperate for news of Port Lathilly.

And then all thoughts flew out of her head as Alyna Dumnorix emerged at the top of the steps. Her gaze went straight to Talyn, eyes widening, before she lifted a trembling hand to her mouth.

"Mama." Talyn ran to her.

"Talyn." Her mother enveloped Talyn in her third crushing hug of the week. If she hadn't been so happy, so relieved, she might have started to worry about bruised ribs.

"What happened?" Alyna demanded when she pulled back. "Where have you been? What is the status of Port Lathilly? Did you come from there with Cuinn?"

"Port Lathilly is ours, the Firthlander force defeated," Talyn said. "As for the rest, it's a long story, Mama, but trust me when I say that I came as soon as I could."

"Stories can be told somewhere more comfortable than this windy rooftop." Cuinn stepped forward. "Talyn, I have no doubt there is a Wolf waiting downstairs to take up his protective duties. He's been as worried for you as I have."

And just like that, Cuinn managed everything. Alyna opened her mouth, probably to protest, but Talyn was already turning to search the roof for Zamaril and Andres. Zamaril was watching her as always, and when she caught his gaze he gave a little nod, eyes bright.

The three of them ran for the stairs, the other Wolves not far behind.

The entrance foyer of the castle was busy with folk coming in and out, but Talyn spotted Theac immediately as she paused above the bottom steps, Zamaril and Andres just behind. Her throat closed over as she took in the sight of her grizzled second, looking no different than when she'd last seen him.

He saw them a moment later and went rigidly still, the scowling face she remembered crumpling with emotion. Talyn jumped to the bottom of the steps and threw herself into his arms heedless of those around them.

Theac held her fiercely, voice gruff with unshed tears. "You came back."

She laughed, wiping tears from her eyes as she stepped away. "I missed you, old man."

"I missed that scowl of yours more than anything." Zamaril came forward then. Andres said nothing, but his eyes were sheened with tears too.

Theac cleared his throat. Tried to say something, failed.

"Me too," Zamaril said quietly.

Theac smiled, then his gaze caught on something behind them. Cuinn had followed her down, and now stood a few paces away, giving them time. "He has been magnificent."

She nodded, eyes welling with tears again. "We haven't had much of a chance to speak yet."

"Then go. We'll talk tomorrow." Theac reached out to grip her arm. "I can't tell you how happy I am to see you, my Ciantar."

"Take us to Corrin's mam and sisters?" Zamaril asked.

"We'd really like to see them," Andres added.

Theac leaned over and wrapped a brawny arm around the thief's shoulders. "And they'll be happier than I can say to see you both."

ARIAR CLEARED the dining hall of anyone but family and then ordered an early dinner as dusk fell outside the castle fortress. Soar flew in from a SkyRider patrol and came to a dead halt when he saw Talyn gathered with the other Dumnorix in the dining room.

Then came definite bruised ribs. She didn't care.

"Did you—?" Cuinn asked.

Soar's shining eyes were on Talyn, but he nodded. "Now that you're back we can start talks."

Cuinn's shoulders slumped in relief. She made a note to ask him about it later.

They sat clustered around the table: Talyn, Cuinn, Alyna, Ariar and Soar, and waited until the food had been served and the servants departed before speaking.

"Where's Allira?" Talyn asked in an attempt to forestall the inevitable questioning. Her food steamed in front of her, but she wasn't hungry.

"In Ryathl, basically running Calumnia and the Lords' Council on our behalf while we manage the war," Soar said with a little smile of pride for his daughter.

"Tell us what happened, Talyn." Alyna's tone brooked no refusal.

Talyn glanced at Cuinn, seated across the table from her. She felt almost suffocated by the nearness of him and the presence of others. It had been so long and she just wanted to bury herself in him and have everything else fade away.

"Zamaril and I were ambushed by Savin," she said, meeting Cuinn's eyes before glancing away. Then, summoning a breath to fortify herself, she told them. "The short version is that I was beaten and badly wounded." She touched her tattoo. "I woke up in a Montagni slave camp, near death."

A strangled noise came from Cuinn. His jaw had tightened so hard it must be painful, and heedless of those around them, Talyn reached across the table. His hand immediately moved to take hers.

They stared at each other a moment longer, then Talyn cleared her throat and let go. "A friend in the camp looked after me and eventually I pulled through." She couldn't help the shudder that shivered through her at the memories. "I didn't realise for a while, but Zamaril had also been dumped in the camp."

She paused to glance around the table; they looked equally horrified and angered by her tale. None of them had started eating. Dumnorix were not going to take news like this about one of their own well, and already anger was a palpable presence in the air.

"In the end it was Jasper who got me out." She smiled at Cuinn. "Somehow he found me, then led Saniya to me. She got Zamaril and I out of Montagn and safely to the SkyReach where the rest of the Wolves are. From there we got ourselves to Dock City, then stole a ship to come here." Hopefully Doran would be arriving in a few days. She made another note to warn her family about that.

"There's more than what you're telling us," Ariar observed.

"There is." She rubbed at her forehead. At some point she was going to have to tell Cuinn about Mithanis, still locked up at their base in the SkyReach. But she didn't have the energy for that right now. "But those are the main points. It's not an easy story to tell."

Cuinn stood, giving Alyna a warning glance. "We'll convene first thing tomorrow to talk further. There's still a Montagni war fleet to deal with and we should get started with Rados as soon as possible."

Alyna tossed an irritated glance at Cuinn then came over to Talyn, wrapping her in a warm, affectionate hug. "I love you, Talyn, and I cannot tell you how sorely you were missed. Rest as much as you need."

"I'll be here tomorrow," she promised. "I have some information about the Montagni ships that might help."

Cuinn followed her as she left the dining room, his hand tangling with hers. Kingshield fell in behind them; two details at a quick count. "They're wearing silver stars now," she murmured.

"I am regent, not king," he said. "And it might be silly, but until we know for certain Aeris is dead, I'd like to keep hope alive."

She squeezed his hand. "It's not silly."

TALYN AWOKE as the slowly rising sun shifted across the floor and onto her face. She stirred sleepily, then stilled at the realisation that Cuinn was wrapped around her, his arms holding her tight to his chest.

"I'm here," he murmured, pressing a kiss to her ear.

"How long have you been awake?"

"A while. I was afraid to close my eyes in case it all turned out to be a dream."

She rolled to face him. "It's not a dream."

"No." He smiled softly.

She took a long breath, studying his face in the morning light. It had taken so much to get here, had been so long, and now she'd found him. "What do we do now?"

"Breakfast," he said promptly. "I'm starved. And then war planning with our family."

She slapped his chest. "You know what I mean."

"I do. I'm just extremely reluctant to say it aloud." He frowned, pulling back from her. "I know you're going to go straight back to Mithranar. I know why."

"You think me so predictable," she murmured, reclaiming the distance and pressing a kiss to his mouth.

"Am I wrong?"

"No. But I am not leaving this very instant."

A reluctant smile returned to his face as she pushed him onto his back, straddling his hips. "Who's Rados? You mentioned the name at dinner last night. Has he got something to do with why Soar wasn't in Port Lathilly?"

"A story for after breakfast." He leaned up to kiss her, hands sliding over the bare skin of her legs, pulling her closer. "And after this."

She chuckled, pressing her palms against his chest. "There's a lot more muscle here than there used to be."

"Oh, is that right?" He arched in eyebrow in an imitation of her. "Admit it, I'm much more your type now."

"I do approve." She kissed him. "Very much."

"You were worried," he said, turning suddenly serious and capturing her hands to still them. "I sensed it in you last night, back in Port Lathilly too. You worried about what I would think... of the tattoo and the scars."

"Cuinn—"

"You are no less magnificent than you ever were." He sat up quickly, almost sending her toppling off him. His hand framed her cheek, refusing to let her look away.

"I know," she said quietly. "I know that I'm still me, still strong. In my head I know that. But I was a slave for months, and I couldn't... Jystar fixed me, Cuinn, but my back was so bad I could barely move. There was a real possibility I'd never be able to fight again."

"We would have figured it out." His green eyes bored into hers. "No matter what happens, to either of us, we will figure it out, Talyn."

She swallowed, pressed her forehead against his. "I never imagined, not in a million years, finding someone like you."

A laugh escaped him. "From the first moment I saw you, I thought you were the most magnificent thing I'd ever seen. I never dared hope that you could love me."

"I do." She kissed him, then laughed as he rolled them in one quick movement, pressing her to the bed so his mouth could slide down her neck. "I do."

．　．　．

HER FAMILY WOULD BE WAITING. Impatiently. But after a quick break-fast with Cuinn, Talyn went down to see Theac and his family. Errana looked so stunned to see her that several moments passed before she bowed. "Your return brings us so much joy, Ciantar."

"Come now, you know there's no need to bow to me," Talyn said awkwardly. "I'm glad you're safe, and well."

Corrin's sisters were equally excited by her appearance, even though they looked bleary eyed. Zamaril and Andres' arrival had made for a sleepless night for everyone, it seemed. Currently, the thief was snoring on the couch, Andres prone on the floor beside him.

"You turned Evani into a Wolf?" Talyn said with a smile when she and Theac finally had a moment alone. She'd left the young woman standing guard outside Cuinn's quarters.

"After Halun, she insisted," Theac said quietly. "And I couldn't refuse her."

"I'm glad you didn't." Talyn swallowed through the lump in her throat. The mention of the big man's name would never not break her heart a little. "She looks like him—she has that same watchful expression he always had when he was on guard."

Theac cleared his throat. "What now, Ciantar?"

She rose to her feet. "Now I'd best see my family before they send out a hunting party looking for me." She hesitated. "I have to go back to Mithranar. Soon."

"And what do you want of me?"

"You seem to have become the primary bodyguard to the regent of the Twin Thrones," Talyn said wryly. "If you're happy to stay here, with him, then that's where I want you."

"He won't be going back with you?"

"We haven't discussed it yet."

"Right." Theac came to his feet as well. "Family meeting. Best be getting along."

．　．　．

TALYN DELIBERATELY TOOK A LONGER route to the great hall, making her way there via a servant's entrance rather than the main doors.

She was happy. Beyond glad to have been reunited with her family. Despite that, nerves fluttered in her stomach. She'd been gone such a long time, even before what had happened in Mithranar—when she'd given herself to Cuinn and the people there and left the Twin Thrones to fight for itself. It wasn't logical, but she felt oddly out of place now that the adrenalin of the battle for Port Lathilly was gone.

She ignored Theac's increasingly pointed glances as she lingered in the doorway rather than entering the hall. She was being foolish, she knew it, but still... she just wanted a moment. To take it in. Prepare. Then she'd be fine.

"Ciantar?" Theac asked, scowling.

"Give me a moment, Theac."

Ariar, Soar and Alyna were clustered around the main table, along with Ariar's second, Rior McTavish, and Lark Ceannar. Ariar and Rior were studying one of the maps, a little frown on the Horselord's face, while Soar and Alyna conversed quietly with Lark.

She was about to step forward when the main doors opened. A man was shown in, escorted by two Kingshield. He was tall and lean, the thick wolf pelt he wore emphasising his broad shoulders. Talyn started in surprise—judging from his bearing and attire, this was a Firthlander prince, one of Tarcos' many cousins. What was he doing in Port Lachley?

And then it clicked. Rados. Tarcos had a cousin named Rados... and if she remembered correctly Tarcos had never liked him.

"Lord Hadvezer," Alyna greeted him, confirming Talyn's suspicions.

"Lady Dumnorix," the man replied, stiffness in his shoulders and bearing. He wasn't thrilled about being here, then. "I'd hoped to have begun negotiations by now."

"We'll begin today, if that suits you?" Alyna said graciously, all courtly politeness. "We have some urgent business to discuss before-hand, but if you don't mind waiting with your escorts, I promise we won't be long. If there's anything you need while you're waiting, we'll be happy to fetch it for you."

Rados inclined his head. "Thank you, Your Highness."

The Hadvezer prince returned the way he'd come, the Kingshield watching him carefully. He ignored them, head held high.

Behind Talyn, Theac cleared his throat. She waved a hand at him.

"*Are you scared, or just getting the lay of the land?*" Sari's voice enquired.

"*The truth? Mostly the latter, but also a bit of the former,*" Talyn admitted, then, "*You've been gone a while.*"

"*You've been naked a while. With Cuinn.*" An embarrassed shudder.

"*Right. Mind sticking around? I hate that I feel slightly intimidated and out of place, but I can't get rid of the feeling.*"

"*I'll be here.*" Sari paused. "*This is your family, Talyn.*"

"*I know.*" The discomfort would pass. She just hoped it did so soon.

"I don't know, Rior." Ariar's words floated to her. "If we make the wrong call, we could lose that whole section of the mountains."

"What does His Grace say?"

The warmth in Rior's voice surprised Talyn. Again, Theac cleared his throat. Sari gave her an equally clear mental nudge. Sighing, she braced herself to enter the room, then stopped when Cuinn's voice rang out.

"Did I hear my name spoken in vain?" He walked into sight, shadowed by two SkyRider Kingshield and Evani.

"Talyn?" Alyna's voice snapped through the room before Ariar could reply.

"On her way here, I'm sure. She went to visit Theac." Cuinn reached out to touch her mother's shoulders. "She's okay."

Alyna nodded. "Lord Hadvezer was just here. He's getting impatient."

"And we have a dilemma to run by you." Rior flashed Cuinn a welcoming smile.

"Such a burden to be so wanted." Cuinn's mouth quirked.

Soar snorted. "Don't let that head of yours get too big. If you'd just deign to give us your advice on one particular aspect of the war, we can probably muddle through the rest."

"Why limit ourselves? I can probably fit the whole war in before lunch." Cuinn chuckled.

Talyn stared. He was changed.

She'd seen it already, in his bearing, his physical form, the new strength in his eyes. But this... he carried himself with a confidence she'd never seen, and from the moment he'd walked into the room, his presence had demanded the respect due a Dumnorix from every single person there.

But as proud of him, as delighted by the change as she was, she also couldn't pretend the niggle of discomfort wasn't there. She'd fallen in love with a criminal, a prince in hiding, but now that man was a king in every sense of the word. Staying with him meant being a queen.

Her Wolf cleared his throat uncomfortably. "Can we stop hiding now?"

"I'm not..." Talyn began, then stopped herself. She *was* hiding. "Let's go."

They noticed the moment she stepped out from the entryway, of course, but the looks were welcoming, relieved, happy to see her. She relaxed. "Why are we hosting a Hadvezer prince?"

"Cuinn's idea." Ariar jerked a thumb. "Has he mentioned to you yet that he demanded to be made regent?"

"He did." A smile teased at her mouth as she accepted a warm hug from her mother, squeezing tightly for a long moment before she let go.

"I have given my word to relinquish the regency the moment I take the Mithranan crown," Cuinn said.

"The alliance agreement still stands, then?" she asked casually.

Something like guilt rippled over both Alyna and Soar's faces. Ariar looked away. Rior and Lark looked at each other, then took a discreet step into the background. Alyna opened her mouth to speak but Cuinn beat her to it. "Talyn, your family understandably did not want to tie the stability of their kingdom to a lesser prince who'd just had his throne taken from him and his wings torn out. I do not fault them for it."

Three Dumnorix gazes swung to Cuinn in astonishment.

"But we were wrong," Alyna said, voice ringing out clearly. "We should have agreed to honour the alliance when Cuinn first came. Instead we forced him to demand the regency."

"None of you should be sorry." Talyn included all three Dumnorix in her gaze, then Cuinn too. "It was me who kept secret from you who Cuinn truly was. You knew only my stories of him."

"So to be clear, all of us are equally to blame," Ariar said cheerfully. "We admit our mistakes and are now moving on."

"On the understanding that Talyn and I will still be marrying," Cuinn said clearly.

She met his gaze, smiled.

"Obviously," Alyna said, a hint of impatience in her voice.

"Burn bright and true," Soar said into the following silence.

Those words hung in the room for a long moment, then Alyna turned to Cuinn. "Best tell Talyn why Rados Hadvezer is here."

Cuinn waved them all to chairs, then took the one at the head of the table. "Ariar told me that Rados was another of Tarcos' cousins that the previous warlord had seriously considered making his heir."

Ariar added, "In the time Tarcos spent with me in the mountains, he spoke often of his hatred for Rados. I ended up disliking him as much as Tarcos did, but on review, I can see how carefully Tarcos set that trap."

"He did the same with me," Talyn murmured. Tarcos was a sore point, a name that summoned white-hot anger. Her hands curled into fists on her chair, but she buried the emotion before Cuinn's song magic could pick it up.

"No he didn't." Laughter edged Cuinn's voice. "Despite his best, and repeated, efforts, you refused to marry him. You were what he needed for a smooth acquisition of the Twin Thrones, especially once Aethain was dead. You made him start a war instead."

She hadn't considered it like that. Still. "I should have seen it coming. I'm sorry that I didn't."

"We're not apologising anymore, remember?" Alyna said dryly.

"Exactly," Ariar said. "Now, it's clear Tarcos didn't like Rados because he considered him too close to the warlord, too wedded to his ideas, too loyal."

"And not inclined to start a war because of the fact Firthland technically owes allegiance to a Dumnorix king," Talyn said.

"Exactly." Cuinn turned to face her. "So, here's my plan to finish the war with Firthland and turn our attention north. We replace Tarcos with Rados."

"Which sounds simple, but will be far from it," Alyna said bluntly, and with the tone of someone who'd voiced this argument before. Clearly they were going over it again for Talyn's benefit. "Tarcos commands the loyalty of the Bearmen and niever-flyers. Even if the Dumnorix officially appoint Rados warlord, only half the country will follow him. Not to mention Tarcos will have Azrilan's might to bolster his claim."

True, but... Talyn spun to Cuinn, rapidly starting to see what he was planning. "But *why* does Tarcos command their loyalty?"

He smiled at her.

"They hate the fact Firthland must swear ultimate allegiance to us," Ariar said impatiently. "What of it?"

"I think Cuinn is suggesting that we make Rados High King of Firthland and formally remove any right to their sovereignty," Talyn said.

Cuinn sighed. "I was, but you go ahead and take the credit for my idea."

Silence fell in the hall.

Alyna and Soar wore equal expressions of horror and shock. Ariar glanced rapidly between Cuinn and Alyna with wide eyes. By now McTavish and Ceannar were practically pressed against the far wall, rapt looks on their faces. Talyn had to smother a smile.

"*This* was your ultimate plan?" Alyna demanded, rounding on Cuinn.

"You want to give up Firthland?" Soar spoke at the same time.

"King Alendor forced them to swear allegiance to the Twin

Thrones because he'd just won a long and bloody war that Firthland had started," Cuinn said. "But decades have passed. None of those alive in Firthland today had anything to do with what happened in the past. Let's give them back their country."

"Doing that would take away their only grievance with us," Talyn added. "What motive do they have for war, then? Even the majority of Tarcos's supporters will see there is no reason for further bloodshed."

"We hope," Soar muttered.

"It's not only hope, Soar," Cuinn said firmly. "Saundin has confirmed that the Shadowlord and Armun Council are already wavering in their support for Tarcos. As are many of the lords. We just have to give them a reason to switch loyalty to Rados."

"Saundin?" Talyn asked, staring in astonishment. She hadn't seen the Armun since before Sari's death. Hadn't forgotten him, but hadn't made an effort to see him either... too many once good memories that had turned painful.

Cuinn shrugged. "I figured if Azrilan could use a single Shadow to de-stabilise Mithranar and hand him power, we could use an Armun to do the same in Firthland. And to be honest with you, after getting to know both men, I'll take Saundin over Savin any day."

"*So would I,*" Sari breathed. "*Saundin... oh, Talyn, Cuinn might actually pull this off.*"

Talyn couldn't help but agree. She'd liked working with Saundin, trusted him as she had few others. And he was highly regarded amongst other Armun, quickly rising in the ranks the last time she'd seen him. If anyone could sway the Armun Council's loyalty their way, it would be him.

"Saundin has handpicked a few trustworthy Armun who are opposed to the war and they've been working to identify Bearmen and niever-flyer commanders most loyal to Tarcos—he's given us a list of those he considers will follow Tarcos to the end," Alyna said. "The Shadowlord will have Shadows in position to assassinate them when Rados is ready to take the throne."

Cuinn flinched, but didn't look away.

"This is war, Cuinn," Ariar said softly.

"I know. It was my idea, remember?" he said.

A heavy silence, then, "It has to be a negotiation," Alyna said. "We hand Firthland their throne and sovereignty on the condition Tarcos is handed over to us."

"Agreed," Cuinn said.

"You think the niever-flyers and Bearmen will turn on him?" Soar asked.

"I think his people will choose peace over war. Especially a war that has no purpose," Cuinn said. "I'm not pretending our favourable trade arrangements with Firthland won't take a hit if we hand them full sovereignty, but we can sustain the losses, far better than we can the losses from ongoing war."

"It's not just trade. We lose the powerful armed forces that have until now been ours to command," Alyna said.

"Those same armed forces making war against us?" Talyn pointed out.

"What of Montagn?" Soar asked, sharing a glance with Alyna. "We just won Port Lathilly, but lost warriors in the process. We're still holding the Firthlanders to the mountains, but my SkyRiders are tiring, and I have little to spare to face the war fleet that is coming."

Cuinn settled back in his chair. "And even if my plan for Firthland works, Azrilan could decide that he wants it all himself. Montagn dwarfs all of us even at full military strength, which we aren't anymore."

"From what you've told us, Cuinn, Azrilan is a very different man from Tarcos. With Tarcos out of the picture, he has no need to hold to their alliance any longer. And he's a smart enough ruler to be happy with the empire he has in the north without risking it to try and take more," Ariar said.

Cuinn conceded that with a thoughtful nod. "You might be right. Especially if we make war with us too costly for him."

"Perhaps I can help there." Talyn spoke up, smothering a smile when several anticipatory gazes turned her way. "I don't suppose you've managed to find the ships carrying the niever-flyers Tarcos sent to protect the Montagni war fleet?"

A series of shaking heads.

"Damn." She sighed. "Even so. The ship that carried me here was one of six sent to Feather Bay to stock up on izerdia before joining the fleet. We destroyed the other five on our way out of Mithranar. All that izerdia is gone, and the rest we brought with us."

She took a breath, but they were all still listening raptly.

"The Callanan in Acleu, working alongside Cuinn's underground network, have been working to disrupt the war fleet any way they can. They won't have had the resources or numbers to take out the whole armada, of course, but it will be smaller than it was by the time it gets here."

"Not to mention their izerdia supply is gone. That could delay their departure south, as could the Callanan sabotage," Alyna said. "Giving us time—"

"To end the war with Firthland through Rados!" Ariar said excitedly. "Then we can marshal all our forces north to defend against the fleet. Which might not even be needed if Azrilan withdraws from the war, which he would be smart to do."

Hope began leaking through the room.

Cuinn looked over at Talyn, easily reading her. "You have more?"

"*If* we manage to install Rados on the Firthlander throne and end the war, and *if* we do it in time to be able to redeploy the army north to meet the fleet, we still have Azrilan sitting on both the Mithranan and Montagni thrones. Even if he withdraws now, we'll never be able to trust him. We'll have an enemy to the north for years to come."

Soar lifted an eyebrow. "You've got an idea."

"I do." She glanced towards the back wall. "First Shield, Captain McTavish—perhaps you'd like to join us for this part?"

Without a word they came to the table, pulled out chairs, sat down. Talyn rifled through the maps lying scattered on the table and pulled out one showing Mithranar and Montagn.

"My Wolves and Falcons and Saniya's network have been making life difficult for the Kingcouncil this past month." She jabbed a finger at Darmour. "We've stopped all wood transport out of Darmour, meaning the Montagni have been forced to resort to finding alternate wood supplies before they can build more ships. They have trees of their own, of course, but not of the quality of Mair-land wood. We've drastically reduced their export of copper too, and by now our people in Dock City will be starting to affect izerdia extraction."

Cuinn sat forward, mouth thinning, but Talyn met his gaze. "We don't hurt Falcons unless we're forced to, but Bearmen or Montagni soldiers are fair game. Corrin and Windsong built us an army while we've been gone, and we need to use it."

He lifted his hands in the air in surrender, settled back in his chair.

"You're not worried about Armun and Shadows hunting them, learning where you are? We've had casualties in Acleu because of them," Alyna spoke up.

"We took out those in Darmour, freeing up our operating space, and as we speak, we will be flushing out the Armun and Shadows in Dock City." Talyn shrugged. "They're good, but on home ground, my Wolves working with Saniya's people are better."

"People will still get hurt," Cuinn said quietly. "The City Patrol and WingGuard will tighten their control of the city."

"They are and they will," Talyn said bluntly. "But if we want Azrilan off the throne and you on it, then we need to have everything in place to make that move. We need the WingGuard and Kingcouncil to be on the back foot, defensive, unprepared. We need to use their laziness and ignorance against them."

Ceannar glanced between Talyn and Cuinn. "Can I point out the obvious? Even if you somehow manage to eject Azrilan from Mithranar, you've still got Montagn to deal with. You've stalled their construction of new ships, fine, but they still dwarf us in size and resources. They still have the ability to come for us—and Mithranar will be the first country he takes back."

Talyn smiled.

Months she'd been in that slave camp. Desperate to escape, so desperate she'd had to find ways to distract herself. So she and Sari had planned. And she'd had days and weeks of tedious labour and restless nights to not only come up with a plan, but refine it, tweak it. A plan that trusted Cuinn and her family would have worked out how to defeat Firthland, so they could bring the Twin Thrones behind them. "Well obviously I have a plan for that too."

Ariar burst out into peals of laughter. Even Cuinn lost his dismayed look and smiled. Alyna reached over to squeeze her hand. "Let's hear it, Talyn."

She leaned forward, cleared away the maps apart from one that showed all four countries. "Let's assume we successfully put Rados on the throne and Firthland withdraws its troops in time for us to redeploy and face the fleet coming from the north."

Soar lifted a hand. "That's a lot of assuming. What if that doesn't happen?"

She shrugged. "Then my plan won't work and we're all in a lot of trouble."

"Okay, good. Just wanted to clear that up."

"Ariar, how many Aimsir do you estimate you'll need to hold the northern coastline?" Talyn asked.

"If we make some *educated guesses*," he shot a smirk at Soar, "that the fleet will try to hit us in two or three different spots to try and spread our forces, then I'd want all my riders in Conmor positioned across the north. That's a thousand."

"I'm confident that between my SkyRiders and the navy, we can pick up the war fleet's approach soon enough to have some idea where they're heading. *If* I use all my legions, leaving only one or two based at Mothduriem to ensure the Firthlanders fully withdraw," Soar said.

"The single benefit of the open coastline is that we can use the cavalry too," Alyna pointed out. "They're holding the foothills north of the Ayrlemyre at the moment, but it should only take a week to get them north. They'll be tired, but it's doable."

Talyn studied the map, going over the plan she'd developed, making sure there weren't any gaping holes.

"Ariar, Soar, can you spare me a few hundred riders and a single legion, plus a ship or two to transport them?"

"Yes," both said without hesitation.

Ariar glanced at Soar. "Depending on how quickly you need them,

I'll draw upon our reserves in Lyall. They can be over the mountains and here in a week or two."

"You can't have a legion until Firthland is out of the mountains," Soar said. "But then I'll have a spare you can use. No more than one, though, I'll need every SkyRider I can get to deal with the ships and nievers protecting them."

"Good. Here's what I'm thinking."

They spent the rest of the day closeted in that audience chamber.

They argued. They countered.

They planned.

LATER THAT EVENING, Talyn found her mother on the western fortress wall watching the sun setting over the harbour.

"Hi," she said, settling against the cold stone.

Alyna regarded her for a long moment, then smiled a little. "Are you all right, Talyn?"

"That's a complicated question to answer." Talyn smiled a little to take the heaviness out of her words. "But mostly, yes, I am."

"You've talked to Cuinn about it?"

"He knows everything," Talyn said simply.

"Talyn." Alyna turned and took her hands. "We fought bitterly about you. I blamed him for your loss, I accused him of not trying to find you."

Talyn's shocked gasp was loud. "Mama!"

"You know what he said to me? He told me that you don't save him, and he doesn't save you. That you save yourselves, that you make yourselves strong, *for* each other."

She nodded, biting her lip to keep the tears from spilling. "He was right."

Alyna smiled. "Your father would be delighted by him. Cuinn told me Trys's story, what his life was in Mithranar. Why he had to leave. I wish I'd known."

"I wish *I'd* known."

They stood together for a long moment in comfortable silence.

Then Alyna shifted, that sharp look coming back to her face, and Talyn braced herself. "We still have a succession problem, Talyn."

"You're not worried that Cuinn will go back on his word?" She was only half-joking.

"No. He has proved himself and more." Alyna waved a dismissive hand. "But Ariar will refuse the crown. So will Soar and Allira. And I can't take it either."

"Why? You'd be perfect. I'm surprised you didn't take the regency the moment I left," Talyn said. "Mama, you're strong, clever and you manage the lords as well as you manage your Callanan sword."

"If I take the crown, then my heirs are any children that you and Cuinn have," Alyna said carefully.

She let out a breath as realisation hit her. "Which would create another empire. And nobody wants that."

"I'm not so sure." Alyna hesitated. "I don't think I'd do a better job than Cuinn. I'm tempted to make him king, let him learn to manage both thrones. Ariar has already spoken to me of it and I'd be astonished if Soar didn't feel the same way. I believe he's the leader we all need. And your children can learn from him."

Talyn winced and turned away.

"It's not what you want." Alyna wrapped an arm around her shoulders.

"I don't want to be queen at all, let alone queen of an empire. But that doesn't mean you're wrong."

Alyna was silent a moment. "I get the feeling that you understand my choice now."

Her mother didn't have to elaborate. Talyn knew exactly what she meant. "I do. At least, I understand now what it is to love someone like that. But that doesn't mean I would make the same choice." Guilt writhed through her at that admission, but it was the truth.

Her mother tightened her embrace. "You might not have to."

Talyn straightened. Pushed off the wall. "Let's just win the war first. Then worry about what comes next."

CHAPTER 42

*a*fter their planning session, Cuinn went over to the SkyRider base to visit Trystaan, ensuring the young eagle was settled in his nest and not bothering the keepers or other eagles. He tended to get restless when Cuinn didn't give him enough attention.

He'd only just gotten back to his rooms and bathed—and was debating whether to join the family for dinner or try to claim some time alone with Talyn—when she came in. He knew she'd been planning to get some sparring in with old Kingshield comrades, and as expected, her eyes were bright, her skin flushed, breathing still coming a little fast.

"You're here." She came straight over to him for a kiss. He obliged happily, but she squirmed away when he tried to pull her closer. "I'm all sweaty."

"There's a bath ready for you." He tugged on her hand. "And I want to hear all about your dramatic escape from Dock City while you bathe. I still can't believe Mayor Doran stole a ship!"

He managed to keep his hands to himself while she stripped off her clothes and stepped into the tub, then sat leaning against it while she told him the tale. By the end, he was once again asking himself how he'd ever been lucky enough to end up with this woman at his side. "It sounds like you had fun," he said instead.

She shrugged, turning her head towards him. "I wanted to leave a little present for Azrilan on my way out."

"You're a wonder."

She shifted under the water, a small frown creasing her forehead. The wave of reluctance that hit his magic had him stiffening and trying not to panic. She was keeping something from him and trying to figure out how to tell him. "What is it?"

She huffed in irritation at his easy reading of her. "There's something I need to tell you."

"Then tell me." His tone brooked no argument.

"I told you we escaped the slave camp with Saniya's help?" She waited for his nod before continuing. "Zamaril and I weren't the only ones branded as slaves and sent to the labour camp—and because I was so hurt... we needed help to get out. We took Mithanis with us, Cuinn."

Cuinn reared back, shock flaring through him. "What?"

"Azrilan did the same thing to Mithanis that he did to you—tore out his wings when he refused to swear loyalty. Only Mithanis didn't escape. Azrilan tossed him away like he did with Zamaril and me."

His mouth opened, closed. He ran a hand through his hair. All this time he'd assumed Mithanis was dead, gone, dealt with by Azrilan. He'd thought about his eldest brother occasionally, but not with grief, even though that shamed him a little. "I assumed Az killed him."

"In some twisted way I don't think he could bring himself to kill either of you."

"Where is he now?" He turned away, trying to process the thoughts tumbling through his head. Mithanis was alive. That opened a whole new world of uncomfortable possibilities. He should be glad, shouldn't he? Mithanis had bullied him and ordered the executions of Falcons Cuinn liked and respected, but he wasn't the monster he'd always imagined his elder brother to be. It also meant the path to the Mithranan throne was once again crowded.

"Locked up in the SkyReach." Exasperation filled her voice, before her face turned sober. "We wouldn't have gotten out without him." Talyn lifted a hand out of the water to touch his face, turning him back to face her. Those sapphire eyes were dark with concern. For him. "Are you okay?"

"Yeah." He managed a smile. "Do you mind if we eat in here tonight? I'm reluctant to share you."

"Yes, please," she said with fervor, then closed her eyes and slid underneath the water. A moment later she popped back up, water streaming down her face and hair, and levelled him with a wicked grin. "Join me?"

"So, you're going back to Mithranar."

They'd eaten and were curled up together before his crackling fire. It was growing late, the castle settling down for the night. She was silent for a long moment, then abruptly she stood, leaving him to walk over towards the window. "Not immediately, but soon, yes."

Frowning, he stood too. "What does that mean?"

It was another long moment before she replied, and he tried to be patient, even though her reluctance to speak was hitting him loud and clear and making him itch with discomfort.

"I don't enjoy killing as a rule, Cuinn." She continued staring out the window as she spoke. "It's something I'm willing to do when necessary—to save myself, a loved one, an innocent—and I do it without hesitation. I'm good at it. But I don't take pleasure from it."

"I already know that," he said quietly, beginning to see where this was heading.

"You remember me telling you about the crazy theory Leviana and Cynia had? That Sari's death, my father's death, leaking my true identity to Mithanis—that they were all attempts by some unknown person to get me to come back to Ryathl. To join the Dumnorix court."

"You think it was Tarcos." It wasn't a question.

"I know it was Tarcos." Talyn's hands curled into fists where they lay on the stone windowsill. "He needed me to join Aethain's court so that when we married he would have a legitimate claim to the Twin Thrones, or at least powerful leverage to force the other Dumnorix to accept him once he allied with Azrilan and took the warlord's title."

"Talyn, I—"

"He was so upset when I went back to Mithranar, even more upset when I turned down his offer of marriage. Like a fool I thought it was because I'd hurt him, because he was in love with me. What arrogance." Her words were bitter, and he let them pour out, giving her the space to say what she needed to. "I missed it."

"Like I missed Azrilan doing to me what I'd been doing to everyone my whole life," Cuinn said, his own bitterness surging. "You think I don't hate myself for that?"

She nodded once. A silence fell, and eventually she turned to face him.

"He killed Sari. He killed my father." She shrugged, met his eyes.

"I know."

"I'm going to kill him, and I'm not going to be nice about it, Cuinn. I'm going to sneak into his fortress and kill him in his bed and I'm not even going to give him the chance to fight back." Her voice was cold, dark, remorseless.

"What does Sari say about it?" he asked.

"It doesn't matter. Because if our situations were reversed, she'd already be on her way to Firthland to hunt him down."

Of course she would.

"Okay," he said.

She huffed a breath. "Really? Just like that? I know how you feel about violence."

He took a step towards her. "I love you, Talyn. More than that, I love all the things that make up who you are. Tarcos killed the person you loved most in this world, he killed the father you adored, and you are warrior born. I accept that you are going to kill Tarcos, that it's not in you to do otherwise, even though I might not like it."

She smiled faintly, and her shoulders sagged as if in relief. "Thank you."

"I..." He cleared his throat, needing to make his own confession. "I know what it is to kill now."

Fire popped into the silence that fell, and he couldn't meet her eyes. She came to him, took his hands. "How did you feel?"

"I hated it."

"I'm glad." She leaned up to press a warm kiss to his jaw. "I'm sorry that it was necessary, but I'm so proud of the strength you've shown. After everything, you found a way to fight back."

Unable to speak, he wrapped an arm around her waist and led her back to the cushions by the flames, stealing a long kiss as he did.

"Do you want me to come with you to Firthland? I assume you're going straight on to Mithranar after."

Talyn shifted in his embrace, turning so that she could face him. "That's up to you. What do you want to do?"

"I never want to be more than three feet away from you ever again," he said firmly. "But I also think that in negotiations with Rados, my song magic will be invaluable."

She closed her eyes, rested her forehead against his chest. "It's not just your magic. It's you. You were born for this. They need you."

"Just like you were born for carrying out daring plans that would have no hope of success if anyone else was involved," he murmured. "And as much as I hate to lose you, I'm glad you're going back home. The guilt I constantly feel for being so far away... knowing what they must be suffering... it eats at me, Talyn."

"You did the right thing. If you'd stayed, you would be no closer to unseating Azrilan. Not when he has Montagn behind him." A smile curled at her mouth, and she reached up to touch his cheek.

"I refused to let you down. I couldn't," he whispered. "You'll go back home, and I'll stay here to deal with Firthland. Once that's done, I'll come to you, and I'll bring the Twin Thrones behind me."

"I'll be waiting." Her sapphire eyes glimmered with resolve.

CHAPTER 43

Talyn stayed two days. Long enough to go over her plan and make it a better one. Long enough to wait for Doran and his Montagni ship to arrive and give him and the crew a day on land to rest.

Not anywhere near long enough.

But while Talyn planned strategy with her family and the Dumnorix commanders, Cuinn opened negotiations with Rados. He started slow and with honesty. He told Rados what had happened in Port Lathilly, what the status of their forces was.

Cuinn told him in no uncertain terms that the Dumnorix wanted the war over and that was why Rados had been brought to Port Lachley.

"Why me?" Rados challenged. "What is it you think I can do?"

"Tarcos hates you."

The Firthlander's fierce expression tightened. "True enough. And I assume you know why he hates me. I wasn't enough of a firebrand for him."

"You were loyal to your uncle. To the Twin Thrones."

"I don't know who I'm loyal to anymore." Rados turned away, beginning to pace. "I am Firthlander to my bones. I'm Bearman trained and heir to a lord. I love my country."

"And you don't want to see your countrymen die for no good reason," Cuinn said softly, threading his voice with his sincerity. "I feel the same way, Rados."

"That doesn't make us friends. I'm not your puppet and I never will be. We have been punished for decades for a war nobody alive today started," he snapped. "I was loyal to the Twin Thrones because your kings have treated us with respect and fairness, but that doesn't mean we like the yoke around our necks, and it doesn't mean we don't fear what happens when a less-great Dumnorix ascends the Twin Thrones. Not to mention the fact Tarcos hates me means I have little influence in Samatia. So I ask again, why am I here?"

Cuinn met his fierce look and held it. "You are here because you agreed to be. Because when Saundin came to you and offered a way out of this war, you took it. Because you are a better man than your cousin." He took a step forward. "And because the Dumnorix want to work with you, as an ally, to end the war none of us want."

A moment's silence, then, "It's not as simple as you make it sound. Tarcos has dragged Montagn into this thing."

"I know. But we have to start somewhere."

"Saundin told me you have a strategy for ending it without more bloodshed."

"We do. But we can't pull it off without you."

Rados straightened his shoulders. "I will deal with the Dumnorix directly, or not at all."

Cuinn smiled faintly. "You're dealing with the regent right now. But yes, if you agree, you'll be negotiating directly with all of us."

Rados offered his hand. "Then let's talk."

Cuinn shook.

TALYN LEFT THE FOLLOWING MORNING. She was out of bed before dawn, no doubt off to prepare. When he woke, Cuinn went looking and found her in a small courtyard by one of the side gates in the castle saddling FireFlare—the mare would be travelling with her back to Mithranar.

He lingered for a moment, watching her as she checked the saddle and stirrups, before affixing a bow and quiver of arrows to their places and then finally buckling on her saddlebags. The space at the small of her back was empty, Sari's daggers lost the night she'd killed Savin with them. His magic told him this wasn't a wound she'd allowed herself to deal with yet.

She was leaving already. It hit him like a punch. Not just leaving, but going to sneak into an extremely well-guarded fortress to kill a warlord no doubt surrounded by fierce warriors. His chest squeezed fiercely and for a moment it was hard to draw breath. "I am finding this extremely difficult," he said aloud, alerting her to his presence.

She turned at his voice and came straight over. The look in her eyes told him she knew exactly what he meant. She didn't say anything, didn't need to, just reached out and squeezed his hand.

"Zamaril and Andres and the Wolves?" he asked.

"Already aboard the ship—I wanted to speak with you all privately." Talyn made a face. "I think I'm going to be spending the entire ship journey to Samatia fighting Zamaril and Andres on not accompanying me into the city. They're not happy."

"They might be extra protection for you," he tried arguing, but she was already shaking her head.

"Three people can evade detection; I don't want to risk a larger group. Besides, if it all goes wrong, Zamaril is our next best chance of getting to Tarcos."

Something in her voice changed when she mentioned the thief's name, and he cocked his head. "He's not just your talon anymore, is he?"

"Don't," she warned him.

He lifted his hands in the air in surrender, very familiar with what that tone from her meant. Push any further and he might lose a valuable limb. She was nowhere near ready to accept that she might one day have another Callanan partner. That was fine. Zamaril had endless patience where Talyn was concerned. And Cuinn was glad that it was him.

"What's with all the mystery?" Ariar bounced into the yard, cheerful as always, saving Cuinn from the fierce scowl on Talyn's face. He was dressed for riding too, no doubt having been out for a gallop on Greylord before confining himself to the castle for the rest of the day. The Dumnorix had a lot of work ahead of them with Rados. "Can't you just leave by the front gates like a normal person?"

"No, because I'm not going straight to Mithranar." Talyn paused as Alyna and Soar appeared, waiting for them to join her.

A brief silence fell. Alyna looked at Cuinn with a questioning eyebrow. He gave her a little shrug.

"Go on," Soar said eventually.

"For Cuinn's plan with Rados to work best, for a clean finish to the war with Firthland so that we can quickly reposition to deal with Montagn, Tarcos can't be allowed to live." She spoke briskly. "I'm going home via Samatia."

Ariar's eyebrows shot skywards. "You're going to assassinate Tarcos Hadvezer?"

"Talyn, no, you can't. That's too dangerous a precedent to set," Alyna said. "We cannot go around assassinating fellow rulers because we don't like them."

"Tarcos did it," Talyn countered. "He sent a Shadow to murder *our* king."

Those words resonated sharply. Cuinn glanced between Talyn and the rest of their family. Ariar was already nodding slightly, Soar and Alyna undecided.

"Mama, Soar, we can't afford for the war to linger. If Cuinn's plan works and Tarcos is left alive, you will have the lingering issue of rebellion in Firthland and more army desertions. He has to be gone for Rados to take undisputed leadership of the country."

"And what if some other rebel Firthlander decides to retaliate, send a Shadow after one of us again?" Alyna countered. "It's bad enough Tarcos did it once. We cannot reciprocate."

"She's right," Soar said heavily. "As badly as I want to see that man gone, this isn't the way."

"I would agree, if that's all it was about," Talyn said. "But he killed Sari. I won't let that lie."

Alyna opened her mouth. Closed it. A grim look filled her face as if for a moment she could forget she was Dumnorix and remember the Callanan warrior she'd been. "And he murdered Trys. Kill him, Talyn."

"You always have my support, Cousin," Ariar spoke then, "But going into Samatia alone to kill a man no doubt surrounded by Shadows, Armun and Bearmen is a close to impossible task, even for you."

"I'm not going alone." A small smile teased her mouth. "I'll be leading a three-warrior Callanan strike force. I don't care how good Tarcos's protectors are. They won't see us coming until it's too late."

Cuinn looked up as Leviana and Cynia walked into the courtyard, perfectly on cue. They were dressed in full Callanan gear and heavily armed. At the sight of four Dumnorix turning to stare at them, they bowed gracefully, but didn't say a word.

Cuinn chuckled. "I'm not betting against those three getting to Tarcos."

Talyn gave him a quick look of gratitude before settling her gaze on Soar. The Sky Chieftain eventually gave a slow nod. "All right."

Talyn stepped forward to throw her arms around her mother and the two hugged for a long time. "Stay safe."

"Don't do all the work of winning the war for us," Ariar complained as he hugged her next. "Leave something for my Aimsir, won't you?"

"Your Aimsir are going to have plenty to do," she promised. "I look forward to seeing you in a couple of months."

"Come home safe," Soar said soberly.

And then she was turning to Cuinn, sapphire eyes roving over his face as if committing it to memory. "Be ready for when he's dead."

"We will," he murmured. "Burn bright and true, Talyn."

She leaned up to kiss him. His arms settled around her and pulled her close, deepening the kiss. Eventually she pulled away, leaning up to murmur in his ear. "I love you."

They lingered there for a moment, reluctant to part, then she tore herself away with a sigh and went to FireFlare. Leviana and Cynia offered waves to Cuinn, and then all three of them were riding out of the courtyard.

Cuinn watched until they vanished from sight.

When he shook himself and turned, he found all three Dumnorix doing exactly the same thing. Even Theac and Evani were staring through the open gates, a wistful look on their faces.

He chuckled. "Come on. Let's go and open negotiations with Rados Hadvezer. Soon the warlord of Firthland will be dead, and we need to have a new high king ready."

CHAPTER 44

"This is the best mission ever!" Leviana announced with glee.

Cynia glanced down the precipitous cliff face, then back at her partner. "Sometimes I wonder about your sanity."

"Sometimes?" Talyn asked.

"At least I'm not balancing right on the edge like that massive drop is no more than a little jump." Leviana pointed at Talyn.

She smiled. "That's my winged folk blood."

"Yes, well, your winged folk blood isn't going to save you if a wind kicks up suddenly and knocks you off," Cynia said pointedly. "So if for no other reason than my anxiety levels, could you please step away?"

Talyn did as requested, scanning the rapidly darkening skies as she did so. They looked clear—no niever-flyers in sight patrolling above the city. All around them were trees, the ground rocky and dry, the area uninhabited.

"I couldn't see much inside the fortress this high up, but there were no visible watching posts or guards on the cliff face," she said. "There's no room for them; it's nothing but rock."

"You're sure nobody has ever tried this before?" Cynia asked now.

Far below their feet, built into the bottom of the rugged and precipitous cliff face they stood on, was the warlord's fortress. Sama-tia, the capital of Firthland, sprawled out across a wide, flat valley beyond it. Several main roads snaked out of the western end of the valley, joining the rest of the country to its capital. At the eastern end were the mountains, the fortress built deep into stone and rock so that it perched above the city.

"If anyone has tried it before, I doubt they were successful," Leviana said. "You definitely couldn't get an army down this way."

"You'd think a Shadow would have pointed it out as a vulnerabil-ity, though. Don't tell me one of them wouldn't think to access the fortress via the cliff to carry out an assassination," Cynia persisted. "There could be trip wires or guards waiting at the bottom."

"We can keep an eye out for tripwires on the way down." Leviana shrugged. "And any guards waiting at the bottom will not be expecting us. We'll have the advantage of surprise."

"Cynia, you're the best markswoman I know. If there are guards waiting, you can take them out from above before they even see us," Talyn added.

"That's if I don't fall halfway down," Cynia grumbled, but then conceded. "When do you want to go in?"

"Not until that sun has fully set." Talyn gave the skies another uneasy glance. "If a patrolling niever-flyer spots us mid-way down, we'll be open target practice."

"Yes, much better idea to scale a dangerous cliff face in the dark," Cynia said, but a smile curled at her mouth. "Should we wait until after midnight? Catch them when most of the fortress is asleep and guards are least alert?"

"Normally I'd second that, but in this case we have to give ourselves time to escape," Talyn said. "Assuming we can get to Tarcos without raising the alarm, we still have to make the climb back up this cliff. We'll need the full night for that."

None of them had to say out loud what it would mean if the alarm was raised while they were still in there. They'd have a fortress full of armed warriors to face down. Chances of escape in that scenario would be slim to none.

Leviana grinned. "I told you. This is going to be fun!"

LEVIANA WENT FIRST, acting as spotter for her partner, who was climbing second. Talyn came at the rear, her job to scan the skies for patrolling niever-flyers. They were clad head to toe in black, woolen masks covering their faces so that nothing but their eyes showed. Even their weapons were wrapped in black cloth to prevent metal flashing for anyone who might be glancing up at the cliffs above the fortress.

Talyn wore a sword slung over her shoulder and a knife at her hip. Cynia's bow and quiver were slung over her shoulders as usual, but she also carried a knife in her boot. Leviana claimed to have eleven knives clustered around her person.

The climb was long and brutal. Darkness and minimal handholds in the rock made for slow, cautious progression. Leviana, a skilled climber, identified the best path for Cynia and Talyn to follow. They weren't even halfway down when Talyn realised that it was doubtful either she or Cynia would have been able to make the climb without Leviana helping them find the way.

The light varied too—it was a cloudy night with a brisk breeze flowing from the east. Cloud cover intermittently dimmed the moon's light before clearing to make it brighter. Leviana deliberately chose a path down that made use of the folds in the rock, hiding them in shadow as much as possible. They inched ever downwards, the fortress below a beacon of hundreds of individual pinpricks of orange light.

Talyn had only ever been to Samatia once, while on Callanan assignment with Sari, but Cynia and Leviana had been there multiple times. Even better, Leviana had stayed in the fortress during trading trips her father had made to Samatia when she was growing up.

As the fortress grew close enough to make out the shapes of the patrolling guards on the western wall facing the city, Leviana began angling them sideways across the cliff face, heading towards the northeastern corner. According to her, the warlord's quarters were on the top level there.

"Historically, the high kings liked the idea of looking down over their city," she'd explained. "Of having nobody living higher than them."

"I bet Tarcos loves that too," Cynia muttered darkly.

Talyn had said nothing. Even the mere mention of his name made her so angry and guilty that her chest constricted and her stomach threatened to expel her previous meal. She hated that he'd successfully played her, but more than that, she hated *him* in a way she'd never hated anything or anyone before.

Both Sari and her father were dead because of him. Her life almost ruined, her mother's heart broken, Azrilan given the ability to take Mithranar and kill Wolves, *Halun*, in the process.

No, hate wasn't even a strong enough word for how she felt about Tarcos Hadvezer.

Much of the fortress extended back into the rock, dug out generations earlier, but the front of it emerged from the mountainside in a series of stone balconies and stairwells linking the various levels. Samatia reflected its fortress, a city that bustled and housed thousands, but without the hint of magic and spices that wrapped Dock City or the bright ocean of Ryathl.

Her attention was drawn back to the present when Leviana halted below, lifting a hand. Talyn stilled against the cliff. Her arms burned and sweat slicked her skin, but her breath came easily. The anticipatory joy of a coming fight began winding through her blood.

This was what she did. It was who she was. Nothing would ever change that.

They'd paused above a private garden emerging from the mountainside. A locked gate sat at its western end, and three high stone walls enclosed it. Beyond the gate a path shrouded in shadow wound down to a wide walkway. That was all she could make out in the dim light.

It appeared to be deserted, and after they'd hung there for several moments, Leviana gave the go-ahead signal. She scrambled down the remaining distance, landing lightly in the garden. Cynia paused a moment, leaning into the rock, bow drawn and knocked in case Leviana's appearance brought guards running, but nothing happened.

Talyn hit the ground only moments after Cynia did, right hand reaching up to curl around the hilt of her sword.

Silence filled the night around them, broken occasionally by faint snatches of conversation coming from somewhere nearby—an open window, maybe?

"This should be the warlord's level," Leviana murmured. "But the direct approach to his quarters will be bristling with guards."

They'd already discussed this. Three Callanan could fight their way through a hallway full of guards—*if* there weren't any Bearmen—but by the time they did that the alarm would be raised and it would be close to impossible to get out alive.

"We go over the balconies," Talyn said. Leviana had assured her that the warlord—and all the important lords—had quarters at the front of the castle with their own private balconies to view the city. Lesser lords and other residents lived in rooms further back in the fortress where there were no windows, let alone balconies.

Leviana frowned, her gaze sweeping their surroundings, clearly trying to place where they were in relation to what she knew of the fortress layout. Cynia padded to the gate, glancing through to keep an eye out for anyone approaching.

Talyn fought to maintain her usual cool calm before a fight. Tarcos was close. The anger that had been simmering away since learning what he'd done to her pushed at the controls she'd placed around it.

"North," Leviana said eventually. "I *think* we've come down in the middle of the warlord's residential level and I'm fairly certain his personal quarters were down at the end of a long corridor—my father showed me in passing once after we were invited up to his dining room for a welcome meal."

Unable to stay still any longer, Talyn jogged for the northern garden wall, *leaping* up to grip the top of the wall and haul herself onto it. There, she lay flat on her stomach, not wanting to reveal her profile to anyone glancing up. Immediately below and to her left were more levels of the fortress snaking down to the impressive stone wall and entrance gates at the ground level. Beyond that the city was visible, thousands of pinpricks of lights filling the massive valley floor.

A stone wall ran perpendicular to the one she was lying on—parallel to a pathway for patrolling guards—and ran up to the edge of a wide balcony. The opposite side of that balcony ended in rocky mountainside.

If Leviana was right, that was the warlord's balcony.

Steadying her breath, she lay there as bootsteps sounded and a pair of guards marched down the long pathway. They reached the end, turned, and marched back.

Talyn shifted to drop silently back down into the garden. "Leviana, you're amazing."

The woman brightened. "You found it?"

Talyn nodded and described what she'd seen. "We'll have to crawl along the top of the perpendicular wall slow and quiet. All it will take is a single noise to make those guards look up."

Cynia frowned. "Coming back that way increases the risk of us getting caught—particularly if Tarcos makes a sound or otherwise grabs the attention of the guards."

"We won't need to." Talyn explained about the opposite side of the balcony ending in mountainside. "We just start our climb back up from there."

Leviana straightened, a fierce grin flashing over her face. "Let's get this done."

"When we reach the balcony, I want the two of you to stay there. Keep an eye on the guards patrolling below and deal with them if the alarm is raised," Talyn instructed. "I'll go in alone but I promise to shout if I need help." If she was quiet enough, any guards posted on Tarcos's room door wouldn't hear a thing, and she could creep out the way she'd come in.

But it was still relatively early. He might not be asleep. And if he was awake, he'd put up a fight. Talyn found herself half-hoping he would—she wanted him to see her face as she killed him, to know that his death was coming.

"That's not you, Talyn."

"It is tonight."

Sari hesitated, then, *"I won't argue because I know I would be saying the same thing in your shoes. Just... make your priority getting out of there alive, okay?"*

"Don't worry about that." Going home to Cuinn, the Wolves, her family. That meant far more to her than killing Tarcos did. *"But we both know I can kill him and get out of here alive without breaking a sweat, especially with Levs and Cynia at my back."*

"Maybe just a little sweat. But yes, I couldn't agree more. Go get him, partner."

"We'll cover your back," Cynia assured her.

The journey along the top of the wall was as painstaking as the climb down the mountainside had been. Sliding forward on their stomachs, they had to place every hand, every foot, carefully so as not to make a sound. And they had to keep it slow—quick movements could catch the attention of the guards' peripheral vision.

The balcony was dark when Talyn reached it, dropping lightly to the stone and freezing into stillness. Nobody called the alarm. Nobody came running. No light leaked from under the door either.

Anxiety beat at her—what if he wasn't inside?

Leviana's hand landed on her shoulder, and she silently pointed to where she and Cynia would take up positions on the balcony. Talyn nodded and moved for the door.

It was unlocked, and she slowly turned the handle and pushed it open. It swung inwards without making a sound, revealing a dark room. Talyn slipped inside and closed the door quickly behind her, halting a moment until her eyes adjusted to the dim light. Once they did, she could make out a large bed with rumpled covers, a dresser, and a sword leaning against a table by the bed.

"Overconfident, Tarcos," she murmured. If he was unarmed, this was going to be a lot easier than she'd imagined.

If he was here.

She pushed aside her doubts. If he wasn't here, she would get out without detection and try again.

"I wish I was with you,"

"You are," Talyn said swiftly.

A burst of warm regard, then Sari went silent, allowing her to concentrate.

She moved lightly across the stone floor to stop her boots from making a sound, then paused by an inner door that stood half-ajar. Beyond the bedroom was a much larger lounge area. A fire crackled in the grate and the double front doors of the rooms were closed.

No guards were visible on the inside. The lounge was empty.

Edging the bedroom door further open, she surveyed the lounge. The fire likely meant someone was in here, or was about to be. Then she heard a snatch of conversation and the tinkle of cutlery.

Several paces to the immediate left of the entrance doors was an archway. Light spilled into the lounge from beyond the arch—where the sounds were coming from.

Talyn's gaze swept the lounge one more time to ensure it was empty, then she moved, quickly crossing the distance between the bedroom door and the wall by the archway. Pressing herself against it, she cautiously leaned around to get a glimpse of what was beyond.

It was a dining room. Though the space was almost as large as the lounge, the part of the dining table that she'd seen in that quick glimpse seemed small in comparison. A serving table ran along the same wall as the entrance doors and it was laden with steaming platters of food and a jug of wine.

Comparing what she'd seen crawling along the wall with the layout of these quarters, she guessed the wall directly opposite the serving table probably held at least one window. There was no way to tell what else was in the room without leaning all the way around the arch and revealing her presence.

Someone spoke again, and her hands curled into fists at her side. The voice was unmistakably Tarcos's, and by his tone she judged he was giving an order, asking someone for more food. Metal clinked against a plate and then silence fell again.

So there was at least one other person in the room, probably a servant. But she heard no indication of anyone else. If someone was dining *with* Tarcos, they were eating in silence.

"*Go, Talyn,*" Sari urged. "*A guard or someone else could walk through those front doors any moment.*"

Talyn pressed back against the wall and took a long breath. She thought about that night—when Savin had ambushed her and Zamaril, almost killed them both. She thought about the years Tarcos had pretended friendship, had taken her as a lover, had betrayed her with every word and touch. And finally she thought about losing Sari. Of how she was never going to recover from the pain of that loss.

Then she stepped around the corner and into the room.

Tarcos was seated at the dining table facing her, his back to the window. His face went rigid with shock when she appeared.

"Hello, Tarcos."

He half-rose from his seat, mouth opening, but she had her knife out of her belt and ready to throw in a heartbeat. "Don't. Or I will bury this in your throat before you finish shouting the alarm. You know I can."

His mouth tightened, but he slid back into his chair. The immediate threat momentarily dealt with, Talyn scanned the room. Nobody else was there. Nobody but the servant. Her eyes flew wide with shock as she saw who it was.

Tall, gangly, around fifteen years old with too-long raven hair, grave features and starlit grey eyes. He was equally shocked at the sight of her, and both of them froze for a moment.

"Aeris," she breathed.

Tarcos took advantage of her momentary distraction, hurling himself from his chair and grabbing for the boy.

But Aeris Dumnorix saw it coming and dived to his right, jumping away from Tarcos' lunge and hitting the floor at Talyn's feet.

Or where her feet *had* been.

Because she was already leaping forward, crashing into Tarcos as he rose from the chair and using her momentum to force him back against the wall. He shoved at her, his brute strength almost dislodging her grip, but she slammed a knee into his groin and he doubled over, gasping. Before he could think to shout for help she pressed the blade of her knife to his throat.

"Aeris?" she said without turning around. Her gaze was locked on Tarcos. His hazel eyes writhed with frustrated anger, lips curled in a snarl. He was thwarted and he knew it. She savoured that look.

"What do you need?" Aeris sounded calm.

"How many guards are usually posted outside the front doors?"

"Two Bearmen. Shift change will be in about a full-turn or so, and they always check on the warlord then."

Her shoulders relaxed slightly. A full-turn was plenty of time. "If they hear anything and open that door, you find a way to allay their concerns."

"Can do." Aeris' footsteps sounded as he moved to the archway, ready to step out and deal with it if the guards opened the doors.

"Why are you here? You know you'll never get out alive," Tarcos hissed, face twisted in a rictus of fury. There was nothing in his expression of the man she'd cared about, respected. The one who'd shown gentleness after Sari's death. How much of that had been an act?

"You know why I'm here," she said coldly, throwing the words at him with all of the fury burning inside her. "Your death was inevitable from the moment you organised Sari's death. How could you not have understood that?"

"I saved your life," he rasped, lowering his voice when she dug her knife warningly into the skin at his throat. "Azrilan was going to kill you and the thief both. I asked him to spare you."

She barked a laugh. "I'm sorry, do you want me to be *grateful* for that? For being beaten within an inch of my life and thrown into a slave camp?" She lifted an eyebrow. "Sparing me was the stupidest mistake you've ever made."

"You can't really be here to kill me," he snarled, anger making his body rigid, desperate to lash out at her. "You'll be dead before you get two steps beyond the door."

"You continue to underestimate me, Tarcos Hadvezer," she murmured, then she pulled back the knife and with one brutal move slammed it between his ribs, angling the blade up to slide through muscle and tendon, holding it there for a long moment.

He gasped, shock and pain flaring over his face, and he went boneless in her grip. She moved her mouth to his ear. "You're dead, Tarcos. Dead without a throne or an empire. And if you think Azrilan is going to finish what you started, maybe it's time to stop underestimating me and realise the truth."

She drove the knife all the way in, to his heart, then stepped back and yanked out the blade. Tarcos slid down the wall, one hand covering the blood-soaked patch on his tunic, eyes already glassy. His mouth moved, but only a croaking sound came out. She crouched down, wiped her knife on his tunic, and smiled. "I'm going to marry Cuinn, and I'm going to give him the empire you wanted to take. Think on that as you're gasping out your last few breaths."

He shook his head, mouth curling in a snarling rictus, but nothing came out. Soon the life faded from his eyes and he slumped there, dead.

"Well done, Cousin."

Talyn rose to her feet and spun, sheathing the knife in one movement. Triumph warred with satisfaction and the tiniest bit of remorse for what she'd just done as she faced her cousin. "Aeris! You're all right?"

Aethain's son and heir, the fifteen-year-old boy they'd all assumed was dead, met her gaze without flinching. His unruly mop of curling black hair had grown out, nearly obscuring his luminous Dumnorix eyes. Anger had turned them stone-cold. "He liked the idea of me serving him, so he made me his personal attendant. He thought it served our family right for years of subjecting Firthland to the same treatment."

"I—"

"We should get out," he continued. "Tarcos has a lover that sometimes visits after his dinner, and the Bearmen will check in at shift change. You've a plan?"

Talyn blinked. She'd never known Aeris particularly well—had only really spoken to him on a handful of occasions—but standing before her was a slightly smaller version of Aethain. Grave, controlled, even-tempered.

And after months of captivity.

So instead of coddling, or asking again if he was all right, she simply lifted an eyebrow and asked her king, "How good are you at climbing?"

CYNIA WAS the first to see Aeris as Talyn led him onto the balcony, and her eyes widened with shock. "Levs, we can't climb back up the cliff," she said instantly. "We'll have to find another way."

Leviana turned at her partner's voice, letting out a hissed curse when her gaze fell on Aeris. "Is Tarcos dead, Tal? Because if he's not, I'm going to go in there and murder him myself."

"He's dead." Aeris moved for the edge of the balcony. "You came down the mountainside above the fortress? I've been trying to work out how to get free so I could escape that way. Don't worry, I can do it."

The partners exchanged a glance. "Your Highness, I don't think—"

"If Aeris says he can do it, then he can," Talyn said firmly. "Cynia, you'll go first this time. Leviana, as our best climber you'll shadow Aeris, help him if he needs it. I'll bring up the rear. Let's go."

"You okay, Tal?" Cynia asked quietly, reaching out to touch her hand.

"I'm glad he's dead." And no matter what those words made her, they were true.

They made it two thirds of the distance up the cliff face before a hubbub exploded below. By then cloud cover had dimmed the moonlight and they were high enough up that Talyn hoped nobody could spot the dark shapes on the rock face.

"We need to hurry," Cynia said. "They'll have nievers up searching for us in no time."

They scrambled over the edge, panting and exhausted, just as the first niever scream sounded in the night sky. Talyn was the first to clamber to her feet and then all four of them were running, moving deep into the forested terrain so that any niever above wouldn't be able to spot them. She kept a careful eye on Aeris as they ran, but he kept up without complaint.

Once well clear of the cliff face, they stopped briefly to confer under a thick copse of trees.

"We could hole up here for the rest of the night and tomorrow, use the tree cover to keep hidden from the niever-flyers," Leviana said, outlining their options. "Then hike back to the coast tomorrow night under cover of darkness. But I'd prefer to keep moving. By tomorrow they could have figured out how we got in and out and have trackers and Bearmen up here searching."

"I agree," Talyn said. "I want to cover as much ground as we can before daylight."

"Your Highness?" Cynia asked, turning to Aeris.

"I'll do whatever you and my cousin recommend," he said quickly. "Tarcos kept me captive, but he didn't starve or hurt me, so I can keep up if we need to hike all night." He paused, as if he was going to say something else but thought better of it.

"What is it?" Talyn asked softly.

"He thought he was injuring my pride, my dignity, making me less than him, by treating me as a servant." Aeris's luminous grey eyes met hers. "The man had no idea what those things truly mean."

"No, he didn't," Cynia said.

Talyn reached out, squeezed her cousin's shoulder. "Let's go."

BY DAWN they'd made it to the coastline north of Samatia where they'd beached their small boat in one of a myriad of small caves along the rugged shore. Talyn eyed the growing light, the empty skies, trying to decide on the best course of action—there were risks no matter what she decided. "I say we go now rather than waiting for nightfall. The niever-flyers don't seem to be searching this far north yet, and the sooner we make it back to the ship the safer we'll be."

Aeris, Cynia and Leviana surrounded the boat and began dragging it into the shallows without another word.

Leviana and Talyn rowed while Cynia stood balanced in the prow, bow in one hand, arrow in the other, ready to start firing if they were spotted by a niever-flyer search party. Aeris sat between them, silent, gaze inward.

Talyn let out a long breath in relief when their stolen Montagni ship came into sight, anchored where they'd left it. Their approach was spotted and a rope ladder dropped over the side. Cynia once again kept watch while Aeris went first, then Talyn and Leviana.

All her Wolves were lining the deck, clearly relieved to have her back safely. Zamaril's expression was mutinous—he'd been furious at her decision to leave him behind.

"Welcome back, Captain. You brought a guest?" Doran came to greet her.

"Yes. Mayor Doran, meet Prince Aeris Dumnorix, presumptive king of the Twin Thrones."

Doran's eyes widened, one of the Wolves gasped, then everyone was bowing low.

"Please, don't," Aeris said, casting a concerned glance at the sky. "We really should get going."

"He's right." Talyn looked to Doran. "Lift anchor and get us out of here. We could have niever-flyers all over us any moment."

"Northwest for Mithranar?" Doran asked.

She shook her head. "Change of plans. We're headed back to Port Lachley. We've got a king to return to his throne."

He nodded and turned to call orders in a deep, penetrating voice. Dock City sailors scrambled and soon the anchor was winding up and the sails were snapping as they turned into the wind.

Talyn turned to Aeris. "You should go below deck, just in case. Besides, after last night, you need to get some food and water into you. I'll come find you soon."

He nodded, hesitated. "Thank you, Cousin. I honestly thought I was going to be there for a very long time."

She smiled. "I'm glad I found you."

.   .   .

THE THREE CALLANAN and Zamaril stood on deck for another full-turn, Andres and the other Wolves arrayed around them and ready for a fight, watching the horizon, before Talyn judged they'd travelled far enough southwest to be safe. She left Leviana and Cynia and the Wolves to keep watch and went to find Aeris.

He was in the ship's galley, doing as she'd instructed and eating. He looked up as she entered, gravely pushing aside his bowl and waiting for her to sit opposite him.

She took a breath, met his eyes. "You know about your parents?" she asked gently.

Emotion tightened his features, and he swallowed, gave a single nod. "Tarcos took great pleasure in informing me of their deaths, and then reminding me of it. Over and over again."

"I am sorry." It was a useless thing to say, but she couldn't think of anything else. And no words had helped her when Sari had died.

"There is nothing for you to be sorry for," he said simply.

She reached across the table, took his hand in hers, and squeezed. Their shared Dumnorix blood sang in such proximity and she hoped at least her presence helped him.

"I have a lot to tell you," she said. "We're going to get you back to Port Lachley as quickly as we can."

"You were going somewhere else?" he asked. "I heard you talking to the captain earlier."

She smiled a little. "I was, so keep eating. I have a long tale to tell."

Aeris had finished his stew, then an extra hunk of bread the cook found him, and both of them had drunk their way through a pot of tea by the time Talyn finished her story. Life had returned to his sad eyes during her tale, and she was glad of it.

"The war seems to be at a precarious crossroads. Now that Tarcos is dead, it's crucial we come to an agreement with Rados quickly, or Firthland will be plunged into civil war. That won't help us," Aeris said thoughtfully.

"Aeris..." She hesitated. "I hope you understand that none of us are going to dispute your right to the Twin Thrones."

"I know that." A quick smile. "But I'm also painfully aware of my young age. Do you think I would be a hindrance at the negotiating table with Rados and Firthland?"

"If you think you can handle it, then it is better Rados deals with the same man he will have to deal with in the future," Talyn said.

A boyish smile spread across his too-serious face. "Thank you. Let's get home, Cousin."

CHAPTER 45

"You can't imagine we were ever going to let your cousin live," Alyna said bluntly.

Rados's mouth tightened. "Your family's unilateral authority where Firthland is concerned is what started this whole business."

Cuinn flicked a glance Alyna's way, hoping she would take that comment gracefully. So far, he'd stepped back to allow her to run these negotiations. Ariar and Soar were present too, of course, but he was more useful employing his magic—and concentration—to monitor the tone of the room and keep a damper on tempers if necessary.

They'd been at it over a week, several sessions a day, circling each other and slowly getting to the heart of their negotiations. Rados had stormed out in a fury on day two after both Ariar and Soar had lost their tempers, and it had taken Cuinn's magic to get him back in the room the following day.

Rados was as prickly and stubborn as Cuinn remembered Tarcos being. But he didn't have that undercurrent of bitterness that Cuinn had always felt in Tarcos. Rados was obstinate, and proud, but when he'd said he loved his country, he'd meant it. The man felt his duty down to his bones.

When the Dumnorix opened discussions on what Rados thought it would take for Firthland to withdraw, it became clear very quickly that Saundin's assessment was right; Tarcos had enough of the country's lords and military behind him that he would never withdraw voluntarily unless he suffered an overwhelming military defeat.

Once that was clear, Alyna broached the subject of replacing Tarcos as a way of ending the war, indicating that the Twin Thrones was open to seeing that come about. Warily, Rados had been willing to discuss that scenario. "But you'll have to convince me how you'll manage it. I have little support in Samatia, I won't be able to topple him alone. And I won't agree to a solution that involves a civil war."

If Cuinn was honest, he'd enjoyed every moment of it. Enjoyed being able to use his magic productively, enjoyed the game play of negotiating.

This morning, however, was crunch time—time for Rados to learn that his cousin would soon be dead, if he wasn't already. He'd reacted with predictable fury.

Alyna's mouth opened, and Cuinn knew what she was going to say before she said it. He sent her a quick magical jab of warning, and while she shot him a frown, she reconsidered. "Acknowledged, Lord Hadvezer."

"Our family was attacked, our king assassinated, and Tarcos's death will be a direct consequence of that," Cuinn added mildly. "We respect the boundaries of sovereignty and would never take such action unprovoked."

"We?" Rados shifted dark brown eyes to Cuinn, anger snapping in them. "Are you a Dumnorix or the failed prince of Mithranar? I'm confused."

"I am regent of the Twin Thrones. A title I will relinquish once I take the Mithranan crown back," Cuinn said quietly.

"If your cousin hadn't murdered our king and his son, we wouldn't be in this position." Ariar was losing his temper with the stubborn

Firthlander. He became bored and restless quickly in these long meetings, not at all suited for diplomacy and negotiation. Cuinn discreetly kicked him under the table.

"I was a loyal subject of King Aethain," Rados snapped. "So don't blame me for my cousin's actions. And don't blame me for your family's fault in all this."

"This isn't productive." Cuinn jumped in before Alyna could loose the scathing insult that was about to come flying out of her mouth. "Rados, our family is united. Mithranar and the Twin Thrones are formal allies. You should have no concerns about any agreement you come to with us."

Soar sat forward. "Lord Hadvezer, there are grievances on both sides here. We will put ours aside for the sake of a successful negotiation, an end to war. Will you do the same?"

After a momentary hesitation, Rados inclined his head. "I wouldn't be here if I wasn't willing to do so."

Cuinn settled back into his chair, relieved, and Alyna gave him a little nod before continuing. "Your warlord will be dead soon, Lord Hadvezer, that isn't negotiable. However, I apologise on behalf of the Twin Thrones that it was necessary."

Talyn's mother managed a genuine note of sincerity in her voice and it visibly softened Rados. Cuinn smiled inwardly.

"We will give you everything you need to take Tarcos's position," Alyna said carefully. Cuinn's hand curled on the chair in anticipation as he waited for her to play the trump card. "Including complete sovereignty. We would make you high king."

Rados stilled, his fierce Firthlander face hiding his shock and surprise well. It hit Cuinn hard though, and he sucked in a breath, riding the wave of stunned wonder from Rados. For the first time he truly realised what sovereignty meant to Firthland.

"And what do you want of me in return?" Rados asked carefully.

"Withdraw all Firthland's forces from the Twin Thrones immediately. Agree to a formal military and trade alliance."

"You want us to stand with you against Montagn," Rados said bluntly.

"If necessary, yes."

Rados visibly steadied himself. "Tarcos has a lot of support in Samatia. If I go back and try to wrest that from him, it will take time. I can't promise to be able to immediately end the war."

"He will be dead soon, and there will be a vacuum to step into. We will do whatever it takes to ensure you are the one that fills it," Cuinn promised. "Including giving you all the credit for these negotiations. You are free to say that you demanded the crown from us. You will go home as high king."

"The Shadowlord has already ordered the Armun Council to begin preparing the way for your return," Alyna added. "Once Tarcos is dead, you will find you have little opposition."

"Of course, it will be up to you to solidify that support and hold their loyalty." Cuinn sat back in his chair. "But after spending these past days with you, Lord Hadvezer, I am confident you are the man for the job."

"I don't—" Rados was cut off when the bells over the front gates began ringing loudly in a steady rhythm.

Cuinn frowned. "I've never heard that pattern of ringing before."

Ariar stood in confusion. "For good reason. Those bells only ring to announce the arrival of the king or queen of the Twin Thrones to the city. And we don't have one right now."

Before any of them could respond, shouts and running feet sounded—all heading in the direction of the main entrance hall, growing steadily louder.

None of them lingered any longer than that.

Cuinn was two steps behind Ariar as the Dumnorix ran in a rather undignified fashion for the front entrance. Startled Kingshield came streaming behind, their captain snapping orders at his detail to ensure the Dumnorix were properly surrounded.

The double doors leading outside stood open as always, and people were streaming into the massive open hall beyond them, alerted by the bells and the excited shouts coming from the soldiers up on the walls by the entrance gates.

As Cuinn came into the hall behind Ariar, Alyna and Soar only a step behind, two figures walked through the main doors, pausing in the patch of sunlight spilling across the stone. Behind them crowded several Kingshield guards—presumably those from the front gates— working hard to keep a multitude of onlookers a safe distance from their charges.

"Talyn," Cuinn breathed. Because that's who his gaze went straight to. As usual, the sight of her took his breath away—the casual confidence of her stance, the cool mask over her features and those bright sapphire eyes.

He stepped towards her, but Soar brushed by him, almost making him stumble. The momentary touch sent shock and joy flaring through Cuinn—Soar's emotions—and then he could feel the same from Alyna and Ariar too. And it wasn't focused on Talyn.

Belatedly, he spotted the smaller figure at her side. A boy, gangly, maybe fourteen or fifteen, with a shock of unruly black hair and luminous, starlit grey eyes.

Cuinn's eyes widened and he looked straight at Talyn, who by now had spotted him and was flashing him a grin across the hall. He began walking towards them both. Alyna, Soar and Ariar were already crowding around the boy, Ariar lifting him into the air with a loud whoop.

"Aeris Dumnorix, I take it?" Cuinn murmured when he reached Talyn.

"It certainly is." Talyn's smile widened before she threw her arms around him. He hugged her back fiercely before letting go.

"You must be Cuinn Acondor-Dumnorix, our regent."

The boy sounded so much like his father Cuinn's breath caught as he turned from Talyn. He had the same grave expression too, and he was offering his hand. Cuinn took it, smiling widely. "That's right. It's an honour to meet you, to have you safely home, Your Highness."

Aeris's glance flickered from Cuinn to just over his shoulder, where the Dumnorix emblem hung over the entrance—what had once been amber lightning wreathed around the twin swords was now silver grey. The same was replicated on the chests of all the Kingshield hovering nearby.

"We are family, Cuinn. You can call me Aeris," he said. "Talyn has told me all about you."

Soar stared between Talyn and Aeris. "What happened?"

"Tarcos is dead," Talyn said simply. "And I found Aeris."

Cuinn stifled a smile.

"Tarcos thought keeping me alive so he could lord it over me was more satisfying than killing me," Aeris explained. "He kept me as his personal servant."

"Something I discovered when I went to kill him," Talyn added. "Fool of an idiot."

"Talyn tells me we are in negotiations with Lord Rados Hadvezer," Aeris said. "Tarcos is dead. How far have the negotiations progressed—I'd like him on a ship for Samatia by tonight if possible?"

Ariar chuckled. "We could probably arrange for you to get some rest and fresh clothes first. I'm sure given the circumstances Lord Rados will be happy to wait until tomorrow to continue."

"No." Aeris shook his head. "Ending this war is my priority, not to mention that it would be rude if I didn't formally welcome the future high king of Firthland to my kingdom."

Alyna bowed her head. "Rados is in the audience chamber. Let's go and introduce him to our king."

The rigid set of Aeris' shoulders relaxed, and Cuinn caught his relief at their acceptance of him. "I will need your advice, Alyna. You too, Ariar, Soar. You will let me know if you think I am making a wrong move?"

"We will." Soar smiled and clapped him on the back. "We are your family, and we will stand behind you always."

"We've just advised him that we're willing to give him the high king's crown." Ariar smirked. "So you might find him in rather a stunned state. I doubt he's even noticed we've left the room."

Aeris frowned a little. "Talyn told me of that too. It's a significant move, but I think it's the right one, and I'm prepared to support it."

Cuinn stifled another smile. In one sentence Aeris had supported the decisions made in his absence while simultaneously making the point that he was now king and could have revoked their decision if he chose. His father's son indeed.

Talyn tugged Cuinn aside as the family followed Aeris through to the audience chamber. "Doran, Levs and Cynia are re-supplying the ship as we speak. I can't linger here—the detour to Port Lachley means I've already been delayed more than I wanted to."

Cuinn cast a glance after the retreating Dumnorix. "Your mother will murder you for leaving without saying goodbye."

She gave him a sheepish look. "Smooth it over for me?"

"No." He shook his head.

"What? Why not?" she asked, the indignance in her tone making him laugh.

"Because, beloved." He framed her face with his hands. "I am coming with you."

She stilled.

"Aeris is back. That changes everything. I don't need to be away from home any longer. I refuse," he said, the emotion leaking out of his voice despite his best efforts. "I'm coming back with you, Talyn."

One of her hands reached up to twine with his as she nodded, light dawning in her stunning eyes. "Good."

He kissed her, hard, then stepped away. "We can't both disappear though. At least they're all in the same room. Let's go say our goodbyes."

A BRISK WIND lifted Trystaan's wings as he took off from the SkyRider landing platform, making it an easy flight to the harbour, soaring over the anchored ships until Cuinn spotted the Montagni ship Talyn and Doran had stolen. Two smaller boats were tacking away from the port side, presumably having carried supplies out to prepare it for departure.

Fortunately the ship had a wide, open deck, though several of the Dock City sailors scuttled away in alarm at the sight of Trystaan's wingspan swooping over it. The eagle's challenging shriek as he dropped out of the sky probably didn't help matters.

The bear-sized mayor of Dock City strode over as Cuinn was unbuckling his harness. Zamaril appeared too, seemingly from nowhere, and any Wolves on deck drifted closer, pretending like they weren't.

Trystaan shifted restlessly until the harness was off—the short flight hadn't been enough for him—before soaring back into the sky.

"Your Highness." Doran came to a dead stop in astonishment.

"Mayor," Cuinn said cheerfully. "Talyn isn't far off. Are we ready for departure as soon as she arrives?"

"We are," Doran said slowly.

"You're coming with us?" Zamaril asked eagerly.

"I am." Cuinn's smile stretched from ear to ear.

Several Wolves lifted their hands as if to clap, then lowered them, but all were grinning. A wiry figure dropped out of the rigging and joined them, straightening into a sharp salute—Andres.

"That's excellent news," Doran said, bowing low. "I'll be in the pilot's cabin if you need me, Your Highness."

Andres turned and began snapping orders to the Wolves to deploy in a protective formation around Cuinn.

"You're a SkyRider now?" A curious voice came from the opposite side of the deck.

Cuinn turned to find two Callanan standing there, arms crossed as they studied him. Another smile teased at the corners of his mouth. "Leviana. Cynia. It's lovely to see you again. You're coming back to Mithranar with us?"

"Yes, without any permission or authorisation." Cynia scowled at her partner.

"She's our friend, Cynia," Leviana said quietly. "And you know Sari would want us to have her back."

"Yes, but you know me. I am hardwired to identify the flaws in any plan." Cynia shrugged.

"She will be glad. She misses you both when you're apart," Cuinn said quietly.

One of the sailors called out then, warning of the approach of the ship's boat. Talyn was on board with Theac and Evani. Errana and her daughters would remain safe in Port Lachley until Mithranar was Cuinn's. Theac came up first, scowl firmly in place at having to scramble up a rope ladder.

"Smile, Theac." Cuinn clapped him on the back. "We're going home."

"Good news indeed." A smile wreathed the man's grizzled features.

Talyn came up last before waving down a thanks to the boat crew who'd rowed them out. She exchanged enthusiastic greetings with Cynia and Leviana before coming over to Cuinn.

The deck rocked underneath them as the anchor was raised, and then a series of orders and answering shouts had sailors scrambling over the decks to begin turning the ship and unfurling the sails.

"Are you all right?" Cuinn asked her. His magic told him she was satisfied with her success in Firthland and relieved and joyful that she'd found Aeris alive and brought him home. But Tarcos had been her lover for many years, and she had genuinely cared for him. The betrayal had to bite deep. Not to mention the guilt—she'd been the lover of the man who'd killed her partner.

"He was so angry when I killed him." Her gaze turned pensive, and she looked away. "How was it that I never saw that anger in him? Never saw the bitterness or hate?"

"I ask myself the same about Azrilan all the time." Similar guilt seared him, still as fresh as ever. "I never trusted him completely, because he was Mithanis's man, or so I thought... but I genuinely believed he cared for me."

"Your brother is clever, cleverer than most people I've encountered," Talyn murmured.

"I will regret that mistake for the rest of my life," he said bitterly.

"We all make mistakes. I learned that the hard way." She stepped closer to him. "And even when those mistakes lead to awful consequences, we still have to accept them and acknowledge that one mistake doesn't define us. It's what we do afterward that does."

He nodded, resting his forehead against hers.

"I'm so glad you're coming back with me," she whispered then, her arms winding around his neck so she could pull him close.

He closed his eyes and let himself take strength from her, from what they were together. "Let's go home, Talyn."

CHAPTER 46

*I*t was a journey of eleven days to sail north, tacking far to the east to avoid Feather Bay and Sparrow Island, before angling northwest until the awe-inspiring peaks of the SkyReach became visible on the horizon.

Doran and his crew anchored just off the barren northeast coast, and they began the painstaking process of transferring crew, horses and supplies to shore.

Thoroughly unimpressed with being confined to a ship's stall for over three weeks, FireFlare refused to go calmly into the boat transferring her ashore. Talyn had to work with her for a good half-turn before she finally got the fractious mare into the boat. By then Theac —bless him—had organised the transfer of the other horses and supplies. Cuinn and Trystaan soared on the thermals above, oblivious, a faint speck against the grey sky.

"It's a shame to leave her," Doran said mournfully of the ship as they prepared to head inland.

"It's not like you can sail her back into Feather Bay," Talyn said.

"I'd almost rather a stint in the city cells than sitting on this creature for the next few days." Doran held himself rigid in the saddle, as if he expected his horse to buck him off at any moment.

"It wouldn't be a stint in the cells—it would be death." Talyn glanced around for Theac. FireFlare was yanking impatiently on the reins, almost pulling her arm from its socket. "Theac? Can you get them all going? I'm going to have to run the energy out of FireFlare or she's going to fight me all the way there."

Theac cast a highly dubious look at the snorting mare, then stepped around her and barked an order for the crew, Wolves, and Callanan to gather round.

Breathing a sigh of relief, Talyn left him to it and swung up into the saddle, finally loosing the reins and giving the mare her head.

A helpless whoop of delight roared out of her as FireFlare's head dropped and she stretched out into the famous racing gait of the Aimsir bloodline, the open, snow-covered plains spread out before them.

Talyn crouched in the saddle, using voice and heels to urge Fire-Flare to her top speed. The copper mare needed little urging, eager to test herself on this flat surface.

And then there was nothing in Talyn's world but the blur of speed, the wind racing past her face, the rhythmic motion of the mare under her and joy. Joy in the day. Joy in being an Aimsir astride one of the finest mares ever born.

A scream sounded from above.

Talyn glanced up, over her shoulder, grinned at the sight of Trys-taan dropping out of the sky, wings spread wide, screeching a challenge. FireFlare heard it and lengthened her stride.

She settled lower in the saddle, hands curling around the reins, a grin spreading unbidden across her face. Trystaan swooped gracefully alongside her, wings beating powerfully. She caught a glimpse of Cuinn's face as he turned to flash a smile at her.

And they raced.

FIVE LONG DAYS of slow riding—given most of their crew had never seen a horse in their lives, let alone ridden one—brought them to the foothills of the SkyReach where the old SkyRider outpost nestled on the lower mountainside.

Their approach was spotted well before they got anywhere close, two Falcons lifting into the sky and cautiously approaching, bows drawn and knocked. As soon as they recognised Talyn, they lowered the weapons and landed in the snow, bright emerald and pink wings stunning against the white. Every time she was away for a long period of time she forgot just how *pretty* the winged folk were.

"Ciantar." They saluted, their excitement evident in their shifting stances and rustling wings. "You're back."

"Firas, Tarlen," she greeted them. "Is all well?"

"Aye, Ciantar." Firas nodded. "Welcome home."

"Can you let Corrin and Windsong know we're coming up?" she asked, gaze flicking to the sky where Trystaan was currently hidden by low-flying clouds. "And that Cuinn is with us."

Both Falcons froze, their gazes immediately searching the rather ragtag group gathered behind Talyn and Theac.

"He's up there." She pointed. "Don't worry, you'll get to see him soon."

The Falcons lifted into the sky and headed back towards the hills. Talyn gave the order to dismount, and the group began winding their way up through the foothills.

They'd barely walked a quarter-turn when there was a blur of movement from Talyn's right and a snarl ripped through the air, terrifying several of the nearest horses. Jasper landed gracefully on the trail before her, green eyes flashing. Unable to hold back her smile she dropped to her knees and held out a hand. "How did you know we were back today?"

Jasper bumped his head against her hand once, twice, then turned and padded up the trail, eagerness in every line of the tawncat's body. He knew Cuinn was nearby.

Soon after, Trystaan's shriek heralded the arrival of Cuinn, who landed the magnificent eagle on a patch of flat ground. Trystaan had barely lifted off when Jasper hit Cuinn in the chest, sending him stumbling backwards, laughing.

Talyn smiled, watching as the two reunited. Tears shone bright in Cuinn's eyes as he held the tawncat close. "You found her."

Jasper snorted, bumped his head against Cuinn's chest, then bounded away. Cuinn stood up, still grinning. His cheeks were flushed with cold, eyes bright from flying.

"Ready for this?" she asked, even though she knew the answer.

"Readier than I've ever been for anything," he replied. "Let's go."

CORRIN AND WINDSONG waited at the main entrance, Liadin and Lyra flanking them. Behind, what seemed like every Wolf and Falcon resident in the outpost had crowded into the open foyer area beyond the doors. Firas and Tarlen hadn't stinted on who they'd passed the news to, it seemed.

Talyn slowed her pace, allowing Cuinn to take the lead, the Wolves, Callanan and the Dock City sailors doing the same. Jasper paced at Cuinn's side.

The moment Cuinn came into sight, the Wolves started howling, the eerie noise resounding through the icy air. Windsong, Corrin and the talons bowed, and the howls turned into raucous cheers, whistling and clapping.

The excitement was palpable, sending shivers down the back of Talyn's neck. She could see how their joy affected Cuinn, how it made him momentarily rock back on his heels, and was glad. He deserved this.

"Welcome home, Your Highness," Windsong said, stepping closer so he could be heard over the furor.

Cuinn smiled, his gaze running over everyone gathered, making sure he included everyone in his smile. "Thank you, Anrun. It's good to be home."

"We didn't expect to see you so soon. Is everything well in the south?" Corrin asked, a little frown on his face. His gaze flicked between Talyn and Cuinn.

Cuinn lifted a hand, and the cheering slowly faded into an expectant silence. Talyn shifted from foot to foot, anticipating their reaction to the news they brought with them.

"Tarcos Hadvezer is dead," Cuinn said, pitching his voice so that all could hear, and wrapping it in magic, strength, hope, determination. Even Talyn was affected by it. "Aeris Dumnorix holds the Twin Thrones. And, if all has gone well, then as of this moment Firthland is ruled by a new high king who has agreed to ally with me and the Twin Thrones against Montagn. The war in the south is over."

A hush fell over the foyer.

Hope, precious and fragile, filled the space where excitement and joy had been. And then someone whistled, another followed suit, and the mountain was once again raucous with cheering.

Talyn breathed in the cheers, letting them fill her with their excitement. They'd wanted him home. Wanted the future, the Mithranar, that she and Cuinn had once promised them. But she was sure they'd never truly expected Cuinn to return with such a victory behind him. That he might bring home a real chance of winning Mithranar for their own.

Corrin's eyes shone. Windsong looked equally aglow. Lyra and Liadin were furling and unfurling their wings in giddy excitement, no doubt picking up all the emotions around them as well as feeling their own.

"Talyn, I think I'm in love with Cuinn now too." Leviana nudged her arm. "We might have to fight over him."

Talyn chuckled.

"He is rather impressive." Cynia sighed.

The renewed cheering eventually died down into an expectant silence. Windsong smiled, bowed slightly. "So now we deal with Montagn," he said.

Cuinn glanced at Talyn, and she smiled. "Yes."

AFTER WINDSONG HAD DISMISSED the Wolves and Falcons back to their duties, Talyn sought out Kaeri, leaving Leviana and Cynia in her talons' capable hands.

"You might want to start them training with the newer recruits," she suggested to Liadin and Lyra. "They're two of the best fighters I've ever seen."

"You aren't going to disappear on us, are you?" Leviana asked suspiciously.

"Not at all, I promise. I'll come find you later."

"Will you do a demonstration fight with Talon Lightfinger again?" Lyra asked excitedly as they walked off. "The Wolves would love to see that!"

"Lady Kaeri has been mostly keeping to herself," Corrin explained as Cuinn and Talyn followed him, Jasper pacing behind. "Although she trains with us every day. She's a solid fighter."

"Mithanis?" Cuinn asked.

"We haven't spoken to him at all—we change his guards regularly in case he tries to use song magic on them. And we make sure they're human Wolves, not Falcons, to be extra careful." Corrin came to a halt outside a closed door. "Is there anything else I can do?"

Talyn said, "Can you organise a meeting later? You, Windsong and the talons, plus Levs and Cynia."

He saluted. "Will do, Ciantar. Your Highness."

Talyn knocked, entering after a moment when there was no response. Kaeri stood outside on the balcony, apparently oblivious to the cold, staring across the channel towards her home. Talyn cleared her throat before stepping out onto the balcony, not wanting to startle her friend. Cuinn's light touch on the small of her back indicated this conversation was hers to lead.

Kaeri turned gracefully, and the smile that lit up her face was warm. "Talyn. It's good to see you."

Talyn hugged her, equally glad to see the Montagni princess. After what they'd been through together, Kaeri was a steadying presence. "You remember Prince Cuinn, I imagine?"

"Of course. The betrothed who spurned me." Her words were cool, but a little smile curled at the corner of her mouth.

"Kaeri Venador." Cuinn bowed gracefully, but his green eyes twinkled. "It is a pleasure to see you again. I am truly glad you survived my brother's spill."

"I suppose it's good to see you." Kaeri frowned a little. "Talyn has told me a little of what always hid behind that playboy façade of yours."

"She also told me what you did for her." Cuinn's smile vanished and Talyn's heart clenched at the pain that flashed through his eyes. They both still had so much guilt and grief that had built up over the past months—and it wasn't going to magically vanish just because they were back together. Especially since Azrilan still had Cuinn's throne. "For that I am forever in your debt, Kaeri Venador."

Kaeri huffed an irritated breath and waved him off. "I could hear the shouts of excitement at your arrival, and I imagine your commanders need your urgent attention, yet you came to speak with me first. You want something."

"We do." Talyn settled against the railing, ignoring the ice-cold of the stone soaking through her sleeves.

"Then ask."

Talyn took a breath. Kaeri wasn't one to appreciate prevarication, so she simply came out with it. "I have a plan, and it involves making you ahara of Montagn."

Kaeri let out a peal of uncharacteristic laughter, but quickly sobered when neither Talyn nor Cuinn smiled. "You're not serious?"

"Utterly. How would you like to be Ahara Kaeri Venador? I think it has rather a nice ring to it."

"Whether I'd like it or not is beside the point. It's impossible." Impatience edged Kaeri's voice as she began ticking off fingers one by one. "I'm a woman. Azrilan's House holds power in Montagn now. My House is out in the cold and isn't strong enough to mount a challenge. I have a slave tattoo on my face. Did I mention I'm a woman?"

"What if I could get you an army?" Talyn asked. "One that would dwarf any army that House Manunin could summon."

"The Twin Thrones are at war, and even if your family somehow deals with Firthland without more bloodshed, they still don't have—"

"I'm not talking about the Twin Thrones." Talyn cut her off. "I'm talking about freeing the slaves."

Wind whistled into the sudden silence.

Kaeri stared at Talyn as if she didn't know whether she was insane or joking, or maybe both.

A smile crept over Talyn's face. "How many slaves were in our labour camp? Two thousand? Three? How many labour camps are there across Montagn?" She pushed. "How much of the Manunin foot soldier army is made up of slaves who have no choice but to fight? Offer them their freedom, Kaeri Venador, and you have an army."

"I would have a revolt, not an army," Kaeri said flatly. "No Montagni House would agree to end slavery. Do you have any idea the impact it would have on our trade, our coin reserves? Our leadership stability?"

"To be honest, I don't much care," Talyn said flatly. "No man or woman should enslave another human life, and I would think you have a much better appreciation of what that means now."

Kaeri was already shaking her head. "It won't work. If I go to House Venador and ask them to put me on the throne as ahara, they'll laugh in my face and tell me to embroider some cushions. If I try and tell them they'll have to agree to end slavery to do it... Talyn, it's just not possible."

"Are you sure about that?" Talyn challenged. "I'm aware it won't be easy. But I imagine your House is smarting after what Azrilan did to your father. Won't they welcome an opportunity to strike back, to take their *power* back?"

"Maybe," Kaeri allowed. "But they won't agree to end slavery, not for anything."

"You can make them. I've seen how tough you are. Bend them to your will."

Kaeri turned away. "You have no idea what you're talking about."

"Is it their refusal you're anticipating, or your own?" Talyn asked softly. "After what we went through, you can't truly still agree with the practice of slavery."

"I'm not a fool, Talyn," Kaeri snapped. "You are manipulating me for your own ends."

Talyn didn't deny it. "My question still stands."

"I have a much better understanding of how our trade, our food production, our treasury works than you do. If slavery were abolished, our kingdom would collapse," she said quietly. "So while I admit to having become distinctly uncomfortable about the practice, I can't just end it."

"We would help." Cuinn spoke for the first time, sincerity ringing through his voice. "The Twin Thrones will offer you advantageous trade deals, loans, whatever you needed to make the transition." This had already been discussed and agreed with Aeris. "I give you my word on the same from Mithranar."

"You would put your own kingdoms at risk in doing so," she scoffed.

"Yes," Cuinn agreed. "But to end the practice of slavery... we are willing."

"We also promise to use whatever influence we have to convince High King Rados Hadvezer to offer you similar concessions." Talyn smiled.

Her eyes widened. "High King who?"

"Tarcos is dead, Kaeri."

Kaeri's eyes glowed and she took a step closer. "You killed Tarcos?"

Talyn nodded slowly. "I killed Tarcos."

"Well done, friend." Kaeri gripped her shoulder. "I'm glad for you."

"Thanks." Talyn cleared her throat. "Tarcos's cousin is currently establishing his new rule in Samatia. The Twin Thrones has released Firthland from its kingdom. Rados is high king of an independent Firthland."

"Thereby removing Firthland from the war. Well played." Kaeri stared at the ground, clearly thinking furiously. "Even if I could convince my House to back me as ahara and end slavery, it wouldn't be enough. We'd need at least one more powerful House to join us or my claim will be laughed out the door. As will any attempt to free slaves."

"Then *you* think about how to accomplish that." Talyn offered her hand. "While I plan how to use a slave army to win you the Montagni throne and end this war for good."

Another long silence fell, the wind screaming around them. Kaeri looked torn. But eventually she lifted her hand, clasped Talyn's. "I promise to give it serious thought."

Talyn grinned fiercely. "Then I'll leave you to it."

CHAPTER 47

"My question is, how do we get her into Montagn?" Theac asked. "The Causeway is guarded, not to mention it's a chokepoint—far too narrow to get an army across without being destroyed in the process."

Talyn smothered a smile. Though he'd only been home three days, Cuinn had already formed an advisory council, and tonight they were gathered in the firelit lounge of Cuinn and Talyn's quarters. Empty and half-empty mugs of kahvi were scattered around them and the air was thick with the scent of smoke and spices. Jasper slept by the fire.

Saniya was present—having arrived only two full-turns earlier from Acleu—along with Doran, Windsong, Corrin, and Theac. Leviana and Cynia had declined the invitation, Talyn suspected because they'd been invited to join the Wolves in an impromptu party happening down in the mess. Two members of Cuinn's Wolf detail were inside the room, the rest arrayed outside.

It was late and informality reigned. An edge of relief had relaxed the room following the news Saniya had brought with her.

The departure of the Montagni war fleet had been delayed.

With their izerdia supply gone and six ships destroyed, not to mention more sabotaged at anchor in Acleu and several naval captains and officers killed by Callanan, the order had come from Arataire to wait for more izerdia and ships before leaving for the south.

"It's not the end of the problem, just a postponement," Saniya warned. "Protection around the surviving ships in port has tripled, and we hear the same is true around the new ships being prepared in Darinoue. Acleu is essentially under martial law. We won't be able to get near them again, not without an army, and I expect the fleet to depart within weeks."

"Unless he learns of Tarcos's death and decides to withdraw from the war," Theac pointed out.

"Saundin was prepared for that. The moment Tarcos died, the Shadowlord was to immediately move to recall all Shadows and Armun and halt any messages north to Montagn," Talyn said. "If he succeeded, Azrilan won't learn of what's happened until after he deploys the fleet."

Doran frowned. "Wouldn't it be better he learn sooner, perhaps withdraw the fleet entirely?"

"No," Talyn said coldly. "I want to draw away his strength. By the time that fleet departs, the Twin Thrones will have an army waiting in the north to destroy it. That's thousands of Berserkers and foot soldiers he won't have to throw at Mithranar."

So far their cards were landing just right... a term Azrilan would no doubt love.

But winning remained such a fragile prospect.

Talyn glanced at Corrin, the only one standing, his young face serious. Theac had relinquished the position of Wolf captain to him the moment they'd arrived. "The job's yours, lad," he'd said then. "You've earned it, you've grown into it, and I know you'll lead the Wolves successfully. I'll still be one of Prince Cuinn's guards, but once this is all over, I'd like to have more time to spend with my family."

"Don't look at me." Talyn had smiled when Corrin had stared at her in shock. "This was Theac's choice, and I happen to agree with him."

Windsong's voice brought Talyn back to the present moment. "What do you think about reaching out to some Falcons in the citadel or the Summer Palace now that you're back? The Ciantar name still carries a lot of weight. We've got a sizeable force here, but if we could add more Falcons, that would take strength away from Azrilan."

"We need to be cautious," Cuinn said. "I don't want Falcons killed or imprisoned because Azrilan finds out they've been talking to us. We know he still has some Shadows and Armun at his disposal, not to mention his hounds."

"Liadin and Lyra would know who to approach, not to mention Grasswing." Talyn looked at him. "And they know how to be careful."

"I can suggest names too," Windsong added. "I know some of my men were still in the citadel when Azrilan took power."

"Something to think about." There was a note of finality in Cuinn's voice, despite its mild tone, that immediately had everyone in the room moving away from the topic. Talyn glanced at him, unsure whether she was annoyed or impressed.

"It's getting late," Saniya said, rising to her feet. "See you all tomorrow."

Doran left with her, and Windsong, Theac and Corrin went soon after that. Once they were alone, Cuinn crossed to a sideboard to pour each of them a glass of spirits.

"You winged folk and your extravagances," she teased when he brought her a glass, then dropped onto the cushions beside her.

"I can't help what people leave here," he countered. "It would be rude to ignore it."

She put the drink aside, turning to him. "I understand why you're cautious about approaching Falcons, but we're going to need them on our side to win the fight here in Mithranar. Even if the crazy Montagni plan works, Azrilan will fight to hold onto this throne."

"We won't be winning anything here while Azrilan still holds onto Montagn. I don't want to move too early and give him time to prepare his defences." He took a sip and sat forward. "Or send Montagni forces here to bolster the WingGuard."

"I agree, but we also need to be ready to move here if our plan with Kaeri works. That means having the necessary pieces in place ahead of time."

"I won't have more people dying for me, Talyn."

"Then give up now and cede the throne to Azrilan," she said sharply, and he spun to face her, shocked. "You can't win a war without people dying. Those who choose to follow you know what the risks are. You need to let them make that choice."

His face tightened, but he nodded and drained the glass before slumping back against the cushions. "You are the strategic genius between the two of us. I'll do whatever you think is best."

"I appreciate that," she said carefully. "But that doesn't mean I don't want your input."

A faint smile crossed his face and he leaned over to kiss her. "I'm too wired for sleep. I'm going to take a flight with Trystaan. Want to come?"

"I'm too tired to be bothered moving, I might just stay here and enjoy the fire for a while."

He frowned. "You don't get tired. Everything okay?"

"Absolutely fine." She kissed him, distracting him before his annoying magic could ferret out the unease his question triggered. "Enjoy your flight."

When the door closed behind him, she snuggled deeper into the cushions. Jasper's eyes opened, and he glanced between her and the door. Letting out a soft huffing sound, he rose from his place by the fire and padded over to leap up and curl himself alongside her before promptly closing his eyes again.

She stroked his fur. Maybe she'd not bother moving to the bed and sleep here where it was warm and snug. But sleep proved difficult, her mind toying over a growing certainty that she didn't want to face, and she began to wish Cuinn would hurry up getting back from his flight.

A knock at the door provided a welcome distraction, and she hefted herself off the couch to answer it. Jasper stayed where he was, telling her that whoever was at the door, it was one of their trusted inner circle. Zamaril stood out there, smirk firmly in place, hands behind his back. "Not interrupting anything, am I, Ciantar?"

"What do you want?" She lifted an eyebrow.

"When Petro stayed behind in Dock City after our departure, I asked him to do me a favour." He shrugged. "A bit of wandering around at night, visiting the old haunts, you know?"

"While this is a very interesting story, I'm not sure why you're here now telling it to me," Talyn said, failing to rein in her impatience.

"He went down the tunnel." All mirth dropped from his face and his expression turned hard.

Talyn sucked in a breath, hand curling around the wood of the door. She and Zamaril had been ambushed down there, almost killed, then sold into slavery. "Why would you ask Petro to—"

"I wanted him to look for these. Saniya brought them back with her."

He withdrew his arms from behind his back, holding out a silk-wrapped bundle. Talyn swallowed, reaching out to take it, knowing what it was as soon as the weight hit her palms. Her throat closed over as she pushed aside the cloth and saw Sari's daggers lying there, one still encrusted with blood.

"They were buried in the mud. Petro reckons they were stomped down by one of those hulking Bearmen during the fight. It's Savin's blood," Zamaril said. "Didn't want to wash that off."

Talyn nodded, barely fighting back the tears welling in her eyes. She still couldn't speak, so she wrapped her free arm around Zamaril instead, drawing him into a fierce hug.

He stiffened in astonishment, then cleared his throat awkwardly when she let him go. "You're welcome, Ciantar. Good night."

He left without another word, and she closed the door, staring down at Sari's daggers. The aethlyx metal gleamed green in the firelight. She picked one up, spun it, a smile stretching across her face.

She had her daggers back.

TALYN STRODE through the corridors from one of the training areas late the next morning, finally feeling right again with the weight of Sari's daggers at her back, when Jystar appeared coming towards her, half walking-half gliding, grey wings spread in the wide corridor.

"Ciantar!" he said, looking pleased. "Just the person I was looking for."

"Nothing's wrong, I hope?" she asked with a frown.

"No, not at all." He dropped to the ground and fell into step with her. "I just need a few moments of your time to check you over."

She stilled, unease rippling through her. "Why?"

"Because I haven't seen you in months, and before that you'd just recovered from some fairly severe injuries after a long period of near-starvation and hard physical labour," he said simply. "I want to ensure your body is still healing as it should."

"I feel fine."

"That is good. I would like to make sure you *are* fine."

She huffed a breath. "Jystar, I've just come from sparring. I'm covered in sweat and probably don't smell the best."

"Yet neither of those things will prevent me from examining you, Ciantar." He was resolute.

"Just let him look at you."

"Shut up, Sari."

"My, aren't we in a mood?"

"You're far more stubborn than your brother, Jystar. Have I ever told you that?" she said grumpily, following as he gestured down the corridor leading to his healing room.

"He accused me of it all the time, Ciantar."

It wasn't a long walk. Two Wolves lingered by the fire in a waiting area—one was cradling his arm to his chest, and the other had a livid bruise over her eye.

"Ciantar!" both said cheerfully when she entered with Jystar.

"If neither of you are dying, I'll see the Ciantar first," Jystar said dryly as he eyed the two patients.

"I can wait," Talyn promptly volunteered—she could vanish as soon as Jystar took them into his room, claim later some urgent task had come up.

Unfortunately both Wolves were horrified by the prospect.

"We're fine, Ciantar. I just sprained my arm."

"And I caught a blow to the head. I'm not dizzy or anything so I'll be fine," the other one added.

She considered pulling rank and ordering them to go first, but one look at Jystar had her capitulating with a sigh. If she slipped away now, he'd only track her down.

Once he'd closed the door behind them, she sat on his bench and tugged her shirt off so he had access to her back. "I really feel fine. I fought hard in Dock City, and then again in Port Lathilly, and there was no pulling or anything from my back. Just the usual muscle soreness afterwards."

"I'm glad to hear it." He moved around behind her, and a moment later she felt his fingers trailing lightly over the scar tissue. "Your scars have healed beautifully. If only my healing guild could see me now."

She chuckled. "I'm happy to sing your praises to them when we take the country back."

"I'm going to use magic now," he warned.

She tensed. "Jystar, I—"

"Your body went through a lot, Ciantar, the type of physical hardship that can have long term effects. You don't want that, do you?"

No. She didn't. Especially if... "Go on then."

Silence fell as Jystar worked on her back for a little while, then shifted around to her front. He pressed his fingers lightly to her forehead, the tickle of his magic more noticeable there, before moving over the rest of her.

Then he stilled suddenly, grey eyes flashing open. "You're pregnant."

Shit.

"*Six thrices, Talyn, is he serious? Why didn't you tell me?*" Sari's mental excitement was so loud and intense that Talyn wasn't able to hold back a wince.

"I suspected," she said aloud in answer to both Sari and Jystar.

Shit. Shit. Shit.

"This is why you were so reluctant for me to look at you?" Jystar lifted an eyebrow as he stepped away. "It's very early, about four weeks, but the good news is you're fine. So is the baby."

432

"Thank you," she muttered.

"Does Prince Cuinn know?"

"No."

Jystar cleared his throat into the silence that fell. "Ciantar, nobody will hear it from me. Still, I want to keep a close eye on you. I won't attempt to insist you limit your usual activities, not yet at least, but the tradeoff is that you visit me here every morning. Deal?"

"That's fair." She forced the words out, but she didn't like them one bit. She slid off the table and yanked the shirt over her head. Jystar's confirmation of what she'd begun suspecting several days earlier had left her stomach a pit of anxiousness and uncertainty.

"Ciantar." He touched her shoulder as she passed him. His grey eyes were soft, warmer than she'd ever seen in this serious man. "Congratulations."

"Thanks," she muttered, and left, trying not to run.

HER MIND WAS AWHIRL—PART panic, part anxiety, part trying to ignore both those things—as she pushed open the door to their quarters, intent on bathing away the morning's sweat before eating... and then hiding somewhere all day until she could figure out what to do about her situation.

"What's on your mind?"

Shit.

Cuinn stood by the fire, staring at her in amusement. She'd walked right past him without seeing him there.

"Nothing. I'm just going to take a bath."

The amusement turned to confusion and he was after her in a flash. "Talyn, what's going on? I've never seen you so distracted. Your emotions are all over the place."

She cleared her throat, eyes dancing around the room until reluctantly landing on him. His green eyes clouded with concern the longer it took for her to speak. No doubt he could feel the waves of confusion and unease coming off her. "Well, it's—"

The knock at the door was the sweetest sound Talyn had ever

heard. Ehdra poked his head in, looked at Cuinn. "Lady Kaeri is here, Your Highness."

"Now's not the best—" Cuinn started, but Talyn cut him off.

"Show her in," she said firmly.

Cuinn frowned, but didn't gainsay her invitation. Kaeri strode in as Ehdra stepped away. Talyn made a mental note to give Ehdra a promotion. Immediately.

Kaeri glanced at Cuinn before dismissing him and facing Talyn. "I'll agree to your plan."

Talyn's shoulders relaxed, excitement quickly displacing the uneasiness she'd been feeling. "Thank you."

"There will be conditions."

"And they are?" Cuinn asked.

"First, for House Venador to not only agree to unify behind me as ahara, but for my position to be strong enough to push through an end to slavery, we can't just ask." Kaeri paused. "I have to *take* the leadership of the House from whoever took over after my father's death, probably my uncle. And we won't be able to do that with only a couple hundred of your Wolves."

Talyn glanced at Cuinn, a smug smile curling at the corners of her mouth. "I thought that might be the case. Consider that planned for."

"Fine. But I also told you that we're going to need more than just me. Provided we take House Venador and install me as leader, I've worked out what we can use to bring another strong House to our side, maybe more." She glanced between them again. "We're going to have to let your brother out, Prince Cuinn."

"An alliance with Mithanis? No way," Talyn said flatly.

"He's a Manunin. If he stands with me, it will ease the sting for House Manunin in losing the ahara's seat so soon after Azrilan gained it. It will give lesser Houses a reason to side with us."

"He'll have to do a lot more than stand with you," Talyn pointed out. "You'll have to give him power, influence, enough to satisfy the Manunins."

"I know that," Kaeri said impatiently. "I'll marry him."

Cuinn and Talyn stared at her. Cuinn looked sick. Kaeri's impatience deepened. "I was going to be married off to you for strategic power, Princeling. At least this way it's my choice and within my control."

"But you don't—"

"Oh for goodness sakes, Talyn, I'm not proposing a love match. I'll allow enough to conceive an heir if and when I decide it's necessary, and otherwise the marriage will be in name only." Kaeri huffed. "You're both looking at me as if strategic marriages aren't the way things work for people like us."

Talyn glanced at Cuinn. Looked away. His unease was obvious.

"She's right. You're only feeling guilty because you're doing the same thing and feeling unsure about it."

"I'm not unsure about it, I just..."

"What?"

"I don't know."

"This is the only solution. The only way I can think for my people to accept a female ahara is if they think I have a strong man ruling at my side. And making it Mithanis wins us House Manunin and a lot of smaller Houses."

"You will be battling for the rest of your life," Talyn said quietly. "To hold power, to manage a husband you'll never be able to trust."

"As a woman, that will be the case with or without Mithanis. I'm not a fool. And I'm willing to do it. Do I need to point out this was your idea?"

Talyn tensed. "If we agree to let Mithanis go, and he helps you win Montagn, we still have the issue of Mithranar to consider. He will demand this throne."

"That's not my problem." Kaeri looked at Cuinn. "You haven't killed him yet, which means when Azrilan is gone, you're willing to challenge Mithanis fairly for your throne?"

"I hadn't actually decided yet." Cuinn ran a hand through his hair. "But you're right, I'm not going to murder him just to get him out of my way."

"If things go the way we want in Montagn, then you and he can battle it out over Mithranar. I don't mind at all if my husband lives in

435

another country most of the time, and it will probably help my standing to be married to a king." Kaeri smiled grimly. "And if you win, Prince Cuinn, then maybe Mithanis will be satisfied with the consolation prize of having some power in Montagn."

For a moment all three stared at each other. Talyn hated the whole idea; it didn't feel right.

It was Cuinn who conceded. "Let's go talk to Mithanis."

CHAPTER 48

Cuinn followed a step behind Kaeri and Talyn as they walked down through the levels to the room Mithanis was being held in, his mind so full of competing problems he was having trouble focusing. Whatever had sent Talyn to near panic levels earlier had seemingly faded. She was back to wearing her cool mask, strides long and confident, his magic telling him she was focused on the conversation ahead.

So she was fine, but that didn't ease his worry. What had happened? He'd never felt that level of unease from her before—she was rarely anything but calmly assured.

And now Kaeri wanted to let his brother loose and bring him to Montagn with them. Not only that but make him consort to the ahara. Cuinn still wasn't solid on the reasoning—his focus had been too much on Talyn as Kaeri explained—but Kaeri was insistent this was the only way, and so here they were.

Their fragile plan was feeling more fragile and uncontrolled by the day.

Talyn glanced back at him, as if picking up some of his unease. He scowled at her in response. She knew perfectly well how his magic worked and how sensitive he was to her in particular. Which meant she knew exactly what was bothering him and that it was her fault.

She scowled back before turning away.

Four Wolves stood guard outside the door where Mithanis was being held. Cuinn hadn't been there before—he'd been assured that his brother had been made comfortable.

They saluted at Talyn's presence.

"We need to talk to him," she told the Wolves. "Leave the door open and keep a close eye."

Cuinn frowned. It was unusual for Talyn to request extra backup. He'd fully expected she'd want this conversation to be private.

"Yes, Ciantar."

"You breathe a word of what you hear to anyone and year-long privy-cleaning duty will be the least of your worries," she added.

One of them gulped at the severity of her voice. Cuinn caught Kaeri's stifled smile as she followed Talyn in, but he was in no mood for amusement. His stomach tensed into a tight ball of anxiety.

He hadn't seen his eldest brother since the day Talyn had defeated him in single combat. This was the man that had tormented and terrified him since childhood. The one who had murdered Raya. Or maybe he hadn't. Confusion milled inside him.

Mithanis sat in a chair by the room's single window. A book lay open in his lap, but his gaze had shot towards the doorway the moment it opened. Cuinn's first impression was shock—the prince of night looked so different without his wings. His face was harder, narrowed into gaunt lines, but his natural winged folk beauty made those features distinguished rather than spare. Still, he seemed... *smaller*. Some of that overwhelming presence he'd once carried with him was gone forever.

"Visitors. How delightful." Mithanis remained seated, dark eyes raking over all three of them.

Cuinn stepped forward. "He took your wings too." It was the only thing he could think to say, and he had to say *something*. He couldn't afford to look uncomfortable or vulnerable in his brother's presence.

"He did." Pain flashed in Mithanis's eyes, gone as quickly as it had come. Cuinn knew that pain, still felt twinges of it when the realisation hit again that he no longer had wings. The only moments he was ever free of it was when he soared on Trystaan's back.

Letting the silence fill for a moment, he found the room's only other chair, and pulled it up to sit opposite Mithanis. Talyn touched Kaeri's arm, pulling her away, instinctively understanding what Cuinn needed.

"I have questions. I want honest answers. You'll let me see the truth of them," Cuinn said flatly.

Mithanis huffed a breath, settled back in his chair. "It's not like I've got anything better to do."

"Did you kill Raya?"

"No." The answer hit Cuinn like a brick—Mithanis wasn't shielding his song magic, letting Cuinn read him as he spoke. "When you announced your engagement to her, I went straight to her father to insist he refuse the match. The man was terrified of the consequences of displeasing me and agreed at once. As far I was concerned, the marriage was never going to happen." Mithanis met his gaze steadily. "When she turned up dead, I assumed Raya had killed herself after her father withheld his permission to marry you."

Cuinn forced the next words out, roughly pushing aside the emotion that wanted to rise up and take a stranglehold on this throat. "Ronisin Nightdrift and his detail?"

"That execution order was mine. Azrilan came to me, said he had an informant that told him Ronisin's detail had shifted loyalties. That they had secretly pledged to Talyn Dynan. The Ciantar." Mithanis' eyes shifted to where Talyn stood somewhere behind Cuinn.

He took a breath. "The izerdia explosion in the Wolf barracks?"

"Not me."

Cuinn's jaw clenched. "Mithanis, I—"

"If it had been me, Brother, I would have just signed another execution order. Not destroyed palace property with an uncontrolled izerdia explosion," Mithanis snapped, growing irritation with Cuinn's questioning filling his voice.

Cuinn took a deep breath. Some of this he'd begun to suspect already, but having Mithanis confirm it... he'd been such a fool. The bitterness flared and it took him a moment to fight it back.

"And when you found out who Talyn's father was. That she was a Ciantar. Was that Az?"

Mithanis smiled, but it had no warmth in it. "More information from his spy. Az told me he wanted me to take the credit for it, ever the loyal brother. We were both thoroughly outwitted, Cuinn."

Cuinn glanced away, then stood up. "Yes, we were."

Talyn's gaze searched his. He gave her a little nod. Her hand brushed his arm in silent support as she passed him and then it was her Mithanis was staring at.

"We're going to take both Azrilan's thrones away from him."

"You mean you're *not* planning on hiding out here forever?" Mithanis said. "I hope you've come up with a way of achieving either of those goals, because from where I sit, we've been thoroughly beaten."

"We?" Cuinn asked.

"The enemy of my enemy and all that." He waved a hand. "I am your rightful king, Cuinn. I was named by the Queencouncil as heir."

"Putting that issue aside," Talyn said dryly. "We do have a plan for replacing Azrilan as ahara. We're travelling to Montagn soon to get things started."

Mithanis slowly rose to his feet. There was nothing threatening about the gesture, but Talyn tensed nonetheless. Cuinn took a step closer to her.

"I'm starting to get the impression you're going to let me out of this room," Mithanis drawled.

"There will be conditions."

Mithanis smiled, gaze shifting to Kaeri. "Let me guess, you're going to try and make her ahara."

"You will agree to a temporary alliance between us," Talyn continued as if he hadn't spoken. "We will give you your freedom, and in return, you will help us remove Azrilan from the Montagni throne."

"Why would I agree to that without knowing the details of your plan?"

"First, you're an angry man. You must be absolutely burning to get your vengeance on Azrilan," Talyn said confidently. "Taking his throne away is the perfect way to do that. Second, your only other choice is to sit here in this room until the war is over. That's not your style."

She had him. Cuinn might be the one with song magic, but Talyn's instincts about people were razor sharp.

Mithanis crossed his arms over his chest. "And when would this hypothetical alliance end?"

"Once Azrilan is off the Montagni throne and Kaeri is on it, we're done," Cuinn said. That promise had to come from him. The moment their alliance was over he and Mithanis would be in a battle for the Mithranan throne and everyone in the room knew it. But that was all right.

One step at a time.

"You will give your word, with your magic open to me, here and now, and I will do the same," Cuinn continued. "If you break your word, I will have you executed without a second thought."

"I won't be of any help to you in Montagn unless Kaeri offers me something substantial. I might be a Manunin, but I'm a relative stranger to them," Mithanis pointed out. "They don't know me like they know Az. They love him. I'll have to win them some other way."

"You and I will marry," Kaeri said coolly. "Don't mistake me, I will be ahara. But you will have the power and influence of being consort to the ahara."

His dark eyes met hers. "And if it's the Mithranan throne I want, not Montagn?"

"Then take it, and be an ornamental husband. You'll get no argument from me."

Mithanis turned, walking to the window, his back to them. Anger, frustration and bitterness seeped from him in snatches underneath his characteristically sloppy shielding. He hated the thought of allying himself with a younger brother he'd always dominated. Mithanis needed to be the one in control, the one running everything.

One hand reached down to idly trace the pages of the book he'd been reading.

"All right, Cuinn." He turned back, his magic leaping across the room to slide against Cuinn's. "In return for my freedom, I will help you and your Ciantar put Kaeri Venador on the throne of Montagn."

"Good."

Mithanis took a step closer. "And once our alliance is over and Azrilan dead, I will take the throne of Mithranar."

"You will try," Cuinn said simply. "And so will I."

CHAPTER 49

"It's dangerous." Talyn paced before their fireplace. "Allying ourselves with Mithanis. I don't like it."

"I agree." Doran spoke up. "Doing this gives him the opportunity to learn our strengths, the size of our forces, for when it comes time to fight for the Mithranan throne."

"If things go the way I'd like them to, there'll be no need for a fight," Cuinn said mildly. "I don't want war. It's bad enough we're going to get that in Montagn."

"Mithanis is a member of House Manunin," Kaeri said flatly. "He will be an asset to us in our negotiations with my House. More than that, he's a carrot to convince House Manunin to cave once Azrilan is defeated. We need him and his blasted song magic."

"We'll keep a watch on him at all times," Theac said gruffly.

"No." Cuinn shook his head. "I promised him his freedom."

"Cuinn—" Talyn began but he cut her off.

"I gave him my word. If we try and cut corners in any way he won't react well. I know my brother, and I sensed his magic earlier. He will hold to his word."

"Until the alliance is over." Saniya spoke. "This is a terrible idea. The man is a monster."

"A monster we need," Kaeri repeated.

Saniya looked at her across the room, then sighed in capitulation. "Acknowledged."

Talyn had finally stopped her pacing but her stance was tense, face set in a slight frown. Cuinn's worry returned with a vengeance. What was going on with her?

"Who will you take into Montagn?" Corrin asked.

Silence fell, all eyes turning to Talyn. She didn't seem to notice, instead frowning at the floor. The two Callanan glanced at her. Cuinn picked up their curiosity too.

"Talyn, Kaeri, Mithanis and myself will go. Levs, you and Cynia too. Windsong will stay here to run things. Corrin, you'll bring most of the Wolves," Cuinn answered instead. Talyn had already discussed her plans with him a few nights earlier.

"How are you going to get across the Causeway?" Windsong asked.

"We can't just ride up to the Venador holding and ask them to put me in charge. I have to take the mountain territory in a show of strength," Kaeri said.

"Your family will hand over the leadership of their House to you after you attack their holding and kill their soldiers?" Theac sounded skeptical.

"Montagni respond to strength. I have to give them no choice but to accept me."

"We'll smash our way across the Causeway, cut off the escape routes out of the mountains, then ride on to the fortress." Talyn finally joined the conversation. "Kaeri, you'll need to show us the mountain paths on a map."

"Us and what army?" Kaeri asked. "I told you the Wolves wouldn't be enough—they'll never get across the Causeway without being cut down. Venador cavalry will be manning it on Azrilan's order in case we try something exactly like this."

"And I told you I planned for that. Within a week or two, all going well, three hundred Aimsir and a full legion of SkyRiders will be arriving on our doorstep," Talyn said. "The SkyRiders will take out those guarding the Causeway, and the Aimsir were born for the narrow trails of those mountains. We'll cut off all routes out, then the fighting force of the Wolves will help you take the Venador fortress."

Silence fell. The fire popped in the grate. Everyone but the Callanan, who already knew the plan, looked thoroughly impressed by it.

Kaeri considered a moment. "That could work."

"You bloody Montagni and your obsession with strength," Saniya muttered, shaking her dark head.

A smile teased at Kaeri's mouth. "You'll come too?"

Saniya returned the smile. "Yes, I'll come too."

That seemed to catch Talyn's attention, and she glanced between them. "I'd planned for you to stay here to keeping running our underground network, Saniya."

"Andres and Len can do that—they don't need me to babysit them," Saniya said casually. "Besides, apart from Kaeri, I know Montagn better than any of you."

The meeting broke up then, Cuinn's council filing out one by one, most of them deep in conversation, leaving him alone with Talyn.

Cuinn sank back into the couch with a sigh. "You used to think *our* love affair was impossible. I don't know how Kaeri plans to be ahara when she's in love with the leader of a rebel network that helps escaped slaves."

Talyn's gaze shot to his, then she gave a rueful shake of her head. "I wouldn't say anything out loud if I were you. Kaeri and I talked about it once in the slave camp. I've never heard anyone give such a scathing dismissal at the idea of falling in love. Why do you think she's so willing to marry Mithanis?"

He smiled at her. "I bet you did at one time too."

She chuckled, face brightening. "Sari is rather loudly agreeing with you."

A brief silence fell.

"Are you ever planning on telling me what is wrong?" he asked softly.

"Cuinn, I..." Her voice trailed off and she turned away. "It's nothing."

He let that sit for a moment, then he rose from the sofa, moving to stand a short distance away from her, but not too close. Something was making her deeply unsettled, and the last thing he wanted to do was add pressure to whatever it was she was feeling. "We don't keep secrets from each other, Talyn. I know that a lot has happened to us in the past year, and neither of us are the same, but you have to know that I will love you no matter what."

She let out a shaky breath, still not looking at him. "I do know that."

He swallowed, sudden terror beating at him. "Is it you? You don't feel the same anymore? If that's it, then be honest, I'll—"

"No!" She spun, stepping into him and resting a palm over his heart.

"Then stop making me guess. Please."

"I'm sorry." Her gaze shifted away and she put some distance between them. Eventually she took a steadying breath then lifted her head to look at him. "I'm pregnant."

For a moment he wasn't sure he'd heard her correctly. He thought she'd said *pregnant*, but it couldn't be... but that combination of nervousness and unease on her face, in the way she was shifting her weight back and forth. Of course that was how Talyn Dynan would feel about being pregnant.

"With..." He cleared his throat, tried again. "We're..."

"Yes," she said.

He simply had no words. A child. Hers. How was he going to keep a tiny baby safe? A child. Joy was a monster unfolding in his chest, squeezing aside all his organs and keeping him from speech or even coherent thought.

"We weren't particularly careful in Port Lathilly, when we reunited," she said, seeming to feel the need to fill the silence. "A week or so ago I started feeling odd. More tired than usual. Ill. It's early, but... Jystar confirmed it this morning."

He took a step closer to her. "You're terrified."

"How do *you* feel?" she demanded, tears welling in her eyes.

"Talyn, I'm not sure words exist to describe how I feel." He lifted a trembling hand to her cheek. "Overwhelmed. Terrified. But most of all... joy doesn't even begin to cover it."

The tears spilled down her cheeks and she abruptly pressed her face into his chest. He gently pulled her close, giving her the comfort she so clearly needed. "Talyn, if this isn't what you want..."

She shook her head against him, her words mumbling into his vest. "Not that. Never that. I'm just not sure what to do about it. We're in a war, Cuinn, and I'm a warrior. I need to be able to fight. I can't be pregnant."

He chuckled, sliding a hand into her hair. "You're not just a warrior. You have a brilliant tactical mind. Besides, as far as I'm aware, pregnancy lasts nine months only, no?"

She made a face. He laughed, the sound ringing with joy. He loved this woman so fiercely it literally took his breath away, and he let her feel it with his magic, holding nothing back.

"Okay," she breathed. "We're having a child."

He smiled, kissed her. "Yes."

She eyed him. "Tell me you know something about keeping a baby alive?"

"We may have to consult with others," he mused. "Theac will help."

She burst out laughing. "You want to trust our child's survival to Theac?"

"Errana, then. She's managed to raise three children successfully." He gave a firm nod, comforted by the excellence of that idea.

Talyn sobered. "I don't want anyone knowing, not until we have no choice but to tell them."

He understood. The Wolves were already protective of her—if they knew she was carrying his heir... and she wasn't going to respond well to even more protective behaviour.

"And if you try to suggest that I shouldn't go to Montagn, to lead the battle for the mountains, we're going to have a massive fight," she warned, fierce light flashing in her eyes. "I absolutely refuse to accept you turning into an overprotective, hovering husband."

He lifted his hands in the air. "I wouldn't dare. You *are* going to listen to Jystar, though, aren't you?"

"That depends on what he tells me to do."

He left that alone. For now. "You just called me husband."

She let out a breath. "We need to get married."

"This child will be my heir whether or not we're married when he or she is born," he said. "The last thing I want is you marrying me just because you're pregnant."

"Isn't that something I'm supposed to say to you?" she teased.

"Talyn, I'm serious. Our wedding needs to be a proper one, with your family and mine, to confirm the legitimacy of our formal alliance. You know that."

"We can still do that once the war is done. But that doesn't stop us from marrying now." She hesitated. "I'm unsure about a lot of things. Whether we can win this war. What will happen afterwards even if we do. What my life will be like as queen. Having a child. But I *am* sure that no matter what happens next, I want to do it with you."

A smile began spreading over his face as his magic finally picked up that this was something she wanted. And not because she was pregnant.

"Stop looking at me like that," she muttered.

"I'll marry you on the day of your choosing." He swept her into his arms. "But first we need to celebrate our forthcoming parenthood."

CHAPTER 50

*I*t took several days before she reluctantly broached with Cuinn the realisation that had been playing on her mind since they'd arrived back in Mithranar, since seeing how the Wolves and Falcons had reacted to his arrival. She'd tried over and over to figure out a way around it. But there wasn't one.

She waited until they were alone, on the balcony of their quarters, a brief moment together before starting the day. The wind whistled around them, numbing her cheeks, almost tearing the words away before Cuinn could hear them. "I think you need to stay."

He didn't respond immediately, no doubt reining in his emotional response so that it wouldn't hit her. "Why?"

"If this thing in Montagn works, then we need to be ready to move here."

"I already know that. Windsong and Andres can—"

"They need to see *you*, Cuinn." She cut him off, annoyed that she had to say this, that her strategic mind was leading her to the last thing she wanted. "The Wolves know and love you. The court of Mithranar doesn't. Not properly. And you've been gone since Azrilan took the throne. If you want to be king, it has to be you coordinating things here. It's not the humans or the Wolves who will give you the throne. It's the winged folk."

His mouth tightened. "That shouldn't be the case."

"No, but it is. If you don't win them, you'll be fighting them the rest of your reign... and it will only reinforce the divide between winged folk and humans. That's not what either of us want."

"That's not the only reason you're saying this." His green eyes searched hers. "You're worried about Mithanis."

"I am. The winged folk have known him their whole lives. He's a known quantity. He will no doubt be a reassuring return to what they know. Until recently you've been nothing but a dissolute fool to them. They need to see who you really are."

He stepped away, lifting a hand to rub over his face. "Talyn. I'm not leaving you, especially not now."

"You've always trusted me, always had faith in me," she said quietly. "Don't stop now, please."

He nodded wordlessly, reaching out to pull her close against him. She buried her head against his chest, wrapped her arms around his waist and held on fiercely. "What about Mithanis?"

"You never promised him you would be travelling to Montagn too." She huffed a breath. "I guess we'll see how willing your brother is to hold to his word."

"If he tries to hurt you..."

"I'll kill him," she said simply, leaning back to meet his eyes again. He took reassurance from that cool confidence of hers.

"You keep Jystar with you at all times. Zamaril too. Promise me."

"I promise." She leaned up to kiss him.

He tugged her back for a longer kiss, his hand sliding over her stomach to cradle their child. "I love you both. Come back to me."

"You stay alive for us," she said.

A heavy silence fell, but then Cuinn frowned, moving away to stare over the balcony. "What's that?"

She squinted, spotting the faint snow cloud on the horizon, and a smile spread over her face. "Ariar's here."

. . .

A QUARTER-TURN LATER, Talyn was still leaning out over the drop, a smile tugging at her face as the distant cloud on the horizon resolved into three hundred racing Aimsir, a golden-haired rider astride a big grey stallion in the lead.

Her peripheral vision was caught by the sparkle of Trystaan's underwings as he took off from higher above, soaring into the skies and winging his way over to meet the legion of SkyRiders circling in the air above the Aimsir.

Remaining where she was, she watched as the horses rode up to Corrin and the Wolves who were waiting to greet them, circling around in an exuberant gallop. Ariar and Corrin spoke for a few moments, then Ariar lifted a hand and riders began dismounting. Once satisfied everything was to his liking, he followed Corrin up the trail. Soon both men disappeared from sight.

Despite their overall appearance of rowdiness, the Aimsir efficiently unpacked tents from saddlebags and began setting up a neat camp—not far from water and grazing for the horses and in an area of the foothills protected by mountain slopes on three sides.

A half-turn later, her cousin stepped out onto the balcony behind her, a wide smile of greeting lighting up his face. "Talyn!"

"Welcome back to the SkyReach." She hugged him. "You're well?"

"Never better," he promised. "You?"

"Raring to go." She speared him with a look. "Where are we at?"

Ariar took his slouch hat off, settling against the railing. "Rados has been back in Samatia for about a month. Saundin is keeping us informed as best he can. I think it was a bit rough at first, but the Shadowlord and Armun Council rallied behind Rados. The first Firthlander troop ship arrived on our east coast to start ferrying their soldiers home just before I left. Alyna and Aeris were scheduled to depart after me to go to Samatia and formally renounce our claim on Firthland and sign an alliance agreement with Rados as high king."

"Isn't it dangerous, sending Aeris to Samatia when things are still uncertain?"

"Alyna is with him, and your mother is one fierce fighter, Tal. Aeris must show he isn't afraid. That he trusts our new allies."

It was true. Still, she worried. "Soar and Allira?"

"Our young king has put Soar in charge of dealing with preparing for the Montagni war fleet in his absence, while Allira will step in as regent in case something happens to him." Ariar smiled. "We're all very busy little Dumnorix."

Talyn stiffened. "The war fleet is moving?"

Ariar nodded. "Word came from Acleu the day before I left Port Lachley—Azrilan has re-stocked izerdia and re-formed the fleet. Not only that, but the ship of niever-flyers Tarcos sent to protect the fleet carried on to Montagn when the Montagni ships never showed up for the rendezvous."

It was what they'd wanted. Still, she worried for the Twin Thrones. "Did the Callanan have any idea when the fleet would depart?"

"They weren't sure, but didn't think it would be longer than a week or two. They may be leaving as we speak."

Talyn thought that over. "Well, let's hope Rados can be trusted. Soar will have to divert several SkyRider legions and most of the Aimsir to the north to fight that fleet. The Ayrlemyre Mountains will be vulnerable."

"It's a dangerous moment," Ariar agreed. "It will only take one thing to fail and this whole scheme could turn to disaster."

Talyn leaned over and nudged him hard. "Since when are you the pessimistic one?"

"Never." He beamed. "Where are you at?"

"We have Kaeri's agreement and three hundred Wolves and Falcons primed for a fight." She met her cousin's gaze. "It's now or never."

"How soon before Azrilan hears about Tarcos, do you think?"

"It's hard to know. Unless Azrilan has spies of his own in the south, which I doubt given how heavily he's relied on Tarcos's Armun, he won't know until Rados sends him a formal missive. Gossip from the limited merchant traffic might get there first." Talyn shifted. "Montagn's army still dwarfs ours. We need House Venador to destroy Azrilan's support in Arataire if we hope to win."

"Then we'd best get to it. When do you want to move?"

"Day after tomorrow." She hesitated. "How do you feel about attending a wedding?"

CUINN AND TALYN were married before three-hundred-odd Wolves and Falcons, fifty SkyRiders, three hundred rambunctious Aimsir, a Callanan pair and Prince Ariar Dumnorix.

Talyn found the whole thing distinctly uncomfortable—the hundreds of pairs of watching eyes and Sari's constant ripples of glee in her head were not helping at all. Cuinn attempted to keep a straight face as they stood in front of all those people and swore their marriage vows, but failed miserably, his delight escaping into the widest smile she'd ever seen.

Windsong officiated—winged folk marriages could be sworn by any male member of the court, and the Falcon was from a small but noble family. He certainly looked the part, distinguished and handsome with his greying hair, the lines on his face conveying character rather than age.

Ariar witnessed on behalf of the Dumnorix, unable to keep a straight face either as he delighted in her awkwardness. Leviana and Cynia stood to Talyn's right, Leviana literally hopping from excitement, while Theac and Corrin stood for Cuinn. Saniya and Kaeri observed from a short distance, both pretending like they thought the whole air of excitement and celebration was a bit over the top.

"Isn't this great?" Sari asked.

"Which part?"

"You getting married. And after all those times you swore it would never happen."

"I know."

"Is this what you want, Tal? Truly?"

"I love him." She had no doubt about that. "Marriage, ruling a kingdom, it wasn't what I would have chosen. But I will have my Wolves, and I will be in Mithranar, and I will be his. I can be content with that."

When it was over, Windsong bowing before them both, wings

half-furled, Cuinn shared with her the emotions of those watching as they cheered and whistled and stamped their feet.

And in that moment she was happy.

Cuinn's hand tightened on hers. "Tomorrow we go to war," he murmured.

She nodded, turned to him with a smile and let him feel everything she felt. "But first let's celebrate our wedding with those who love us."

"Time for the best part," Ariar bellowed, clapping his hands loudly. "Aimsir, we're in play! Come congratulate your fellow rider on her marriage."

The Aimsir came forward, hooting and hollering, wine spraying from the bottles they carried to douse Cuinn and Talyn and those closest to them. Talyn laughed as wine soaked through her clothes and hair, as entranced by the delight and joy on Cuinn's face as she was by the happiness filling her.

No matter what else came, this was right.

CHAPTER 51

*T*alyn calmed a restive FireFlare with a touch, her eyes focused on the horizon. The Causeway was a short gallop away but not visible in the dim light. Behind her gathered over a hundred riders, uncharacteristically quiet and calm.

A short distance away Ariar sat at the head of another hundred riders. He glanced over, caught her looking at him, and winked. She flashed him a smile.

Talyn looked behind the horses, where just under two hundred Wolves and eighty Falcons were lined up in neat formation under Corrin's command. Kaeri and Mithanis rode with them. Saniya, Leviana and Cynia too. Talyn was counting on the two Callanan to keep Kaeri safe if things went wrong. Without the Venador princess, their plan would be over before it began.

It was dark, the faint blue line on the horizon marking the rapidly approaching dawn.

They waited.

"This is going to be epic." Sari's voice sounded wistful.

"I hope so."

The ache was still there. Where Sari had once been. The palpable absence at her left side. She'd slowly learned to be a formidable warrior on her own, without Sari, but that didn't mean a day went by where she didn't wish with everything inside her that things could be different.

A distant screech had everyone looking to the skies.

Dawn was advancing now, darkness replaced by growing light that illuminated the stark white snow surrounding them in a silver glow.

Another screech, this one a little closer. Talyn squinted, her winged folk vision picking up the dark specks of a SkyRider legion as they flew in from the direction of the SkyReach, dropping lower towards the snow. FireFlare shifted under her, eager to be off.

One eagle dropped lower, insanely fast, and Trystaan's challenging scream echoed through the morning. Midnight-blue flashed underneath his wings as Cuinn brought him low over the Wolves and Aimsir.

And then he was past them, soaring back up into the sky to hover above while his legion flew on towards the Causeway. Talyn's gaze lingered on the distant speck of Trystaan—Cuinn wouldn't fight in this battle, but would instead return to the SkyReach to begin the fight for Mithranar. She worried ferociously about him. About the Wolves she was leaving behind. She hated that it was necessary.

Talyn glanced at Ariar. His wide grin and bright eyes, full of anticipation, dispelled her melancholy. Anticipation began uncurling in her chest.

"Aimsir, ride!" he bellowed, urging Greylord into a gallop with a light touch of his heels. "We're in play!"

FireFlare was only a second behind, the copper mare stretching out into a full gallop. Whoops and whistles and loud shouts echoed through the Aimsir as they flowed into movement, no formal ranks or neat rows, just hundreds of beautiful horses racing through the morning after the SkyRiders.

"Amazing."

Sari's excitement spread through Talyn, igniting her own and smashing through all her caution.

She settled lower in the saddle, hands curling around the reins, a smile spreading unbidden across her face.

The Aimsir streamed towards the Causeway, a thunder of galloping hooves and screaming riders, bright against the white snow. The ocean came into sight first, then the rugged peaks of the Montagni mountains.

Then the Causeway.

The SkyRiders circled in the air above it, eagles swooping down to rake the Montagni defensive positions in flaming arrows. Kaeri had pointed them all out on a map, and it seemed like the SkyRiders hadn't had any difficulty in locating them.

Spots of orange flame glowed along the mountainside flanking the Causeway. As FireFlare raced towards it, Talyn's gaze picked out Montagni soldiers as they fled the flames. They all made for the main road below, where it wound deeper into Venador mountain territory.

The moment FireFlare's hooves hit the stone of the Causeway, Talyn leaned down and unhooked her bow from the saddle, slid it into her left hand, then reached up with her right to draw an arrow from the quiver hanging down her back.

Riding without the reins, a half-pace behind Greylord, Talyn drew and fired at the closest Montagni. Her arrow took him in the arm. Blood spurted, but he barely heeded the injury, instead turning to shout a warning to his comrades. She swore at her poor aim and fired again.

The closest soldiers immediately began forming into defensive lines, but by then the Aimsir were pouring across the Causeway, their arrows whistling thick and fast through the air. More orders were shouted back. Talyn got off another three arrows—Ariar even more— before Greylord and FireFlare hit the lines.

Aimsir weren't built for standing and fighting, so Talyn and Ariar pushed their horses through and down the road, trusting to the riders behind them to take out any threat to their back.

"Incoming!" Ariar bellowed.

Talyn loosed an arrow and lifted her right hand. Her sapphire energy shield snapped into place just as several arrows came flying down the road towards them. The Montagni had already set up a secondary defensive position.

They were good.

"Above and to the north!" Ariar shouted again.

Talyn nodded, scanned the rocky mountainside where he'd directed her, but before she could do anything, three eagles dropped out of the sky. They passed overhead in a blur of speed and icy wind and then firelit arrows pounded into the defensive outpost.

"Keep going!" Talyn shouted, urging FireFlare back into a gallop.

A glance back showed all the Aimsir were across the Causeway now, filling the narrow road leading into the mountains. This was their most vulnerable moment, when they had to trust to the SkyRiders above to identify and remove any threat.

If they faced heavy cavalry assault here in these narrow spaces between slopes, they'd be slaughtered. But the Aimsir horses were fast, and soon the retreating Montagni cavalry came into sight ahead —they were all fleeing, none stopping to try and set up an ambush. Just as they came into sight, they reached a fork in the road and split up.

"The roads through the mountains are numerous, and soldiers of the Venador House will know the way out without having to think about it. They'll split up to break our pursuing force and hope to lose us in the wilderness," Kaeri had warned.

"Once the Aimsir have their tail, they won't be able to lose us," Ariar had said confidently. "Our horses are too fast. And they're accustomed to the Ayrlemyre Mountains—the Montagni terrain won't be difficult for them."

He proved right. Without a word Talyn sent FireFlare after the cavalry taking the southern fork while Ariar and Greylord turned north after the others. The Aimsir split neatly into two behind them.

FireFlare galloped, hooves racing effortlessly down the rockier road. The space between the Aimsir and cavalry decreased enough that the lead riders could get off a few shots. Two horses and their riders fell.

The road branched again. Talyn urged FireFlare after the group veering around to the north. "Arn, wheel east!" she snapped.

Arn shouted confirmation, deftly turning his chocolate mare to follow the smaller group continuing along the main trail. Aimsir again split neatly to follow Talyn and Arn.

This trail was narrower, and steeper, but the Montagni hadn't realised that this gave the fleet Aimsir horses the advantage. Naturally faster and more agile, and not weighed down by riders wearing armour and weapons, Talyn's group quickly caught up.

As the trail opened up to grassy hillside, she gestured to the Aimsir closest behind her, pointing him left, then spurred FireFlare on. "Ha ha!"

The copper mare lengthened her stride further and they raced up along the right side of the fleeing cavalry group. Talyn started firing, hitting where she could, while trusting FireFlare to avoid the sword thrusts of their quarry.

Soon her group of Aimsir had completely encircled the cavalry, weaving and dodging until most had fallen and only a few riders remained in the saddle. One of the riders barked an order and the cavalry slowed their horses, gradually coming to a complete halt.

"We surrender!" a man shouted, yanking his helmet off his head and tossing it away before putting his hands in the air.

"Aimsir, halt firing!" Talyn bellowed. "Bows nocked and ready."

The hail of arrows stopped.

"Throw down your weapons and dismount," she snapped at the cavalrymen.

They did as ordered with various degrees of reluctance. Once they were all standing together in a huddle in the middle of the path, Talyn snapped an order and several Aimsir began spooking the cavalry horses, panicking them into galloping off.

She waited until the horses were long gone, then flashed a smile at the helpless frustration of the bearded Montagni standing in the road. "It was a pleasure, gentleman. Arn, you'll escort them in?"

"Aye!" He nodded.

She kicked FireFlare into a gallop back the way they'd come, a series of whooping victory cheers following her.

It was going well so far.

CHAPTER 52

Talyn galloped up to the rendezvous point to find the others had already arrived.

Kaeri was speaking as Talyn dismounted and joined her, the Callanan, the legion captain, and the Wolf talons. Mithanis was there too, armed, expression calm and focused. "Over that rise the road leads down to the main gates," Kaeri said.

Corrin cleared his throat. "This is the part where the Ciantar would insist we go over the plan once more, just to make sure."

"And so she should," Cynia said primly.

Talyn smirked, though it quickly faded. She was too on edge, worried that this would fail, that someone she loved might get hurt. "Drift, you take the SkyRiders in first," she said crisply, hiding any trace of worry from her voice. "Your job is to force any guards on the walls to flee inside—if they won't, you need to provide us enough covering fire to get to the gates safely."

"I'll bring the winged Wolves and Falcons in from the sky after you've begun your attack," Liadin said. "We'll target any remaining archers on the walls first."

"Then I bring a third of the force around from the north," Corrin added. "Once the archers are out, we smash through the back entrance."

"While Talyn and I lead the rest of you through the main gates," Kaeri said in satisfaction. "Plan officially gone over. Let's get moving."

"We try to avoid killing unless it saves lives, and we hold fire the moment the fortress surrenders to Kaeri," Talyn said firmly.

"Agreed." Their assent was quick and steady. Mithanis said nothing, gaze dark as he glanced at her.

"These are my countrymen, my family," Kaeri said quietly. "I will do what I have to, but I won't hurt any more than is necessary."

SITTING in a wide valley between particularly rugged mountains, the Venador fortress was as forbidding as its surroundings.

That was Talyn's first thought as she watched the SkyRider eagles crest the valley summit and drop down towards its high stone walls. Her second was that if she were an archer guarding the walls, she'd be quailing in her boots at the sight of fifty fearsome eagles filling the sky, screaming challenges as they swooped towards their target.

Drift led a handful of SkyRiders straight for the front gates, spread out in a line, and firing at any movement they could see. The rest of the legion spread wide to cover more of the walls.

Despite their obvious shock, the guards reacted impressively quickly. Return arrows hissed through the sky by the time the eagles banked and rocketed skywards to come around for another run.

As they hit the walls again, Liadin and the winged Wolves and Falcons joined them, using the cover of SkyRider arrows to pick out the archers on the walls and take them down as quickly as they could.

Despite how disciplined and fierce they were, the Venador guards were utterly unprepared to deal with an aerial force, and the defence along the walls of the fortress collapsed within minutes of the SkyRiders screaming overhead and the winged folk dropping out of the skies and using their warrior magic in targeted fashion to take out anyone still firing back.

"Your SkyRiders are impressive," Kaeri murmured from her spot beside Talyn overlooking the fight.

"They are." Talyn's gaze surveyed the situation. "Time for you to make your entrance."

WITH THE GUARDS in total disarray, Corrin's force broke through the back gates without any major problems, filing in to encircle the main yard right as Kaeri and Talyn and their force broke through and quelled any further resistance.

Drift's legion grouped together and came in low, eagles screaming, circling the yard protectively in case the Venadors mustered a secondary attack.

The yard was wide and empty. Armed guards inside the compound had dropped their weapons in surrender and knelt by the wall, presumably at Corrin's order. Talyn cast an apprehensive glance up at the walls, but was reassured to see Falcons and Wolves standing there in the place of defenders.

They would keep Kaeri safe.

Talyn dismounted and came to stand a half-step behind Kaeri just as three men emerged from the front doors of the fortress. Leviana and Cynia stood close by, green Callanan cloaks swishing around them, Cynia with bow drawn and Leviana with a knife in each hand. Mithanis stood a half-pace behind Kaeri. Zamaril appeared at Talyn's side, sword drawn.

The approaching men were bearded like all free Montagni, and dressed richly but practically. The middle one was substantially older than the other two, broad-shouldered, with short-cropped greying hair. Talyn's eyes narrowed; he looked enough like the previous ahara that she wondered if they were brothers.

All three were angry; it snapped from them, obvious to anyone even without song magic. But when they realised who was standing before them, shock and bewilderment, along with a hint of relief and joy, eclipsed much of the anger.

"Kaeri!" The older man stared at her. The other two came to a halt a pace behind him. "We thought you were dead! What are..." He trailed off, his mystification sending his expression slack for a long moment. "What are you... what is going on?"

"Uncle Tashon," she said curtly, making no allowances for his shock. Her back was ramrod straight and her voice had no give in it. "My father couldn't hold onto his throne, and you gave it away to a winged prince from another country. I'm here to take House Venador and reclaim the seat of ahara."

Tashon opened his mouth, glanced at the two men beside him. They looked as befuddled as he did. "You can't."

"I think you'll find I already have. Surrender House Venador to me now, and I'll withdraw my forces. I don't want any more soldiers of our House to die unnecessarily."

"I—you're a woman."

"Clever of you to notice," she snapped.

"Kaeri, be sensible, a woman has never led a Montagni House." This from the man beside her uncle, younger, taller, but the happiest of the three men to see her alive, as far as Talyn could tell.

"That doesn't mean it can't happen, Tarif." She looked her uncle in the eye. "How exactly do you plan to deny my claim? I've just taken your fortress."

Silence filled the yard. If what they were doing wasn't so vital, Talyn would have been hard pressed not to laugh.

"Is that..." Tashon shook his head, gaze landing on Mithanis. "You're Mithanis Manunin."

"I am." Mithanis even managed a *very* slight bow. "And I stand with Kaeri Venador."

The shock and confusion deepened. "You're standing with another House against your own?"

"Azrilan cut out my wings and threw me in a slave camp. Your niece offered me power and a chance to strike back. When she re-takes her father's position as ahara, I will bring House Manunin to heel behind you." His voice rang with confidence, both innate and magical. A little shiver went down Talyn's spine. Mithanis could be a formidable force in Montagn. She hoped Kaeri hadn't made a mistake involving him.

"As my husband," Kaeri added, waiting a beat before continuing. "Push me, and I will kill every single man here, you included. I have demonstrated that I have the superior force. You can't stand against me."

Her uncle's face darkened. "A foreign force."

"What does that matter? And in case you're thinking the SkyRiders and Aimsir currently hunting down the guards on the border posts are all I have, don't. I have formally allied with King Aeris Dumnorix of the Twin Thrones and Prince Cuinn Acondor of Mithranar."

"You..." The poor men seemed to have no idea what to do or say.

"It is done," Kaeri said. "All you need do is accept it, accept *me*, and we will restore House Venador to power."

Still they hesitated. They couldn't seem to get their heads around a female leading their House, despite the fact they already stood defeated. But they loved her. That much was obvious. She was one of them. A Venador. And no doubt Azrilan's defeat of Kaeri's father had stung badly.

"I am Talyn Ciantar-Dumnorix." She stepped forward then, keeping her shoulders loose and voice confident. "I verify the alliance. As will Prince Ariar Dumnorix, once he's finished chasing your cavalry through the hills." She paused. "Give Kaeri your House, and then we can go inside and discuss how we make Venador the most powerful name in Montagn once again."

Tashon glanced at the two men beside him, stared up into the sky, then sighed. "Kaeri Venador. I hereby surrender House Venador to you."

Talyn saw the shock ripple over Kaeri's face. Followed by delight. Then triumph.

But the succession of emotions happened so fast it barely showed in her expression or bearing. Instead she stepped forward, laid her hand on her uncle's shoulder. "It's good to see you, Uncle Tash."

His head bowed, then raised to run his gaze over her face. His expression hardened. "They made you a slave?"

"They did. But we're going to do something about that."

Tarif stepped in closer then, as did the other cousin. All of a sudden it was as if nobody else in the courtyard existed but the four Venadors. Their bonds were tight, bound deep by loyalty and honour and tradition. "Tell us how, Kaeri."

CHAPTER 53

*C*uinn sat on a chair before one of the many wooden tables filling the room. They were covered in dust, having stood unused for months. His leg jigged constantly despite numerous attempts to stop it. His grip on the shadows in the room was fierce, ready to pull them around him so he could disappear into darkness in an instant.

The likelihood of betrayal was uncomfortably high.

Despite that, the Wolves remained outside, leaving him alone for this meeting. Even Jasper was back at their hiding place, no doubt snarling his fury at anyone who dared come close. Theac had been predictably against the idea. Cuinn had insisted. He had to show these men he trusted them.

Even if he didn't. Not yet.

A low whistle sounded. Three sharp whistles followed. Everything in Cuinn tightened. That code meant the meeting attendees were approaching. A second series of whistles... four this time.

That meant they were alone and weren't being followed.

Tirin Goldfeather was the first to enter what had once been the Wolves mess. An eager air hung around him, his expression open, golden wings relaxed at his sides. Charl Nightdrift, only two steps behind, was the opposite. He held his wings rigidly behind him, as if prepared to fly off at any moment. His face gave nothing away of what he was thinking.

But Cuinn could feel his fear. It was potent, sliding against his song magic like an oily residue. He tried not to let it affect him.

Cuinn stood, letting go of his grasp on the shadows. "Lord Nightdrift. Lord Goldfeather. Please have a seat."

Both men started in surprise, then equal looks of horror flashed across their faces as they registered Cuinn's lack of wings. The emotion hit him in a wave, and he couldn't stop a wince, though he quickly buried it.

"You know he would kill us if he found out we were here," Nightdrift said without preamble, striding forward to take a chair.

"I do. Thank you for coming."

Cuinn hadn't been named the prince of song for no reason, and he used every inch of his magic now to understand these men before him. He needed them, had chosen them deliberately, but if they betrayed him… he'd be dead well before he had any chance of taking the throne back from Azrilan.

Nightdrift tensed, as if he guessed exactly what Cuinn was doing, but said nothing. He wasn't trying to hide his emotions either. He had come to this meeting because Mithanis had murdered his son. That didn't mean he enjoyed any part of sneaking around. It wasn't his life he cared about—but he was a traditional winged man who'd sat on the Queencouncil since young adulthood. He didn't like change, and he didn't like the old ways being turned over. Cuinn didn't detect any malice, however, or nefarious intent.

Goldfeather was an open book. He still grieved the deaths of his father and Ronisin, knew Azrilan and Mithanis were responsible, and was more than willing to help put Cuinn on the throne. Although his lack of fear worried Cuinn; it indicated he didn't fully understand the danger he was in by being here.

"You must guess why I'm back," Cuinn said, settling in his chair.

"It's not exactly difficult to figure out," Nightdrift barked. "You want the same thing as your brothers. Our throne. Why are *we* here?"

Cuinn shrugged. "I want you to help me take it back."

"You mean you want us to get ourselves killed in a useless endeavour. The throne was never yours to *take back*, Prince Cuinn. The Queencouncil chose Mithanis. Azrilan took his position by force. All you did was run away and hide."

"I won't deny that." Cuinn squashed the guilt that wanted to rise. "But I left so that I could grow stronger. Find allies. Have a better chance of unseating Azrilan."

Goldfeather sat forward, earnestness in every line of his body. "Prince Cuinn, I would vote for you on the Kingcouncil any day. But Charl is right. If we openly challenge Azrilan, we'll be executed."

"All I'm asking you to do is vote for me at Kingcouncil when the time comes," Cuinn said simply. "And between now and then I want you to talk to those you trust. Tell them I've returned. That I want to get rid of Azrilan and make life here better for everyone."

Nightdrift barked another laugh. "Foolish idealism. Life already is good for us, Prince. Why risk our lives to change it? Unless you think jabbering to our friends about treason isn't risking our lives."

Cuinn leaned forward, capturing Nightdrift's gaze. "If I'd been king, Ronisin would still be alive today. You know it. *I* know it. I want you to make sure the court knows it."

Silence fell. Nightdrift's mouth tightened, but he looked away, his grief caustic against Cuinn's magic.

"I'll do as you ask," Tirin said hesitantly. "But there are few I trust enough to speak to about this. If I start spreading the information more widely, I can't guarantee it won't get back to Irial or Azrilan, or the WingGuard."

"Only speak to those you trust with your life. Ask them to do the same." It was risky no matter how much they trusted their friends. Cuinn hated how much danger they would be putting themselves in. But Talyn was right. He wouldn't ever achieve his goal without being willing to place lives at risk.

Nightdrift shot a glance at Tirin, then shrugged. "You'll need us to do more than that if you're truly planning on deposing your brother."

"That's true," Cuinn admitted. "I need information, whatever you can pass me. When does Kingcouncil sit? What are the loyalties of the lords? Who will be most opposed to me? How many Falcons guard Kingcouncil meetings? That sort of thing."

"Done." Tirin nodded.

Nightdrift shot him a scowl. "Even if you succeed, which isn't likely, what do you plan to do about the fact Azrilan is also ahara of Montagn?"

"Let's just assume that problem is dealt with. I won't move here until it is."

Nightdrift's dark look deepened, but eventually he gave a terse nod. "How do we contact you?"

"You don't. I want to make sure you both stay safe. One of my Wolves will come to you. It will be a different one each time. They'll ensure nobody sees you meeting with them."

"A word of warning." Nightdrift leaned closer, lowering his voice. The fear that had been hanging around him since he'd arrived grew even stronger, making it hard for Cuinn to sit still and meet his eyes. "Azrilan's hounds are back in the citadel. Their leader was at King-council yesterday. Don't know where they've been... but they know you're here, Prince Cuinn. I'd watch my back if I were you."

Nightdrift's fear became Cuinn's then. It squeezed his chest and set his heart thudding. "How many are they?"

"Ten Shadows, five Armun, ten Bearmen."

Cuinn swallowed, sweeping every trace of terror from his voice before speaking. "Thank you."

Nightdrift stood, chair scraping back. "Tirin, best you wait a bit before leaving. Not a good idea for us to be seen together."

"I'm glad you came back," Tirin said fervently once Nightdrift had gone. "We've been hoping you would."

"We?"

He nodded. "Some of the Falcons here are loyal to Windsong, though they pretend loyalty to Brightwing every day. And the lesser families... many of them liked the idea of you being king. I make sure to stay in touch with them."

"Be careful." Cuinn worried about the risks Tirin was taking.

"Azrilan's hounds won't just be looking for me. Take extra precautions."

"I'll be fine, Ronisin taught me a few things." Confidence beamed from Tirin as he stood. "I'll see you soon, Your Highness."

Cuinn worried for him. For all of them. Azrilan had out-maneuvered them all once before.

He desperately hoped it wouldn't happen again.

CHAPTER 54

Talyn couldn't keep still. She'd been tossing and turning ever since she'd gone to bed. Eventually she shoved the covers off and started dressing. Ehdra, on guard at her door, gave her a surprised look when she opened it. "Go and wake Drift. Quietly. Tell him to take his eagle up."

He hesitated. "Is something wrong?"

"I just..." She shook her head. "Something's off. Tell him to scout the area, make sure I'm worrying over nothing."

A full-turn later, Talyn, Corrin, Ariar and Liadin waited on the chilly rooftop and watched as Drift and his eagle dropped out of the sky over the fortress, a more rapid descent than any sane person would attempt at night. The eagle landed gracefully on the stone, but Drift was already unbuckling and jumping down.

Anxiety knotted in Talyn's chest.

"An army is marching toward us along each of the three access roads," he said without preamble. "Slave infantry and cavalry. The Causeway is wall-to-wall with foot soldiers and I think I spotted Berserkers too. Lord Ariar—your Aimsir scouts are maybe a half-turn away with the warning."

"How did you know?" Liadin turned, wide-eyed, to Talyn.

Corrin dismissed the question with a wave of his hand. "Drift, how long have we got before they surround us here?"

"Two full-turns, maybe a little more."

Talyn swore long and fluently under her breath. "We warn Kaeri first."

"I'll rouse the Aimsir discreetly." Ariar nodded. "We can be ready to ride in a half-turn."

All four followed Talyn in a run down the stairs. They reached the bottom and Talyn slowed her pace to a brisk walk. Ariar turned left to head to where the Aimsir were billeted. At a quick word from Corrin, Liadin peeled off to prepare the Wolves and Drift to the SkyRiders that had remained in Montagn with them.

Talyn knocked once at Kaeri's door before walking inside, not giving the Montagni guards stationed in her hallway time to voice the protests forming on their lips.

"Kaeri!" Talyn snapped the moment the door was closed. "Out here, now."

An internal door opened from the bedroom seconds later. Kaeri appeared, impatience and surprise warring on her face. At least she was dressed. "What the hell is going on?"

"Saniya, you too!" Talyn used her command voice, the one that meant instant obeying or dire consequences. She didn't wait for the other woman to appear though. "A small army is marching on us. They're using all three routes in and they've cut off the Causeway."

A snarl of fury rippled across Kaeri's face and she strode for the door, hauling it open and pointing at the Venador guards. "You—go straight to your watch captain and rouse the household guard. You—go to my uncle. Tell him to meet us in the audience hall now!"

"How far off?" Saniya came through from the bedroom, buckling on her knives.

Corrin relayed the info quickly and concisely. "Just over two full-turns for the first lot. A little longer for the second."

"If we can't escape via the Causeway, which way do we go?" Talyn asked Kaeri.

"We can scatter via trails over the mountains, but then we dilute our force and lose our defensible position. If we can't escape to the Causeway, though, we don't have a lot of other options." Kaeri sat to yank on boots. "We'll have to stand and fight—this fortress was built with defence in mind. Your SkyRiders should make the difference."

"Not against these numbers." There were only twenty SkyRiders left with them—the rest had returned to the SkyReach in preparation for Cuinn needing them—and there would be archers with the cavalry and foot soldiers. The Aimsir couldn't stand and fight against a powerful cavalry line, not to mention they'd be useless inside the walls of the fortress. She mulled the problem over.

"Sari?"

"What if you do the one thing Azrilan would least expect?" Sari suggested.

"Right. That would mean…" Talyn's head shot up. "What if we don't try and escape Montagn? What if we use the mountains as cover and begin striking at the slave camps like we originally planned?" she suggested.

"We *planned* an orderly series of attacks using my family's forces and your own to steadily build an army," Kaeri said. "If we start randomly attacking slave camps without a base to bring them back to, we'll just create chaos."

"Exactly." Talyn nodded. "Chaos that will hinder any pursuit of us, and chaos that will begin to affect their food supplies, and their weapons' manufacture, especially if we hit the right camps. Maybe it's not the orderly invasion we planned for, but it could still work."

Kaeri's eyes narrowed in thought. "True enough. We'll slip out of the fortress before they get here, scatter into the mountains and re-form further south, closer to the camps. They won't know what's going on."

"Wait!" Corrin stopped them before both women went running for the door. "Ciantar, you're talking about staying in Montagn indefinitely without a base or reliable access to supplies. What do we do with our wounded? Or the slaves we rescue who are hurt or sick or just malnourished and weak?"

"The villages throughout the mountains will shelter and protect us," Kaeri said. "They are loyal to our House."

"And what happens when Azrilan's army starts attacking them too?" Corrin said, a stubborn line to his mouth. Talyn wasn't sure whether she was annoyed or impressed.

"They can't be everywhere at once. And our villagers know how to protect themselves, not to mention how confusing the trails are." Kaeri sounded impatient.

"Corrin, I truly think it will still work," Talyn said. "Jystar will be with us, after all."

"Ciantar, I don't think you should—"

"She's pregnant, not an invalid," Saniya snapped, cutting Corrin off. "Can we please get a move on?"

"No!" Kaeri held up a hand when everyone turned to stare at Saniya. Corrin's eyes had gone wide as saucers. Talyn's anxiety shot through the roof. "We are NOT standing here having a debate about how Saniya found out your little secret while an army is marching on us. Let's go."

The women ran for the door. Talyn levelled at look at Corrin. "Not. A. Word."

He swallowed, still wide-eyed, and saluted. "As you say, Ciantar."

WITHIN A QUARTER-TURN the castle was a hive of activity. Kaeri and her family had decided not to ring the warning bells, instead taking extra precious time to manually rouse all the soldiers and residents.

"Better they not know we've been warned," Kaeri said, quickly convincing the others. "I like the idea of them storming up here to find us all vanished."

"We need to be gone inside a full-turn," Tashon barked. "Yet barely half the castle is awake and moving."

"We can do it."

"We can," Tarif said firmly.

Talyn glanced at him. In the days since they'd been here, Kaeri's eldest cousin had very quickly become her loudest voice of support within the family. If she didn't have the sense to make him one of her most senior advisors when she took the throne, Talyn planned on suggesting it very strongly.

She would need someone around her like that, someone to offer unquestioning support when she couldn't trust her own husband or any rival House. Speaking of Mithanis, he'd woken, become predictably furious at the news his brother was attacking them, and was now more usefully occupied using his song magic to keep the gathering soldiers calm and moving quickly.

They spent a quarter-turn dividing the Venador soldiers into groups—some would escort non-combatant residents of the fortress out to nearby villages for safety, while others would split into smaller, mobile forces that could manage the winding trails up through the mountains. The fifty remaining Wolves would travel with Talyn and Mithanis, with Saniya to guide them. Ariar would lead the Aimsir and SkyRiders.

"You don't stand and fight," Talyn warned Ariar. "You—"

"Talyn, I love you, but you're talking to the Horselord," Ariar said tersely. "We'll be like ghosts on the wind, unable to be caught. But if we get the opportunity to loose a few arrows as we go, I mostly certainly will take that opportunity."

All groups would meet in an isolated valley in three days' time. Kaeri and Talyn chose it after a careful study of one of the family's maps. It was barely two days' ride from the first slave camp they wanted to hit.

The bustle devolved into chaos as more and more people woke and time began running out. Each Venador family member was responsible for one of the departing groups, and shouts and running feet sounded from every direction. The horses in the stables were restless, made anxious by all the noise, and Kaeri sent the order not to light any more lanterns than would normally be alight at this time of night.

Corrin had the Wolves already out of barracks, dressed, weaponed and ready to ride before they all emerged from the escape planning. That meant the Mithranan contingent would be the first to go.

"Mithanis is out there with the gathered Wolves." Corrin strode up as Talyn and Saniya appeared. "He's got blood all over his hands. He says he found the spy reporting to Azrilan."

Talyn shuddered, not at all confident the prince of night hadn't found some poor innocent to take his anger out on. There was little she could do about it now though. "Get them moving. Saniya will be taking point. I will be right behind you."

Corrin saluted and jogged off, Saniya with him.

FireFlare was agitated, greeting Talyn with a sharp whinny when she appeared in the stables. It took longer than it should to buckle on the saddle given the mare's restive movements.

"Come on, FireFlare," Talyn murmured as she swung onto the mare's back. "Time to free some slaves."

CHAPTER 55

"Six Falcons on guard in the Kingcouncil chamber during meetings, all stationed indoors." Andres reviewed the latest information from Tirin Goldfeather. "That's light security."

"What do they have to be afraid of?" Lyra asked.

Andres conceded that. "If we can simultaneously subdue the six Falcons before the alarm is raised, at the same time as we take out Brightwing and his most loyal flight-leaders—"

"Without killing them," Cuinn said pointedly.

Lyra and Andres shared a look, but both nodded. Windsong crossed his arms over his chest.

"We still need information on the Falcons loyal to us," Andres finished. "So that we can ensure they're in position to take command."

"This is still a coup," Theac grumbled. "If we force the Kingcouncil into voting for you, none of the winged court is going to consider it legitimate."

"It's exactly what Azrilan did, and they're happily following him," Cuinn said.

"Because they're afraid of him. You want them to be afraid of you?" Windsong said pointedly.

Cuinn sighed. He was right. "You know I don't."

"We need to use the human population," Lyra said. "If they march up to the citadel and fill the open spaces to show their support for Prince Cuinn, then—"

"No, we can't guarantee the Falcons won't attack. Brightwing isn't above issuing that order." Frustration tinged Cuinn's voice.

Andres looked equally irritated. "Your Highness, we are your soldiers. If you keep refusing to follow our suggestions because you're afraid of violence, we'll never get anywhere."

Cuinn held onto his temper. She'd trained these men, and they were good at what they did. But how could he be king if he achieved it off the blood of his people? "We subdue the guards and the Falcons most loyal to Az. We negotiate a truce with the remaining Wing-Guard. Then we hold an open Kingcouncil with equal numbers of my soldiers and Azrilan's present. Whoever Kingcouncil votes in will be accepted as king."

"And the agreement you made with Mithanis?" Theac asked.

Cuinn's jaw clenched, but he nodded. "He'll need to be there too."

Windsong scratched his jaw. "And if they don't vote for you?"

"Then we accept that."

Windsong and the talons stared at him like he'd lost his mind. He tried not to wince. "The goal is to make sure ahead of time that they *do* vote for me."

Theac looked at Andres, who gave a little shake of his head, then Lyra, who stared at the roof. Almost rolling his eyes, he turned to face Cuinn. "Your Highness, we love you and you know that. You keep saying that you are responsible for all the people of Mithranar... but if you lose that vote and accept it, then what happens to the humans? Or the winged folk that showed loyalty to you? Those are the people whose lives ride on your decisions now."

Cuinn tried not to squirm in his chair, but failed miserably. "I'm aware of that."

An owl hooted outside Cuinn's small hut, breaking the tense silence that had fallen. Cuinn almost jumped.

Night had fallen several full-turns ago, but Cuinn and his talons had been up late after an unexpected visit from Andres with the latest message from Goldfeather. It wasn't like he would have been sleeping, anyway—and it wasn't just because he was currently hiding out in Vengeance's old compound behind the wall, where they were treated to a nightly chorus of tawncat snarls and other terrifying noises.

He'd been on edge since the news that the hounds were in Dock City and looking for him. He woke frequently during the night expecting a Shadow to jump out from the darkness. Not even the double guard of Wolves on him at all times reassured him.

Mainly because he could sense that it didn't reassure them.

The hounds were coming for him. And it was only a matter of time before they got to him, in one way or another.

The hooting came twice more as Cuinn and his talons headed towards a large clearing at the centre of the compound. The grass was long after months of being abandoned, but it provided no problem for the SkyRider dropping out of the sky.

"Plummet?" Cuinn recognised the woman unbuckling her harness and dropping down. Fear and dread warred in equal measure in the pit of his stomach—they hadn't expected to receive a SkyRider messenger this early unless something had gone wrong.

"Wolf." A smile creased her face, partially dispelling some of his concern. "Quite a nice hideout you've got here. Very difficult to find in the dark though."

"It's not like we could leave a lantern lit for you," Theac growled. "Blasted winged folk in this country."

"What's going on?" Cuinn demanded.

Plummet's smile faded a little. "Azrilan learned that Princess Kaeri and the Ciantar were hiding in the Venador fortress. They sent forces to attack, but—"

"Are they okay?" Cuinn cut in, every part of his body going tight with fear.

"When I left, they were all fine. They slipped out before the attacking forces could arrive, scattering into the mountains." Plummet hesitated. "Azrilan cut off the Causeway though."

"They're trapped in Montagn?" Theac asked gruffly.

"Yes," Plummet said.

There was a moment's silence, then Andres sighed. "What crazy plan has the Ciantar come up with now?"

Normally Cuinn would be amused by the question. Instead anxiety roiled in his stomach until he felt sick with it. Talyn was trapped in Montagn. With only a few hundred Aimsir and less than a hundred Wolves. Swallowing, he forced himself to pay attention to Plummet's response.

"She's going to use the mountains as a base to attack the slave camps. Same plan, just happening sooner." Plummet reached into her flight tunic and pulled out a crumpled sheet of parchment. "She told me to give you this."

Cuinn turned without a word and strode back to his small hut, the Wolf talons trailing behind him silently. Once he'd closed the door, he checked the blackout curtains were firmly covering the windows, then lit a lamp and unfolded the parchment on the table so they all could read it.

You need to gather the Wolves and Falcons and make your move on the citadel soon, within a week of getting this. We have an opportunity now, a brief one. He'll be distracted by what we're about to do here in Montagn—it will draw him in. Take Mithranar away from him before he even realises what's happening... and when he does, it will be to find Montagn has slipped from his grasp too. I will win this war for you, but you have to claim your country, Cuinn.

Love always,

Talyn

Windsong scratched his nose. "Interesting."

"She's barking mad," Theac growled.

"She has a point, though." Lyra tried not to quail in the face of Theac's scowl, but didn't quite succeed. "Factoring in the three or four days it took for Plummet to fly here, the Ciantar is probably hitting the first slave camp around about now. Within a week, she'll probably have freed another two camps, if all goes well. Azrilan will be focusing on dealing with that threat."

Andres shrugged. "I guess this should have been the plan from the beginning."

Cuinn began pacing, running a hand through his hair. "We're not ready to move."

"We could get the Wolf army into the underbelly of the palace like we planned within three days," Windsong said. "Kingcouncil is in six days. It could be done."

"We still need the names of the Falcon officers most loyal to us, not to mention those that need subduing along with Brightwing," Cuinn said.

"I'll supervise the transfer of Wolves into the palace, then I'll go to Nightdrift. We'll send Ehdra to Goldfeather tomorrow," Theac said. "We can have those names within a few days."

"You should stay here until the last minute, Prince Cuinn, in case the hounds catch word of our movement," Andres said. "Few people know how to get in here, and we can lock you down."

It was too soon. He didn't feel ready. If they rushed this and got it wrong, then everything they'd worked for would be gone in a blink. Several moments passed before he realised the three of them were staring at him, waiting for his decision.

Abruptly he wished Talyn was here. This was her forte, not this. But she'd told him to move, and he trusted her more than anyone else in the world.

"We'll start moving the Wolves in tomorrow."

CHAPTER 56

*T*alyn calmed FireFlare's restive movements with a touch, her gaze focused on the slave camp visible through the trees. A light rain tapped on the hood of her cloak. Zamaril sat silently at her side, watchful as always.

Five days since fleeing the Venador compound. Three days since re-assembling, not a single group lost, at their rendezvous point.

And now they were about to make their very first hit, at a location Talyn and Kaeri had chosen together. She wasn't sure what she was feeling as she stared down at the familiar wire fencing, the buildings, the front gate. The slaves working. They'd already rebuilt the front gates and guard posts either side of it.

"That's the camp you were held in?" Corrin rode up beside them.

"Yes."

"I vote for killing every guard in there."

Talyn glanced over at the Wolf talon. "I'm glad you're with me, Corrin."

He smiled, hard expression lightening. "So am I."

The excitement was already seeping through her—the anticipation of battle. The Venador soldiers were howling for blood on Kaeri's behalf and the Wolves, while calmer, were equally focused on exacting revenge. The Aimsir milled excitedly, ready to be let loose. Their half-legion of SkyRiders remained at their valley base to protect the villagers nearby in case of unexpected attack.

"*You're still a crazy person.*" Sari sighed through her mind. "*But I know this is you. Just be a little more cautious than usual, Tal.*"

Talyn smiled, hand pressing briefly against her stomach. From anxiety and fear, she'd settled into something approaching cautious wonder and matching nervousness. She wasn't going to do anything that would put her child in danger.

Hoofbeats sounded as Kaeri and Saniya rode up with Ariar. Kaeri's sharp green eyes raked over her. "The command is yours, Talyn."

Talyn blinked in surprise. They'd already planned and agreed on the attack strategy the day before, but she'd expected Kaeri would take command of the actual fight.

"I'm no slouch, but you're a tactical genius and the best fighter I've ever seen. Let's get this done."

"I like her," Ariar commented.

Saniya snorted.

A smile spread over Talyn's face as she turned, her gaze taking in the forested slope around them where four hundred Venador cavalry, fifty Wolves and a hundred-odd Aimsir were poised.

Then she faced back down the hill, lifted her arm, and sent a bright sapphire energy burst flying into the sky before kicking FireFlare into a gallop. "GO!"

The mare was as excited as Talyn to be in the midst of battle again, and she thundered down the slope towards the compound with a burst of speed that left Talyn's eyes watering and Corrin and Zamaril quickly falling behind.

Behind them a series of howls broke out, echoing through the forest. They held a hungry note, predators anticipating the hunt.

And then the Montagni cavalry burst out of the trees behind her. Their bellows of challenge added to the cacophony of howling and the Aimsir whoops as they let their horses loose at the rear.

Despite the shock of the sudden appearance of a large assault force bearing down on them, the soldiers in their posts at the main gates moved quickly. Warning bells began ringing through the compound, and figures moved as they reached for arrows to nock their bows.

Talyn waited as the archers took aim.

She waited until they drew.

Then she dropped the reins, gripped with her knees, and thrust both palms outwards. Blue sapphire sparked in the dull morning and two bursts ploughed into each of the posts.

In seconds, more brightly coloured bursts began exploding; Tirina, Nirini, and Kiran, swooping down from above to contribute their own warrior magic.

The gates blasted open seconds before FireFlare reached them, and Talyn gathered up the reins. Mud sprayed from her mare's hooves as Talyn pulled her to a halt in the clearing beyond. Around them, slaves filing out of the mess hall to begin their day's work stared in astonishment.

"I am Talyn Ciantar of Mithranar!" she cried at the top of her lungs. "And with me is Kaeri Venador, rightful ahara of Montagn. We are here to free you!"

There was a moment of shocked silence as the slaves stared, not comprehending her words.

And then the Venador cavalry thundered through the gates, led by Kaeri and Saniya. At a few crisp shouts from Talyn, they divided neatly into smaller groups to spread through the compound. The bells resumed, only adding to the clamour.

The Aimsir rode to surround the fence line and cut off any guards seeking to escape.

It wasn't long before the well-trained and disciplined Montagni soldiers began to scramble in defence. The Berserkers roared as their battle rage took hold.

"Make for the field!" Talyn shouted to the slaves. "Go straight there! Tell everyone you see, make for the field."

With that, the Wolves swept into the camp, Corrin at their head. The core of their force made directly for the largest concentration of slaves, surrounding them in a protective formation and helping to shepherd them towards the field. The rest moved to intercept the approaching Montagni soldiers.

Talyn scanned the area, kicking FireFlare into a gallop when she spotted a group of archers emerging onto the roof of the eating hall. From there they were in position to fire on the moving slaves and Wolves protecting them.

Talyn steered FireFlare towards the building, turning the mare to gallop alongside the outer wall. Then, she kicked her feet free of the stirrups and rose until she was standing in the saddle. Judging her moment, she *leapt* upwards.

She landed on the roof in a graceful crouch. Un-slinging her bow, she was up and firing arrows into the gathering archers as she ran across the roof towards them. Spotting her, one of them barked an order and several turned to begin firing at Talyn. She lowered the bow and ignited her energy shield a mere second before the first arrows reached her.

Undaunted, they drew swords and edged towards her as a disciplined group. Talyn drew her daggers and engaged the first man, forced to duck and weave at lightning speed to avoid their thrusts. She took one man down, but sustained a burning slash to her arm in doing so.

Then, boots thudded on the roof beside her and Zamaril was there. He waded into the fight with his sword, all quick moves and skill, and together they killed the remaining soldiers.

"Thanks," Talyn told him, catching her breath.

He scowled. "If you could wait for me to catch up next time, that would be great."

She flashed him a smile. "I was doing fine."

They moved to the edge of the roof to survey the compound. The attack seemed to be going well. They'd had the element of surprise, so that even though there were over a hundred soldiers resident in the camp, they hadn't been able to gather into a sufficient force before the Venador cavalry was there to tear through them.

Hundreds of slaves were already filling the training field, protected by her Wolves. The Berserkers fought on, though, undeterred by the superior number of their enemy. The Venador cavalry were fighting a bloody battle to try and contain them.

"They'll come after us," Zamaril said.

"Not if we kill them all."

He glanced at her.

"There's a time for mercy, Zamaril, but this isn't it. We can't afford soldiers escaping here to sound the alarm and come after us. Our force is too small. The stakes too high."

"I wasn't arguing," he murmured.

Talyn shook her head. "We're still going to be vulnerable. We'll have to leave here on foot—there aren't anywhere near enough horses stabled here for all the slaves. Even if none of the guards escape it will only be a day or so before the nearest village misses visits from off duty soldiers and raises the alarm."

"We'll be back in the mountains by then, and with a surprise waiting for any pursuers," he said, voice ringing with confidence.

Talyn nodded. "Come on, let's get down there."

She and Zamaril dropped down from the roof and re-mounted. They killed more soldiers from horseback as they rode to where the slaves were gathering.

"It went well," Saniya said gruffly as they rode up to her.

Thudding hooves signaled the arrival of Kaeri. Mud and blood splattered her face and clothes but she looked unharmed. "We need to start them moving. My cavalry can ensure the soldiers here are taken care of before bringing up the rear."

"I'm going on ahead to make sure there aren't any surprises waiting along our escape route," Talyn said.

Kaeri nodded acknowledgement of that and turned her horse to begin issuing orders to form up for departure.

TALYN RODE ahead of the slow-moving trail of escaped slaves for the rest of the morning and afternoon. This part of Montagn was only lightly inhabited, and the route Kaeri and Saniya had picked out stayed clear of main roads and villages.

The rain kept up a light drizzle before fading as dusk fell. Satisfied that they weren't going to accidentally stumble across a convoy of soldiers, Talyn rode back along the trail she'd left at a gallop.

It was close to midnight when she rode into the camp the army had set up. The slaves were clustered together in a clearing, and several Wolves roamed the surrounding woods on watch. Those not on watch-duty were passing out water and food rations to the slaves.

"Tal. I've got Aimsir scouts out in a ten-mile radius. We'll know anything that's coming at us well before it gets here." Ariar fell into step with her.

"Good."

"Anything?" Kaeri looked up as Talyn and Ariar approached.

"All clear," Talyn said, glancing around. "You've made good time."

"We'll be much slower tomorrow," she said. "The slaves were full of adrenalin and excitement today because of the escape, but they're already tiring and we haven't got a lot of food for them."

"It's a three-day journey to where we want to go; I don't think pursuit can catch up to us before that." Talyn hoped she was right.

Saniya joined them. "If they do, a group of us can ride back and harry them a little."

"My Aimsir can handle that if necessary," Ariar said confidently.

"Nobody should be treated like that." Corrin gestured to where the slaves sat huddled, jaw tight, his glance flicking to the slave tattoo on Zamaril's cheek. "It makes my stomach turn, the thought of these people being treated like sheep."

Kaeri glanced away. "It's time for me to talk to them."

Talyn lingered in the shadows with Zamaril, Corrin, Ariar and Saniya while Kaeri went to stand amongst the slaves. She estimated over a thousand had escaped with them, though nobody had had time yet for a full head count. The murmur of conversation between those who had enough energy for it slowly died when they recognised who was walking amongst them.

Eventually Kaeri came to a halt in the centre of the huddle. "I am Kaeri Venador, daughter of Shonin Venador. I claim the Montagni throne, and I ask for your help to support that claim." She paused.

Even now, it was hard for her to turn away from centuries of Montagni tradition. "In return I promise to end slavery in Montagn."

Whispers rustled through the night air, and not just from the slaves. Although Kaeri had made her position clear to her family and the cavalry that rode with them understood it, it still made them uneasy. Talyn wished Cuinn were here with his song magic to help smooth any lingering resentment.

She hoped he'd received her message. That he trusted her enough to do as she'd urged him. Azrilan couldn't focus on both countries at once—forcing him to split his attention would give them a significant advantage.

"You have tonight to decide. Tomorrow morning, you can either march with us into the mountains and help me fight for the throne and the freedom of every other slave out there. Or you can leave and make your own way. The decision is yours, nobody here will try and force you to follow me."

With that, she turned and left them to think.

TWO DAYS LATER, as the cavalry and approximately seven hundred slaves slowly wended their way higher into the more isolated terrain of the mountains, winged Wolf scouts reported a large squad of Montagni cavalry hot on their trail.

Talyn reined FireFlare in beside the column of people and horses and stared up at the higher peaks rearing above. Rain had persisted since their escape but this morning had dawned with blue skies and sunlight.

"They'll be on us within a couple of full-turns," Tirina warned.

Talyn rode at a gallop down the column, Tirina swooping behind, until reaching Kaeri, Ariar, Saniya and her Wolf talons at the rear. Their expressions tightened as she passed on Tirina's news. "Let's move all the Wolves back here as a buffer to protect the slaves," Talyn said.

"The cavalry pursuing us will struggle on these narrow paths and steep inclines," Kaeri warned. "They are no Aimsir, nor are they House Venador."

"I'm aware." Talyn slid her gaze to Ariar. "Time for you to ride, Horselord."

JUST OVER A FULL-TURN LATER, Talyn sat FireFlare at the rear of the marching column, on a flat plateau that provided a perfect view of the foothills. Behind, Kaeri's force wound its way ever higher into the peaks. Below her, handpicked members of the Venador cavalry were using their superior knowledge of the mountain paths to lead the Aimsir at the pursuing Montagni to intercept them in a flanking maneuver.

"Sitting this one out, Ciantar?" Zamaril struggled to hide the puzzlement in his voice.

After exerting both herself and her magic in the attack on the camp only a handful of days ago, Jystar had stridently warned against participating in this one. She'd accepted his advice with reluctance, confident Ariar and his Aimsir could succeed without her. She glanced at Zamaril. Glanced away. "I'm pregnant."

At first there was only a faint coughing sound from Zamaril's direction. When she gathered enough courage to look at him, it was to find the thief gaping at her, ears pink, eyes rounder than she'd ever seen them.

"I don't want to hear a word about it," she snapped. "And you're not to say anything to anyone."

"Jystar..." he managed.

"Is keeping a close eye."

He nodded. Closed his mouth. Then laughed.

She swore for the umpteenth time she was going to murder him. Then, her attention returned to the battle beginning to unfold below.

The Montagni remained disciplined when they found themselves hit from both sides by whooping Aimsir. Those on the outside raised shields to help protect the group from arrows. They didn't halt to fight, but instead urged their horses to a faster pace.

Talyn shifted in the saddle, worried. But the Aimsir eventually broke through the outer shielding of the cavalry and then the fight dissolved into the chaos of a normal battle. The Venador cavalry closed in around them like a noose, keeping any from escaping.

And then it was done.

"This might actually work, Ciantar," Zamaril murmured.

Sari roused. *"Azrilan won't take this lying down."*

"No, he won't," Talyn replied. *"You've been gone a while."*

"I'm always here when you need me."

"That's true." There was no sinking panic at Sari's absences anymore. She'd finally grown to trust that her partner would always be there, one way or the other. *"Azrilan will make his counter move soon. We just need to be ready for it."*

CHAPTER 57

"*E*verything okay, Your Highness?" Lyra asked.

"I'm just a little uneasy." Something was prickling at his magic. It had been all night—ever since finally joining his army inside the bowels of the palace. At first he'd put it down to restless dreams, but dawn hadn't brought any relief.

"No wonder." She smiled. "A hundred Wolves and thirty Falcons are crammed into the lower levels of the palace and could be stumbled across at any moment."

Cuinn chuckled. "When was the last time any of the winged folk came down this low?"

Lyra's smiled widened. "We're more likely to get eaten by tawncats."

Those had stayed away so far as well—although venturing through the forest from the Vengeance compound to climb up into the citadel from below had made for a daunting journey. Cuinn wasn't sure whether it was due to luck or Jasper's presence, but whatever it was he was grateful for it.

Two more days until Kingcouncil. It felt like too long.

"Andres says almost everyone is organised." Lyra seemed to read his thoughts again. "We have the Falcon names and their likely locations."

"Your Highness?" Ehdra stuck his head in the doorway. "Lord Nightdrift is here."

Cuinn frowned. "Show him in. Is the Falcon around?"

"He's out checking on our watch posts. Shall I fetch him?"

"No, leave us to it. Thank you."

Ehdra saluted, standing back to let Nightdrift enter the room before leaving it and closing the door behind him.

The man looked much older since the death of his son, with grey threading his black hair and some of the shine gone from his scarlet wings. He still held a sour expression, but he'd done everything Cuinn had asked of him so far. Or at least he'd said he had.

"I thought we'd agreed you wouldn't come down here," Cuinn said, frowning. "Theac could have brought back any urgent information you had."

"I haven't seen him," Nightdrift said. Tension filled his stance.

Cuinn stopped the cold fingers of fear before they paralyzed him completely. "What do you mean?"

"I haven't seen any of your Wolves in days." Nightdrift's gaze narrowed. "You sent him to me recently?"

Cuinn shared a glance with Lyra, who'd paled. "Last night. I'm sure he just got stuck getting back here unseen in daylight hours." He spoke the words to reassure Nightdrift, whose fear was threatening to spill over. "I take it you have something important for us?"

"Swiftwing received a message in the middle of a dinner he was hosting last night. He and Irial went out, didn't come back. I haven't seen them all morning."

"Do you normally see Tarich that frequently?" The heads of the Nightdrift and Swiftwing families had never gotten along well.

"It's odd, that's all." Nightdrift's jaw was clenched.

Nightdrift was a song mage. If Tarich's unaccountable absence had brought him all the way down here, risking his life, it wasn't for no reason.

Cuinn didn't let any of his unease show. "Tirin Goldfeather is still safe?"

"Yes." A jerky nod. "I saw him before coming down here."

"Two days, Nightdrift. We move as planned during Kingcouncil. Everything will be fine until then."

Nightdrift nodded, glanced around. "Are you sure you're strong enough?"

No. "Absolutely."

"I'll see you there, Prince Cuinn."

"You remember my instructions?" Cuinn wanted to make sure.

"No violence unless strictly necessary." Nightdrift barked a laugh. "You don't have to worry on that score. None of the lords with us want to risk their feathers."

Cuinn wanted it to be bloodless. If he walked into the council meeting and convinced the lords to stand down, he hoped to subdue the WingGuard without a fight. Then it would just be a matter of Talyn winning in Montagn and bringing Mithanis back for a vote on the crown.

But he needed to wait. For the Wolves to be in position to surround the council chamber, for his old Shadowhawk network and Vengeance to be ready to either fight or stand down.

Even then, he had to prepare himself for the fact it would come to violence. His Wolves might have to kill. They might die.

And he would have to be strong enough to bear it.

Once the door closed behind Nightdrift, Cuinn forced himself to wait long enough for the man to get well away. The door had barely shut when Jasper rose from the corner where he'd been sleeping and began to pace.

Cuinn's patience snapped. He hauled the door open, looking at the nearest Wolf. "Dorsan, where is Talon Parksin?"

"I'm not sure, Your Highness."

"Find him. Now."

.   .   .

CUINN, watching the morning turn into afternoon and then evening out the window, turned to study the pacing tawncat. "What is it, Jasper?"

Jasper flicked green eyes in his direction and let out a little hiss. Cuinn stilled.

Something was worrying his friend.

Clouds scudded across the sky from the west, bringing nightfall early. They were firmly in the middle of monsoon season, but the rain had died off since early morning. Maybe more rainfall was coming and that's what was bothering Jasper.

But he was uneasy too. And Nightdrift had come all the way down, risking his neck to do so.

A knock came at the door and Dorsan poked his head in. He looked worried.

"You can't find him?"

"Nobody's seen him since he left to meet Nightdrift last night."

Fear took a stranglehold on Cuinn's chest. Lyra moved across the room to talk to Dorsan; she was using her song magic to try and calm them both. "Dorsan, send someone to let Andres and Len know Talon Parksin might be missing. Ask them to keep a lookout for him."

Dorsan saluted and left.

"I'm going to look for him," Cuinn said, striding for the door.

"You can't." Lyra looked horrified at the thought. "The hounds—"

"Stop me." Cuinn slammed the door behind him.

THAT NIGHT, for the first time in a long time, Cuinn donned the mask of the Shadowhawk. A long shapeless cloak swung around his quick strides, though he needed far less glamour now he no longer needed to hide the bulge of his wings. For anyone looking, his features wore their scruffy human visage, and shadows dogged his footsteps. He kept the mask in his pocket, just in case, part of him craving the feel of it sliding up over his mouth and nose.

Despite his panic and fear, he took his usual circuitous route through the Poor Quarter, then over the Rush and into the Market Quarter to ensure nobody was following or paying undue attention to him.

The city *felt* different than he remembered. The air of unease, of danger, that had always permeated the deepest reaches of the Poor Quarter had spread further, into the other quarters. Fewer people walked the streets at this time of night, and more Patrolmen were obvious, standing on street corners or patrolling in pairs.

His steps slowed as he approached his destination. He leaned against the corner of the alley wall, drawing the shadows close around him to carefully erase himself from sight.

Then he watched.

A few people passed, a man drawing a cart. Two Patrolmen who didn't even look his way.

After a quarter-turn, he was satisfied he hadn't been followed, and that nobody was watching the alley from *outside*.

Which meant if a trap had been laid, it was waiting for him inside. But they would never expect him to come alone like this—if they were even expecting him at all. He might be completely wrong in his wild guess.

Gripping firmly to the shadows, he edged around the brick wall and into the alley. He used every inch of song magic he possessed to scan the area for emotions of any kind. He sensed nothing at all.

Painfully slowly, remaining wrapped in darkness, he slid along the wall, feeling his way with his palms, magic poised and ready. When he reached the loose brick—the space behind it where he and Navis had always left messages for each other—he cautiously pulled it out.

A tiny scroll of parchment sat inside.

Cuinn's heart thudded. If there was an ambush, now it would be sprung.

But nothing jumped out of the shadows at him. Heart still racing, skin slick with sweat, he pushed the brick back in and just as slowly edged his way out of the alley.

Once he was several blocks away and confident he hadn't been followed, he stopped and unrolled the parchment, using the light of a nearby street lamp to read it.

Our hounds have your Wolf. Give yourself up at the palace, by sunset tomorrow, or we kill him.

You don't come, we capture and kill another of your beloved Wolves.

I would hurry if I were you. The sooner you come, the less damaged your Wolf will be.

He crumpled the paper in his palm and gasped out a breath. Fear and panic were so strong he had to lean against the wall for a moment simply to hold himself together. Hatred churned with the fear in his stomach... for his brother. For Tarcos's hounds.

It took a long time for him to pull himself together, to be able to focus enough to hold his glamour and walk steadily. Once he could he started making his way back.

To deliver the worst news they could possibly have received.

A horrified silence filled the room as Windsong and his talons read the note. The Falcon looked grim. Andres and Lyra had tears sheening their eyes and held themselves so rigidly it was as though they were literally trying to hold themselves together. Jasper paced relentlessly, tail lashing from side to side.

"Kingcouncil is the day after tomorrow," Cuinn said, managing somehow to speak.

"If you give yourself up, they'll never let you get near Kingcouncil," Andres said carefully. "They'll kill you."

"Not if we get Talon Parksin out before then," Lyra said. "We've got two hundred Wolves here."

"We don't have any idea where he's being held," Windsong said carefully. "And Azrilan's hounds have him. That many Shadows, Armun and Berserkers... that's a deadly force to try and get past given we can expect Falcons will be guarding him too."

Fury flared on Lyra's face. "We can't just leave him to be killed."

"We don't have a choice." Andres looked sick. "The Falcon is right."

Cuinn lifted a trembling hand to run through his hair. "I'll have to give myself up. Azrilan couldn't kill me before. Maybe he won't now."

"Azrilan's not here. It's Swiftwing running the show." Lyra's shoulders sagged.

"Think about what Talon Parksin would want. He's your bodyguard, Prince Cuinn, he would never want you to give yourself up to save him," Windsong said. He held Cuinn's stare, firm and unremorseful, but the hint of song magic he added to his voice was full of empathy.

"What about their threat to take another Wolf if I don't show up?" Cuinn rasped.

"We'll keep them all locked down in here until it's time to move. No foraging, nothing. We can keep them safe," Windsong said.

Cuinn stood abruptly, his chair going flying with the force of his movement. Misery churned in his stomach. "I *can't*. I can't do it. I'm not the man that can let someone else die for him."

With a single sweep of his wings, Windsong stood in front of Cuinn, his hands reaching out to grip Cuinn's shoulders. "You are the man who has *always* put the people of Mithranar first. You are the man who has *always* sought to protect those people, no matter what obstacles were placed in your way. You are a king, Cuinn."

His shoulders crumpled and he almost burst into tears right there. He wished Talyn were with him. He needed her quiet strength more than anything. He loved Theac, with all his heart he loved that man. So did she. Even the thought of the look on her face, her grief, if Theac died... "I don't think I'm strong enough, Anrun."

"Then Azrilan wins," Windsong said quietly.

Andres cleared his throat into the silence. "I'll go and search for him. If we can find out where he is before sunset tomorrow, then maybe we can get him out."

"If you go out alone, you'll be a target too, Talon," Windsong said quietly.

Andres' dark gaze shifted to meet Cuinn's. "I would do anything for Theac, for the chance at finding him. But if they catch me, then you let me go, you let them have me. Is that clear, Your Highness? This is my choice and I make it willingly."

"Thank you, Andres." Cuinn cleared his throat, his heart feeling like it was rending into a thousand pieces. "Go."

CHAPTER 58

Talyn strode up to the tiny campfire outside her tent, Zamaril a shadow at her shoulder as always, and dropped wearily onto the log that had been placed there to use as a seat.

As always when she had a moment to herself, her thoughts turned to Cuinn. A month he'd been back in Mithranar, hopefully moving the Wolves and their other supporters into place.

"You need to eat." Zamaril shoved a hunk of bread roll and bowl of steaming stew into her hands.

She took the offering without complaint and ate hungrily. Being pregnant seemed to have doubled her appetite, and she gave her belly a wary glance. At some point she was going to have to stop riding and fighting.

Not yet. That was a few more months away.

The sound of an eagle shrieking had everyone in the vicinity leaping to their feet. Talyn scanned the darkening skies, taking a few moments to spot the roving specks high in the sky. Shortly after that one of them spotted their camp and quickly spiraled lower. The other eagles fell in behind.

She ran, Zamaril only a step behind, to where the four eagles had found open space to land on the eastern edge of their haphazard camp. The lead rider was already jumping down from his eagle's back, and Talyn ran straight at him.

"Soar!" She collided with him, throwing her arms around his neck.

The big man caught her easily, crushing her tight. "Talyn!"

She matched his wide smile. "You're well! Everyone else? The invasion fleet?' Sadness flickered over his face, and her breath caught, heart plummeting. "We didn't—"

"No." He waved away her fear. "The fleet is no more, and in fact in the end, we had to do very little."

Her gaze roved his face, reading the sadness still there. "What happened?"

"Rados felt it was not the Twin Thrones' responsibility to lose lives defending against a fleet protected by his nievers," Soar said heavily. "He sent word to the Callanan in Acleu. The Firthlander ships carrying the nievers to protect the Montagni war fleet were anchored in the Acleu port with the fleet readying for departure. The Callanan managed to get out to one of the Firthlander ships and show Rados's orders to the captain."

She frowned. "What were his orders?"

Soar took a steadying breath. "To attack and destroy the fleet. The legion of niever-flyers attacked without warning... they destroyed it, but their ships were destroyed in the fight and the nievers had nowhere to retreat to."

Talyn looked away, swallowing. "They were killed."

Soar rubbed a hand over his face. "Honourable and dutiful to their bones, Firthlanders. They saved the lives of our warriors in honouring our new alliance and taking out that fleet."

Tears pricked at her eyes. Tarcos had been a manipulative, power hungry monster. His people hadn't deserved to die for it. But they had.

She took his arm, blinking away the tears. "Come through, get some rest and something to eat."

"Things are on track here?" Soar asked as they walked.

"We attacked our second slave camp six days ago, and added just over seven hundred fighters to our army in doing so," she said. "Is Aeris well?"

"He's safely back in Port Lachley, throwing himself into tackling the fallout from the war." Soar smiled again.

She relaxed a little. "And you brought legions too?"

"Not as many as I'd hoped," Soar warned. "The fighting has been nasty and long. I've got a lot of wounded and tired—birds and riders both. But a hundred of the healthiest and freshest are moored just south of Montagn, out of the shipping channels in the hopes they won't notice us. McTavish got fresh Aimsir ashore with the help of your people in Acleu and they're already heading through the mountains to join up with those you have here. We've been out scouting for a place to set camp."

"Cousin!" Ariar came striding over, blue eyes alight. "You brought me more Aimsir?"

"I certainly did." Soar chuckled, and they hugged briefly. "Where's Cuinn?"

"Back in Mithranar," she said briskly. "Preparing things on his end. One way or another, this is all going to be over soon."

THEY'D BARELY REACHED the command tent when running feet sounded outside and Kaeri and Saniya burst in.

"Good, you're here," Kaeri said briskly. Talyn wasn't sure whether that was directed at her or Soar. "We have a problem."

Talyn glanced between them—Saniya looked worried. Her cousin *never* looked worried. "What is it?"

"Azrilan isn't in Arataire."

"Where is he?" she asked quietly.

"Mithranar." Saniya spoke tightly. "It appears he's been gone for at least a week. Our informants didn't learn of it until this morning. He deliberately hid his departure."

Soar frowned. "Why would he do that unless..."

"The prince of games has a trick planned," Talyn murmured, beginning to pace. "He's worked out what we're doing."

"Even if he has, how could going to Mithranar help him?" Kaeri asked with a frown.

"You continue to underestimate how devious he is!" Mithanis burst into the tent suddenly, face as usual dark with anger. "Azrilan is making a play. He thinks if he sneaks up on Cuinn in Mithranar, he can neutralise that threat first—turn the coup you're planning around on you. Then he can turn his full attention to holding Montagn."

Talyn went cold. "Shit, why didn't I think of that?"

"Because you think you're the smartest tactician in this war, and you're not," Mithanis said flatly. "Azrilan has met you step for step every way, Talyn Dynan."

"At least he didn't successfully manipulate her for decades," Zamaril burst out furiously.

"There's more!" Saniya shouted over the outbreak of angry voices. "He didn't go alone. He took Berserkers with him—two hundred of them. If you add those to the thousand-strong WingGuard, he's got a force that dwarfs your Wolves and rebels."

"Azrilan is smart. He wouldn't have moved unless he'd learned where our rebel force is and what they were planning," Talyn said, glancing at Mithanis. He nodded tightly.

Shit.

"He'll have to move fast." Soar spoke into the heavy silence that followed. "You tell me he's no fool, but if he leaves Montagn for too long while you're all roaming around freeing slaves, he *is* a fool."

"I agree." Mithanis spoke. "It will be a clean strike, aimed to wipe out the Wolves, Cuinn and any of his supporters left in Mithranar. He might have moved against them already."

Talyn froze. "I'm going back, tonight. Soar, you'll take me. We'll bring the SkyRiders with us."

"You can't just leave," Kaeri protested. "That's what he wants. You'll be walking into a trap and letting the effort here fall apart."

"No." Talyn shook her head. "What he's done is clever and unexpected, but it's also a big gamble. We have to beat the prince of games at his own game. We're going to double down."

"How?"

"You are going to abandon the mountains and ride for Arataire tonight. Take the Aimsir, your Venador soldiers and the slaves willing to fight with you. Hit any slave camp on the way and bring them with you too. If you move hard and fast you can be there in three or four days. Initiate a spill and take Arataire before they know what's coming. That way, even if Azrilan succeeds in Mithranar, he'll come back to find his capital taken out from underneath him."

"Taking the capital doesn't give us the country," Kaeri argued.

"No, but it gives you a defensible stronghold and a powerful symbolic victory that the other Houses will be swayed by." Saniya looked at Kaeri. "And it's exactly what Azrilan did, right? So the other Houses can't claim to have a problem with it."

"Not only that, but you'll have almost five thousand slaves living free and passing the word to other slaves throughout the country of what will happen if they support you on the throne," Talyn added.

Kaeri turned to Mithanis. "Time to hold to your word."

"No." He shook his head, for once not sounding angry or unreasonable, just firm. "Time for you to hold to yours. If Cuinn is making a move for the Mithranan throne, then I'm going with you, Dynan. You promised."

Talyn hesitated. Took a breath. Wanted to refuse. She could... she could hold him here, a prisoner, keep him out of the fight. It's what she *should* do, what she would do if it were up to her.

But it wasn't what Cuinn would want.

"You come with me, then once the throne is sorted, no matter which way it goes, you come straight back to Arataire to stand by Kaeri. You hold to *your* word."

He held his hand out, astonishing her. "I swear it."

She didn't take it. Couldn't. Not after everything that had happened. Instead she turned to Kaeri. "Start the spill. If all goes as we hope in Mithranar, Azrilan won't be returning to challenge you."

"Good. Because it will be difficult enough to win even without him here."

"I'll leave all my Wolves with you under Liadin's command, as well as Leviana and Cynia." She winced inwardly at the thought of *that* argument. "They're the best bodyguards you could hope for and their sole job will be keeping you safe." This would all be lost if Kaeri died; she trusted nobody else to rule Montagn. "The Aimsir will stay too with Ariar—if you don't mind?"

"Happy to do my part, Cousin." Ariar flashed her a smile.

"Zamaril, Corrin, Jystar, you'll come with me." Talyn wanted those she trusted most at her back. And Cuinn's. Relief crossed their faces, and she realised the three men had been prepared to fight her on staying behind.

Kaeri turned to stride from the tent, paused to glance back at Soar. "You brought your forces to bolster mine. I won't forget it, Lord Dumnorix."

He bowed his head. "King Aeris asked me to remind you that he intends to honour his promise to provide whatever support Montagn needs to transition to a country not based on slave labour."

She gave a grim smile. "One step at a time. We march for Arataire and start the spill."

CHAPTER 59

*C*uinn sat, his back against the wall, knees drawn up against his chest, staring sightlessly at the opposite wall as the sun slowly set behind the trees of the forest outside the window.

A small knock came at the door.

"Come in," he rasped.

It was Andres. His face was drawn, eyes dark. He gave a little shake of his head. Tears filled Cuinn's eyes and he had to look away.

"I'm so sorry, Prince Cuinn."

"It's not your fault, Andres." It was his. He'd started this whole thing. Talyn had warned him there would be violence and death, but this… he wasn't sure he could survive it.

Andres hesitated. "What are you going to do?"

"I'm going to sit here and stare at the wall until the sun sets over the horizon. And I'm going to spend every single second of that time fighting bitterly to stop myself walking up to the palace and handing myself in."

The Wolf said nothing to that, but a moment later, he slid down the wall on Cuinn's left, crossing his legs, their arms just touching. Jasper finally stopped his pacing and came to curl up on Cuinn's other side. The soft snort he let out was confused. He could clearly see how distressed Cuinn was but didn't know what to do about it.

As the light through the window slowly faded, Cuinn's stomach and chest grew tighter and tighter, into a knot so tense he could barely suck breath in.

Silent tears streamed down his face.

And he willingly let another man die for him.

He wasn't sure how much time had passed, but the room had grown fully dark when the distant sounds of running feet roused him. At the same moment Jasper uncurled and leapt to his feet, snarling.

Beside Cuinn, Andres shook himself and scrubbed at his damp face. "That doesn't sound right."

Cuinn hauled himself to his feet and strode to the doorway, hauling it open. Jasper took the opportunity to weave between his legs and shoot out into the hallway beyond. He looked back at Cuinn as if to say, *aren't you coming?*

Lyra, outside the door, turned to him. Her eyes were suspiciously red too, but he also picked up the unease in her song magic. He frowned. "What is it?"

"Something is off. I—"

Running feet cut him off, followed by the distant sounds of shouting. Cuinn started running, Lyra and Andres following suit.

They hadn't made it very far before running into Ehdra and Windsong. They were carrying a bleeding and pale Nightdrift between them. The older winged man sagged in their hold and was losing a frightening amount of blood from a wound in his chest. Fear and pain were bleeding out of him and both Cuinn and Lyra staggered backwards from the force of it.

"Nirina?" Andres snapped, asking for their best healer after Jystar.

"Dorsan went for her. Ehdra was on guard up on the higher level and saw him staggering towards the entry. Nightdrift managed a few words while he was more alert. I've sent Kiran to do a quick sweep of the area and confirm his news…" Windsong trailed off, face grim. "Azrilan is here, Your Highness. Falcons and Berserkers are sweeping through the citadel and Dock City. They're killing anyone they believe is linked to us."

"He… knows." Nightdrift gasped. His eyes rolled and he groaned in pain. "He has… Berserkers. Too many. The lords will never risk his wrath to join you now."

His heart plummeted. He'd sacrificed Theac only to be beaten anyway. There was no way to avoid a fight now. Everything in him just wanted to sink down in that hallway and cry like a baby.

It was over.

Windsong looked at Andres. "Go, rouse and arm the Wolves!"

"And send them where? There are just two hundred of us, who do we focus on first?" Andres straightened.

Windsong looked at Cuinn, waiting for orders. He stared back, momentarily frozen by grief and shock. They needed Talyn here. She would know exactly what to do. Anxiety and fear and heartbreak threatened to crush him under their weight.

You are the man who always puts Mithranar first, no matter what.

He grabbed onto those words, flailed around until he found that determination that had always been there inside him. He gripped both with white-knuckled fists and used them to shove away the grief and fear and force himself to focus.

He'd gone to Mothduriem, become a fighter, learned to be strong, and he'd done it all for exactly this moment. When his brother once again threatened to crush him under the weight of despair… so that this time he could rise above that and fight back.

Violence it would have to be.

"Andres—send a small group into Dock City to rally the Shadowhawk network and Saniya's people. They're to fight and kill any Berserker they see. Windsong, you rally the rest to go and protect our allies. Goldfeather and Nightdrift's family first, then the families they named as likely to side with me." He had to assume Azrilan's Shadows or Armun had figured out who they were—they might already be dead. He took another steadying breath to fight off the urge to sink into despair. "Go!"

Andres and Windsong ran.

Nirini appeared then, almost bowled over by Windsong as he leapt into flight. Cuinn knelt before Nightdrift. The man's face was slack and his gaze was glassy, barely conscious. The strength of his emotion had faded, a bad sign.

"Nightdrift. Where is Azrilan?" he asked.

"Don't... know." Nightdrift gasped.

"Was he the one who did this to you? How much does he know?"

Nightdrift shuddered. "He... dinner Irial organised. Tried to escape... to warn you... got me..."

"Goldfeather?"

"Wasn't... there. I..." Nightdrift's eyes rolled back in his head. The blood seeping into the floor was making a spreading puddle despite Nirini's work.

"I've got him!" Nirini said as Nightdrift passed out completely this time, almost dropping to the floor. Her gaze turned to Lyra. "Stay with Prince Cuinn. I'll do what I can for Nightdrift."

"We have to keep you bunkered down here, Your Highness," Lyra said immediately. "Hopefully they won't find us and—"

"They're coming!" Kiran yelled down the corridor. "Heading down from the top levels."

Shit. Azrilan knew too much. This had been planned carefully. Of course his brother had planned for Cuinn not giving himself up.

"Go and tell Windsong and Andres they'll need to take the lower levels out," Cuinn shouted. "Be out of here before the Falcons get this far. Go!"

Cuinn rose to his feet and ran toward Jasper. The tawncat waited for him at the opposite end of the corridor. His breath rasped in his chest and his heart was beating too hard. The fear was threatening to get the best of him. He didn't know how they were going to get out of this, dispersed and fighting through Dock City and the citadel against superior numbers.

He couldn't leave those loyal to him unprotected. Couldn't leave them to be slaughtered. But his Wolves would be slaughtered helping them.

He wanted to scream.

They'd planned so carefully. Prepared. And it had all gone to hell. And Theac... a sob crawled up his chest, desperate to escape. His hands curled into fists at his sides as he fought the emotions down.

Lyra followed him as he took a series of stairways and walkways through the bowels of the citadel—one of his old Shadowhawk routes. The one he'd used to get in and out of Dock City undetected.

A beat of wings above had them both reaching for weapons, but it was just Windsong, landing a pace behind. "Your orders are passed," he said before Cuinn could protest. "And my talons know their jobs. I'm your Falcon. I'm not leaving your side, Prince Cuinn."

"Fine." He didn't have time to argue. He had to see what was going on for himself. Maybe then he could work out what to do.

If only Talyn were with him.

Eventually, sweat slicking his skin, muscles burning, he sprinted up a wide marble stairway and onto the top of the wall. He wasn't far from the wall walk; in fact he was standing almost at the mid-way point to Dock City, the waterfall pounding down into the Rush a good distance to his left.

Either side of him, Lyra and Windsong lifted into the air, ready to protect him if he were attacked.

The air was completely still, thick with the humidity of approaching rain. Not a whisper of a breeze. Nothing to impede the sound of the battle raging in Dock City below.

Falcons swept through the streets of the Poor and Dock Quarters, clearly searching for Shadowhawk or Vengeance safehouses. They burned as they went, pockets of them battling against residents, probably mostly ex-Vengeance network members. In that quick, frantic glance, it looked like City Patrolmen were fighting on both sides.

His chest heaved. Fear, pain, anger, hate, it all swirled up from the city, fed by the fighting.

And in the citadel too.

Howls broke out as the Wolves emerged from their hiding places, some out of the tunnel and into the streets of Dock City, others spreading through the citadel as they headed for the homes of the lords allied to Cuinn. The clang of steel ripped through the rapidly darkening sky, along with shouts of fear and pain.

It made him sick, watching Falcons and humans fighting each other, killing each other. They were all Mithranan. Countrymen. *His*.

And the Berserkers. He could see them now too. They cut down any resistance the humans put up with ruthless ease, too big and strong and manic once the battle rage was upon them.

It had to end.

All the pain. All the violence. All the hate. Azrilan had brought it with him, had nurtured it his entire life, had used Mithanis to grow it amongst the palace and the entire winged folk society. Had been allowed to do so by their mother and a weak Queencouncil.

Cuinn hadn't sacrificed Theac's life for this. For more hatred and bloodshed and violence. Talyn said it was necessary in war, and maybe it was, but he couldn't fight a war this way. It wasn't him. As strong as he'd gotten, as much as he'd hardened and steeled himself to be capable of this... he wouldn't do it.

He had to stop it. And he couldn't do that by using more violence and more hate.

Which left only one option open to him. His song.

At first it was just a humming under his breath. He slowly gathered his magic, blocking out the dark emotions hammering at him. Then he steadied his breathing... in and out.

In and out.

His focus sharpened. He gathered more and more of his magic.

He allowed himself to think of Theac. Of the man's scowl. His strength. His steady, unflagging loyalty. Of his love for *him*. He allowed that love and that grit and that fierce protectiveness to fill him.

Another breath and he dug deeper, finding everything there that he needed to power his magic. The need to help that had spurred the

Shadowhawk on, the shame that he hadn't been able to do more, the hope that Talyn had brought with her to Mithranar, the strength she'd taught him.

He tipped his head back and let his magic loose on the world.

He sang for Theac Parksin.

He wasn't sure what he was singing, couldn't have repeated the melody if someone asked him. But he *threw* his song out there. Jasper pressed against his leg, a solid weight, anchoring him to the ground as the magic roped through him.

His voice rose, grew stronger, louder, spread out into the sky and the air and the people around him. The wordless song turned into words.

Long ago in the dusk we came,
Mithranar through the cold and rain

And then another voice joined his, rich and deep and thrumming with magic. Cuinn glanced to the side where Windsong stood, head back, wings outstretched. He hadn't realised the man had such power.

A third voice weaved into the song, softer, more melodic, not quite as strong but used with obvious skill.

Lyra Songdrift.

As one, dear heart, as one.
We fly as one.

It hit those closest first, a group fighting on the street immediately below where they stood. When Cuinn's music reached them, clear through the still air, the fighting slowed.

A Falcon blinked. Lowered his sword and shook his head as if in puzzlement. His opponent didn't take advantage of the distraction. And then they stepped away, swords dropping. Cuinn let them go and moved on, eyes closed now as he buried himself in magic, finding the next battle, washing them in hope and light and the reluctance to fight.

A better world.

A better Mithranar.

Battle by battle, the fighting began to ease. Falcons and humans put down their swords.

And then a thunderclap sounded.

Cuinn reeled backwards as opposing magic slammed into him, cutting off his focus and making his voice falter. He took a rasping breath, opened his eyes.

Azrilan had come.

CHAPTER 60

*J*t was almost nightfall by the time the SkyRiders came in over the west of the citadel. Dark rain clouds had followed them in, cutting off the light as they flew and turning afternoon into dusk.

They were all tired, having flown directly from eastern Montagn without stopping to rest, but there'd been no time. Azrilan might already have attacked. Talyn rode with Soar on Hunter, while Mithanis, Corrin and Zamaril rode with other members of his legion close behind.

"We'll do a high level runover first," Soar spoke into her ear. "If all looks calm, we'll drop you at the compound they've been hiding in, then head north for the SkyReach to bunker down until we get word we're needed."

Talyn nodded.

The eagles came in low and fast to reduce the chance of being seen by any winged folk out on the evening thermals—not that there were any. The air was thick and still, not a single hint of a breeze. Even up in the air Talyn sweated.

Soar used the cover of the mountains behind Dock City to hide their approach. He leaned back, made a sharp hand gesture to the legions circling behind them. They broke off into groups, all but one soaring higher to allow Soar to scout first. Moments later Hunter soared through a narrow gap between two mountains and out over the citadel.

Talyn swore.

"Berserkers!" Soar pointed.

They were battling a large group of Wolves who looked like they were trying to get into one of the residential areas of the citadel. More fighting filled the walkways and the air around the palace.

And then the wall passed beneath them and she could see flames. Several fires lit up the Dock Quarter, and the light turned the evening orange. Smoke sat thick in the still air. More Falcons, Patrolmen, and citizens formed knots of fighting in the streets. Berserkers too.

Once they'd had a good look, Soar turned them sharply upwards and they flew above the smoke. Nobody seemed to have noticed the quick circling of an eagle high above them, which was no wonder given what was unfolding below. Talyn felt sick to her stomach.

Azrilan had beaten them there. And he'd turned her home into a battleground.

Where was Cuinn?

"We'll split the legions," Soar suggested. "Half to support your Wolves in the citadel and the other to provide cover down in Dock City. Maybe we can stem the bleeding."

Talyn banished her fear and thought quickly. "I can't think of anything better, but it's going to be almost impossible for your SkyRiders to pick out friend from foe down in Dock City."

Not to mention the thought of mowing down Falcons made her ill. They might be loyal to the wrong prince but that didn't mean they should be cut out of the sky by a foreign army.

"They're killing humans," Sari reminded her.

"They're just following orders."

"Those Berserkers are easy enough to spot. We'll just go for the big angry men wielding massive swords," Soar said. "We might be able to do something about those fires too—any thoughts on where we could pick up containers to carry water in?"

"I wouldn't risk your riders getting too close to the ground, not until the fighting is better contained."

It didn't take long for the Sky Chieftain to summon the legion and give them their orders. "Don't shoot unless you're certain they're the enemy. Focus on helping innocent lives if you can." He roared into the still air, hand signals repeating his orders.

Talyn turned to him. "We have to find Cuinn."

She was terrified for him. Absolutely sick with worry.

The legions cried out their affirmation, eagles adding their own challenges to the mix. Talyn settled back against Soar as his hands tightened on the harness, and then he was urging Hunter into a steep dive.

The closer they got to the fighting, the worse it looked. More Falcons were arriving in Dock City, and the Berserkers were mowing down anyone trying to attack them.

The SkyRiders dropped out of the sky, drawing bows and arrows as they plummeted. The eagles banked then, moving from a steep dive into a smooth glide that would allow their riders a better and more steady shot.

And then Talyn heard the music. A snatch of it on the still air.

It came from somewhere along the wall.

Cuinn's voice. Unmistakably Cuinn's voice. She craned her neck, listening as the music grew stronger. His magic filled the song, more potent than she'd ever felt it. And she knew at once what he was trying to do.

"Hold fire!" Talyn turned, screaming the order at the eagles closest behind them. "Hold!"

Soar didn't dispute her order. He lifted a hand, made a sharp gesture, and one by one the legion broke off the attack, swooping up into the sky. "What is it, Talyn?"

"He's trying to stop the fighting." Talyn scanned the top of the wall —it was almost completely dark now, and hard to make out individual figures. So she closed her eyes and focused on the sound of Cuinn's voice, allowing his magic to draw her to him.

Her eyes snapped open when she found him. Windsong and Lyra

hovered in the air above him, and they were singing too. Jasper stood at Cuinn's side, tail waving. But even as she watched, the magic cut off suddenly, and a dark-winged figure dropped out of the sky before Cuinn.

"Get me down there!" she bellowed at Soar.

He turned his eagle instantly, bringing Hunter to a graceful landing on top of the wall. Talyn tore the harness off before the eagle was down, jumping off and sprinting along the wall behind where Cuinn stood.

As she ran, she summoned her own magic.

Sapphire light flashed into existence around Cuinn, a bright beacon that highlighted him to the world as well as protecting him. Funneling more power into the shield, she pushed it outwards into the space between Cuinn and Azrilan, forcing the prince of games and his guards to take several steps backwards.

Cuinn glanced back, and instead of relief on his face at the sight of her, all she saw was terrible guilt and grief. "Talyn, his hounds have Theac."

She stumbled to a halt, her heart dropping into her stomach so fast the breath escaped her in a shocked gasp. Her hold on the shield wavered. "Where?"

"I don't know. They were going to kill him at sunset if I didn't give myself up."

And he hadn't. The torturous pain of his decision was stark in his voice and on his face. Tears welled in Talyn's eyes. She couldn't bear the thought of … not Theac. Her hands curled into fists so hard her nails drew blood.

Beyond them, Azrilan was snarling something at his Berserker guards, but there wasn't much they could do to get past her shield.

Cuinn's face crumpled at her reaction. "I'm sorry. I'm so sorry."

"You made the right decision." She stepped towards him, opening to his song magic so he could read her sincerity.

But she wasn't a king or a queen. She was a warrior. She didn't have to make the same decision. She didn't have to abandon one of her dearest and most trusted comrades.

She glanced sideways, where she knew Zamaril would be standing, then further behind to Corrin. "Zamaril and I will find Theac. Corrin, you go down and take control of our forces in Dock City."

"What about Prince Cuinn?" Corrin asked.

"This is my battle to fight," Cuinn responded before she could, glancing back through the shield towards Azrilan, who lifted a fist and sent his warrior magic flying at Talyn's shield. She winced at the impact, her shield shuddering, barely holding.

Talyn reached out to Cuinn, squeezed his hand. "Sing. I'll find Theac."

"He's not…" Cuinn's breathing hitched. "You know he's gone."

She bit her lip. "Yes. But I'm going to bring him home anyway."

A sad smile briefly crossed his face. "I'll see you later."

She searched his emerald gaze, pressed her forehead into his chest for a brief moment, then stepped away. He swallowed, straightened his shoulders, then he closed his eyes and began to sing again. Windsong and Lyra's voices quickly joined him.

Energy rapidly draining, Talyn let go of the sapphire shield. Azrilan's protective guard instantly moved towards Cuinn, the prince of games lifted his hand, and she faltered. If anything happened to Cuinn…

No. She had to trust him. Like he trusted her.

"I'll watch our cousin," Soar said, moving closer. "Go, do you what you need to do, Talyn."

"Thank you." She took a deep breath and turned to Zamaril. "Where do you think he is?" she asked.

"No idea. But I'm going to ask the first Falcon we find." Zamaril's expression was flat and hard. "And I'm not going to ask nicely."

CHAPTER 61

*W*ith Talyn's shield gone, Cuinn tried to focus on his magic and watching Azrilan at the same time. His brother stood less than ten paces away, eyes unwavering on his, humming rather than singing, but throwing every bit of song magic he had at Cuinn. The threat of Azrilan's warrior magic hung in the air between them, but for now he chose not to use it.

"Be ready to shield me," he said to Windsong anyway. "Do you know how?"

"I do." Windsong's voice was strained, but steady.

Cuinn took a steadying breath. "Lyra, Anrun, you hold the song. Let me handle Az."

A shiver of emotion from both winged folk signaled their agreement. Azrilan's lips curled in a snarl, and he made a sharp gesture with his left hand. The three Berserkers approaching cautiously drew their swords.

Cuinn refused to flinch. He held Azrilan's dark gaze, focused on his magic, on catching and containing the fear and despair and helplessness Azrilan was trying to push out. His brother was skilled, and strong.

But so was Cuinn.

Jasper was a blur of teeth and claws as he leapt forward to contend with the first Berserker. Amusement flashed in Azrilan's gaze as the second moved around the tawncat battling his companion and sped up when he saw Cuinn making no effort to defend himself. Windsong tensed at his side. Lyra's song faltered briefly.

And then an arrow slammed into the Berserker's heart. His eyes went wide, and he was dead in the next second, his massive body crumpling to the ground.

Cuinn glanced back to find Soar standing there, SkyRider bow already knocked with another arrow.

"Keep fighting, Cousin, I've got your back."

Nodding thanks, Cuinn returned to matching wills with his brother. Soar fired at the next Berserker, who took the arrow and kept coming with a roar of anger. Soar's third arrow buried itself in his eye. He fell almost right at Cuinn's feet. A heartbeat later Jasper tore the first Berserker's throat out with a vicious snarl.

Cuinn's music was growing louder, Azrilan's focus faltering as his bodyguards were slowly cut down.

He hadn't expected Soar to be there. Or the SkyRiders. His plan had been to take Cuinn by surprise while Talyn and his army were still in Montagn. The winged Wolves close enough to hear the music were joining in now too, their song spreading further as more and more voices swelled with magic and music.

We fly as one.

The wind will guide us home

"The prince of song indeed," Azrilan mused, calm and collected despite what was going on around him. "I wasn't sure you had it in you."

Cuinn read affection on Azrilan's face, and a sadness that surprised him. But both those emotions were almost entirely eclipsed by the calculating expression that replaced it.

"I can't say that it's good to see you again, Azrilan," he said.

"My offer still stands." Azrilan abruptly stopped his onslaught of magic, and Cuinn took a deep, steadying breath. Exhaustion roped through him. "Give yourself up now, and I'll let your Wolf free."

Cuinn didn't allow himself to hope. "You think I'm going to fall for that? You were going to kill him at sunset."

"I *was*." Azrilan shrugged. "But then it occurred to me that he was far more useful alive. I knew that my move on you would come as a surprise, but I also have a lot of respect for that Ciantar of yours. I couldn't see how she'd get here in time, but in case she did... well, I knew she'd choose her precious Wolf even if you wouldn't."

Dread took hold, strong enough that Azrilan could feel it. "You set an ambush."

"Two birds with one stone, as they say." Azrilan's smile widened. "And don't worry... I made sure to surround your Wolf with enough guards to take down even a warrior of her renown. I hope they hurry. He's not in good shape. I *may* have left him with a very hungry wild tawncat."

Cuinn didn't try to hide the guilt and fear he felt. It would have taken too much energy, energy he was going to need. Talyn had trusted him to take care of this. And he would trust her now. Despite the odds. So he took a deep, steadying breath. "You think it was the best decision to come here and face me with only a handful of Berserkers?"

"Your Wolves are occupied trying to *save* people, which is what I banked on." Scorn filled Azrilan's voice. "And our magic is evenly matched. I think those are good odds."

"Always the prince of games." Cuinn shrugged. "I think you bet wrong."

"You didn't kill Mithanis. You're not going to kill me." A cold smile spread over Azrilan's face.

"No." Cuinn glanced behind him, his song magic having warned him minutes earlier about who lurked back there. "But I think our brother might have a different view on the matter."

Mithanis appeared then, coming forward from where he'd loitered in the shadows behind Soar, who still held a drawn bow. "Hello, Az."

Mithanis stalked past Cuinn, sword raised, metal glinting. Shock and surprise rippled over Azrilan's face as he watched his brother come. "You, allied with Cuinn and the Ciantar? Impossible."

"Your Highness!" Windsong murmured, strain evident in his voice. For a moment his song hung in the dark sky, its echoes fading slowly.

Cuinn glanced down—and saw immediately what he meant. Flames licked over buildings and bitter fighting continued where Cuinn's song hadn't reached them. He met Windsong's gaze, gave a little nod.

Then he stepped back, conceding Mithanis the fight with Azrilan.

"Soar!" He turned to his cousin.

"What do you need?" His bow was still raised, arrow nocked and ready.

"Take your legions out over the harbour, make sure Azrilan doesn't have any surprises waiting for us. If he does, destroy them. Once you've done that, start working on putting out those fires. I'll make sure it's safe for you to fly that low."

He nodded, turning to run back for his eagle. As he did so, Jasper let out a snarl. He nudged Cuinn's leg with his nose, then turned and ran, disappearing into the citadel.

Cuinn took in a deep breath, pushed away his exhaustion and his fear for Talyn, and began to sing again.

And then a bellowing roar tore through the night—Mithanis launching himself at Azrilan, metal ringing as their swords clashed.

CHAPTER 62

They'd expected to find a body, and so she and Zamaril hadn't bothered to conceal their approach as they sprinted through the citadel towards the location given to them by the first Falcon they'd cornered.

Instead they came upon a trap.

She and Zamaril slid to a halt at the top of a wide citadel walkway, open-aired down one side, and filled with Bearmen, Shadows and Armun. She didn't have to look behind them to know their exit was quickly being cut off by more warriors.

Despite the impossibility of those odds, Talyn's first response was a brief flash of hope. If Theac were truly dead, would they have bothered to set such a trap? She squelched it as quickly as it came. There was no time for anything but cool focus.

At the other end of the walkway, the original doors had been removed from their hinges and replaced with a locked iron gate. She couldn't see inside from where they stood, but assumed Theac was in the room beyond.

Zamaril glanced behind them, then back at her. "We could probably break through those behind us, run and get backup."

Talyn surveyed their opponents, weighed their options. Cuinn needed every soldier he could get right now, and there was no way to know how hurt Theac was, if he was even alive. There might not be time to get backup. Something told her even if Azrilan had kept Theac alive, he'd be playing some kind of game.

"What do you think, Ciantar?" Zamaril was calm, ready, despite the closing net around them.

Her chest tightened. She knew how to get this done.

"*Sari, do you—*"

"*You don't have to ask, Tal. You never have to ask.*" Sari's response was immediate and unwavering.

She shook her head, swallowing the tears that wanted to come. "*I don't know if I can… I don't want to.*"

"Yes, you do," she said gently. "*You've known for a while now. Go save your Wolf.*"

"Ciantar?" Zamaril's voice brought her back to the present.

Her eyes slid closed. Opened. "*Sari…*"

"*Talyn, it's truly all right.*"

"*Okay.*"

Talyn turned to Zamaril, held out her hand. "Not Ciantar anymore, Zamaril. Just Talyn."

His eyes widened in understanding, but he didn't hesitate to reach out and close his fingers around her forearm. She gripped his just as tightly. Both closed their eyes, took a deep, steadying breath. Then opened them and held each other's gaze.

Sapphire and pale blue magic flared, so bright she had to look away for a moment.

Just like once, many years ago, sapphire and silver had flashed together.

It was the briefest of things, no time for anything more, but the warrior bond snapped into place without pause or hesitation, steady and true and rippling with power.

And then she and Zamaril were turning, facing down the walkway. Steel rang as she drew her twin aethlyx blades in the same smooth movement Zamaril drew his sword.

Talyn took a deep, steadying breath, allowed the focus of an upcoming fight to settle over her like a perfectly tailored cloak. Her awareness narrowed to the walkway full of adversaries and one of her dearest friends waiting at the end for her.

And, for *always* now, the warrior at her left side.

Time slowed.

Her breath came fast, her grip on her daggers sure, stance loose and ready.

Enemies all around.

"Let's get this done," Zamaril said.

Then time snapped back into focus. And they moved.

The adrenalin of battle thrummed through her veins, hot and powerful. Running forward, one foot in front of the other, her steps light and sure—confidence surging through her, the confidence of knowing that the odds were against them but that she and Zamaril would come out victorious anyway.

She stepped aside to avoid the first swing of a blade at her neck. He shifted quickly to shove his elbow back into her head, but she twisted aside before thrusting her dagger deep in between his ribs. He coughed blood and she shoved him against the wall where his heavy body slid to the ground with a crash.

More warriors converged on her from every direction.

At first she fought as if she were alone, keeping all sides covered, closing any vulnerabilities. But it made her too conservative, not quick enough to push through when so many warriors converged on her at once.

Her body moved at its utmost limit of agility, dancing between opponents. She felt every pull of muscle, each rasp of breath in her lungs, the slickness of sweat on her face and the damp grips of the daggers in her hands.

But Zamaril fought at her side, his sword licking out with a quickness almost beyond belief to take advantage of every opening, his footwork moving in perfect synchrony with hers.

And she began to adjust. To fight like she once again had a partner. To leave her back open when he was there, to overextend and leave her side vulnerable when it meant pushing the advantage. To fight like she knew someone was protecting her back always, each instinctively knowing where the other was.

Every step part of a dance she and Zamaril wove together.

Parry, slash, drop, weave. Lose the blade, gain another with a quick *sabai* move. Bring her shield to life. Drop it again. Breathe in. Breath out. Feel the air rush over sweat-soaked skin. Teeth bared in a silent snarl the whole time.

She had no idea how much time had passed before she killed a Berserker and stood, chest heaving, staring towards the gated room before them. Her breath steamed in the cold air. Blood and gore covered her from head to toe.

"Something's off," Zamaril said, breath rasping in his chest.

He was right. The single remaining Armun stood right by the gate, staying where he was rather than coming to fight them or to get reinforcements. He didn't even seem taken aback by the corridor full of dead and dying bodies that a single Callanan warrior pair had just torn through.

Instead, a little smile flickered on his face as he began to lift his hand towards a rope hanging from above the doorframe.

Talyn moved closer, daggers raised, eyes searching the room beyond. It was lit by several flickering torches, and Theac sat chained to a chair in the middle of the room. He was bloodied, bruised, his head hanging down.

"He's breathing," Zamaril rasped. "Probably unconscious. But his chest is moving."

"You give us the keys, we let you live," she told the Armun. "You don't and we do to you what we did to your friends back there."

"Talyn!" Zamaril's voice turned sharp, his voice calling out at the same time a deep snarling sound came from inside the room. "They've got a tawncat in there."

Shit. Her chest turned to stone as she glanced where Zamaril pointed. A tawncat the size of Jasper was prowling inside a wooden cage, its yellow eyes flat and murderous. Old and new whip scars decorated its tawny coat.

The Armun's hand moved again, faster now, towards the rope, and Talyn understood suddenly what he was doing.

The prince of games, indeed. Sick, twisted games.

"No!" She hurled her dagger as the word tore out of her. It flew true, burying itself in the man's heart.

But it wasn't quick enough. It landed a heartbeat after he'd yanked on the rope.

Zamaril was already throwing himself at the gate, one hand grabbing hold of the lock, the other reaching for the lockpicks he always carried in his right boot.

It wasn't going to be quick enough.

The rope yanked up the door to the cage holding the tawncat, and with a triumphant snarl it broke through, claws flashing.

Zamaril dropped the lockpicks, his breathing coming fast, pale blue eyes meeting hers. "It's a solid one, it will take me too long to get through."

"Then we'll use magic."

She tried to ignore the fact the tawncat was already prowling towards Theac's bound body. She lifted a hand, pressed it against the lock, tried to flood it with her warrior magic so it melted through. Setting off a blast in such a confined space could kill Theac if shrapnel exploded inward.

Zamaril laid his palm over hers, concentrating fiercely. The pungent scent of melting metal filled her nose and she put more and more into the effort.

A hungry snarl came from within.

Desperation roped through her, fighting with her focus. "Come on, come on." She kept repeating the words over and over.

And then the bolt melted through.

She kicked the door open and lifted her dagger, ready to throw.

But the crazed tawncat was already leaping for its prey. Her dagger wasn't going to reach across the space in time.

Then a blur of movement from the left, a violent snarl, and something collided with the tawncat mid-air. The wrestling creatures hit the ground, a flurry of swiping claws, snarling and yowling.

"Jasper." Her breath shuddered out. How had he even... but as her gaze automatically scanned the room for any other threats to herself or Zamaril, it landed on the air vent high in the southern wall. The tawncat had come through it, just like his mother once had to assassinate Goldfeather and Iceflight.

Zamaril moved, running for Theac and dropping to his knees by the chair. Talyn joined him a moment later, sparing only a brief glance for the fighting tawncats. Thick chains wound around Theac's midsection, bound together by a single lock.

"Guard will have the key." Zamaril rose and ran for the door.

Talyn reached up with trembling fingers to Theac's neck, letting out a sobbing breath of relief when she felt a faint pulse. Then Zamaril was back and unlocking the chains. Across the room the tawncat fight was vicious, blood spattering the ground and walls around them.

She wanted to help, feared for Jasper to the depth of her bones, but the fighting creatures were so closely entwined she could risk inadvertently hurting him if she tried to attack Azrilan's creature.

"Let's get him to the healer's centre." Zamaril wrapped an arm around Theac's left side while Talyn did the same from this right. Together they gently lifted him from the chair and staggered from the room.

Azrilan's tawncat saw them trying to leave, and momentarily broke free of Jasper to come at them with a bloodcurdling yowl. Talyn turned, drew her dagger, but Jasper was faster. He landed on the tawncat and they rolled across the floor, spitting and snarling. Blood already dripped from gashes along his dark coat.

"We'll come back for him." Zamaril read her hesitation easily. "As soon as Theac has help."

Talyn nodded, spared one last glance for her friend, then continued out the door.

TALYN AND ZAMARIL moved as quickly as they could through the cloud of ash and smoke that was rising up from Dock City. The healing residences would no doubt be protected by WingGuard, but if she had to fight through a hundred Falcons to get Theac help, she and Zamaril would do it.

And then they crossed into the bubble of magic Cuinn's voice had settled over the city and citadel. The tune was haunting, hopeful, dancing over her skin and draining some of the anger simmering inside her at what had been done to Theac.

She was surprised at how far it had spread. But it wasn't just the prince of song. Where his voice ended, others began, winged Wolves and Falcons both. Not as powerful, but using their song magic in the same way. Dispelling hate and anger and fear.

She paused for a moment, Zamaril at her side, and listened, allowing the song to give them both strength and purpose. Between then, Theac's eyes flickered open, and he peered groggily around.

"Hey there, Parksin." Zamaril steadied his grip. "Think you can walk on your own, or you want us to keep carrying your heavy corpse all through the citadel?"

He managed a half-hearted scowl. "Shut up, Lightfinger. What's that music?"

We raised our banners to greet the sun.

For our strength shines bright from here to afar.

Zamaril and Talyn kept moving then, Theac taking some of his own weight but still swaying alarmingly. They hit a small knot of fighting outside the main entrance to the healing centre—several Wolves battling Berserkers, trying to prevent them from getting inside.

Without a word, Zamaril and Talyn gently settled Theac against the wall, then waded into the fight, sword and daggers slashing in a blur of movement. After a few more moments of fierce fighting, the Berserkers were dead. Zamaril stamped out the torch one of them had been holding.

Talyn was already taking a step forward, heading back for Theac, when Zamaril's shout of warning stopped her. But it was only Andres coming from the direction of the wall, three more Wolves with him, face streaked with dirt and sweat.

"Andres!" Relief shot through her. "You're well?"

"Not a scratch on me." He saluted with his usual crispness despite the fact he was splattered with blood and ash and dirt. "Ciantar, look!"

His eyes were wide and he was pointing towards the wall. They all spun. The healing centre sat high on a hillside looking down over the wall and city, providing a clear view of the battle laid out below them.

Where before seven winged Wolves had been in the sky above Cuinn, now there were at least triple that number of winged folk. Not Falcons. Not Wolves.

Civilians.

As Talyn watched, another three winged figures rose into the sky above the citadel, joining the rest.

She'd been so focused on fighting that she hadn't realised the singing had grown louder, stronger, its influence spreading wider. Song mages were combining their magic to drown the citadel and Dock City in Cuinn's song.

The words almost shimmered in the air with the strength of a hundred song mages, their voices raised in song.

After all our battles were won,
We raised our banners to greet the sun.
For our strength shines bright from here to afar,
SkyReach, the Ice Plains and now Mithranar

"It's not just them." Ehdra's voice sounded behind them as he came running out of the healing centre. "The healers are treating everyone. Wolves and Falcons alike. Goldfeather's here and he insisted on it, but none of them protested."

"The fighting is all but over," Andres said. "The Berserkers down in the city are battling on—they seem unaffected by the song magic—but their numbers are dwindling fast. Corrin has rallied the city's defences against them."

The Wolves threw their heads back and howled.

Across the citadel, the rest of the force of Wolves heard the howl and added to it. Soon the eerie howls of a wolf pack intertwined with the music, ethereal and magical and powerful.

Talyn took a deep, steadying breath.

Cuinn had won the day.

"Is Azrilan still at the wall?" she asked.

"Last I saw he was. Mithanis is there too—they're fighting."

Worry lurched in Talyn's chest. Whichever one of them won that fight would be an immediate threat to Cuinn. "Andres, take any spare Wolves and spread through the citadel, make sure all the fighting is over, then organise to have any injured brought here." She turned to Zamaril. "Can you make sure Theac is looked after? Then go—"

"And find Jasper." Zamaril reached out and gripped her arm. "You know I will."

Talyn turned and ran.

CHAPTER 63

*H*is song magic filled him, roped through his veins and spilled out over the city. Windsong and Lyra sang unfaltering at his side, propping him up when he grew tired, bolstering his song with everything they had.

And his people sang with him, joining his cry for an end to the bloodshed. Slowly, very slowly, it worked. He could *feel* it working... feel as the hate and fear dissipated, the anger going with it. Sensed the desire to fight fading from bright flames to ashes. With every voice added to his in song, a fighter stood down.

But eventually the last of even his great magical strength faded, his throat turning raw, his strength dwindling to nothing. His song gradually slowed to a halt. Some of the Wolves had already stopped, drained of power and energy.

And as the music faded, the sharp sounds of a fight quickly filled the space.

His brothers.

Cuinn lifted a trembling hand to run through sweat-soaked hair, his chest heaving, legs unsteady.

Mithanis and Azrilan were a blur of movement as they battled back and forth on the top of the wall. It was something Cuinn had seen a hundred times before growing up, his two elder brothers sparring, both displaying their sublime skill but also Mithanis using every opportunity to display his dominance.

Now it was for real.

Now Azrilan was no longer hiding or pretending.

He glanced up—the winged folk who'd come to join him still hung there in the sky, floating on the night thermals. What was left of his magic sensed unease and trepidation... but also a resolute desire to stay and see this through to the end.

A glance down. Flames licked buildings in three different areas of Dock City, but all those areas were drawing more and more people. Corrin had gathered the Wolves and his network to help, just like the night of the floods. And SkyRiders were flying in from the ocean, carrying water to drop on the flames.

The fighting had stopped.

He'd done it.

A hand landed on his shoulder. Windsong, head bowed, as exhausted as he was but with triumph and delight seeping from every part of him. "Well done, Cuinn. I've never seen anything like what you just did."

Cuinn reached up to grip his arm. "Thank you. But it's not over yet."

Together, he and Windsong turned to watch the fight.

A grunt escaped from Mithanis as Azrilan pushed him back towards the edge of the wall. Without his wings, he wobbled precariously, but cold determination filled his features and he gathered himself, pushing back hard.

Running feet behind had Cuinn turning, shoulders sagging with relief at the sight of Talyn—bloodied and dirty but alive and well. Without a word he drew her against him for a fierce hug. "Theac?"

She pulled away quickly. "He's okay. Beaten up but okay."

Cuinn shuddered with the relief that flooded through him, but Talyn's focus was already moving to the fight, her concern for what happened once one of them emerged the victor obvious as day to the remnants of his song magic.

"You could take both of them now." She lifted her gaze to his.

"She's right, Your Highness," Lyra said. "They're vulnerable and distracted. Two knives is all it would take."

"Windsong?" he murmured.

"Your choice, Prince Cuinn."

Cuinn turned from Talyn, looking up at the winged folk above, who were watching all this unfold. And then he turned back to his brothers.

Brothers who had tormented and betrayed him. One who'd made him afraid his entire life. The other who'd almost killed him, who'd killed Raya and his Wolves. Who'd made Talyn a slave.

Brothers who were right at this moment trying to kill each other. Who would no doubt try and kill him once a victor emerged. A victor who would go right back to oppressing the humans if he took the throne of Mithranar.

It suddenly felt like the whole of Mithranar was watching him decide what to do.

"Cuinn?" Talyn asked softly. "Finish this cleanly."

His eyes closed. He took a single, deep breath. He wanted to be different. To do better.

He always had.

"No." Then he stepped away. "My people deserve a choice."

Talyn stared at him, a mix of pride and disbelief flashing over her face, and then she dropped her hand from the hilt of her dagger. Lyra followed suit. A little smile flickered over Windsong's face.

And they all stood to watch the fight.

The prince of night and the prince of games were skilled fighters, good enough to be Callanan, evenly matched. Mithanis had strength where Azrilan had the grace of his wings. Mithanis had passion and fury where Azrilan had cleverness and footwork.

Over and over they went at each other, blades slamming together, sometimes sliding through a guard. Blood trickled from minor wounds on both princes. Their breathing grew heavy. Mithanis slipped and almost went over the edge. Azrilan cried in pain when Mithanis's sword sliced through feathers.

Cuinn stood, jaw clenched, waiting to see which of his brothers would die in front of him.

"We could stop it without killing them." Talyn spoke at his side.

He reached out for her hand, twined their fingers together. "No. This is their choice. I will respect that too."

At one point the flurry of blows slowed and came to a halt, the two men tacitly agreeing on a breather.

They circled each other. Neither had noticed the battle ending around them. Neither noticed that hundreds of eyes were watching them fight. Instead they were focused only on each other—on the decades of bitterness between them and their shared ambition for power, shared willingness to do anything to get it, including killing innocents.

Cuinn sucked in a breath as Azrilan broke the tacit truce without warning, blade lunging straight at Mithanis's chest.

But Mithanis had been expecting his brother's betrayal.

He moved at the same moment as Azrilan. In a single sideways step he avoided the lunge, bringing his own sword up and swinging it at Azrilan's over-extended body. A powerful man even without wings, Mithanis's sword bit deep into Azrilan's neck, shearing his head clean off his shoulders.

Silence.

Cuinn and Mithanis both stared as Azrilan's body swayed and hit the ground, his blood gushing into a large pool, his head coming to rest a short distance away. Mithanis's chest heaved and his sword dropped to the ground with a clatter. Cuinn sensed both grief and triumph in his quickly hidden emotions.

The prince of night straightened then, something like clarity coming into his dark eyes. Then he turned, gaze sweeping over Cuinn, the Wolves gathered behind him, the winged folk hovering in the sky above. It was clear when he realised nobody had moved to stop or otherwise interfere with the fight.

"You could have killed us both." Mithanis's voice rasped, laden with weariness.

"We both have a right to the throne," Cuinn responded. "I would like to give our people the choice."

Mithanis nodded slowly, glanced around them again, then looked at Cuinn. "Kingcouncil. Tomorrow. We'll choose Mithranar's king then."

Cuinn simply nodded. "Agreed."

"I'm really not convinced this is a good idea.," Talyn spoke up as Mithanis walked away, heading to the palace, nobody trying to halt his progress. "I don't trust him."

"I don't either."

"You're woefully idealistic," she said with a sigh.

"And you're woefully murderous."

"I don't care what either of you are." Windsong spoke up, steady and strong. "The entire force of Wolves will be watching you between now and that Kingcouncil meeting tomorrow, Your Highness."

"Fair enough." A smile spread over Cuinn's face. He was exhausted, heartsick, guilty over the people who'd died before his song could slow the fighting. His gaze travelled over the Wolves standing before him. "Andres? Zamaril?"

"Andres is fine." Talyn reached out to touch his hand, the shadow in her eyes making his stomach clench. "Zamaril's with Jasper."

"Is he okay?"

Her fingers tangled with his. "Let's go and see."

CUINN DIDN'T REALLY SEE the bodies lining the wide bridge over to the unused tower where Azrilan had clearly been keeping his tawncat. All he could see was the melted iron doors and the chair that Theac had been chained to.

His strides quickening, he yanked his hand loose from Talyn's, his heart thudding in his chest. The rasping sound of laboured breathing filled the air. Jystar's grey wings hung loose against the ground as he kneeled by Jasper.

Zamaril watched from the tawncat's other side. His gaze went straight to Talyn when Cuinn walked in, then over to Cuinn. Without a word, he stood and moved away, going to stand by Talyn near the door. Cuinn's song magic picked up the new bond between them, and wonder filled him at the shining beauty of it, but it was only a moment, and then his attention was all on his friend.

Jasper's green eyes focused on Cuinn the moment he stepped inside. They were duller than Cuinn had ever seen them, dark with pain, but they brightened at the sight of him. Cuinn knelt by the tawncat's head, reaching out to stroke the soft fur around his ears. "Hey there, Jasper."

Jasper snuffled, tried to move, but clearly couldn't. Blood matted his dark coat and seeped into the floor under him. His pain filled Cuinn's senses.

"The other tawncat ripped him up pretty good," Jystar murmured. "I'm doing what I can, but I don't know if..."

"Do what you can. Please." Cuinn tried not to let his voice break on the last word, but failed.

Talyn kneeled at his side, her arm sliding around him, her forehead pressing against his shoulder.

"He knew," Cuinn whispered. "He knew that it would break me to lose Theac. He knew."

She held him tighter. "Stay here with him. I'm going to go down to the city and make sure we're doing everything we can to ensure there's a bed and food for those who lost homes or loved ones. I also want to coordinate with Soar and Windsong—prepare for any unexpected interruptions tomorrow."

He nodded.

She pressed a kiss to his jaw. "I'll find you later."

He turned his head to meet her sapphire gaze. "You're okay... you're well. You and baby?"

She smiled. "A boy, Jystar thinks."

A son. He couldn't breathe. Couldn't swallow around the lump in his throat. He merely nodded and clutched her tighter until she stepped away. Zamaril followed her out the door but Lyra remained.

Cuinn settled more comfortably on the ground, gently lifted Jasper's head into his lap, and smiled into those green eyes.

And then he began to sing. It was a raspy, halting hum with the tiny pieces of magic he had left.

But Jasper's eyes closed and his entire body relaxed.

"I'm here, Jasper," he whispered. "I'm not going anywhere."

CHAPTER 64

$\mathcal{T}$alyn managed a half-turn nap in between coordinating with Soar, Windsong and Doran. SkyRiders flew patrols out past Feather Bay, keeping a protective cordon around Dock City and the citadel. Meanwhile, the fires in the city were out and the residents were busily engaged in restoration and fare-welling their dead.

The Wolves were quiet too. They'd lost comrades in the fight. If Talyn weren't so anxious about the outcome of this Kingcouncil, so focused on making sure Cuinn would be safe and there would be no surprises, she'd have been grieving right along with them.

She'd only seen Cuinn briefly, to check in on him and Jasper. The tawncat was still in a precarious condition—Jystar was powerful, but no winged healer knew much about tawncat anatomy or the mechanics of healing one—and Cuinn hadn't left his side yet.

So she was already in the Kingcouncil chamber when he entered, slightly early. Mithanis was there, the remaining chairs around the Kingcouncil table empty—ready for the five council lords to arrive.

Cuinn came straight over to her—he'd bathed and changed into fresh clothes, but dark shadows hooded his eyes—and pulled her into a quick hug. "He's still unconscious but Jystar is hopeful."

"He's a tough one, Cuinn. I'm betting on him pulling through." She managed a smile. "You ready?"

His glance took in the room, the empty chairs waiting for the lords. "I've been ready for a long time."

Talyn hesitated. They'd already gone over this, but... "We promised Saniya."

"And I intend to hold that promise." Cuinn glanced back to her. "But I want to win this nomination by all the winged families choosing me—I don't want to be left open to claims I only won because I added humans to the voting and skewed things my way."

"*He's right*," Sari said.

"*I know*." Talyn gave a little nod. "I'll be watching. If anything happens—"

"I know you and your Wolves will keep me safe." He smiled softly, then leaned down to kiss her. His magic surrounded her briefly, showing her how confident he felt.

Before she could say anything further, he strode towards the table. The door behind her opened again, admitting Theac, Zamaril and Corrin. Theac leaned heavily on a crutch, his face swollen and bruised, his free arm in a sling. But when Corrin attempted to offer him a chair, he levelled the talon with a scowl so fierce Talyn almost laughed.

Corrin and Zamaril left Theac to stand guard at the door where Lyra stood too and crossed over to join Talyn in standing only a handful of paces away from the table. Instantly something in her relaxed as Zamaril took up the space at her left side. Corrin glanced between the two of them with a little smile.

The next to arrive was Tarich Swiftwing, Flight-Leader Brightwing on his heels. Swiftwing nodded at Mithanis as he sat down, while Brightwing went to take up a similar position to Talyn and her talons on the opposite side of the table.

A rush of air and Anrun Windsong swooped through from the open space that served as the fourth wall. He bowed to both Mithanis and Cuinn. "Prince Mithanis, you named Brightwing your Falcon, and

Prince Cuinn named me his. May I suggest that in the interests of fairness we both get a vote at the council table today?"

Anrun had suggested this to Cuinn and Talyn earlier, so only Mithanis reacted to the suggestion. He levelled a dark look Brightwing's way. "Brightwing was my brother's Falcon. He should be in chains for what he did. Neither of you should get a vote."

Cuinn shrugged. "Fair enough. The vote will be made by the five lords and the two of us."

Seven men. No chance of a tie.

Talyn tried to calm the anxiety roiling in her stomach. If Cuinn lost the vote, she had no doubt they would have to fight their way out to survive. Mithanis would never show them the same mercy Cuinn had him.

"If it comes to that, your Wolves will take his Falcons any day." Sari was confident. *"You know that."*

She did. It didn't soothe her anxiety.

Jurian Stormflight and Ridan Nightdrift walked through the double doors next. Charl Nightdrift hadn't made it through the night despite the healers working tirelessly on him, and his younger brother had abruptly found himself thrust into a Kingcouncil seat. His face was expressionless, making Talyn's unease deepen. She'd never met Ridan, had no idea where his loyalties lay.

As he and Jurian took their seats, Tirin Goldfeather flew in. He looked painfully young amidst the senior lords of the kingdom, but was unbothered by it, offering Cuinn a friendly smile.

Finally Werin Blacksoar strode in, a faintly annoyed look on his face as he took the final seat at the table. Feathers rustled as Falcons spread through the room—no doubt those loyal to Mithanis. They stood side by side with the Wolves. There was no overt hostility between them, yet if things went awry, there would be bloodshed.

Talyn took a deep breath, forcing herself to calm. Cuinn would win this.

"Thank you for coming." Cuinn rose to his feet, offering a polite bow. "Let's not prevaricate. Azrilan is dead and today's Kingcouncil will decide the next king of Mithranar."

"There is no serious choice to be made." Mithanis rose as gracefully as Cuinn had done. Despite the fact both had lost their wings, they were still impressive men, dark and light, Dumnorix and Manunin. "I have been the presumptive heir to this kingdom since birth—I was raised to rule Mithranar. I am a powerful warrior and song mage. The throne is mine."

His magic was blunter, harder than Cuinn's. It filled the room with his sincerity, the confidence he held that the throne would be his. He showed them his strength, the depth of his power.

Cuinn paused until Mithanis's words and magic faded, and then he spoke. "I have been working to build a better Mithranar since I was seventeen years old. I know that some of you do not agree with my views, that you think the way we rule, the way we treat our human citizens is a good thing. But I want to lead a better kingdom. One where we respect all our people and earn their respect in turn. You have seen for yourselves the way I would rule. You have seen how Mithanis would rule. The choice is yours, my lords."

Cuinn bowed again, fist over heart, then straightened and stood calmly, hands behind his back. A muscle ticked in Mithanis's jaw, but he too gave a terse nod, and stood, waiting for the council to decide.

Talyn scanned the room, alert to any possible danger or betrayal. Mithanis was no better than Azrilan and she found it hard to trust that he was going to let this process happen without intervention.

"*I think he's certain he's going to win the vote,*" Sari murmured.

She was right. And that confidence raised doubt in Talyn. She shifted, moving her left hand surreptitiously to check her daggers were within reach.

"*Stop fidgeting. Whatever comes, you know you can handle it.*"

"There is no doubt for me." Tirin Goldfeather rose to his feet, the young son of Ausul Goldfeather, murdered by Savin and Azrilan. "For my friend Ronisin. For my father. For the future I want for my children. I choose Cuinn Acondor."

The words hung in the room. Tirin gave a little nod, then resumed his seat, ignoring the dark glance Mithanis sent his way.

"Prince Mithanis was right. He was born to be our king." Tarich

Swiftwing rose as if his choice too had been made long ago. His voice was filled with scorn at the idea anyone could think different. "He will keep us strong rather than making us weak. I choose the prince of night."

For a moment there was silence, the remaining three lords glancing at each other around the table, maybe wondering whether they dared go next, perhaps still making their decision. Talyn shifted slightly, focused on Cuinn, who seemed calm. At his side, Mithanis was tense, simmering anger ready to burst alight.

Then, a chair scraped and Jurian Stormflight rose to his feet, wearing the manner of a man who was taking a dive off a very high cliff into unknown seas below, without wings. He took a breath, gaze distant, not looking at either prince. "I choose for my sons Tiercelin and Jystar. I choose Cuinn Acondor."

Ridan's fingers drumming on the table broke the hush that fell after Stormflight's announcement. His shoulders were rigid, his jaw clenched. He was afraid, but forcing himself to push forward anyway. "I spoke to my brother before his death. His wishes were clear, and I must respect them. I choose Cuinn Acondor."

Hope started beating through Talyn, a surging tide of barely repressed joy. That was three votes already. One more and the crown was undeniably Cuinn's. One vote against and he would only have a slim majority.

Her hands curled into fists at her sides, heart thumping in her chest. Cuinn's magic reached out to her then, betraying his own dawning hope, his anxiety, his wonder. Mithanis's entirely body had turned rigid.

Every single gaze turned to Werin Blacksoar, and the hush that had fallen over the room was that of every man and women present holding their breath, waiting. Some hopeful. Some afraid. If he voted for Mithanis, Cuinn would still win, but there would always be room for doubt with such a narrow margin... but if chose Cuinn...

Blacksoar took a steadying breath, then slowly pushed his chair back and stood. "Prince Mithanis offers us the stable rule we have always enjoyed. Prince Cuinn offers us alliance with the Twin

Thrones, along with a new way of ruling. Both are powerful mages. Both have demonstrated the ability to lead." Werin paused, clearly weighing his words.

Mithanis couldn't help himself. "Get on with it, man," he snapped.

The room went utterly still.

"Very well." Blacksoar bowed his head. "I choose Cuinn Acondor."

At those words, chairs scraped back as all four other lords rose to their feet—Tarich Swiftwing a little more reluctantly than the others —and bowed, wings furled, towards Cuinn.

What happened next was a blur.

Mithanis stopped holding back his building fury—his song magic sent it flooding through the room. Everyone within range staggered with the force of it, air whooshing from lungs, cries of alarm echoing out. Fighting off the emotion, Talyn reached for a dagger, instinct telling her something was wrong.

Mithanis spun towards Cuinn, faster than lightning, knife out and slashing for his unprotected throat.

Only to roar in pain, the blade falling from his hand to clatter on the marble floor, Corrin's knife embedded in his wrist. Talyn raised her arm, her dagger ready to throw, to see her Wolf captain, green eyes hard, another knife already in his hand.

But Cuinn had shifted, faster than thought, using a move that could only have been taught to him by the Kingshield he'd trained with in Port Lachley. He swept his brother's legs out from under him, threw his shoulder into Mithanis's chest and pinned him to the table, forearm across his throat, his own dagger at his brother's kidney.

The entire room froze.

"Everyone stand down!" Anrun Windsong bellowed into the brief silence before utter chaos broke out. "Stop! Sheathe your weapons!"

His command was wreathed with song magic, and the Wolves and Falcons froze mid-draw, weapons sliding slowly back into their sheaths.

"Mithanis, stop!" Cuinn spoke, clear and firm, no magic. "Don't do this. I have won. Be better than Azrilan. You still have a life. Go to Montagn. Fulfill your word."

Mithanis's rasping breath was loud, blood dripping to the floor from his wrist, shoulders rigid. "The throne is mine, Cuinn. It always has been mine."

"No, it hasn't." Cuinn's voice was gentle. "Please don't make me kill you and lose another brother. Please. Let Mithranar go. Find something better."

Talyn had to remember to breathe. Everything in her wanted to go over there and ensure Mithanis was never a threat to Cuinn ever again. But she trusted Cuinn to handle this his way.

"Please," Cuinn murmured. "Respect our lords and their choice."

The two brothers stared at each other, eyes locked. What felt like an eternity passed.

Then Mithanis's entire body sagged. "Okay, Brother."

Cuinn stepped away, kicked Mithanis's fallen knife across the floor, then offered Mithanis a hand. Mithanis took it, cradling his injured wrist to his chest. Cuinn helped him away from the table. "Go, get out of here. Have Jystar stitch your wrist up before you bleed out."

After only a single hesitation, Mithanis turned and walked out of the room, shoulders stiff with anger.

"The Kingcouncil has chosen Cuinn Acondor as king by a clear majority." Windsong spoke into the stunned silence. "There will be no more bloodshed."

"My Falcon is right," Cuinn added, sparing a glance for his departing brother. In that glance was pain and grief and relief all wrapped up in one.

Talyn sheathed her dagger, and reached out to grip Corrin's shoulder with a fierceness that was probably painful. "Thank you."

He smiled. "You trained me to save his life, Ciantar."

Zamaril slung an arm around Corrin, hugging him fiercely. "Well done, Corrin."

"My lords, if you could please sit down." Cuinn's voice rang out again. His green eyes shot to hers, clear and strong, assuring himself she was all right. She gave a little nod. "There are some urgent orders of business for us to discuss."

The lords promptly sat, glances tearing away from the splatters of

Mithanis's blood still on the floor. Cuinn caught Lyra's eye and made a gesture. The talon opened the door and slipped out.

"First. Anrun Windsong. Please take your seat at the table as Mithranar's Falcon—ultimate leader of our army."

Several glances shifted to Talyn, surprised at this announcement, having expected her to have been named to the position. After all, she was Ciantar. She ignored their looks. Cuinn had already spoken of his plans with her... well, most of them. And as for the rest, she trusted him implicitly.

Windsong bowed low, wings half-furled, then pulled back the empty Falcon's chair and sat down. He looked like he belonged. And he sat like he knew it. He and his new king shared a small smile.

The doors opened then, Andres appearing with Tirina and Ehdra. All three carried a chair each over to the table. Lyra propped the door open.

"Next." Cuinn threaded his voice with magic so that he instantly commanded the wandering attention of the lords, some staring at the new chairs, others at Mithanis's blood on the floor. "I restore the Ciantar family to its rightful place at the Kingcouncil table. Saniya Ciantar?"

If they'd been surprised by Windsong's appointment, then now the lords were downright shocked. A little smile curled at Talyn's mouth when they all turned to stare at her, then looked away as Saniya stalked through the door, crossed the room, and dropped into one of the new chairs. She gave Swiftwing a dirty look, then assumed a watchful expression.

"From now on, the mayors of Dock City and Darmour will also have a seat at this table. Mayor Doran? Mayor Patroy?"

The two men walked in together, neither showing any signs of being overawed about where they were or what was happening to them. They took their seats at the table and turned their attention to Cuinn.

Before he could say anything else, Swiftwing cleared his throat. "I presume you want me to resign my position, Your Grace. May I ask that you consider—"

"Why would I ask you to do that?" Cuinn frowned slightly.

"I... I voted for Prince Mithanis."

"Goodness, Tarich, I don't want yes-men on my council." Cuinn shook his head. "You're perfectly entitled to your views, and you may argue them as vigorously as you like, provided you accept my final rulings."

Tarich's mouth opened, closed. Goldfeather shot him a smug look. Then Swiftwing settled back in his chair, composure returning. "I can do that, Your Grace."

"Good, because our new Ciantar will no doubt be joining you in challenging me as often as she possibly can." Cuinn flashed a smile in Saniya's direction. Her hard expression softened. "I look forward to it."

Windsong chuckled, and just like that, the tension was broken. The nine seated at the table turned to their new king, attention firmly focused on him.

"Too many old men."

"Agreed. We'll have to do something about that."

Sari sniggered. *"You're a queen now."*

"Shut up."

Cuinn remained standing, resting his palms on the table, a wide smile spreading over his face. "Welcome to my Kingcouncil. Shall we move on to our next order of business?"

CHAPTER 65

*C*uinn led a legion of SkyRiders, many riding double with a Wolf, and two carrying Mithanis and Saniya, along with a full wing of Falcons to Arataire. Talyn flew with him, strapped tightly in front of him. With them travelled Soar, an additional formal representative of the Twin Thrones.

Alyna was going to be so mad she'd missed all this. Cuinn smiled inwardly; he'd have to invite her for a visit soon.

Neither he nor Talyn were sure of what they were going to find. If Kaeri had taken Talyn's advice, then she would be in Arataire. Either she'd won the spill, lost it, or could still be fighting.

If the latter was the case, he hoped to bolster her forces with his SkyRiders and Falcons to help her to victory. Not that he wanted any more fighting… maybe he could try singing again.

The SkyRider scouts reported that the fields outside the city were empty, the slaves who usually worked them absent. And large numbers of soldiers surrounded Arataire, wearing the bright scarlet Venador sigil.

They reported the Aimsir were there too, encamped to the east, patrolling riders circling the area. That reassured him somewhat.

"You should let me go in first, make sure it's secure." Talyn twisted to look at him.

He grinned. "What would be the fun in that?"

Her eyes flashed. "You almost died three days ago."

"I'm all right." He held her tighter.

She leaned against him, then straightened up. "Let's do this."

He nudged Trystaan, sending the eagle in a steep dive for the Arataire castle fortress. Behind him, Soar and ten other SkyRiders dropped out of the sky in pursuit. The rest remained aloft in case of trouble. Windsong followed too, along with Lyra.

They did a quick run over the walls first, making sure nobody was going to start firing arrows at them.

Nothing.

Cuinn gave the order and they landed on the bridge over to the castle, just outside arrow range, allowing the eagles to settle before unstrapping and climbing down.

The gates opened, silently admitting them.

"That looks welcoming," Talyn muttered.

"Not at all like a trap," Soar said mildly.

Cuinn smiled at them both. "My song magic isn't raising any alarm bells."

"Mine either," Windsong added. "We'll go first though, Your Grace."

The Falcon swept forward, Wolves behind him, Falcons hovering overhead. Talyn smirked at Cuinn before following. Cuinn glanced over his shoulder, settling his gaze on Mithanis. He wasn't sure exactly how his brother was doing since his defeat. Wrist tightly bandaged, he wore an expressionless mask as good as Talyn's, his emotions tightly shielded. Cuinn still wondered if he shouldn't have killed him when he'd had the chance, removed what could be a future threat.

But he didn't have it in him to kill. Especially not his own brother. He never would.

"Are you going to stare at me all day, or are we going in? I have a wife and throne to claim," Mithanis barked irritably before striding past Cuinn.

Cuinn hurried after him, inwardly wishing Kaeri the very best of luck.

A scowling Venador soldier met them in the entrance courtyard, Windsong and his protective guard reluctantly stepping aside to allow Cuinn, Talyn, Soar and Mithanis through. "I am General Carvin Venador."

"Well met, General. I'm King Cuinn Acondor." It still felt odd saying those words, *processing* those words. "This is Lord Aerin Dumnorix." He gestured to Soar. "Prince Mithanis Acondor-Manunin, and my wife, Talyn Acondor-Dumnorix."

Something rippled over the general's face when Cuinn introduced Mithanis. He thought it might be dislike. Or fear. Maybe both. Whatever it was, it didn't bode well for Kaeri.

"Who's the ahara these days?" Soar asked mildly.

"We thought we'd come and introduce ourselves," Cuinn added with a cheerful smile.

Carvin saluted and stepped backward with alacrity as Kaeri's sharp voice rang out. "You did it!"

All gazes turned to her as she came down the front steps and headed towards them with quick strides. Ariar was only a couple of paces behind her, grinning from ear to ear at the sight of them. Trailing them was Liadin and two Callanan; one of whom was waving frantically at Talyn while the other smiled brightly.

Those smiles took all the remaining weight off Cuinn's shoulders, and he felt Talyn relax beside him as well. They wouldn't be smiling like that unless everything had gone as they'd hoped.

Kaeri stopped before them, gaze going straight to Talyn, then Cuinn. "You have Mithranar?"

"We do." Cuinn glanced at Talyn. "Azrilan is dead. I am king."

"And you?" Talyn asked Kaeri, hope ringing in her voice.

"For now, I am ahara of Montagn." A smile teased at Kaeri's mouth, but quickly vanished. "It is by no means a stable situation. Already food production has stopped now the slaves have been freed, and three Houses are on the verge of outright mutiny."

"I came to deliver your new husband. He might help with that." Cuinn nudged Mithanis with a little smile. Mithanis glowered at him, but stepped forward and offered a polite bow.

"He let you have the throne?" Kaeri looked all kinds of dubious.

Cuinn opened his mouth, hesitated, then said, "He did. When I won it after a full Kingcouncil vote."

"The throne is Cuinn's," Mithanis agreed, causing several astonished stares to swing his way.

"Perhaps a formal offer of alliance with the Twin Thrones and new, advantageous trading agreements would assist also?" Soar offered. "Ariar and I have full authority from King Aeris to negotiate with you, Ahara Venador."

"As does Lady Ciantar." Cuinn pointed to the final member of the party. "Saniya is my new Kingcouncil lord responsible for foreign relations. Mithranar will do what we can to assist, Ahara Venador."

Kaeri's shoulders relaxed. "I can't promise that will solve all my issues, but it will help. It will help substantially. Thank you."

"Talyn and I can't stay long." Cuinn offered his hand. "But we'll make a show here for a day or two, so it's obvious you have our backing, and then I'll leave Saniya behind to hammer out the new agreements. Lord Nightdrift, my trade councilor, will also be joining the negotiations shortly." Once he got his head around his new role.

Kaeri took his hand, shook warmly. "Welcome to Arataire, King Acondor. I look forward to being allies."

EPILOGUE

Talyn took a deep breath of thick, humid air, savouring the hint of flowers and kahvi spices. It was a typically hot Mithranan afternoon, the monsoon season finally easing. Her cotton shirt stuck to her sweaty skin, and tendrils of hair were plastered to the side of her face.

A few paces away Jasper slept on a blanket in the afternoon sun, bandages swathing most of his body. He was past the worst, Jystar assured them, and now just needed time to heal. The relief in hearing those words had been profound. Jasper had saved her life when he'd pulled her out of that slave camp, in more ways than one. She'd never forget what he'd done for all of them.

"You've been very patient with me."

She turned at the sound of Cuinn's musical voice, smiling when he appeared at the top of the ladder leading up to her rooftop garden. A day since returning from Arataire and the two of them were still sleeping in her old captain's quarters in the Wolves' barracks. Neither had wanted to move into his tower, though she supposed they'd soon have to take quarters in the central area of the palace.

"What do you mean?" she asked.

He came to settle beside her, sparing a fond glance for Jasper before turning his attention to her. "Well, I've given the Wolf captaincy to Corrin, your place as Ciantar to Saniya, and the overall command of our army to Windsong. I haven't even formally acknowledged you as queen yet."

She made a face. "I have no issue with you delaying that as long as you like."

"The thing is, I'm not going to," he said carefully.

Surprised, she lifted an eyebrow. "What are you talking about?"

"Talyn, you will always have a place at my side in ruling this country. You need only say the word and I will hear your views, welcome you into my council, let you wrangle with my lords." He reached out to take her hands, squeeze them. "But that's not what you want."

"Cuinn, I chose to marry you. I knew what that meant when I made the choice, and I did it without hesitation." She meant those words, let him feel it. "I wouldn't go back, even if I could."

He smiled. "I'm aware. And I will never stop being grateful that you love me enough to make that choice. But I love you just as much, and I want a happy life for you."

"I'm not following," she said, truly lost.

"The Wolves have grown too numerous for a protective wing." He cleared his throat, stepped back and let go of her hands. "Windsong is going to promote Corrin to Flight-Leader—he'll command the full protective flight of the WingGuard, Wolves and Falcons both. Theac will return to being Wolf captain, and he will lead a single wing in charge of my protection."

She had no idea where Cuinn was going with this. "And?"

"After our son is born, you will captain a second wing of Wolves." His green eyes were steady on hers. "I want Mithranar to have a Callanan-Armun hybrid unit capable of operating beyond borders, collecting information, killing when necessary, capturing when not."

Her heart began to thud as he spoke, her throat closing over.

"Your first priority might be undercover work in Montagn helping Kaeri keep her throne. Perhaps you might also look to contain the more violent gangs operating on the docks here and in Acleu." He paused. "Of course, Zamaril would join you in this unit. Cynia and

Leviana too, I suspect. I very much doubt they're going back to the Twin Thrones."

A life with her fellow warriors, fighting, planning, travelling. A life as a warrior, not as a queen or a commander. The life she'd never stopped wanting.

"What about our son?" She tried to squelch the hope before it took hold. "What you're describing, I'd be away a lot, I'll—"

"Our son will have a father always by his side, and sixty devoted Wolves to ensure his safety. He will have an aunt on the Kingcouncil, and a mother who will love him every moment she is here." Cuinn smiled a little. "And when he is old enough, he will have a home in Ryathl with Aeris and the rest of our family for a time."

"And you?"

"I will miss you fiercely when you are gone." He stepped closer, framing her face with his hands. "But I will be happy knowing that you are happy. Being king is my destiny, Talyn, not yours, and I must be strong enough to shoulder it alone."

"Thank you," she whispered, pressing her forehead into his chest, his shirt soaking up her tears.

"Thank you." He breathed into her hair. "For a life fulfilled, Talyn Ciantar."

"*Talyn?*"

"*Yes?*"

"*Would you still give anything? To go back to the life you had before I died?*"

Her breath caught. But the answer came without hesitation. "*No.*"

"*I'm glad.*"

An unrestrained smile of joy spread over her face, still pressed against Cuinn's chest. "*We're going to be Callanan again, Sari.*"

"*You and me and Zamaril. I can't wait.*"

A rush of air had them breaking apart reluctantly, Talyn scrubbing at her wet cheeks. It was Anrun Windsong, dropping to the ground and bowing respectfully. "Your Grace. I apologise for the interruption, but Lord Swiftwing has asked to begin Kingcouncil early this morning. He plans an early afternoon departure for Acleu."

Cuinn huffed a good-natured breath. "I should be glad he's volunteered to go and assist Nightdrift and Saniya over there. And I could use his sharp mind on those agreements. I'll see you later, Talyn."

He kissed her, lingering when she tugged him closer, then left with a smile and a hint of song that wrapped her in his love. Windsong remained once Cuinn had disappeared down the ladder, looking after him in a contemplative fashion. "In many ways, he is his mother's son."

Startled, Talyn glanced at him. "Why would you say that? He's nothing like her."

Windsong turned his contemplative gaze to her. "I believe I knew her a lot better than either of you did, Captain Dynan."

Talyn stared at him. The emotion in his voice sent her instincts sparking powerfully to life, and Zamaril's puzzlement over Windsong came back to her in a rush. All this time it had been playing at the back of her mind. Zamaril had seen Windsong before. Before ever going to the SkyReach. And Zamaril wasn't the type to mistake something like that.

"It was you. You put them all in the pardonable cells that day," she said slowly. "How did you even know?"

A little smile crossed his face. "Sarana and I corresponded frequently, though always discreetly. I was the only one she told about her plans to request a Kingshield for Cuinn." Windsong shrugged. "I merely ensured you had the right men in your unit. But not even I could have imagined what you turned them into. Your arrival in Mithranar saved us all, Talyn Dynan. I don't know how we can ever thank you."

Talyn stared. Windsong smiled and turned, wings lifting for flight.

"Windsong!"

"Captain?" He turned.

"Cuinn's father never died, did he?" she said slowly.

Windsong smiled again. And in a breath. A single heartbeat. His glamour vanished. And there, staring across at her in the hot afternoon sunlight, was a pair of luminous sea-green eyes.

Bright as the stars in the night sky.

* * *

Here ends *A Tale of Stars and Shadow*

* * *

Want to delve further into the world of *A Tale of Stars and Shadow*? By signing up to Lisa's monthly newsletter, *The Dock City Chronicle, you'll get* exclusive access to advance cover reveals, book updates, and special content just for subscribers, including:

- A short ebook - *A Tale of Two Callanan*
- Maps to download
- A download of *We Fly As One* - a song written and recorded for A Tale of Stars and Shadow by Peny Bohan

You can sign up at Lisa's website
lisacassidyauthor.com

ABOUT THE AUTHOR

Lisa is a self-published fantasy author by day and book nerd in every other spare moment she has. She's a self-confessed coffee snob (don't try coming near her with any of that instant coffee rubbish) but is willing to accept all other hot drink aficionados, even tea drinkers.

She lives in Australia's capital city, Canberra, and like all Australians, is pretty much in constant danger from highly poisonous spiders, crocodiles, sharks, and drop bears, to name a few. As you can see, she is also pro-Oxford comma.

A 2019 SPFBO finalist, and finalist for the 2020 ACT Writers Fiction award, Lisa is the author of the young adult fantasy series *The Mage Chronicles,* and epic fantasy series *A Tale of Stars and Shadow.* The first book in her latest series, *Heir to the Darkmage,* released in April 2021. She has also partnered up with One Girl, an Australian charity working to build a world where all girls have access to quality education. A world where all girls — no matter where they are born or how much money they have — enjoy the same rights and opportunities as boys. A percentage of all Lisa's royalties go to One Girl.

You can follow Lisa on Instagram and Facebook where she loves to interact with her readers. Lisa also has a Facebook group - Lisa's Writing Cave - where you can jump in and talk about anything and everything relating to her books (or any books really).

lisacassidyauthor.com

ALSO BY LISA CASSIDY

The Mage Chronicles

DarkSkull Hall

Taliath

Darkmage

Heartfire

Heir to the Darkmage

Heir to the Darkmage

Mark of the Huntress

A Tale of Stars and Shadow

A Tale of Stars and Shadow

A Prince of Song and Shade

A King of Masks and Magic

A Duet of Sword and Song

Consider a review?

'Your words are as important to an author as an author's words are to you'

Hello,

I'm really hoping you enjoyed this story. If you did (or even if not), I would be humbled if you would consider taking the time to leave an honest review on GoodReads and Amazon (it doesn't have to be long - a few words or a single sentence is absolutely fine). Reviews are the lifeblood of any book, especially for indie authors like me. Not to mention a review can absolutely make my day!

Thank you so much for reading this book,

Lisa

Printed in Great Britain
by Amazon